The Brass Rail

LD Robison

Copyright 2017, LD Robison

All Rights Reserved

No part of this book may be reproduced, stored in a retrieval system, or transmitted by any means, electronic, mechanical, photocopying, recording, or otherwise, without written permission from the author.

ISBN: 978-1-970024-65-4

DEDICATION

The story is dedicated especially to all the men and women in the United States Air Force with whom I had the honor to serve, and to all the women and men in all the branches of our armed forces past, present, and future who have proudly worn or will wear the uniform of our country and defended our liberties.

Table of Contents

CHAPTER 1	Land of the Rising Sun	1
CHAPTER 2	The Encounter	13
CHAPTER 3	Memories of the Sea Journey	21
CHAPTER 4	Barracks Life	33
CHAPTER 5	Duty Station	41
CHAPTER 6	Waylaid	51
CHAPTER 7	The Assignment	61
CHAPTER 8	Saturday	69
CHAPTER 9	Mama-san's Story	79
CHAPTER 10	The Search Begins	95
CHAPTER 11	Mama-san and Butler	107
CHAPTER 12	The Drunk and the Entrepreneur	115
CHAPTER 13	The Chase	123
CHAPTER 14	Stitched Up	133
CHAPTER 15	Back to the Brass Rail	143
CHAPTER 16	Visitor	157
CHAPTER 17	A Lesson Learned	171
CHAPTER 18	Rendezvous at the Laundry	179
CHAPTER 19	Tranquility and Surprise	191
CHAPTER 20	Return	197
CHAPTER 21	Skepticism and Reward	205
CHAPTER 22	June 18, 1953	219
CHAPTER 23	The French Embassy	223
CHAPTER 24	Irish to the Base	231
CHAPTER 25	Run for the Gate	247
CHAPTER 26	The Ride	257
CHAPTER 27	The War Is Over	267
CHAPTER 28	Gaijin	279
EPILOGUE	Citadel	287

CHAPTER ONE
Land of the Rising Sun
2054 Hours – Friday – 1952

The pop-top bottle of Dai Nippon beer he'd nursed most of the night was now empty. If he was going to make what little money he had left in his pocket stretch until payday, there was no extra cash for another brew. When it was time to leave he glanced around the bar, surveying the crowd for a few minutes, and then returned to his doodling. Delaying his departure, he created saloon art, the interconnecting of wet circles on the bar surface with the bottom of his glass. His total concentration was on the artwork, and while he was signing his name, Andy Anderson, on the moist surface, a soft feminine voice asked, "Want 'nother *buru?*"

"Huh?" With all the background clamor and deeply engrossed in his own thoughts, he hadn't fully heard the question. Looking up he gazed into the exquisite face and then down the low-cut blouse of a curious, gorgeous young Japanese barmaid who had leaned over the countertop to see what he was doing.

"You want 'nother buru?" The lovely woman lifted the empty pop-top beer bottle and waved it in his face to show him he needed another round. She winked and, with a seductive smile, purred, "'nother buru?"

Covering the glass with his hand, he shook his head. "No thanks,"

Andy had been stationed at the nearby air base for the past year, and the Japanese tavern had become his home away from home, a place where he felt comfortable. When you lived in an open-bay barracks with seventy-two men, even a crowded bar could give you a sense of privacy. Crammed wall to wall with patrons that night, the atmosphere of the saloon, or *izakaya,* echoed with the endless noisy chatter. Someone bellowed for another round of beer. The language was so foul and vulgar that even Satan, if he'd been there, would have turned away. The young enlisted men drank heavily, consuming more alcohol than necessary. But who cared? They were having a good time.

A few older retreads from World War II bellied up to the bar or slouched drunkenly in chairs. These men, reduced in rank for various misdemeanors, swapped lies and told war stories recalling their younger days of glory and sorrow. Andy personally knew only three of the older men, though they weren't all that old, maybe in their thirties. Irish, once a staff sergeant and now a private, had been arrested when he'd sold a Jeep on the black market. Sentenced to five years' hard labor in Leavenworth prison, he'd managed to cut a deal with the government prosecutors and turned informant on the buyers. In return for the information, he'd received a reduced sentence of six months in the stockade, reduction of rank, and been permitted to remain in the service. Irish bragged that he'd sold four Jeeps and a couple of truckloads of Jeep parts the government didn't know about. The proceeds of the illegal transactions had provided him with a comfortable little nest egg.

Then there was Private First Class Blankenship, a former master sergeant who'd once worked in the finance office. Blankenship would approve a voucher for early pay if you needed money—for a fee, of course. That is, until Uncle Sam discovered his little scheme. Sergeant Butler, an enlisted reservist, had been recalled to active duty at the beginning of the Korean War. He had been a captain at the end of World War II and had earned a chest full of medals and campaign ribbons that a four-star general would envy. Sadly, Butler still dealt with the stress of combat fatigue and drank heavily on occasion to repress the memories and nightmares.

Loud voices at a nearby table caught Andy's attention, and he swung around on the barstool to see why the group of R and R guys from Korea were arguing. The ensemble of Army and Air Force men sat around a table, arguing about which Asian women were the best in the sack—Korean, Japanese, or Chinese. The heated discussion intensified. A tall, skinny kid with peach fuzz on his chin slapped his hand down with enough force to rock the table and topple a bowl of peanuts.

"Ya don't know shit from Shinola!" he yelled. "Last night was the best lay ever. That little jo-san knew every move in the book!" He uttered the words, "What a night; what a friggin' wonderful night."

Then he sighed, and a grin big enough to make the Cheshire Cat jealous spread across his face.

"What the hell do you know about women?" taunted a pompous-looking Air Force two-striper. "I've spent more time in whorehouses in Seoul than you've been in the service. I bet you ain't got screwed more than once in your life, an' that was last night. And you were prob'ly so dang drunk you were tryin' to hump a pillow." He fiercely grabbed his bottle of beer and chugged the contents down in one long gulp. Then he wiped off his mouth with his grimy hand.

The skinny kid wanted to say something in response, but an Army PFC broke in. "You wimpy-assed flyboys are full of crap. My last R and R was in Hong Kong. Now, those are the women. They know how to take care of you! They got all the moves an' ain't lazy like them sluts in Korea."

The arrogant-looking character took exception to the comment. "Them cheap whorin' gals in Hong Kong all got the clap. You ground pounders are so dumb. Prob'ly thought the bitch was givin' ya VD as a birthday present all wrapped up in a fuzzy little box." He smirked and continued, "Y'all's so dumb you didn't even know what was goin' on until the gonorrhea got you hurtin'. Then the drippin' and burnin' became so bad when you pissed, ya almost ripped out the pipes from the urinal 'cause of the pain in your pecker."

The insult was perhaps partially correct, because the only comeback the Army grunt had was to double up his fist and cock back his forearm. "You're a smartass son of a bitch!" he yelled.

A scuffle commenced, with pushing, shoving, and derogatory remarks exchanged. They continued discussing and questioning each other's lineage as the quarrel heated up.

Along with half a dozen other regular patrons, Andy began to wonder if they needed to step in to quell the brewing fight. There were no bouncers in the bar; the regular patrons policed the joint themselves. If someone felt they needed a physical confrontation to settle their differences, the regulars requested the opponents take their argument outside. If the foes were reluctant to abide by the bar's unwritten protocol, or if the rivals had difficulty in locating the door, there were plenty of men in the bar who would happily help them to the exit. The regulars didn't cotton to the idea of the provost marshal closing the bar down and putting it off limits just because a few goofballs couldn't control their tempers.

During the argument, one soldier, a guy with an authoritarian manner, sat at the table and watched the exchange of heated words. Ordering a round of beer, he signaled to the waitress to place all the bottles in front of him on the table. "Damn it, knock it off!" he roared, noticeably annoyed.

This soldier stared at the two combatants and said sternly, "Come on … sit down! Shut up an' drink up or leave." He shoved a full bottle of beer in front of each of his companions at the table. "The night's still young, and I'm not goin' to spend the rest of my R an' R in the hoosegow!" He lifted his bottle toward them. "Drink up," he ordered in a commanding tone.

A couple of icy stares, some grumbling, and a tense moment ensued as a chair leg scraped against the floor, but no one left. One by one they lifted their bottles in a silent toast to one another, drank, and the conversations grew friendly. The turmoil had settled down to everyone's satisfaction without a punch being thrown.

Perhaps the Brass Rail wasn't the nicest of drinking establishments, and the décor did not meet everyone's taste. The building needed painting and repairs, and there was no uniform pattern to the room's furnishings, but the interior was clean, fastidiously so. Five polished cherrywood picture frames, displaying scenic calendar pictures of Japan, hung haphazardly on the freshly scrubbed plaster walls. The beautifully handcrafted frames seemed out of place in the tavern's humble chamber, as did the elaborate cherrywood bar that stood elegantly alongside the mismatched scruffy, scarred tables and chairs. The well-crafted appointments were of such quality they deserved a more sophisticated setting. Cracked and peeling red oilcloth covered the padded seats of the scratched barstools. The electric lighting was subdued, not by design, but because the overhead fixtures were inadequate to provide the illumination needed. A dim glow from two small lamps behind the bar cast a faint light. The wood floor, white from daily scouring with chlorine bleach, reflected no light. For most of the men, how you viewed the saloon depended on your pay grade. The bar was an off-base hangout for the lower-rank enlisted men, and it was the best Andy could afford.

Having lost interest in watching the group at the table, he swung his stool back around and turned to look at his buddy sitting next to him. "Hey, Mel!"

Coming from a wealthy Philadelphia family, Mel Schultz was a kid determined to put aside his prep school mannerisms and Ivy League style for approval and acceptance as one of the guys. Receiving no financial assistance from home, he was like the rest of the peons—broke most of the time.

All of Mel's attention was concentrated on ogling the shapely backside of the bar girl standing in front of Andy. The girl twirled lasciviously and strolled to the far end of the bar to serve other customers.

"Hey, Mel!" Andy said again, louder than necessary to bring the kid out of his lustful paralysis. "You ready to head back to the base?" Andy stuck a Lucky Strike in his mouth, stoked it up, and let out a lungful of blue smoke while he waited for a reply.

Mel couldn't take his eyes off the girl as she bent down to pick up a discarded cigar wrapper off the floor and her loose-cut top exposed her bosom. "Nah, don't think so. Gonna stay here a bit and then head on over to Chibi's joint and check out the entertainment. What about you?"

"Thought I'd walk over to the RTO and catch the bus back to the barracks." *Why can't they just call it a train station or depot rather than use the military acronym for Rail Transportation Office?*

A few dribbles of beer remained in the glass he had poised to his mouth, and Andy was ready to let the last few drops trickle down his throat when Mel jabbed him in the ribs. The jolt caused the lingering liquid to drip on the front of his uniform. "Shit, Mel, look what you made me do!"

"Sorry—didn't mean to, but check out Butler! The guy's got a snootful. Whoa, talk about being snot-lockered."

"He's gonna fall off that barstool in a second," Andy answered, a little fretful of what might happen if he actually did.

Way beyond the reasonable limits of sobriety, Butler sat precariously on the edge of the padded stool, both of his elbows firmly anchored on the countertop as he struggled to preserve his stability.

In a cynical manner, Mel commented, "He polished off that last jug of *sake* faster than most people can drink a shot. Got to give him credit; the guy can put the booze away!" Then he added in a condescending tone, "By morning he'll be down on all fours hugging the commode and wallowing around in his own stinking vomit."

The mama-san who owned the Brass Rail stood quietly behind the bar in the sedate fashion customary of older Japanese women, yet also with a regal elegance which declared her independence. The only name they ever addressed the woman by was simply Mama-san. She replaced Butler's empty *sake tokkuri* with a fresh decanter of warm rice wine, and she watched him with a concerned expression, as if saying, *You've consumed more than enough tonight, my friend. Go home.* She then positioned the newly filled tokkuri in close proximity to his hand but where he would not carelessly knock it over. Politely she bowed and backed away, and for a second, a glimpse of empathy broke through her solemn expression.

Andy worked in the same hangar, lived in the same barracks, and ate in the same chow hall as Butler. Although he was around the ex-officer most of the day and night, Andy didn't know him all that well. The scuttlebutt was that Butler still held the rank of captain in the inactive reserves. The guy kept to himself. He was a colleague, or perhaps more of an acquaintance, not quite a buddy. The difference in their ages played a large role in their relationship as well.

"I think we ought to try to get him back to the barracks before he passes out," Andy said. "He's ready to crash any minute."

"The old fart won't listen to us," Mel said, looking over his shoulder at Butler. "He goes by his own set of rules; it isn't our responsibility to babysit him. The guy's a snob. The man is the heir of some old aristocratic Southern family, and just 'cause he was an officer once, he thinks enlisted people are beneath him—we're like dirt to him."

"He ain't an officer anymore," Andy shot back. "If he's too hungover to do any work tomorrow, we'll have to pick up the slack, and he's not that bad of a guy."

"You don't need to defend him. The man is old enough to take care of himself, and he doesn't want our help. Besides, I betcha all those combat stories about him are a bunch of crap."

"You're probably right, but maybe there's some truth to them…. Butler's not a bad sort of guy…."

Andy quit talking, as Mel had focused all his attention on Sumiko, an attractive Eurasian hostess he'd been endlessly pursuing. Mel always described her as "a dish, a real winner, a complete knockout!" To use an expression he had picked up from a guy in the barracks, Mel would add that "she is built like a finely constructed outhouse with every brick in place."

Sensing they were looking at her, the fair-skinned young Eurasian woman turned to stare at them. As she shifted her position, the luster of her light brown hair shimmered in the subdued light for an instant. When she glanced at the two guys and smiled, there was a sparkle in her hazel eyes that Andy found irresistible, and he understood why Mel was so smitten with this young woman. She stood apart from the other Japanese women with their darker hair, and at times Andy knew it bothered her a great deal that she looked different. He and Sumiko had become close friends during the past year, since he had begun dating her roommate, Yoriko. Andy had chatted numerous times with Sumiko while waiting for Yoriko to finish work or when the three of them were out sightseeing. However, the only family and personal information Sumiko ever conveyed to him was that her parents were dead and she had grown up in an orphanage and foster homes.

Fiddling with the empty beer bottle, Andy observed Butler. The man's actions were comedic. He'd nod and doze off, and then he'd snap his head upright as he started to wake, and then he'd doze off again; you'd think he'd break his neck the way he popped it back. Slipping partway off the stool, Butler's elbows slid awkwardly from the bar top. He made a wild, desperate grab for the side of the bar, scraping and banging his knuckles harshly against the wood until his fingers found a grip. Funny, yes, yet Andy found it depressing to see Butler in such a drunken state.

Those who stood around him laughed at his antics, yet no one bothered or befriended him. When Butler was sober, he had an air of distinction about him. He was a classy guy, well educated, a graduate of the Citadel, the distinguished West Point of the South in Charleston. Andy liked him, but when Butler was drunk he was withdrawn and aloof.

A different bar girl, unknown to Andy, peered at him with a scheming expression that reminded him of a rattlesnake ready to strike. "Hey, you want buru? You sit, stare all time, or goin' drink? Want buru or sake? *Tabru*—food?" She paused for a second and then wheedled, "Me need keep job. What you want?"

He didn't say anything; he simply looked at her as she continued her tirade in a very gruff and unpleasant manner.

"Mama-san say we sell buru or lose job. Lose job, must go work on street. You no want see me on street. Street no place for nice girl like me. Me cherry girl." She glanced over her shoulder and shuddered. His eyes followed her gaze. Mama-san stood by the door to the kitchen, intently scrutinizing her with a disapproving stare.

He wondered what the deal was between this girl and Mama-san. In the year he'd been coming to the Brass Rail, he'd observed Mama-san interact with her employees. Mama-san always seemed fair, and the girls appeared to like her. Between these two, though, there was venom.

"Mama-san no like me; she watch me all time. I no like her." The words were spat out, full of hate.

"Why don't you quit; get another job?" he replied sharply.

"No can do. Have…" There was a long pause, as if she needed to think of an acceptable reply. "Have sick mother. Must work."

Perhaps I misjudged the woman, Andy thought, and trying to be polite and make amends, he asked, "What's your name?"

"My name Peggy," she replied.

"No, no, what's your Japanese name?"

"I no tell my Japanese name to no one," she spat back at him.

"Why not?"

"I no want you know," she countered in a nasty tone.

That little bit of negative chitchat put an icy frosting on their discussion. Time for him to go. He didn't think she would get into trouble because he wasn't buying any drinks. Moreover, he didn't think she was a cherry girl either. There was a deceitful and almost conniving quality about the woman; no wonder Mama-san watched her. He stood up and tapped Mel on the shoulder. "Hey! Leavin'. You gonna stay here, right?"

Mel had his arm draped over Sumiko's shoulder, trying to cop a feel, and was not about to let her go. "Guess so. Besides, I'm not ready to go. It's not even 2100; curfew's not till 2400. Over three hours left before we need to be back."

"OK, but I'm goin'. I've had enough beer. Going to hit the latrine first or my kidneys are gonna explode."

Andy finished his call of nature and walked out into the main room. He was standing by the door ready to leave when a small, supple arm slipped around his waist. A feminine body soft and warm cuddled invitingly against him, and with only a slight, subtle movement, her hip and leg sensuously caressed his. A light whiff of jasmine perfume wafted through the air; just by the fragrance he knew it was Yoriko, an eighteen-year-old Asian beauty, cute and sexy with a well-proportioned petite figure. He struggled against the influx of hormones that began to surge through his body.

"You leave now, Andy?" she whispered with a desperate, misty voice. "I no chance be with you. Mama-san say I must talk with the boys over there from Korea, much money to spend. I want be with you, but no can do."

Her touch was warm as velvet and smooth as silk.

"If not tonight, when?" Andy whispered. A flood of sensations began to overwhelm him, and he was ready to explode like a Roman candle at a Fourth of July fireworks celebration. Putting his arms around her, he brought her slim, tantalizing body close to his in an intimate hug. Bad mistake. All it did was increase his already heightened libido.

"Tomorrow night, no have work. We be 'gether."

The suggestive lilt of her voice sent a shiver of anticipation through his body. He needed to leave fast. With a quick, passionate kiss and a fast "See you tomorrow night," he swung open the door and fled the tavern before something embarrassing happened.

The languid spring night was a refreshing change after being inside the pub. The evening was warm and tranquil, free of cigarette smoke and the stench of stale beer. Drawing in a deep breath, he noticed the aroma that permeated the darkness was different. The air, so unlike the smell of the windswept plains of eastern Colorado, did not carry the same fragrances as home. An unknown faint pungent odor, unique to the lands of the Far East, hung in the gentle wind. The difference in the essences was unmistakable in the not-so-subtle scents.

Stores and shops were closed for the evening, their windows and doors boarded against intruders and thieves. It was quiet; little traffic moved on the street, the occasional bicycle and motor scooter or, now and then, a taxi. Couples lingered in secluded, darkened corners and doorways, trying to stay out of sight as they fondled and embraced. Streetwalkers propositioned GIs, while in turn the servicemen haggled to get a lower price for an evening of enjoyment. The world's oldest profession was not an uncommon way to make a living in a war-torn, occupied country. Ladies of the evening touting their services were a standard aftermath of war; they had a commodity that sold, and it was a way to survive. The war had been over for six years, but its disastrous consequences called for unorthodox solutions in the critical struggle for basic human survival.

A billboard for the local cinema attracted his attention. The sign advertised John Wayne's 1934 cowboy presentation *'Neath the Arizona Skies*. It was hilarious to listen to the Duke speak in dubbed Japanese. The one time he and Yoriko had gone to a Japanese movie, there had been no popcorn. Instead, they'd snacked on rice crackers and tangerines.

A few yards past the theater, a viaduct bridged the small river that bisected town. The bridge's concrete railing was the right height to lean on and loll against on this warm spring night. He stopped, propped his elbows on the rail, and gazed at the river. Light from the stars reflected on the surface of the slow-moving stream and glistened in the darkness. The mirrored glow of the moon, distorted by the water, undulated in constantly rising and falling patterns, much like how his perspective of the world and life had transformed during the months he'd been in Japan.

Growing up on a farm near a small, isolated town, Andy's perception of people had been somewhat limited. His view had been greatly altered by the different individuals he had met since joining the military. Most of the acquaintances he had made were casual, but a few were more than chance meetings, and they were people he would remember all his life. They included the unforgettable Remmey, whom he had met on the troopship; a guy nicknamed Skeeter, whom he had met in tech school and who was also stationed there in Japan; Mel and Butler; Yoriko; Sumiko; and Mama-san.

He diverted his attention as he spotted a woman walking down the road toward him. The dim light and the distance between them made it difficult for him to make out her features. For a second, elation swelled. He thought it might be Yoriko and she had somehow managed to get off work and follow him. As the person drew nearer, though, disappointment took over when he realized it was an older woman. As the lady drew abreast, she said, "I give you short time for three thousand yen. Best ever; maybe I so good you want go all night. OK, GI?"

What a shame. The woman doesn't look and isn't dressed anything like a prostitute. How sad that consequences from the war have driven her to sink to the depths of soliciting on the street. "No have yen," he said, thinking it proper, polite, and discreet to say he didn't have any cash rather than tell her he wasn't interested. He shrugged his shoulders in a negative reply and she walked on by, staring out into space without even looking at his face.

Andy had observed Mama-san, who owned the bar, staring like that sometimes. A wistful look of fleeing into the past, seeing objects and places only she could see. There were rumors Mama-san had been a geisha before the war. She displayed the characteristics of a trained geisha, the short, gliding, graceful walk; the perfect posture; and the elegant traits and mannerisms associated with the renowned profession. It was rather ironic one of Japan's elite geisha would now be running a second-rate bar for a bunch of American GIs.

A splash in the water below startled him. Craning his neck he looked under the bridge, searching the dark shadows for the source of the noise. The dim moonlight highlighted a few ripples in the sluggish-moving water but revealed nothing else. Upstream, indistinct figures scurried cautiously on the banks of the canal. The silhouettes slipped clandestinely in and out of the darkness, pausing and looking back at the bridge, giving the impression they were checking to see if someone was watching. He couldn't make out who or what they were. Squinting, he peered into the night, trying to keep track of them until the darkness obscured their movements. There was no motion by the bridge or under it, and nothing happening by the water. After waiting quietly for a few minutes, listening, Andy walked across the bridge and stared downstream. Fifty yards away, he could vaguely distinguish human forms lurking by the river's edge. His attention was riveted on the indistinct figures as they inched toward the bridge.

CHAPTER TWO
The Encounter

No one saw as she slipped the opiate drug cocktail into the man's sake tokkuri. It would be twenty to thirty minutes before the sedative started to work, so when he left the bar he should be amenable to almost any suggestion. At least that was what her pimp had told her, and he'd gotten the drug from the Chinese, who'd said they were using it in the prisoner of war camps in North Korea. The Chinese had supplied the drug as part of the deal when her pimp, Koji, had agreed to steal American military identification cards for them. *We should have no trouble rolling the GI*, he'd explained to her, *taking his money and ID card.* The money they could keep. The identification cards went to the Chinese. *The Americans are so gullible, especially when drunk or drugged; I don't understand how they won the war.*

"What do you want, young lady?" Butler snapped. Sensing a presence opposite him, he opened his eyes to see a woman standing across the bar from him. Something troubled him; the only one who served him was Mama-san. *Why is this girl messing with my drink?* But the wine clouded his ability to reason, and the questions vanished.

"You mo' something drink," she sneered, positive that he'd not seen her slip him the Mickey Finn.

"No! No!" He waved her off. "Wait a minute." He looked around. "Is Andy still here?"

"Who Andy?"

"That sandy-haired kid who was sitting on the barstool over there. You were talking to him earlier in the evening."

"Not here…. Think they all gone now. Go other bar."

"If they come back in, tell me…. No, never mind," he muttered and then continued droning on to himself. "Don't need any help getting back to the base. Can manage it alone; better alone." Approaching within earshot of the conversation, Mama-san intervened and instantly shooed Peggy away. The only English words she knew and had managed to hear were "help" and "base," but she'd immediately grasped what he needed. In a mixture of English, Japanese, and gestures, she communicated, "You stay here and I'll find you help to the barracks."

Butler watched the bar owner and nodded in a perfunctory way. Then he reached for his sake cup and downed the altered contents. Mama-san refilled his cup. He pushed it aside, laid his head on the bar, and closed his eyes.

The bar owner turned from Butler and saw Peggy, who, with a sleight-of-hand movement, swiped her bar towel and scooped up the change a patron had left lying beside his drink. Deftly depositing the money in her skirt pocket, she smiled at her victim. The unsuspecting customer never spotted his cash had disappeared.

There had been reports of someone pilfering money, and now Mama-san had caught the culprit. She moved with amazing speed, grabbed the thief by the scruff of her neck, and hauled her into the kitchen, slamming the door behind them.

The older woman was livid with anger and, using her open hand, she cuffed the barmaid on the cheek.

"Why did you hit me?" Peggy wailed.

"Because you're a worthless piece of gutter trash. I gave you a job, a chance, an opportunity. How do you repay me? By robbing my customers?" The girl had deliberately betrayed her trust, which infuriated Mama-san. She smashed the cowering Peggy across the face with the back of her hand.

Sobbing, the barmaid began making excuses and seeking sympathy, although she had been caught in the act. "He gave me the money! I didn't steal it. I'd never take money that is not mine."

"Shall we go and ask him?" Mama-san replied.

"No, don't. I'm sorry! It was the first time. I'll never do it again, I promise," she continued, crying and pleading.

"Disrobe, now," demanded Mama-san. "I want to search your clothing."

The younger woman sniveled and blubbered. "Here in the kitchen? What about my pride, my modesty; you would take that from me? You slapped me, and now you wish to further demean me here in front of everyone!"

Mama-san unsympathetically responded, "You stole from me. You have no idea what real pain, humility, and suffering are. You are worthless. You're a whore, a streetwalker. You have no morals about stealing, so why should undressing bother you? Take off your clothes or I will I call the police."

Peggy reluctantly began to peel off her clothing, and Mama-san inspected each garment as she did. Finding the hidden pocket in the petticoat, Mama-san retrieved the rest of the night's ill-gotten money, and she was satisfied.

"Enough!" Mama-san ordered, "Now out and never come back, or I'll have you jailed. Out! Out!" Through the back door of the kitchen Mama-san forcefully shoved the thief, happily rid of the *doroboo*. "Dress out in the street like the rest of the tramps," Mama-san added as she threw the discarded clothing at the younger woman, who was now clad only in her bra and underwear. Then the bar owner closed and locked the door.

***

Butler lifted his head off the bar; he took no notice of the mellowing effects of the opiates in the Mickey Finn he'd unwittingly ingested. Bleary-eyed he stared at the sake cup. The small ceramic mug kept shifting in his vision from a single to a double image and back. "Enough booze; time to stop, but better finish this one before I leave," he slurred, each word incoherent.

The thought of finishing the sake, however, slipped from his mind as effortlessly as an olive slides to the bottom of a martini glass. Getting off his stool proved to be a challenge, however. Holding onto the bar with one hand as he slid off the stool, he managed to stabilize his equilibrium. Legs unsteady, he staggered toward the john to relieve himself. A cool breeze brushed across his face, and he mindlessly turned toward it, forgetting his objective. The open front door of the bar beckoned him and he wandered outside, stumbling across the threshold.

Once outside at the tavern's entrance, a dizziness overwhelmed him, and to keep from falling he propped himself against the doorframe.

Enraged by Mama-san's treatment, Peggy had managed to recover her clothing and get dressed. She was furious as she walked around the corner of the building to the front door. Then she stopped and smiled to herself. Even though Mama-san's slaps hurt, they were nothing like what her pimp would do to her if she returned empty-handed. But it was karma; the GI was still there, leaning against the wall like an old broom. The opportunity of taking his cash was even sweeter now. The American was one of Mama-san's favorites, and Peggy was determined to make him pay for the humiliating treatment she had received from the old geisha. *Who does that uppity, scar-faced bitch think she is, anyway?* she grumbled to herself. She would get even with that callous old witch even if she needed to kill the old lady.

"Mama-san tell me help you back base."

Butler dimly heard a soft woman's voice as it spoke from shadows. A hand grabbed his arm, pulled him from the stoop, and hustled him away from the bar, around the corner and down a back alley. *She said Mama-san sent her, so it's OK.* He trusted Mama-san. Somewhere in the recesses of his mind a little voice was telling him to wait until his head cleared, that something wasn't right. But in his permissive, opiate-clouded state, procrastination was simple, and objections were of no importance.

Peggy held his arm firmly as she swiftly guided him through the dark and dingy back alleys. At one point he questioned her, saying, "This doesn't look like the way to the main gate."

"Short way. Round corner; you see" was her response.

His reasoning abilities weakened, he trod along beside her as they passed through an area of decaying buildings. The woman slowed her pace as they approached a dilapidated shack which fronted the alley. They paused, and she rapped loudly on the closed shutters. A treacherous-looking man peered out through a small opening; Peggy motioned for him to follow.

"Why did you do that?" Butler asked.

She didn't answer and only tightened her grip on his arm, compelling the man to accompany her on her trek. In his mellow mood he offered little resistance, permitting the woman to take him in tow as he blindly followed her down the dark, secluded, and narrow alleyways. Yellow slivers of light shone dimly through cracks in the shuttered windows, suggesting habitation, but none of the shacks or hovels invited entry.

Peggy glanced back over her shoulder, looking for her partner. *Where is he? He should have caught up by now.* Was she going to have to rob this GI by herself? She guessed she could do it. The American was as tame as a puppy dog and asleep on his feet. What would she do if he passed out here in the alley? *I must find a spot, a safe place to hide him.*

Eventually, they stopped and entered a ramshackle shed. Fatigued, he leaned against the wall as he fought to stay awake. His mind spun in endless circles, a kaleidoscope of meaningless, confused emotions. The dreams were there, just under the surface of his consciousness, groping and clawing to manifest their terror. A memory of his past came tearing across his mind, a panorama flashed in his subconscious; it waved and beckoned as scenes projected onto a silver screen. He was part of the memory and suffered the anxiety and pain, yet he viewed the incidents as an observer.

On that fateful fall morning in 1942, the gritty and grimy dirt of the African desert caked the inside of his mouth. He was thirsty, desperately craving water, his throat parched beyond relief. The sun's intense rays beat down upon him, penetrating his clothing as if the material were cheesecloth. No shade or habitation existed in the wilderness in which he might rest and escape the ruthless heat. His sweat-crusted shirt clung to his body like a ravenous leech sucking the last few drops of moisture from his skin. The sergeant, shot in the leg during the skirmish and again in the shoulder, limped along beside him across the darkened terrain, his lifeblood seeping from his wounds. Physically unable to go any farther, he collapsed and lay helpless on the forsaken wasteland.

Struggling laboriously to breathe, Butler carried and dragged the wounded and unconscious platoon sergeant over the endless miles of scorching sand. Without the perception of movement he traversed the hot, barren landscape inch by inch, constantly moving toward a distant point where he hoped there was an American aid station.

An 8mm German slug had raked across Butler's thigh, tearing and ripping away flesh and muscle. The wound ached and burned, and dried blood stiffened the fabric of his trousers. With each step, the hardened material rubbed and irritated the inflamed gash.

The platoon sergeant might die. Butler refused to give up and was determined to carry the wounded man across Africa to find medical aid if he must. Stopping to rest was not an option; he'd never find the strength to start again. *Move, must keep moving, slow and endlessly, placing one foot in front of the other, over and over.* With each plodding step, his feet grew heavier until he no longer had strength to lumber forward.

It had been late in the afternoon when they'd run into the enemy ambush. Butler was a first lieutenant, his mission to lead a search, rescue, and recovery mission. With the platoon sergeant, the group was comprised of remnants of Butler's original platoon as well as stragglers and injured soldiers they had come across during the operation. Butler ordered the squad to retreat in the half-track back to the Allied lines and they should take the wounded and dead with them while he and the sergeant stayed behind. They would provide cover fire against the advancing Germans and Italians.

"Sir!" the corporal had shouted. "They'll pin you down; too many of them!"

"Don't argue with me, Corporal. Get going. We'll clear out once it's dark. That's an order."

Dusty plumes of sand thrown up behind the plodding half-track faded as the armored vehicle disappeared beyond the hills of sand. Then he and the sergeant were alone to face the uncertain odds of life and death. Pinned down by the superior number of Axis troops and firepower, they were unable to move. Conditions worsened as the day wore on. Short on ammunition and water, it would be only a short time before the inevitable happened.

Cast by the dunes, the eerie evening shadows lengthened as sunlight began to melt into darkness. A lone American P-40 Warhawk fighter sped through the evening sky, its engine roaring as the plane passed overhead. As the German machine guns opened fire, tracer bullets streaked through the dusky sky in pursuit of the speeding plane. The pilot of the P-40 paid no heed and continued on his course. Then the plane unexpectedly banked and came thundering back. Skimming the tops of the dunes, the plane made a single strafing run against the enemy position, the six wing-mounted guns spitting out destruction and death. The firing pass complete, the Warhawk circled and returned to its original heading. As it raced low over Butler, the pilot tipped the plane's wings in recognition and vanished into the dim light on the horizon. The diversion created by the P-40 presented the opportunity to make their escape, and they bolted into the desert.

The memory faded as Peggy shoved Butler, trying to push him farther into the shed. He had limited control over his movements and, losing his balance, he fell and slammed against a wooden wall. Momentarily, he was conscious of his surroundings. He knew he must flee and tried to straighten his unwilling body and attempt to run. Seized by the terrifying fear that he was going to get away, she beat on him with her clenched hands, the pent-up anger against Mama-san alive in her flaying fists. He felt nothing but a slight pressure from the blows, as the opium conquered both his ability to reason and any sensation of pain. Tremendously tired and exhausted he felt his knees buckle, and he collapsed to the floor in an agonized slumber.

Images of the blistering desert plagued his memory, and the vision was devoured by a tormenting hallucination, no longer a memory but a terrifying delusion.

Night faded and it became late morning. Their canteens were empty and a hot, blistering sun beat down, searing his skin. The weight of the body draped across Butler's shoulder pushed him down, forcing his feet deeper and deeper into the fiery inferno of sand. The sergeant's blood had soaked through Butler's shirt and encrusted his arms and hands. His own blood already drenched and discolored his pants. *Blood, so much blood. Will it ever wash from my skin?* He was unclean. He wanted to stop and scrub his body with sand, scour his skin with the rough granules, ridding it of the red parasite that coated and infected him. He needed to be cleansed.

The body slipped from his shoulder, and the motionless sergeant lay prostrate on the yellow sand. A ring of crimson appeared and gradually grew as it encompassed the motionless human form. Butler stood transfixed as the red circle continued to grow larger second by second, expanding and magnifying until the sands from horizon to horizon were sodden with a brilliant red. Blue sky changed its hue to pink, then red. The earth trembled and the heavens erupted, bursting into blistering flames and raining fire, and he closed his eyes tight against the terror.

Unexpectedly he stood alone, surrounded by an ominous barren desert that stretched forlornly outward in all directions. The ground became spongy, the soft granules of sand dissolving under his feet. Struggling to preserve his balance, he realized the soft, shifting sand no longer supported his weight. His knees buckled as he collapsed, and the earth opened and drew him beneath the surface. A relentless whirlpool of wind and sand drew him deeper into the depths of a bottomless abyss, down through the burning gates of hell, sucking out his breath and smothering him. The rancid, foul odor of burning and rotting flesh filled his nostrils and constricted his throat. Thrashing his arms wildly, he fought to escape to the surface as he labored for air, shoving and clawing against the weight of his suffocating prison. The heavy sand smothered him as he churned his hands wildly, flinging his arms in every direction in a desperate attempt to remove the substance that covered his nose and mouth.

***

In a moment of lucidity, he struggled to rise and his attempt was thwart by a blow to his head, and a searing pain encased him. Darkness enveloped him, and all sounds ceased.

A peaceful force guided him along an invisible path, and as yielding as a child, he moved toward the tranquil radiance of the celestial light. A silhouette of someone standing at the fringe of the luminosity beckoned to him … oblivion.

CHAPTER THREE
Memories of the Sea Journey

Unseen in the opaqueness of the night, small ripples of water washed against the riverbank. The disturbance of the water was the consequence of the dumping of a human body, which now floated face down on the surface. The cadaver bobbed gently with the serene movement of the water. As they crept farther away, the men responsible for the disposed person's demise looked back, checking on their handiwork, and speculated on the inquisitive man loitering on the bridge.

As the corpse floated on the sluggish water, the current was not strong enough to move it with any noticeable perception until it began slowly drifting towards the riverbank. Bare, tentacle-shaped branches of a tree snag-grasped the unconcerned prey, attaching themselves tightly to the soggy clothing. With the additional weight the branch twisted and bent, and the portion of the bough buried in the mud loosened. The obstruction held for a few minutes and then reluctantly gave way to the additional burden and motion of the water. Gradually drifting through the shallow water, the dead man's shoe caught on a submerged clump of mud. With a quagmire grip the muck held onto the shoe leather, laying claim to the remains it had captured. The inertia of the small river struggled against the goo and mire and recouped its prize. Unintimidated, the little river languidly carried the tree snag and the remains downstream in a bizarre watery burial procession.

Andy followed the movements in the darkness as the two figures from downstream walked closer to the bridge. As they neared, he could make out they were a couple of GIs who stood by the river's edge, staring at the water. *Were those two the source of the sound? I'd swear that the noise in the water was on the other side of the bridge.*

One of the two suddenly said, "Bet I can skip this here rock across."

"Bet ya can't. You got a round rock, and you need a flat one. 'Sides, you're nex' ta bein' too loaded to throw it. Ya can't even stand up straight," replied the other man with a slight Midwestern twang.

"I'm not the one who stepped into the damn water. You did, not me."

"Reckon we best oughta head back now. Ain't feelin' so good. Maybe were that raw fish an' noodles I ate."

"Let's go…. Ya gotta puke?"

There were choking and gagging noises, coughing, and finally spitting. The one with the twang commented, "That were nasty."

"OK now? Come on." They stumbled up the riverbank and headed down the thoroughfare.

The two compadres made their way along the street, incapable of walking in a straight line as they wove and staggered. One started singing a ditty to the melody of "Across the Alley from the Alamo." His friend joined in, and together they howled at the moon like a couple of drunken coyotes.

> Across the alley from the RTO
> Lives a short-time gal named Sayoko.
> She sings a doko e iku no
> To the GIs passin' by.
> One day, I went a-walkin'
> Down by the railroad tracks.
> Sayoko came a callin',
> GI, you come back.
> Oh, across the alley from…

Their voices faded away in the distance. Andy's eyes trailed them as they meandered toward the main gate, two friends trying to take care of each other. *What about Oren Butler? There are times when you need a friend. I hope he realizes he does have friends.*

When Andy could no longer see or hear the two, he turned and walked to the bus stop at the Rail Transportation Office. His internal deliberation of whether Butler could manage to find his way to the barracks without assistance came to an abrupt conclusion. A bus was waiting, scheduled to leave in five minutes. *The guy is a grown man, and he can take care of himself.* He boarded the conveyance as concerns about Oren Butler and his plight slipped from his mind.

Having found an empty seat, he slid in and slouched down, taking up the entire padded bench, and began thinking about the trip over from San Francisco. He had been at Camp Stoneman in California for three weeks, in the Air Force for only six months, and then he'd shipped out.

***

Water broke over the bow of the USNS *General Howe* as the ship, bound for Yokohama, plowed through the rough waters of the Pacific. The second day out, the choppy seas became the culprit for a rash of seasickness onboard. Andy trudged up the companionway stairs from the lower depths of the ship where he'd been assigned a bunk. His assigned compartment was so far under the waterline that he imagined the fish were swimming next to him and perhaps Poseidon slept in the next bunk. The ship's loudspeakers were always blaring some announcement, do this or don't do that, some rule or regulation the troops were supposed to obey. This time, the monotonous voice of the unseen person droned over the speakers, "Now hear this. Now hear this. Everyone remain below deck until the weather clears. Everyone remain below deck until further notice. Dangerous conditions topside."

Ignoring the droning voice, he and a few others ventured topside for fresh air, heedless of the weather and the warning. Cows, horses, and pigs were smells he was used to, but not that of so many boxed-in *Homo sapiens*. The locker room odor of four thousand male human beings cooped up in enclosed cramped quarters was more than a farm boy like him wanted to take.

Andy had read magazine advertisements touting ocean voyages, luxurious cruises where you lounged comfortably in varnished wooden deck chairs. While a crew member in a white starched uniform catered to your every need. All you did was sit and enjoy a sophisticated life. Or so the magazine ads read, but this ship was by no stretch of the imagination in the same class as the grand luxury liner the *Queen*

Mary. A fourteen-day cruise on a troopship wasn't a grand passage, and the days were not glorious. You were either pulling some crummy detail or hiding from the duty sergeant.

When he had lugged his overstuffed duffel bag up the gangplank, he had a chance to glance around. *This is where I'm going to live for the next two weeks. I doubt this beat-up old tub will stay afloat, let alone make it all the way across the ocean to Japan.*

The first day out he found that if he wanted to find an empty place by the rail, he needed to roll out of the sack by dawn and be up on deck before most of the men were even awake. By a chance discovery he had located a niche, a little open space between the railing and a folding ladder. This cranny was a bit small, but there was enough room to rest his back against the rolled-up rungs and stretch his legs through the metal balustrade that prevented him from sliding into the sea. There he planned to sit for the next two weeks, eyes closed, soaking up the sunshine.

The view from the cubby space allowed him to gaze at sea and sky or study the movements of others roaming the deck. The only problem was if he needed a latrine break or wanted to go to chow, someone always commandeered the spot as soon as he left.

On the third day at sea he met Remmey, a burly guy from Chicago, a two-striper who said he'd been in the Air Force for a couple of years. An agreeable person, he looked to be twenty-one or twenty-two, but occasionally he would say or do something to make Andy think he was older, little slips of the tongue that Andy thought were peculiar but never questioned him about.

Remmey's aid became beneficial; at least one of them occupied the site during daylight hours. If one wanted to go to eat or stretch his legs, the other stayed and kept watch, keeping intruders away. The best part of throwing in with Remmey was that the guy had a medical excuse that exempted him from details and left him always available to help guard the location.

Andy was curious. The guy didn't seem to be ill. So one day he ventured, "Remmey, how'd you get that sick slip that keeps you from havin' to pull crappy duty like the rest of us?"

A scowl exploded on Remmey's face. "Ain't none of your business!" he growled.

Unsure whether the question had made Remmey angry or if the curt reply was part of his tough act, Andy never inquired again. He needed Remmey to secure the cubbyhole, and it made no difference how he had managed to obtain the medical slip; it was just important that he didn't have to pull details.

Bored of watching the endless waves crest and break, Andy started picking at a flake of loose gray paint on the deck in front of him. He poked and meddled with the paint chip until it worked loose, revealing rusting metal underneath.

"Take a look. See how rusty this old tub is?" He pointed out the brown color to Remmey, who was leaned back with his feet stuck through the rails. "You would think they'd junk this boat before it falls apart and sinks."

Remmey looked over at him, not replying for a few moments, and then said thoughtfully, "What do you know about this ship?"

"Nothin' other than its name and there are too many people aboard and the food is crappy."

"Well, this old tub, as you call her, has an impressive history." Remmey's voice softened as he continued. A noticeable thing about Remmey was that when he began speaking of history or past events, he lost the vulgar and coarseness of his speech pattern and spoke as a refined, cultured person. He abandoned the street jargon he spoke most of the time. Andy often wondered about this abrupt change in speech but thought if he probed into the reason, Remmey might quit telling his stories. This was an ornery guy from the South Side of Chicago, supposedly self-educated, yet when he spoke it was with elegance and the knowledge of a historian.

"The USNS *Howze*—launched 1943. I don't recall in which shipyard she was built. But the *Howze* ferried troops back and forth during the war in the Pacific to the various islands as they were recaptured from the Japanese. Also, it transported Japanese prisoners of war at one time."

Andy was astonished at what Remmey was telling him and even more surprised that Remmey knew the ship's background.

Remmey looked to see if Andy had shown any interest in what he was saying. The young man was listening intently, so Remmey continued.

"The *Howze* became a refugee ship and provided transport for individuals and families displaced by the war from Europe to Melbourne. In fact, the ship made two of these humanitarian trips to Australia, one in 1949 and another in 1950. The *Howze* made numerous voyages between Europe and the United States with displaced war victims as its passengers. Once it served as a floating POW camp, transporting over three thousand German prisoners of war. After the war, it carried American servicemen back home from Europe."

Andy's furrowed brow sent the message that he was puzzled, and Remmey grinned at him. "I did a little research about the ship before we came aboard." Then he continued relating the story of the boat as if it were a living being. "If you knew a third of the stories of what and who has been on this ship, I think you would look at her in a different light. She has been the bearer of both joy and sadness. She's saved and changed people's lives by taking them to safe havens and new beginnings. She's carried others to war and to their deaths."

He paused. "She's served her country proudly and should be allowed to have a little rust." Then he stopped talking and gazed out over the rolling blue waters of the Pacific.

"You need to take in the whole picture, Andy, not just what's on the surface, before you pass judgment."

***

The bus door slammed shut, the engine started, and the driver revved the motor, the sound of which rudely interrupted Andy's reminiscences of the past. The shuttle pulled out of the parking area, and the driver maneuvered it along the bumpy street to the base, hitting every pothole he could find. The bus slowed at the bridge. The flashing lights of an ambulance and several MP Jeeps lit up the area. Andy strained to see what was going on, but an MP directing traffic motioned for the bus to pull forward. At the gate, the driver swung the conveyance over to the curb, parked with the motor idling, and flung open the door.

One of the gate guards, a one-striper with an attitude and a cocky swagger, boarded the bus. "Passes and IDs out," he commanded, flaunting his authority. A passenger in one of the front seats asked, "What's happening down at the bridge?"

"Can't tell ya nothin'. Ongoing investigation." The guard strutted up and down the aisle, checking and double-checking everyone's identification. His task completed, he strutted off, and the shuttle started moving again.

Andy started to slump back in the seat and close his eyes when he noticed the two inebriated guys from the river sitting in the back of an MP Jeep, but he couldn't tell if they were handcuffed or not. *Wonder why they picked up those two poor slobs. All they're guilty of is trying to skip rocks on the water.*

As the bus sped on into the night and away from the lights of the gate, he settled back in his seat and continued recalling the sea voyage.

***

Remmey was a hard person to figure out. At times he projected the image of a hard-hitting guy or thug, but he was neither. His intelligence, knowledge, and mannerisms did not always fit his character. A living, walking, talking history book, he spoke of the gangs and the turbulent years that had gripped the city of Chicago. His Prohibition-era stories filled the empty days at sea. Andy sat and listened, mesmerized, for hours as Remmey related the sagas of Chicago in the 1920s. Remmey had an overwhelming curiosity and interest in the lives of Al Capone, John Dillinger, Baby Face Nelson, Bugs Moran, and others of the time. He knew all the facts about the gangsters of that era, and he could recount exactly what had happened at the 1929 Saint Valentine's Day Massacre. He told what had been relayed to him or what he had read so fervently you could visualize what had happened as he spoke.

One day, he asked Andy who his heroes were when he was growing up—not Superman or Captain Marvel, but real-life figures.

Andy thought for a moment and replied, "Nathan Hale; he was a man who loved his country enough to spy on the enemy, and in the end he forfeited his life for the betterment of his nation."

The troopship's tutelage included how to avoid the duty NCO. Early in the trip, Andy found out that the lower your rank, the crappier work assignments you pulled. With his pay grade of E-2, he was next to the bottom. Remmey, who was always vigilant in the morning, helped him keep a sharp eye out for the duty NCOs as they strolled around the deck hunting for unsuspecting GIs. If it looked like Andy was about to be garnered for a detail, he moved to a less observable place or walked at a faster pace around the deck in front of duty NCOs so they wouldn't nab him. Remmey, a great lookout, had a knack for sighting the duty NCOs before Andy. When he did spot one, he'd punch Andy on the shoulder and mutter under his breath, mimicking James Cagney or Edward G. Robinson, "Scram, kid, here come dem screws." He liked using the 1920s expression for prison guards or "here comes da dicks," the slang for policeman. One of his favorites was "Cheese it, here come da cops." Andy didn't volunteer for any details and avoided KP like the plague, having learned from different sources that seasickness came with the job down in the kitchen area. The idea of heaving your guts up until you passed out down in a hot, steamy, cramped compartment didn't appeal to him.

One day late in the morning, Remmey had gone walking around the deck. Andy was seated in his usual spot, staring out over the water. The duty NCOs had already been around once, and Andy had let down his normal vigilance and relaxed. An uncomfortable feeling that someone was staring at him made him glance up and into the glaring face of a duty NCO, who said, "We're a little short of people on latrine duty today, and I believe it's about your turn."

He wanted to make up some excuse why he couldn't pull the detail, but thought better of the idea and only said in an enquiring tone, "But Sarge…."

The staff sergeant showed no expression as he uttered, "I'm in no mood to be jerked around, Airman. Don't try it."

Being smart enough to know when he was beaten, Andy sighed, "OK, Sarge, give me a second to gather up my stuff."

The sarge wrote Andy's name and other information in his duty log, copied the information onto a slip of paper that had a map of the ship and the latrines' locations, and handed it to him. "This map is so you don't get lost. You need to contact the sergeant whose name is listed at each location." The sarge pointed to the map. "Anderson, make sure you report within the next fifteen minutes. I don't want to come looking for you!"

"Sure, Sarge, will do." If Andy didn't report, his ass was mud.

He had resigned himself to the fact that someone would grab his sitting spot as soon as he left and was getting ready to leave when Remmey showed up. Andy had someone to gripe to, and he relayed his story of bad luck.

"Sorry, Andy. Didn't think they would be tapping anyone this late in the day, or I would have stuck around."

Latrine detail, or head duty, was not a pleasurable job, even in the barracks. The chore of cleaning a toilet on a troopship where thousands of men used the facility each day was the worst job imaginable.

When he got to the head, he gave the sergeant in charge the duty slip. The sergeant looked at the paper, glanced around the latrine for a moment, and said, "You ever been on head duty before?"

"No, Sarge; been on latrine duty lots of times in the barracks, but nothin' like this."

"Same thing, just bigger and dirtier," the sergeant said.

The sergeant knew from Andy's expression that he wasn't happy pulling the duty. "Anderson, I'm short two men on this detail, and you're the first one to report. You have your choice, the sinks or the shit trough and urinals. You pick."

Scrubbing out the grungy, putrid, long metal urinal and a multiple-hole communal commode, best described as an indoor-outdoor privy, was plain disgusting. The john was just a long trough filled with water that sloshed back and forth with the movements of the ship. A long board seat with holes sawed out every couple of feet covered the opening. Like a vast outhouse, you sat down in public, pants down around your ankles while you took care of business. On the plus side, the seating arrangement did make passing reading material easier.

The smell from where he was standing was bad enough, and he didn't hesitate. "The sinks, Sergeant; I'll do the sinks."

"A good decision, Anderson. Some of the troops have diarrhea so bad they don't care if they hit the hole or not when they take a dump. Grab a bucket, rags, ammonia, cleanser, and whatever else you need, and get to work. Make sure you keep those sinks clean, wiped down, and the floor around them mopped. A lot of traffic in here all the time, and they become dirty fast. You'll be relieved at 1700."

Years of human use had stained the sinks to the extent that they were impossible to clean. The nauseating sour smell issuing from them turned your stomach. With rationing of fresh water, they used seawater for cleaning as well as showering. Soap and ocean water don't work well together—no suds, no power to clean. He scrubbed, mopped, and scoured all day, and then he repeated the process.

The next morning, Andy slipped into his spot and managed to find a comfortable position against the ladder. Just as he closed his eyes, Remmey slapped him on the shoulder and asked, "How did you like the latrine detail?"

Andy's sarcastic but truthful answer was "If offered the choice, I'd rather scoop out a barn full of fresh cow manure with a damn tablespoon than ever clean the head on a troopship again."

"Don't fret; you won't get shithouse duty again if ya did it once! Here," he said, shoving a cup of warm coffee into Andy's hand. "Sorry it's not real hot, hopefully it'll make up for my not covering your ass yesterday."

"How the hell did you manage to drag a cup of coffee out here on deck? If they catch you, all hell will break loose."

"Well, kid, if you're worried about it, then you'd better give the coffee back to me."

"No! No!" Andy held onto the mug and gulped the coffee, thankful for the warmth and caffeine. He didn't question Remmey again about how or where he'd commandeered the coffee. Some questions were better left unanswered.

As much as Andy disliked the troopship, it became an educational trip. His semi-isolated upbringing in a small town on the farm had left him lacking in a lot of areas of life experiences. Of the multiple tutoring experiences presented to, forced on, and exposed to him on the ship, he failed one miserably.

One day, up on deck, a couple of guys asked him if he wanted to play pinochle with them.

"Nah," he told them. "Don't know how."

"We need another person. Come on, we'll show you; it ain't hard to learn."

Teach him they did. The rules were a penny a point and twenty-five cents for a setback. His momentary stash came to a grand total of four dollars and thirty-seven cents. At a penny a point, he didn't think he'd lose much. After one day of playing pinochle, he was flat broke. It wasn't so much that they'd won his money; it was more like he'd given it to them.

After that lesson, gambling held no glamour for him, nor did it seem like a way to make a fast buck. When he'd lost all his money, Andy could picture his grandma standing in front of him, waving her old arthritic finger and lecturing in that stern voice of hers: "The evils of wagering are the ruination of many a man." Once again, the old woman was right.

Andy's waking hours were spent talking with Remmey. They discussed childhood experiences, Andy answering questions about farm life and Remmey telling stories of the city. Andy sat for days, raptly listening to Remmey recount American history. The guy wasn't just knowledgeable on Chicago, he also told stories of the American Revolution and the Civil War. He also knew about the exploits of Louis and Clark and the dangers they'd faced on their trek. The tales he told of the settling of the West held Andy spellbound, along with yarns on how the railroad contributed to the expansion of the country. Remmey recounted history in a fascinating and passionate manner, as if he were telling stories of places he had visited.

His vast knowledge of history was another mystery that he explained away by simply saying he read a great deal.

They discussed the war in Korea, why President Truman had replaced General Douglas McArthur and put General Matthew Ridgeway in charge in Korea. At times they would fall silent and spend hours simply watching the ocean waves swell, crest, and break.

Whether it was the close proximity of being on the ship or the number of hours they spent together, or perhaps their uncertain future, a friendship developed along with a camaraderie that would last for a long time. Remmey became more than a friend; he was also a teacher and mentor.

When the ship arrived at Yokohama, the authorities separated those who were going to Korea from those who would stay in Japan. Sitting on a bus waiting to leave the port, Andy saw a small convoy of Army vehicles weave along the dock. In one of the Army Jeeps sat Remmey—only he was wearing lieutenant's bars on his shoulders instead of Air Force chevrons on his sleeves.

CHAPTER FOUR
Barracks Life

The bus bumped along the base perimeter road in the dark. As it passed the landing strip, the glow of the runway lights illuminated the interior of the vehicle, creating optical illusions. The reflections of the lights quivered on the windows. Andy stared at the hypnotic images as the dancing silhouettes frolicked and then evaporated in a mesmerizing light show.

Shaking off the mesmerizing effects of the light, he wondered if Mel would be back on the base before the 2400-hour deadline. There were times when Mel became so absorbed in what he was doing he would lose track of time, especially if his exploits involved a female. Mel looked at life from a perspective different from Andy's, and Andy guessed that was because of their different upbringings. One of Mel's failings was not being on time. Something outside of Andy's control usually dictated the time he had to do things, so his mental clock was set on what needed to be accomplished from the pattern of farm life: the cows needed to be milked and fed at a certain time, or the school bus would arrive at a certain time. Mel's internal clock ran more on his wants and needs, and he would absentmindedly forget the fact that he was a servant of the Air Force and the military's demands and wants took preference over his own. It had taken a lot of effort for both to adapt and adjust to the military and living with a collection of people from different ethnic groups. Strange how two people, opposites, could hit it off. They had become close friends and relied upon each other's strengths and weaknesses.

Finally the bus arrived at the stop closest to the barracks. Clouds dark and heavily laden with moisture had blown in, obscuring the glow of the moon and blacking out the glimmering light of the stars. A few splatters of rain begin to fall as Andy approached the barracks. At 2300 hours, the building was dark except for exit lights and a subdued yellow circle cast by a single bedlamp.

Home sweet home was the barracks: a low, wood-frame, H-shaped building with a tin roof and white clapboard siding. Two parallel open-bay wings comprised the sleeping areas. These large rooms without interior dividing walls accommodated thirty-six bunk beds. Each wing had the capacity for housing seventy-two men. The center section connecting the two sides contained the latrine, with the toilets, showers, and sinks.

A guy from Mississippi had commented to Andy once, "These buildings are like what're called down South a shotgun house. You can stand in the door at one end and look through the opposite entrance—a straight shot."

Tucked up under the eaves of the building, windows two feet high and three feet wide allowed for slight ventilation. Small exit lights mounted on the interior wall above each of the outside doors provided a faint amber glow in the darkness. After lights out, you navigated to your bunk using the visibility provided by exit fixtures and by counting the number of beds. To know the number of bunks between the door and your bed was important. Consequences of an intruder accidentally climbing into the wrong sack had proven to be disastrous. Bloody noses and split lips were prevalent on such unfortunate occasions.

The alignment of the bunks was the head against the exterior wall and the foot toward the center of the barracks. This arrangement was the same on both sides of the building, which allowed room for an aisle to extend the full length of each wing. The placement of wall lockers on either side of the bunk beds created individual cubicles. Partitions made for cramped living space, but it was better than no privacy.

The institutional-style bunk frames of tubular steel painted battleship gray came complete with wire link bedsprings. These springs, which had an inclination to sag in the middle, served as support for a cotton-filled, three-inch-thick pad. A pillow, mattress cover, two sheets, pillowcase, and wool blankets completed the bed linens. Mosquito netting was a necessary accessory during the summer months.

The barracks accommodations were significantly better than those on the ship. Bunks or berths aboard ship were canvas, stacked four-high, allowing just enough room for you to breathe when sleeping. On the ship they had a pillow and blankets but no sheets. If the occupant of the upper bunk became seasick, the men on the lower bunks were at the mercy of his spew.

Entering the barracks by the door that faced the squadron area, Andy's bed was the eighth one on the right. The light this late at night was minimal, nevertheless it was enough that he was able to distinguish silhouettes and shapes. He counted how many bunks just to be sure … six, seven, and eight.

Not bothering to turn on the small lamp mounted on his bedframe, he opened the door of his metal wall locker as quietly as possible so as not to disturb anyone.

He did not worry about waking up Charley, who had the top bunk; the guy never slept in the barracks. Charley, a buck sergeant, stayed in town at his *uchi*, his house, with his Class B dependent, which was a nice name for a shack job. The expression used to describe this group of men who lived off the base with their unauthorized dependents was "gone native." This collection of airmen immersed and assimilated themselves into the Japanese culture and embraced a way of life in which they felt comfortable.

They adhered to military curfew regulations with a few minor exceptions. They would arrive at the barracks early in the morning, change their clothes, and continue to their workstations. When the duty day was over, they would return to barracks, switch back to Class A uniforms, and leave the base. They were always coming or going, never staying on base at night unless forced to do so. Their habitation preferences were not condoned by the military, but as long as no regulations were broken their actions remained ignored, as they fell within the gray area of morality dos and don'ts.

By military decree, all American personnel had to be off the streets during the curfew hours of 2400 to 0600. The only movement on the isolated avenues was a few Jeeps with military police and their Japanese counterparts seeking violators of the mandate.

The roads of the town would be relatively empty; although permitted to move about the town, only a few of the local citizens did so that late at night. Cur dogs would roam the alleys, searching the trash heaps for stray scraps of food.

At 0500 hours, in the dimness of predawn, there would be little activity to be seen by the casual observer. Gradually, there would be a proliferation of movement in the backstreets and alleys. From houses still draped in darkness, shadowy human figures would emerge. Although negligible in numbers at the beginning, the indistinct forms would glide on noiseless feet, some carrying bundles and others pushing bicycles. The distinguishable outlines would drift forward, drawn by an invisible force toward a single location. These interlopers of the pre-daybreak would move motionlessly, migrating through the alleys to the access points for the thoroughfares. Here they would stop and wait; none would penetrate the entrance until the appointed time.

One had to witness the early morning ritual to understand and appreciate this metamorphosis. The alleyways, bleak and stagnant, would spawn the birth of the morning's transformation. The small enigmatic group of men slinking through the backstreets would grow and multiply in number as they encroached upon the last bastions of safety, waiting to venture into the open. At 0600 hours, the first crackle of reveille would blast over the air base's loudspeaker. The day had dawned. The street would burst into life in an instant. Men, walking or riding bicycles or motor scooters, would hasten to the main gate, arriving before the final notes of music had faded into the sunrise. At 0630 hours, all but a few of these GIs would have entered the military installation. They would then hurry to their duty stations, after changing their uniforms if necessary, and begin their day of work. The alleys and streets would become empty, the beginning and the decline of the metamorphosis having passed until the dawn of another day.

Putting aside his thoughts of Charley and the town's morning transformation, Andy crawled into his sack. He grabbed his blanket, yanked the woolen covering up over his shoulders, and enclosed his body in a cocoon of warmth.

The man in the next bunk had his radio tuned to the Armed Forces Network. The subdued tones of Nat King Cole's soulful rendition of "Too Young" cascaded across the airwaves. Then the song faded into oblivion, and there was silence for a moment before the soft mellow tone of Tony Bennett crooning the ballad "Because of You" filtered through the room. From the alcoves of Andy's memory, thoughts of home and the images of those who had promised to wait flashed through his mind. Tony's final lilting melodious phrase vanished into the ebony of the night, and Kay Starr's lyrical vocal styling of "The Wheel of Fortune" poured forth, as if a gushing stream of water, to fill the stillness.

Andy heard a tiny click as the guy turned off the radio.

Immersed in drowsiness, thoughts of the past drifted into oblivion and provided an avenue for slumber to travel in and encompass him.

"Andy! Andy! You awake?" From beyond the foot of the bunk, a voice interrupted his dreams.

Opening one eye, he faintly made out Mel standing in the shadowy gloom of the center aisle. "Am now!"

"Sorry. Wake me up in the morning for chow, will you? I want to go to breakfast, OK?" Mel said in a muted tone.

"Yeah. Hey, did Butler get back?" Andy murmured.

"Don't know. When I left to go to Chibi's, he was slouched on a stool with his head on the bar. Maybe he was asleep, maybe not; that's the last I saw of him. Night, Andy." Mel headed toward his bunk.

Oh well, too late to do anything about it now, Andy thought. Then he turned on his side and closed his eyes.

Reveille

Saturday morning. Andy was on duty all day. Out of the sack at 0545, he grabbed his towel and shaving kit and headed for the latrine. Quickly pausing at Mel's bunk, he said, "Rise and shine."

"What's the time?" a voice from under the blankets grumbled.

"Five forty-five. Hit the deck."

"No, too damn early."

"You asked me to wake you up, and that's what I'm doing. Fifteen minutes to reveille." Andy didn't have time to stand around and argue. "Get up!" He resumed his trudging, pre-caffeine pace to the showers.

After completing his morning hygiene ritual, with a towel tied around his waist and his shaving bag in his hand, he passed by Mel's bed again. The guy was burrowed under the covers, cozier than a rabbit in a haystack. The man who slept in the bottom bunk had already left, providing Andy the opportunity to roust Mel. Grabbing the steel bedframe, he shook it violently. "Out of the sack if you're goin' to breakfast. Last time I'm gonna tell you."

With the velocity of a spring-wound jack-in-the-box, Mel popped up. "Mu … mu … musta dozed off," he muttered, slipping out from under the blankets.

Andy paid no attention to Mel's sputtering and proceeded back to his cubicle, where he put his shaving gear away. He stuffed his dirty clothes in his laundry bag and struggled into a pair of clean, starched, and ironed fatigues.

You don't slide on starched fatigues; you force your legs through the pant legs in a manner similar to pushing a pencil through a sealed envelope flap. When you finally manage to pull the trousers on and get buttoned up, your reward is an uncomfortable chafing in the crotch. Managing to lace up his brogans while ignoring the irritation, Andy grabbed his hat and made a beeline for the dining hall.

Stimulated by the invigorating rain-sweetened morning air his appetite mushroomed, and he picked up the pace.

Early on Saturday morning, there wasn't a large crowd in the dining hall. With a mess tray clutched in his hand, he hurried through the chowline, heaping enough food on the rectangular metal plate to satisfy his hunger pangs. Finding an empty table, he plopped down on a chair and began consuming the SOS. In military terminology, SOS is "shit on a shingle"; in civilian life it's called hamburger gravy on toast. Many of the troops disliked the flavor; some were of the opinion that SOS was slop and not fit to eat. Perhaps it was the country boy in Andy, but he enjoyed it. It was comfort food, like having biscuits and gravy, just substituting toast for the biscuits.

Halfway through the meal he wondered what happened to Mel and thought, *The guy had best be moving if he wants to eat before we report in. If he misses breakfast, it's a long time till lunch.*

More men entered the mess hall, and the chowline was getting longer. Andy glanced at the crowd but didn't see Mel. Two sailors stood in the line, gaping at the large mess facility. Andy wondered what they were doing so far inland, and his thoughts wandered back to when he was on the troopship.

***

On the USS *Howze*, they lined up in a passageway to start through the chowline. One person after the other, mess trays held out in front of them, they plodded forward like a bunch of well-disciplined robots. The metal plate was divided into different compartments for vegetables, dessert, and your entrée.

The mess attendants behind the counter scooped the food from the cooking pots and launched portions off a large spoon in the general direction of your tray. As with rocks off a catapult, portions of dinner would fly toward you before the airborne food landed with a splat. You'd end up with mashed potatoes in your Jell-O, gravy mixed in with spinach or peas, and pudding with sauerkraut. Once, Andy ended up having a chocolate cake sandwich with a mustard and Spam filling. When they finished flinging food, they ushered you along as if you were animals, funneling the men into an area where rows of tall stainless-steel tables stood like sentinels bolted to the floor. Here the troops stood side by side, hundreds of men bunched together. The tabletops were made of metal, as were the food trays. As the ship rolled and pitched, the tray would slide. Holding it steady with one hand, you'd use the other one to grab your fork in a choke hold and make a gallant effort to shovel food into your mouth.

One particular morning on board the boat, Andy couldn't sleep. He rolled out of his hammock or bunk, whatever the Navy called them, and went to get some coffee. It was still dark out when he got on deck, and he wandered around until he found the mess hall open. There were specific times he was supposed to eat, but he took a chance. No one stopped him as he entered the semi-vacant dining compartment. As the ship pitched back and forth in unstable seas, he grabbed a tray and coffee mug and struggled to retain his balance and maintain control of the tray against the sudden movements of the vessel while he made his way to a table. Clasping the metal platter with a death grip to stop it from sliding around, and trying to hang onto his coffee cup, he wound up with more food on his chin and shirt than in his stomach.

As a rule sailors didn't frequent transient messes, but that morning five or six seamen stood by one of the tables, drinking coffee. A grizzled seaman kept watching him, and Andy was afraid he was going to tell him he wasn't allowed to be in the mess area. The sailor instead said, "Tear the crusts off the bread and stick a small piece under each of the four corners of your tray. The bread will help keep it in place."

Andy gave him a questioning look.

The sailor went on: "Go ahead, give it a try, son. You ain't got nothin' to lose."

Doing what the old salt recommended, Andy found the suggestion to be sage advice. At every future meal on the ship, the pieces of bread went under the tray before he began eating. Recalling the kindness and words of wisdom from the unknown sailor made him smile.

***

The legs of the metal chair scraped against the floor as Mel yanked it out from under the table. Without looking up Andy said, "I was wondering if you were going to make it here."

"Must have been exhausted, 'cause I dozed right back off," Mel said. "Stayed out way too late last night."

"No sweat, you're here. Eat up. I need to be at the hangar earlier today; got to catch up on a bunch of requisitions."

Mel pounced on his food, wolfing it down with all the fervor of a newly weaned pup. Andy stared at him. *I sure hope his table manners are better when he's home. From what he's told me, he grew up with a silver spoon in his mouth. I'd think he'd have perfect table manners, rather than actin' like a pig at the trough.*

Polishing off the last of his SOS, Andy gulped down the rest of his coffee and then said, "Let's clear the hell out of here."

CHAPTER FIVE
Duty Station
0712 Hours

Once inside the massive hangar, Andy and Mel made their way to the production control office, a large enclosed area built at one end of the hangar with an expansive open space with desks for the peons and individual offices for the senior NCOs and officers. They headed for their respective areas in the large office. Charts and graphs surrounded Mel's desk in the statistical analysis work zone, which was situated at the back of the room.

Andy had once asked him, "Did you want to be a statistician when you joined up?" He'd figured that Mel, being a brainy person who liked math and was a whiz at figures, might have wanted the job.

"Shit, no," Mel had said. "They told me in basic training that was what I was going to be based on my test scores."

"About the same deal happened with me. They didn't ask me; they told me I was going to be in supply. I don't even think they took a look at my test scores," Andy commented. "What I wanted was to be a gunner; I've been hunting and shooting guns since I was big enough to hold a rifle. I'm a good shot and thought I'd make one hell of a formidable tail or waist gunner. But no, they said, the Air Force needed supply people and that was what I was gonna do. I tried to talk them out of it and into giving me a different job, no such luck. In fact, I was told to quit complaining. They threatened to put me on permanent KP and make me peel potatoes for the rest of my hitch. I knew the personnel guy could not do that, but there was no use arguing with him anymore. Needs of the Air Force is what they told me. They gave me a job, and I'm stuck with it."

Andy turned away from Mel, saying, "Catch up with you later." He walked over to his desk on the far side of the room and rifled through the stack of requisitions which had piled up overnight.

Sure don't need to be an Einstein to do this job; this routine sorting doesn't require any intelligence. All the priorities are already marked on the requisitions. AOCP is simply Aircraft out of Commission for Parts. Pick up and haul. Everythin' I need to do is a rush job. If the shops need it, my job is to retrieve it. Oh, well. Back on the farm I'd be cuttin' hay and haulin' grain, and I'd be rushin' before it got too hot or rained.

Andy's main claim to fame was he had been assigned his own tug, a small yellow tractor used on the flight line, and a couple of trailers for hauling. At home, he drove his dad's old McCormick Deering tractor or his own '37 Chevy pickup. Now he drove the tug between the maintenance hangar and base supply. On the bright side, he was able to get a little fresh air and sunshine on occasion and a bit of goofing-off time as well. It was better than being cooped up in an office or hangar all the time. Yet the job wasn't what he'd expected to be doing when he'd joined up.

He looked up at the clock hanging over the door. *About time for me to go to work,* he thought to himself, and then sighed. Grabbing the stack of requisitions, he headed across the hangar to where he'd parked the tug.

The monstrous hangar doors were wide open, and the ventilation systems were working at full capacity. Still, exhaust fumes from gas generators, trucks, and tugs moving in and out of the building fouled and polluted the air. The noise in the building was deafening with the hiss of acetylene torches and the *wang, wang, wang* of thin sheet metal as it was shaped and bent to repair the skin on a plane. There was the distinguishing roar of R-4360 airplane engines being run up for testing, as well as the *clank, thud,* and *bang* of fifty-five-gallon oil drums being roughly offloaded from a truck. The conglomeration of sounds surged through the building, amplifying and intensifying until the cacophony pushed the decibel count off the scale.

"Now what the hell's goin' on?" Andy muttered aloud. *They're going to tow that aircraft into the hangar and block my exit route to the tarmac. It's gonna take more than a few minutes before a path is clear.* All he could do was play the waiting game. He slouched down on the seat of the tug and watched them as they hauled in the airplane. It never ceased to amaze him the way they could jockey around the aircraft. *I have trouble backing up a trailer, and that guy's moving the*

C-119 like a little kid pushing a toy airplane around the tree on Christmas morning.

"Anderson! Hey, Anderson!" The brassy voice resounded across the vastness of the hangar. "Anderson, get over here. Now!"

Andy focused in on the sarge, and one glance told him the man was not happy. The sarge's scowl was so intense that the wrinkles on his forehead were as deep as the Grand Canyon.

What did I do wrong? I didn't think I'd screwed anything up yet today.

He doubled-timed it across the hangar, unable to imagine any of his shenanigans would have raised the ire of the sergeant. Granted, occasionally he and Mel bent a few rules—never broke any, just tweaked them a little. There was stuff they shouldn't admit to that they had done, but nothing to make the sarge angry.

"Where the hell is Butler?" The burly old sergeant glared at Andy as if he'd committed a serious breach of military protocol or had even committed treason.

Mel walked out into the hangar, also at the sarge's request, and stood beside Andy.

The sarge studied the perplexed expression on Andy's face, and without giving him a chance to think, growled, "I asked you a question. Where's Butler?"

The sarge's probing accusation careened off the tin walls and metal roof of the massive building. The question hovered over them like a hungry buzzard riding the air currents above its unsuspecting prey. Noticeably irritated, the sarge wore a somber expression, and the commanding timbre of his voice demanded an immediate answer.

"Don't know, Sarge," Andy and Mel said in unison as they shrugged.

Andy stood braced at parade rest on the hard cement floor of the aircraft hangar and attempted to keep his eyes fixed on the sarge. Mel Schultz wore a deadpan facial expression, standing firmly rooted beside Andy, and his spit-polished boots were planted at the perfect angle and ideal distance apart for this particular military stance.

Andy didn't enjoy being reamed out, but he had to stand there and listen to his boss, Technical Sergeant Bowman, question them about a man they couldn't find.

No one ever mentioned to me that I needed to keep track of the guy. I haven't even thought about Butler since last night, when I asked Mel about him. My morning began positively. How did I end up in this predicament?

He struggled to hear what the sarge was saying amid the background racket in the hangar. The sarge continued, "Anderson…." He paused. "Let me rephrase the question. Did you see Butler in the barracks this morning?"

"No, I didn't," Andy replied. Then he added, "I didn't bother to check on him either." *That was a stupid smart-ass answer.*

The sarge lowered his eyebrows, scrutinizing them. "Look, guys, neither one of you is in trouble." The sarge's tone mellowed. "I received a call this morning that Butler didn't return to the base last night, and that is out of character for him. I'm just trying to figure out what happened."

Andy looked at the sarge, thinking, *Wow, they sure keep close tabs on you.* He asked, "Was Butler to be on duty today?"

He received a curt "No" for an answer and then another question. "When was the last time either of you saw him?" After a pause came the revelation: "I know you were in a bar with him at one point."

Mel glanced at Andy. His nod was infinitesimal, but Andy got the message he conveyed: he was going to tell the sarge what they knew. "Andy and I went to town last night and spotted Butler in one of the bars. He'd had a lot to drink.

"He was still sittin' at the bar when I took off," Andy said. What he left out was Butler had been so drunk he couldn't have walked farther than ten steps from the barstool before passing out. "I was back on base by 2230."

Mel piped up, "Butler was still glued to the barstool when I left. No idea what happened to him."

"Did you two think about asking him if he needed assistance? Ever occur to you the man might have drunk too much and couldn't make his way back? And don't tell me that you two pansies never overindulged and had trouble getting back to the barracks."

The conversation paused, and there was only silence. Mel wore a befuddled expression on his face, looking like a sixteen-year-old virgin in a cathouse without a clue what his next move should be.

Andy groped to find the right answer and was ready to blurt out, *I'm not Butler's keeper,* to cover up his guilt, knowing he should have helped Butler last night, or at least tried.

"You think you might know where Butler is?" demanded the sarge.

The answer had to be yes or no. If Andy said no, he would be lying, because he figured Butler was still at the Brass Rail. If he said yes and Butler wasn't there, he would still be lying. It was a win-win or a lose-lose situation either way. Something in the back of his mind told Andy to keep his mouth shut and come up with a better answer because it was not the time to be belligerent.

The sarge pointed his finger and jabbed it in Andy's direction. In an instant, the sarge transformed from a mentor and father figure into a military disciplinarian. His tone of voice changed from honey to molten lead as he commandingly asked, "Can you find him?" The unexpected harshness of the command caught Andy off guard, and he flinched and jerked back as instinctively as a coyote springs back from a striking rattler. He knew he looked like an idiot when he winced.

The instant he fixed his eyes on Mel, who was staring at him, he knew the guy was gloating. With a half-assed grin on his face and an "I saw what you did" smirk, Mel let it be known that he had noticed Andy wince and would never let him live the moment down.

Sergeant Bowman queried, "Well?"

Andy's grandpa had once told him, "Always have your mind in gear before you set your mouth in motion." He didn't want to sound too positive, but they might get some time off to go look for the guy.

"I think we might know where he is, Sarge, I'm not sure. Maybe."

"You're telling me you might be able to locate him?" This time, it was more of a request, and the sarge emphasized the word "might."

They both nodded.

After a long pause, the sarge looked at them. "OK, you two, back to work. Now. I'll let you know if I need you."

With no further explanation he spun on his heel, away from them, and went into the production control office, closing the door a little harder than necessary. They stared at him through the office windows like a couple of peeping Toms. As the sarge entered his private office, he closed that door and walked over to his desk, jerking out the chair. The grizzled, tired-looking man sat with both elbows on the desktop and rubbed his eyes with his forefingers.

Andy speculated that Sergeant Bowman was mumbling something like "What a hell of a way to start the day." The sarge's posture was slumped, and he resembled someone with a heavy weight on his shoulders. Why the image of a picture Andy had seen in his high school art book of the statue *The Thinker*, sculpted by someone named Auguste Rodin, popped into his mind he didn't know, but that was what the sarge looked like. Sergeant Bowman lowered his hands from his face, grabbed the phone, and dialed.

With a shrug of his shoulders, Mel moseyed back into the office, walked over to his desk, took a seat, and started shuffling through the pile of reports.

Andy turned away from the office windows and went back across the hangar. No hurry, they were still working with the C-119. He couldn't fathom why the sarge was so worked up about Butler not making it back to the base. *If Mel or I didn't show up one morning, would they be this concerned about us?*

He sat down on the fender of his tug as they worked on the plane. The C-119 Flying Boxcar had been flown in from Korea last week. Since then, it had stood secluded on the ramp outside the hangar, awaiting repair. The Dollar Nineteen, as the men who flew and maintained that fleet of aircraft had affectionately nicknamed them, needed an engine overhaul and sheet metal work.

Bullet holes dotted one wing and the port side of the plane. The log indicated that while it had been making a low-level supply drop to Allied troops, North Korean soldiers had fired at the aircraft with rifles and handheld automatic weapons. The small arms fire had caused minor damage to the Flying Boxcar. The pilots and crew of the unarmed plane had completed their mission and no one had suffered injuries.

Near the cockpit, three bullets had pierced the fuselage. Someone had circled the cluster of holes with a grease pencil and had written in bold letters, "Alive only by the Grace of God!" Those words echoed in Andy's mind, *the Grace of God ... the Grace of God....* This testimonial of faith reminded him of his unexpected encounter with the most unlikely of holy men a few weeks earlier.

***

While wandering along the wide pathway leading to the temples in Kamakura, he'd caught his first glimpse of the huge bronze statue of the Great Buddha, the *Daibutsu*, which had been on display since 1252. To him, the remnants of his great-grandfather's sod house were ancient. The home had been constructed with blocks of sod cut from the prairie by his great-grandfather when he'd homesteaded the farm after the Civil War. The Soddy had been built in 1866; the statue of Buddha had been put on display 240 years before Columbus set sail for America. It was incredible to Andy that he was actually seeing something created so many centuries ago still standing.

Along the sides of the main corridor leading to the temples, a number of pushcarts containing assorted trinkets and food were parked haphazardly. One particularly antiquated cart caught his attention. Leaning against the rickety two-wheeled wagon for support was a gaunt, aged man hawking his wares. He was clothed in a traditional kimono, and the garment was as old, worn, and threadbare as its elderly owner. The peddler's skin, wrinkled, tanned, and leathery from years of exposure to the sun, added to the mystique of the timeworn merchant. As Andy approached, the vendor struggled and managed to stand with the aid of a battered bamboo staff.

The trader held out a package in his frail hand and beckoned. "Come," he said. "I have what you need. Come look."

Curious to see what the vendor was selling, Andy walked over. The old man held out a small sack of birdseed and weakly uttered in a beseeching tone, "You need."

Andy started to leave, and the man said in an aged and trembling voice, "Buy; all do. All buy. All feed birds. Fortune smile upon you. Feed birds; all peoples do."

Although the merchant spoke English, Andy still motioned with his hands and shook his head side to side to indicate to the peddler that he wasn't interested.

Ignoring Andy's superfluous attempt to communicate, the merchant continued, "Buddha smile you. You feed birds! Give birds."

"No, thanks," Andy replied.

"Young American boy need Buddha bless!" The old man emphasized the words with the steadfast conviction of a devout monk as he intently studied Andy's face.

"Good luck, must have! Feed birds!" the man pleaded, his dark eyes filled with compassion. With an aura of wisdom transcending eternity, the old man fixed a penetrating, concerned gaze on Andy.

Andy had a shuddering thought: *Does this old disciple of Buddha have the ability to see into the depths of my soul?*

The vendor grinned, a toothless smile as pleasant and warm as the spring day. The advanced age and physical feebleness of the merchant made Andy imagine that he must be as old as the statue of Buddha.

Ceding to the peddler's wishes, he placed fifty yen in the gnarled and weathered hand for a packet of birdseed that was worth fifteen.

The trader acknowledged the transaction with an appropriate bow of his head. Displaying the tranquility of a revered holy person bestowing a benediction, he lifted his free arm while his other hand remained firmly clasped on his staff. "Buddha bless young man.... Buddha says, 'Peace comes from within. Do not seek it without.'"

Nodding that he understood, Andy turned to leave as the elderly gentleman muttered, "A true comrade would remember what Buddha foretold and would tell his friend." *Was this old man a Buddhist monk posing as a merchant? A soothsayer? Was he referring to Butler and the man's struggle with combat fatigue? How could he know about Butler's problem?* He suddenly recognized an anomaly. *What happened to the old man's broken English?*

Reluctant to stand in public like a country bumpkin feeding a flock of chickens, he had not intended to open the sack of seed. But as he stepped back on the main path leading to the statue of the Great Buddha, a bird landed on his shoulder, then another and another, their numbers multiplying. Having bought the seed, he thought he might as well feed them. The instant he unsealed the bag, droves of winged creatures descended upon him. Those finding no resting place on his body glided to the earth and encircled the area. Standing with arms outstretched, Andy looked like a feathered scarecrow amid a field of fluttering plumage.

He tossed the packet of seeds to the ground when he realized these were not the graceful doves of heaven but a flock of scavenger pigeons. His quick action resulted in the immediate departure of the flying fowl from his body as they hungrily attacked the discarded bag. Flabbergasted at the sudden onslaught of pigeons and not relishing having more birds rest on his shoulders, it was time to depart. He said good-bye to the old man and took leave from the spot where his newfound winged acquaintances greedily pecked at the strewn seeds.

Relieved of his fluttering burden, Andy continued his exploration of Kamakura. The rest of the day he had a constant uncanny feeling that the old peddler was somewhere watching him, ensuring the blessing kept him safe. Strangely, he felt tranquil and at peace.

As he walked along the path, he mused, *Everyone benefits on occasion by divine intervention, be it by the Grace of God or the Blessing of Buddha. Even a benediction by a pushcart peddler might prove beneficial.*

CHAPTER SIX
Waylaid

The episode in the kitchen with the barmaid Peggy had left Mama-san exhausted and frustrated. She knew she should not let herself become so upset when these kinds of problems happened. *If people hear that the barmaids in my tavern are stealing from the customers, my honor will be in question. The integrity of my business could be in doubt. No one cares about the character of a thieving barmaid, but my reputation will be at stake.*

Recalling her promise to obtain Butler's help to get back to the base, she became uneasy because she had not attended to the problem. Then she procrastinated, worrying about her own situation and telling herself that he would be all right for a little bit. He would not be going anywhere in his inebriated state, and she needed the few extra minutes alone in her quarters to compose herself. Taking the opportunity to inspect her appearance in a mirror, she examined her hair and makeup. Gently, she brushed and smoothed her hair and applied a dab of makeup here and there to blemished areas of her face. A fleeting wave of sorrow and self-pity flowed over her as she touched her uneven nose.

Having made the decision that Sumiko and Yoriko would be the ones to accompany Butler to the main gate of the base, she relaxed a little. The two could wait and watch to assure that he entered the expansive airfield, and they would remain watching him until a bus arrived and he boarded the conveyance back to his barracks.

Gathering herself up to her full height of four feet eleven inches, and with all the poise and grace she could garner, she reentered the bar area. Pushing the door open to the main tavern room, she was stunned to discover that Butler was no longer seated at the bar. She glanced around the room, and an unexpected twinge of panic and the gnawing feeling that something was terribly wrong gripped her.

"*Butler-san wa doko deska?*" she anxiously asked one of the girls.

"*Shirimasen*, I don't know. He left. I saw him go outside and leave with someone."

Mama-san rounded the bar and dashed outside. The door stoop and the street were empty; Butler had vanished into the night. Rushing back inside, she probed other girls for answers. Finally, one girl told her she thought she'd seen Peggy leading a drunken GI away from the bar. *That dirty, thieving wench. Is she using the unsuspecting American to take her revenge against me?*

***

As Peggy scuffed her feet on the dirt floor, pondering what to do next, little particles of dust swirled up and floated in the air current created by the flame of the candle. Butler sat unresponsive where he had passed out, his back propped against the wall of the shack and his head slumped forward against his chest. Her pimp, Koji, hadn't shown up yet. *Where is he? He indicated he would follow me when I signaled him, but more than thirty minutes have passed. What's taking him so long?* The longer she waited, the angrier she became. *I bet he's checking out those new girls he procured for the street. He always likes to screw the new whores before he sends them out, likes to check out the merchandise. After they've slept with the Americans, he doesn't feel they're so desirable.*

She rummaged through Butler's pockets and found military payment certificate money, some yen bills in his wallet, and some yen coins. Altogether there was about a hundred and fifty dollars, more money than she'd ever gotten before. An impulsive thought raced through her mind: *Keep the money for yourself. Why give it to the pimp? You did all the dirty work. You were the one who was humiliated. You deserve a reward; keep the money, or at least part of it.* She knew just where to stash her newfound treasure. While in the process of hiding her share of the money, she heard a noise and pulled down and straightened her dress. No one entered the building.

The melted candle was now only a stub. How much longer the flickering flame would glow was anyone's guess. The idea of being alone in the dark frightened her.

Where was he? She was worried he wouldn't come, but fearful of the physical abuse he would inflict upon her if she didn't do everything right. An hour ticked by. Butler suddenly jerked, his legs twitched, and his hand that had rested on his leg slid awkwardly from its position to the floor. Terrified he might awaken, she began devising a plan to contain the comatose man.

The small vial of drugs was hidden in her bra. *I can pour the serum in his mouth and make him swallow it before he wakes. I'll do the same as that bitchy mother of mine did to me when I was a child to make me swallow that rotten-tasting cod liver oil. She'd pinch my nose and hold it tight as a vise until I couldn't breathe, and when I opened my mouth for air she'd dump the foul-tasting liquid down my throat and then clamp my mouth and nose closed until I'd swallowed it.*

Pulling the small glass tube from her bra, she walked to where the unconscious Butler slouched against the wall. She knelt beside the lifeless form, and with only slight trepidation, she grabbed his nose and squeezed. A second was all it took for his mouth to open. With the container poised in her hand, she started pouring its contents down Butler's throat. He coughed and gagged, and he tried to spit out the opium liquid, but he swallowed and coughed a second time as he struggled to breathe. A rapid unexpected movement of his arm knocked her hand away from his nose. The involuntary defensive reaction was like that of brushing a fly away when a person is sleeping. The small container of opiate flew from her hand and landed on the floor, its contents spewing out and soaking into the dirt.

Startled by his abrupt movement and believing he had awoken, she was now anxious and terrified. She tried to summon enough courage to flee, and then she hesitated in fear as she felt a presence behind her. The dim candlelight illuminated a flash of an object as it arched downward beside her, striking Butler on the head.

Her pimp stood behind her, clutching a short length of lead pipe in his hand. The blow to Butler's temple knocked him from his sitting position, and he lay in a crumpled heap on the floor, bleeding profusely from the wound.

"You killed him!" she cried out, shocked and horrified.

"No, I didn't, and even if I did, it doesn't make any difference. In a war, you kill people," he responded.

She screamed, "The war is over, you stupid!" She was so angry she couldn't find a word to express her feelings, so she added one she'd heard the GIs use: "turd."

He interrupted her, shouting, "I'm a soldier of the Imperial Japanese Army!"

"You were never in the Army. They conscripted you one week before the end of the war. You never reported for duty, never shot a gun or wore a uniform."

"What do you know about it, you scheming slut? Who are you to criticize me? You were digging through garbage heaps, looking for something to eat, and screwing bums for a place to sleep when I found you," he fumed. "I never surrendered; I am still at war."

"Bullshit!" she yelled, using her favorite American expression. "You're playing games, and one of these days you're going to lose." She spat the words with disgust, her hatred for the pimp clouding her judgment; she knew she shouldn't make him mad.

Angered at her outburst and sudden retaliation, he brought the lead pipe up and was within seconds of using it on her.

Peggy threw her hands up to cover her head, cringing in fear, knowing she'd pushed him too far, and she cried out, "I'm sorry!" She pleaded, "Don't hit me, please! Don't hit me."

"I should beat you until you can't walk." A boiling rage consumed him. "You're nothing but scum!" he howled as the length of pipe quivered in his hand and he fought to contain the urge to hit her. *If I beat her, she might not be physically able to help me tonight.*

"I know I was wrong. I won't do it again," she appealed to him. "I'll do whatever you ask. I won't argue. Please don't hit me."

The pimp lowered the pipe, his face still red with anger. "You better, and this is the last time I'm going to put up with your big mouth." *I'll punish her for her insolence later.*

Peggy pointed to Butler. "Can't leave him here; what if he dies?" she whimpered. "You're so smart. You know what to do." In reality, she was thinking, *You're so damn stupid that if I don't tell you what to do, you'll never figure it out.* "This shack is close to where we live. The police will find him here and start asking questions of the neighbors. We need to put him somewhere, someplace they won't look for us."

The man thought for a few seconds, and a sinister grin spread across his pockmarked face. "I have a plan," he said, and he left.

Peggy relaxed and breathed freer when he walked out the door. *I need to run away from him; I'm afraid of what he might do. How do I exist without him? He gives me food and a place to live. And he doesn't beat me all that often.*

Before she could formulate any plans, the pimp returned. He'd brought a two-wheeled cart, and together they heaved Butler's unconscious body into the pushcart, not an easy task as Butler was a much larger man. The pimp stood looking at the disheveled body heaped in the cart. Then he picked up his metal pipe from the floor where he had thrown it and laid it alongside the American in the cart before turning and staring at the woman.

"Where is the money?" he demanded viciously. "I know you've been through his clothes."

She cringed, anticipating punishment for not giving him the money earlier, and she handed him Butler's wallet, which still contained fifty dollars.

"Is that all?" he asked as he opened the billfold.

She nodded yes, and he reached out and slapped her across the face. "You lying whore. I know you better. Give me all of it or I'll rip your face off."

She reached into her concealed dress pocket and gave him Butler's ID card along with fifteen dollars and the change so he would think it was all the money. She'd hidden two ten-thousand-yen bills, the equivalent of fifty dollars; they were tucked safely away in her body cavities.

"Where are we going to dump him?"

"We'll take him down the river by the bridge, unload him, and roll him down to the water. When they find him, they'll think he was so drunk he fell off the bridge or stumbled down the slope," he bragged, confident his plan would work. It wasn't his plan; he had overheard the Chinese discussing different methods of disposing bodies to make it look like an accident.

"What are you going to do with the cart?" Peggy asked. "Someone will see it."

"Don't worry, it belongs to a grocery store on the other side of town. I took it when I stole food from the grocer last night. They will figure it was just abandoned." He lifted the handles and began pulling the cart forward. The wooden wheels creaked as they began to roll. "Push, you damn whore!" he snarled.

She kept pestering him, wanting to know what he planned to do as they moved the cart down the deserted backstreets. It had begun to rain, and they sought the protection of building and roof overhangs whenever they could to stay out of the inclement weather.

Arriving at a spot where shadows darkened the slopes of the riverbank, he abruptly stopped.

He hesitated, and Peggy, tired, wet, and frustrated with having to push the cart, complained bitterly. "What are you doing now? You going to stop and have a cigarette?" *You're a worthless, bloodsucking lout!* screamed in her mind.

"Shut up," he whispered, as he'd noticed figures creeping toward them along the riverbank. "We have to hide. Help me push."

She strained against the cart, and they moved the awkward transport back into the alley.

"You stay here. I'll be right back." He stole forward. One of the figures looked familiar. Keeping low, he crept and then crawled into the deep shadows and lay still as three men ran by him. One was the Chinese operator who had given him the drugs. *They did something. I don't know what yet, but I'll find out, and the knowledge will give me power over them.*

He returned to Peggy, and they waited; someone was standing on the bridge. The Chinese men disappeared into the night, but there were American GIs wandering back and forth on the bridge and street. She became tired and restless; the hour was late. Finally, the pimp said, "Pretty quiet now. Let's get this over with."

Pushing the overladen cart in and out of the shadows made her muscles hurt—she wasn't used to this type of labor. They had covered half the distance to the bridge when someone yelled and flagged down a passing military police Jeep. Red and blue lights flashed as the

Americans began running up and down the banks of the channel, pointing at something in the water. A siren blared from a Japanese police car, and its tires screeched as the car slid to a stop. She saw the blinding glare of searchlights as they scanned over the surface of the water.

The pimp froze, afraid to move. Peggy, tired of his inability to act, hit him on the shoulder. "We need to leave here now!"

He looked at her with a blank stare. Then, finally, he turned the cart around and headed away from the bridge. It was a full fifteen minutes before he said anything, and then it was only "I know of an old boat shed outside of town, down by the river. We can take him there and no one will find him."

Worrying about Mama-san, Peggy said, "What about the woman who owns the bar? She will be suspicious if this GI doesn't come back tomorrow."

"That old woman has something to hide," he shot back. "I don't think she will call the cops." Then he added, "I don't think she wants to attract attention about her past."

By the time they reached the old boat shed, morning light was creeping across the eastern skies. The old abandoned building was in disrepair and had passed its useful days. The gray, weathered wood was warped, and the gaps between the rotting horizontal boards of the siding were sufficient to let in snow and rain. Now the wind whistled through it as freely as if it were a flute. The double doors hung precariously on rusted hinges.

They struggled as they pulled on the sagging door. When the wooden slats scraped and dragged against the moist ground, he yelled, "Put your whore'n back into it! Work as hard as you do when you're screwing some damn American."

Butler, still unconscious and oblivious to all that was happening, lay in the bottom of the cart, as limp as a rag doll. The shed's doors were built wide enough to accommodate a small boat, so the cart easily fit through. They pushed it in and dumped their human contraband out like a bag of garbage.

"You stay here and watch him," the pimp ordered in a caustic tone.

"What if he wakes up?" she sniveled. "Where are you going? What do I do if he comes to?"

"If you gave him all the narcotics, he's going to be dead in a short time. None of your damn business where I am going, but if you must know, I want to see the Chinese. I have a proposition for them." He started for the door and then turned. "You just stay here like I told you and I'll be back."

"I'm hungry. I want something to eat."

"Woman, you can do without eating. Losing a little weight will do you good. You're too chubby, anyway."

She began to whimper. "I don't know what to do with him."

He yelled back at her, "Tie him up and gag him!" Then his mood altered, and with a sadistic glint in his eyes, he snapped, "If he comes to, screw him. Give him a blow job. Do what you're skilled at; just keep him quiet. Don't bother me with your pitiful complaints, you blubbering pussy."

He stomped out and tried to slam the door behind him, but the old rusty hinges wouldn't oblige. Infuriated by the door's lack of mobility thwarting his grand exit, he yelled, "Close the door!"

She was hungry and angry, tired of being treated like a dog. *I have money, and there's a restaurant a few kilometers back. I'll bind the American and go find something to eat. Perhaps I'll come back; perhaps I won't.*

She found some twine heaped along the wall, enough that she could tie the American up, but it was rotten and broke easily. Shelves mounted on the wall still held a variety of items: empty tin cans, bits of old fish netting, rope, all rotten. A folded canvas tarp on the top shelf caught her eye. Standing on her tiptoes, she reached up to pull and yank on a corner of the old tarp. The rickety shelf collapsed, showering her with dust and debris as the canvas tumbled to the floor. She quaked in disgust at the cloud of grime covering her. Coughing and spitting the dirt out of her mouth, she brushed the dirt off her clothes the best she could.

Kneeling down, she unfolded the canvas covering. The stench from the canvas was terrible, and roaches and all kinds of other bugs scurried in all directions when it flopped open. Drawing back with disgust and repugnance, she waited at a distance for a few moments until the insects disappeared into the darkened corners of the building. Then she finished unfolding the tarp.

She stood up, brushed her clothes off again, and went over and stretched out the American. He was still alive. The job proved to be an arduous task. By the time she'd moved him into the position she wanted, she was perspiring and anxious to finish her task. Pulling the tarp close to him, she tucked the edges in as best she could under his body. Struggling, she rolled him over and over into the canvas until, at last, he was as snug as a caterpillar in a cocoon. *He isn't going anywhere. Why should I wait? I'm hungry and thirsty.* She imagined her pimp was out having breakfast. Why shouldn't she be allowed a meal as well?

Reaching her hand up under her dress, she removed one of the ten-thousand-yen bills and wiped the currency on her slip. *This is more than enough for breakfast and a train ticket the hell out of here.* She made up her mind she was going to run, and the time was now for her to separate from her pimp forever.

Walking to the door, Peggy turned and took one last look at the serviceman they had abducted. With the side of his head caked by blood and his face pallid and lifeless, she didn't think he'd live much longer. *I'm sorry, GI; you seemed like a nice person. He made me do it. I had no choice, and I did what he told me. Gomennasai.* Sorry.

When she turned around, terror gripped her, for standing between her and the entrance was her pimp.

He reached into the cart and brought out his length of pipe. "I came back for my weapon." Enraged and furious, he tightened his grip on the metal baton as he hissed between his clenched teeth, ranting, "Hiding money from me, were you? You thieving *bitch*!"

He drove his arm down with all his strength, and the bludgeoning began. He struck her repeatedly, and the feeling of the impact of iron rod against soft human flesh provided him with a sense of satisfaction. *He* was in control, and that bolstered his shattered ego. His anger eventually subsided, and he stopped his senseless flaying.

The pimp bent down to pick up the ten-thousand-yen bill she had dropped and stuck it in his pocket. He glanced at the cart and the comatose figure wrapped in the moldy canvas. *If the American isn't dead now, he will be soon. No one will be looking for him; I'll come back and get rid of the bodies tonight.*

He stooped, grabbed the hem of the dead woman's dress, and nonchalantly wiped the blood off the pipe as casually as one might remove breadcrumbs from a table. Not looking, or caring, he left her mangled body lying in a pool of muddy blood.

CHAPTER SEVEN
The Assignment

The task of parking the C-119 was completed, and they securely tucked the chucks under the wheels. After they removed the tow vehicle from the hangar, Andy had a clear pathway out to the tarmac. It was time for him to crank up the tug and start moving before they began assembling the scaffolding so the mechanics could pull the engine cowlings.

He knew he'd better hustle and be back before the mechanics started yelling for the replacement parts. Andy turned on the ignition switch and punched the starter. It whirred and growled; for a second he didn't think the motor was going to catch, and then, with a spit and cough, the engine fired up and roared to life. He jammed the gearshift into low and was ready to slip the clutch when movement caught his attention; the sarge had just stepped out of his office.

The clamor was so loud and deafening the sarge didn't even bother to shout. He just motioned Andy over and, judging by the manner in which he signaled, he meant pronto.

Now what? Andy cut the motor, hopped off the little tractor, and tore across the hangar, his eyes glued on the sarge as the man turned and went back into the office.

Blatt, blatt, blatt. The blast of a horn startled Andy. It didn't resound like a klaxon, but it was close and loud. The horn was so unnerving he wasn't certain which way to run. His peripheral vision picked out a large yellow forklift speeding toward him on a collision course. The engine roared and the exhaust bellowed smoke as the forklift operator showed no intention of slowing down or stopping.

Andy dove out of the way and the forklift breezed by him, close enough to blow any dust off the seat of his pants. Had he been a couple of seconds slower, the tire tracks would have been running across the back of his fatigue shirt and not on the concrete floor. His heart pounded as loud and fast as an ensemble of *taiko* drums. Perspiration broke out on his forehead, and rivulets of moisture trickled down his face and under his shirt collar, giving him a clammy feeling.

Whipping his head around, he shouted at the driver, "What the hell are you tryin' to do?" while simultaneously shaking his fist in the air. The forklift kept moving. The driver couldn't hear Andy's tirade because of all the noise, however he got the gist of the message. In return, the driver gestured with his arm and middle finger. Not a warrior's salute but a salutation that was not apologetic, friendly, or complimentary.

When Andy reached the office, he grabbed the doorknob and held on to help steady his nerves. Thinking a couple of deep breaths might help the jitters, he inhaled deeply and sucked in a lungful of the floating exhaust fumes polluting the air, making him cough and gag. *Nothing's going right this friggin' morning.*

He yanked the door open and slipped in, slamming it shut behind him. You'd catch a lot of guff from the guys who worked in PC if you held the door open, because the noise and smell coming from the hangar ticked them off. He ignored the obscene and rude remarks and rushed to the sarge's private office.

Lo and behold, Mel was already entrenched by the desk. "You took a long time," he mouthed.

"Close my office door, Anderson," the sarge ordered. Andy reached back and pulled the door shut.

Still a little shaken from the close encounter with the forklift, he tried to concentrate on what the sarge was saying. "OK, here's the deal. I want you two to go and see if you can find Butler. Here is the catch—he must be back here in the hangar by 0730 on Monday. With or without him, you two are to be back here by then. Is that clear? Butler or not, you're on base by 0730 Monday. No excuses."

"But—" Andy started.

The sarge held up his hand. "I talked with the first sergeant; you'll have passes to town and also pick up a pass extension for Butler." He glanced up at the wall clock. "It's 0800 now; get to the barracks and change into Class A's. Then head into town and drag Butler in—I don't care how. Do either of you two have any questions on this matter?"

"But Sar—" Andy started to say.

"Anderson, don't worry; I'll send someone else on your supply run. Focus on finding Butler." The sarge waved them off.

That wasn't what he had wanted to ask. Andy wondered what would happen to Butler if they failed to return with him on time. However, on reflection, Andy realized it was better to let the sarge think he was worried about work.

They must have stood there a beat too long; with the fire of the devil in his eyes, the sarge glared at them and said, "What are you waiting for? If you don't have any questions, haul your butts out of here and find him!"

Andy and Mel didn't wait any longer. Chasing after Butler beat working, and they took off at a fast gallop out of the hangar, heading for the barracks about a mile away. They double-timed up the road and, between breaths, Mel gasped, "Andy, help me keep a lookout; maybe we can hitch a lift with someone."

A quick nod was the best Andy could do; he was having enough difficulty keeping his breakfast down. The two men kept watch, hoping to thumb a ride. A couple of cars and a truck or two went by, but no one they knew. Finally, a truck slowed as it passed. Hoping for a lift, Andy looked at its occupants: a stout young airman he didn't know was holding onto the doorframe.

Then he heard someone yell, "Hey, Andy, whatcha doin'?" With that, the empty vehicle sped along down the road.

Breathless, Mel wheezed, "Who was that?"

"A guy I know who works up at base supply, goes by the nickname of Skeeter."

"Hell, he could have given us a ride," grumbled Mel.

When they reached the barracks, Mel was right on Andy's heels as he dashed inside and ducked into his cubicle. Mel brushed by him in his rush down the center aisle to his area and said something as he banged his locker door open. Absorbed in what he was doing, Andy didn't pay any attention to him as he reached into his footlocker and pulled out a Prince Albert pipe tobacco can. The top half of the can held the can's lining paper and tobacco and, under the lining, he had stashed his life's savings, a whopping 120 bucks. He'd been putting away a little money each month, saving for a car when he got back home. Andy pulled out sixty dollars from the stash, refitted the tobacco, and walked over to Mel.

Just in case there was someone else lurking around, he whispered, "Pry out some of those shekels you have hidden way; we need money to pull this off, and we can't do it on promises and good looks."

Mel looked at Andy as if he'd run a dagger through his heart.

"Shit, Mel. I dipped into my stash, so you need to do the same," Andy said. Then he turned and went back to his bunk.

Regulations were that you could not go off base in fatigues. Japan was still considered an occupied county, and Class A uniforms were to be worn off base. The Class A uniform for winter was the wool dress blues with the blouse (coat), or airmen could get by wearing the waist-length Ike jacket made popular by General Eisenhower during World War II. The summer attire was long-sleeved khaki shirt and trousers. Both uniforms required you to wear a blue necktie, cap (head cover), and black low quarter shoes. The talk was that after the occupation ended next year, on April 28, 1952, they would be allowed to wear civilian clothes off base, and Andy hoped it was true.

He sat on his footlocker to put on his shoes, and when he looked up he saw Mel standing in front of him, all prim and proper, looking every bit the image of an airman in a recruiting poster.

"What's takin' you so long? Need help tying your shoes?" Mel taunted before walking roguishly away.

"No, I don't," Andy grumbled. "An' if I did, I wouldn't ask you." He slammed the locker shut and followed Mel out the exit.

"Andy, don't forget your hat; you left it lying on your bunk."

Not bothering to answer, Andy did an about-face and retrieved his headgear.

The chief clerk, Sergeant Borelli, was expecting them as they entered the orderly room. A decent guy, the chief clerk was a little on the chubby side and always trying to lose a couple of pounds but never succeeding. His problem was all the candy stashed in his desk.

"OK," he said. "Here are your passes. Sign out and enjoy your weekend." Then he whispered, "Look, guys, if you're unable to be here by 0730, just make it back to your duty station. Sergeant Bowman will call me, and I'll sign you in."

"Hey, Borelli," Andy said very softly, hoping no one else could hear him. "How did they know Butler wasn't in the barracks last night?"

Borelli leaned a little closer to him and replied, "Butler was expecting a phone call from the States at 0130; before he went to town, he asked the CQ to wake him. When the call came through, the CQ couldn't find Butler and noted it in the log. The strange thing is that Butler had another call at 0400 from the States. This time it was from someone in the State Department, of all places. They're supposed to call back on Monday."

Andy wanted to ask Borelli more questions, but he noted that the new first sergeant was standing by his office door, staring at them. Master Sergeant William Jones had been in Japan only the last three months and, during that period, he had earned the nickname of Mother Jones. The reason for that particular moniker was that he was always hovering. He kept asking questions and checked on each movement the troops made to ensure that everything was copacetic. He reminded Andy of a mother hen trying to keep her brood of chicks in line.

The master sergeant lived in the barracks, by his own choice, in a private room; rank has its privileges. Waiting for his family to join him in Japan, he had nothing better to do than hang around the squadron area all the time after the end of the duty day. They would all be glad when he was living in family housing and they would be free of him, at least in the evenings.

The first sergeant seemed upset; they assumed it was because of the arrangement Sergeant Bowman had made over getting additional time to locate Butler. The rumor was that this new first sergeant enjoyed pulling someone up on an Article 15, court-martial. The talk was he liked to watch people squirm.

As they hastened out of the orderly room, Andy said, "Think Old Mother Jones has a bet going with Bowman an' he wagered we weren't going to find the guy and make it back on time?"

Mel spat back, "I bet you're right. If the rumors are correct, he'd like to have us screw this up. Don't think he cares much for Butler."

"He probably has the Article 15 for being AWOL already typed up on Butler, hoping we won't find him."

They headed for the bus stop, and Mel nudged Andy. "If we don't need to come back here, why don't we take our fatigues with us? We can leave them at Sumiko and Yoriko's apartment until we need them and change at the hangar after we find Butler."

"Good thinking." They reversed their course and grabbed their AWOL bags, so named because they only held a change of clothing in case you decided to make an unauthorized split. Since they needed the clothing to be presentable on Monday, they folded and packed their clothes in the small satchels, trying not to wrinkle them.

Andy stuffed in his brogans, and the bag bulged at the seams.

He was ready to close the zipper when Mel suddenly said, "We'd better grab fatigues for Butler; I know where he hides a key for his locker."

Mel took a couple of seconds to find the key. Then he wrenched open the locker and started pitching clothes at Andy.

"Slow down; I'll try to jam in his fatigue shirt, hat, and one brogan. You'll have to stuff the rest in yours."

They each took half of Butler's clothes, but were not as careful folding them as their own. Finally, after wrestling to close the bags, they darted out the barracks and raced to the bus stop. They were panting like a pair of old dogs by the time they reached their destination, and they stood for a second before they could talk. From there, they could hop a base shuttle to the main gate.

"Wonder how long it'll be before the damn thing arrives here?" Mel complained. "If we got to chase around looking for the old fart, you'd think they'd let us check out a Jeep. Not have to ride a damn bus, wouldn't you think?"

Andy ignored the first part of Mel's outburst and said, "Usually the bus runs every half-hour, although you can't rely on that." He checked the Timex strapped on his wrist and the bus schedule fastened to the signpost. "If they're running close to the timetable, should be here in a couple of minutes."

Mel rattled on without taking a breath. "You think Butler's at the bar?"

"Where else would he be? Let's hope so. With the shape he was in when we last saw him, don't know how he'd be anyplace else." Andy looked intently in the direction the bus should approach from, but nothing was in sight.

"Yeah, but if he left by himself, he might've passed out. Maybe he's lyin' out cold in an alley, or someone conked him on the head and rolled him. Not all that safe to be out alone that late at night, especially drunk as he was."

"We'll find out when we're there. Wish the damn bus would show up; minutes are wastin'."

They stood wiggling their toes inside their shoes and tapping their feet. They stared at dirty splotches on the pavement and cracks in the sidewalk. Finally, Andy plopped down on the bus stop bench; he felt he might as well take a snooze, relax. There was nothing to do until transportation arrived. He clasped his hands behind his head, stretched out his legs, and closed his eyes.

"Mel, wake me up when the bus comes."

"Airman Anderson."

What a shocker it was to hear the crisp, articulate voice of Master Sergeant Jones right behind him, breathing down the back of Andy's neck. Andy sensed that icy stare as a shiver ran down his spine. Hesitantly he turned his head and stared. He first glimpsed a chest full of campaign ribbons and medals. Then he looked into Sergeant Jones's steely gray eyes. Andy started to stand up, but the sergeant motioned for him to stay seated.

Mel was as stunned as he was, and was already at a parade rest as he stared at the first sergeant.

"Anderson, Shultz, find Butler," Sergeant Jones said in a calm yet forceful manner. It was not a command but more of a request. "I'm putting my trust in you two. Although I'm not well acquainted with you men yet, I'm sure you're capable of doing this task, or Sergeant Bowman would not have recommended you. You have the responsibility of locating Sergeant Butler and having him at his duty station by Monday." He paused for just the slightest of hesitations, but it was enough to make Andy think he was a little reluctant to continue.

"If Butler gives you any argument, just mention Laon. Tell him I told you to say, 'Laon.' Best of luck in finding him."

After a stalwart look and a quick once-over inspection, Jones turned and started down the street with the typical measured stride and perfect bearing often seen in career military men.

They watched until he disappeared, and then Mel smirked. "He walks like he's got a ramrod up his ass."

Andy ignored the remark and shook his head in bewilderment and amazement. "Mel, what the hell's a lay own?"

"No damned idea. Nevertheless, remember the words. They may come in handy when we find Butler. Strange," Mel added. "Who the hell ever imagined the first shirt would follow us here to give us a pep talk and wish us luck." He scratched his head. "I'd always figured the guy was an a-hole."

CHAPTER EIGHT
Saturday

The shuttle pulled to a stop in front of Andy and Mel, the door opened, they piled in and grabbed empty seats. The driver slammed the vehicle in gear and headed down the road. Mel slouched in the seat across from his buddy. Andy was going to say something to him, but Mel was deep in thought, so the question was left unasked.

Lay own, Andy thought, recollecting what Master Sergeant Jones had said. *Lay own; strange thing to say. Would those words suggest something special to Butler? The first sergeant talked about responsibility. I'm nineteen and have enough trouble being accountable for myself, let alone for a thirty-something-year-old guy who got drunk. Maybe I should have tried to roust him out of the bar last night, and I didn't. I was wrong, and I gotta suck it up and go find the guy. I've rounded up a lot of stray cows on the prairie. How different can it be to find someone in town? Look at the positive side: the sarge excused you from duty for a couple of days to search for him.* Something odd struck him about Sergeant Jones's World War II campaign ribbons—*they were almost identical to Butler's.*

Mel was not in a relaxed mood. Andy noted, *The guy's squirming around like a hound dog ready to roll in a pile of fresh manure.*

Mel wore a worried expression on his face as he turned and asked, "Hey, you think they might do something to us if we don't find Butler or we're not back on time?"

Andy chuckled to himself. Then he decided to have a little fun and mess with Mel. "We're in the military; they'll do anything they feel like—restrict us to the squadron area, assign us extra duty, reprimand us. Hell, I guess even an Article 15 … maybe ship us to Korea or to Thule, Greenland. Who knows?"

"Thule, huh? Cold up there," Mel answered a little absently. Then he rebounded and shot back with a little satire. "Don't you muck up this go-find-the-missing-drunk mission. I don't have any long underwear."

"You're the one that's gonna be a lawyer. I'm expectin' you to keep us out of the hot seat. Remember, I'm just a hick farm boy."

To take Mel's mind off the task at hand, Andy added, "Hey, remember you started telling me about the Schultz dynasty once and the quest you all undertake before you go on to college?"

That perked Mel up; he liked to talk about his kinfolk. "Yeah, I did. Well, as I started to tell you, there's a tradition among the Schultzes. After we—the males of the family—graduate from prep school, and before entering Harvard, we go on a trek, or quest. For two years minimum, we venture out to make our way in the world. We're on our own and receive no financial help from home. If you can't make it, you're not frowned upon or seen as a failure, but you're not held in the highest esteem either. Hard to explain to someone outside the family, it's a task we must do."

The bus buzzed by the Post Exchange, mess hall and then pulled in at a stop to let a couple of guys off. Not many people going to town this early in the morning.

After the bus began moving again, Mel continued, "My father's foray had him working as a common seaman on a tramp steamer sailing around the Cape of Good Hope. He was gone for three years. Grandfather Schultz ventured west, herded cattle, busted broncos, and worked as a deputy marshal in Tombstone. When I was little, he would spin the most fascinating stories of Arizona and the West. The old man has this brace of six guns with pearl grips he said he was going to leave to me.

"His father, my great-grandfather, signed on with the Pony Express in 1860 and rode the trail from St. Louis to Sacramento. He claimed he delivered mail in all kinds of weather, riding through a hail of Indian arrows and chased by outlaws and bandits. When the Pony Express disbanded in 1861, he joined the Second Cavalry California Volunteers and fought in the Owens Valley Indian Wars in California until 1863.

"After their individual journeys, the Schultz men came home, completed their Harvard educations, and then assimilated into the family law firm or investment banking business.

"Not all returned to Philadelphia, though. My grandfather's brother's search took him to Alaska to prospect for gold. He didn't strike it rich, but the lifestyle suited him. He remained a prospector and never came home—just stayed in the Yukon, panning for gold. The story goes that the fiancée he left in Philadelphia died of loneliness and a broken heart.

"Me, I joined the Air Force. Kinda tame compared to the adventures the others had, don't you think?"

"No, you're doing your journey. Times have changed, and there's no more Wild West or Alaskan gold rush. You think the military is all that tame?"

He answered with a shrug of his shoulders, and they rode on in silence, passing bus stops where no passengers were waiting or wanted to get off.

"Why did you join up?" Mel asked.

"It was either join or be drafted, not a lot of choice." *Truth was there wasn't much of a future for me on the farm. My older brother will take over the farm from my dad. I was expected to carve out my own path in life. I'd taken the test and applied for West Point when I was in high school, but the rejection letter simply read that I didn't receive the appointment. It didn't elaborate if I had failed the test or if it was because I didn't have any letters of recommendation from our state's US senators or congressmen. No one in my family knew any members of Congress, nor did we have any friends who could leverage such letters of reference. So much for my dream. There's a lot of difference between a dream and reality. Now, if I'm going to do anything about college, I have to depend on the GI Bill.*

Mel shifted his position. "How did Bowman know we were in the same bar Butler was in last night? Someone rat us out and tell him we left the guy crapped out at the bar?"

"They were checking on Butler, not us," Andy answered. "You're jumpin' at shadows."

"Wish the driver would jam his foot down to the floorboard; we're running out of time." With that, Mel slumped down and drummed his fingers on the seatback in front of him.

If Butler wasn't at the Brass Rail, Andy wasn't quite sure where else to look. If Butler had hooked up with some girl last night, he could be shacked up anyplace in town, and they would never find him. It was conceivable he was lying face down in the dirt somewhere, and they would need to check the maze of alleys between Mama-san's and the base.

A paperback book was lying on the seat in front of Andy. *Something to read. It will help me take my mind off Butler.* He reached down to pick up the book, a Zane Gray novel, *Riders of the Purple Sage*. Having already read the story, he tossed the book back on the seat and stared out the window. As the bus drove by the buildings, he began reminiscing about home.

His hometown only had one school, grades one through eight. The town's population was 342 people, and it had a couple of small businesses, a general mercantile, a bar, and a movie house that was open on Friday and Saturday nights. The bus he was now on was so similar to the one he used to ride over to the county high school. The only difference was this one was painted blue instead of yellow. He looked out at the massive buildings and aircraft hangars, marveling at the size of the buildings compared to those in his little farming town.

Andy's family were all farmers and ranchers. His dad was the first of his family to finish high school.

The bus moved along at a fast clip, and with few passengers and not even slowing at every stop, it arrived at the main gate in thirty-five minutes.

They were both standing, ready to exit. Before the conveyance came to a full stop, the door swung open. The bus driver yelled, "Wait!" Nevertheless they jumped off, beat a path straight to the guard shack, and handed their passes to the young air cop on duty. The cop glanced at them and then stared. It was obvious by the way he acted that he needed to flaunt his authority.

The kid couldn't have been more than eighteen and really must have needed an ego boost. "Need ta see whatcha got in them bags," he ordered.

The Brass Rail

Reluctantly they unzipped the bags and opened them up wide enough for the cop to look inside. "Clothes, stuff we're taking to the laundry," Mel mumbled.

The guard poked around with his nightstick, rumpling the clothes. This ticked Andy off. *Come on, guy, quit screwing around. I gotta wear the clothes later.* At last, the cop was satisfied and nodded OK.

Closing the satchels, they walked away from the guard shack. After they were out of earshot, Mel muttered under his breath, "Prick! I have more important things to do than stand there and listen to some snotty-nosed kid."

"Gotta agree with you. Come on; let's move it."

Sporadic puddles from last night's rain lingered in the depressions of the pockmarked street. They hurriedly picked their way down the semipaved thoroughfare, trying to avoid the mud holes.

"Damn it all to hell," Mel complained to Andy. The balance of his discourse was so indistinctly muttered, Andy couldn't make out the rest of his streak of profanity.

"You got a problem?" Andy had an idea why Mel was cussing, but it was fun to provoke him when he was upset.

"Sloppy stinkin' mud screwed up my spit shine!" Mel grumbled. "Just got them cleaned up."

"You can shine your shoes again." Andy hoped Mel hadn't caught the sarcasm in his voice, but the guy was a neat freak, sometimes to the point where it was irritating. Everything concerning his clothes and appearance needed to be perfect. They hired houseboys who cleaned the barracks, latrines, and polished the guys' footwear. Mel, however, would go over his shoes after the houseboys shined them; he always had to put that finishing glistening shine on them. The service wasn't free—they automatically deducted it from their pay—but the houseboys were worth every penny, or rather, every yen they were paid. The men didn't have to pull KP either; locals were hired for that job as well.

Payday was once a month, and after they took out money for laundry, houseboys, and all the other fees, Andy was almost broke before he got to the end of the pay line. After he stashed a couple of bucks in the tobacco can, the money that he had left needed to stretch for the next thirty days. When the money was gone, he'd hang in the barracks and read books or polish his shoes.

They rounded the corner and hurried toward the tavern. The bright red front door stood out like a beacon, a sentinel, a Circe summoning them to her lair. However, the building didn't have the beckoning atmosphere in the daylight that it did in the softening shadows of the evening. The one-story wood-frame structure had been painted a dismal gray color at one time. Exposure to the wind, rain, and sun had caused the aging paint to crack and flake away.

All the bars in town closed at the same hour, allowing time for compliance with the 2400-hour curfew.

They sprinted up the sidewalk, expecting a quick resolution to their task and visualizing a drunken Butler asleep, slouched on a stool with his head awkwardly resting on his arms atop the bar. Andy seized the knob and then turned and pushed, but the door didn't budge. It was locked and bolted tight. The bar wasn't open. Stuck on the door was a small tattered cardboard sign that read:

Close 2330 hour no drink after

After a few knocks, they politely waited. When no one came, they knocked again and waited some more.

Mel's impatient movement behind him made Andy edgy, and he stepped aside as Mel reached around him and started banging on the red panel. When he stopped pounding they listened, but there was no reply.

"Maybe there's a rear way in," Andy said. "I'm sure Mama-san lives in rooms behind the tavern."

Mel took off at a half run, and Andy followed him at a fast trot. They traversed the distance to the side of the bar, where they found a side door that was closed and locked. A seven-foot-high bamboo fence spanning the gap between the bar and the next store blocked their entry to the back of the bar. After close examination, they found the artfully concealed entranceway through the fence. Figuring out how to work the latch, Andy pushed the gate inward.

The gate swung open to expose a meticulously groomed gravel path leading to the rear of the tavern. The walkway was so immaculate Andy didn't want to disturb a single particle of gravel by treading on the path's smooth surface. They picked their way along the corridor, trying not to leave any evidence of their trespassing. The narrow space between the two buildings led them down a passageway to a different world. Rounding the corner, a perfectly manicured and modest garden began to take shape in front of them, a humble botanical oasis filled with vast beauty. Lush bamboo trees and petite, delicate, glistening green bushes grew with exquisiteness, while dainty blossoming flowers filled the air with a fragrant perfume that gratified the senses. There was a small Zen garden, its weathered rocks scoured spotless and impeccably placed, with white flowing sand raked and manicured in swirling concave and convex patterns surrounding each stone. Never had Andy seen anything so luxuriant. Who would have imagined something this serene, tranquil, and exquisite was secluded just a few feet from the dirty bustling street? Awed by the compactness, the complexity, and the beauty of the little garden, Andy was speechless.

Mel punched him on the shoulder, interrupting his meditation. He pointed. "Look, a way in." He crossed the distance to this newly discovered entrance and knocked before Andy came out of his trance and became aware of what Mel was doing.

Andy hurried to join him, anticipating an immediate answer to the knock, but nothing happened. Mel pounded on the door with his fist, and they waited.

When the door at last slid open, they expected to see the woman who owned the establishment. Instead, an older, dignified Japanese man with graying hair stood silently peering at them. Something in the man's posture gave Andy the impression that the man had been a soldier during the war. Something about him—the way he carried himself and his appearance—spoke of a proud and defiant man, a man beaten in war and in battle but not defeated in spirit. Andy didn't remember Sumiko mentioning anything about Mama-san having a husband. The expression on the man's face communicated that he wasn't happy seeing a couple of young Americans standing in his backyard.

Mel stared at the man and started to stutter and stammer, "Ah … ah, aba … ah."

Good ol' Mel; always count on him to do the unexpected, Andy thought. *I shouldn't criticize; I've no idea of the proper way to ask either. Neither of us was expecting a man to come to the door.*

Andy racked his brain, trying to think of what to say. Never having seen this person before, he needed to be a diplomatic.

Mel suddenly blurted out, "Sergeant Butler here?"

There was no visual or vocal response from the man.

Mel tried again, this time with gusto, as if by increasing the volume of his voice he could create a hole in the language barrier. "Oren Butler, you know?"

The Japanese man peered intently with a stern, blank stare at the two Americans.

Andy couldn't remember the Japanese word for good morning. *What's the short version of the greeting? It sounds like the name of a state.* He moved up alongside Mel and bowed toward the elderly man. "Ohio."

"*Ohayo gozaimasu,*" replied the distinguished-looking gentleman in a snippy tone, in conjunction with a slight, trivial bow.

"Excuse me; we're trying to find a friend of ours."

The Japanese man glowered at Andy; he hadn't understood a word Andy had said.

Now what? I'll ask for the woman who runs the bar. But we just call her Mama-san. I've heard her name once, but I've forgotten what it was. In his best broken pidgin Japanese, Andy said, "Mama-san … ah…." He hesitated. *The Japanese are so polite, and I need to add something other than just asking for Mama-san. My Japanese vocabulary is only fifty or so words, but I know the word…. What is it?* Andy was totally baffled for a moment. Then, through all the dark, cluttered mess in his mind, a word came to him, the word for "please."

"*Dozo*, Mama-san, *dozo.*"

The man bowed slightly while still glaring at them and replied, "*Chotto matte kudasai.*" ("Just a moment, if you would.") He bowed with such dignity and pride that Andy was embarrassed by his own meager attempt to replicate the gesture. Without further comment, the man quietly slid the panel shut.

"What did he say?" Mel questioned.

Andy shrugged. "I'm not really sure, but I think he went to get Mama-san. Anyway, I hope so. Otherwise, we could be standing outside all day waiting for him to come back." He was anticipating the man getting the woman. What little he knew about Mama-san's fascinating past was indeed intriguing, and he wished he knew more. But if anyone could help them find Butler if he wasn't here, it would be her.

CHAPTER NINE
Mama-san's Story

A few months prior to Andy standing around Mama-san's back door, he and Mel had been hanging around the tavern. It was a slow night, and there weren't many customers. Mama-san retired early, there being so few customers. Andy and Mel were speculating about Mama-san: if she was once a geisha, how did she end up with the Brass Rail? They knew little about the proprietress except that she was an amiable lady, friendly and well liked by everyone. She ran the bar with an iron fist, letting the customers horse around but controlling the actions of the girls who worked for her. She would not tolerate prostitution.

Having asked the girls about Mama-san's past numerous times and not receiving any information, Mel started pestering Sumiko. "Tell me about Mama-san."

"What you mean, tell me 'bout?" replied Sumiko.

"Where is she from? Why won't she talk about her past? Was she a geisha before the war? Tell me about her."

"Oh, no can do. Mama-san past big secret."

"What do you mean, big secret?"

"No can talk 'bout her; very hush-hush. You no can know."

This only intrigued Mel further. The more Sumiko resisted, the harder he pushed. He went on, "I'll bet Yoriko will tell me. I'll buy Yoriko a drink, and she will tell us everything."

Sumiko shook her head. "Yoriko no know all 'bout Mama-san secret."

"I so know secret," Yoriko fired back.

"You no know all the secret," countered Sumiko.

Andy, wanting to defuse the argument between the girls, interjected. "I suppose you know all about the secrets, huh, Sumiko? I'll buy champagne if you tell."

"No can do."

They bantered back and forth without coming to a compromise, as Sumiko refused to budge. Realizing it was time to up the ante, Mel made an offer. "I'll take you to a nice dinner and movie on your day off if you tell me; maybe we go someplace fun afterward. If you would like?"

Sumiko countered, "What about Yoriko? I no go without her."

"I'll take Yoriko," Andy piped up. "Don't worry about that. We'll all go together if you tell us 'bout Mama-san."

Sumiko and Yoriko started conversing in Japanese. They would stop talking, look at the two guys, and then start giggling. Finally, Sumiko said, "If you take us dinner Peter's Restaurant in Tokyo and then dancing at nightclub, we tell."

Mel's startled expression revealed that the request had rocked him. "Peter's Restaurant is very expensive. It will cost me all my month's pay to take you to Peter's for dinner. Won't have the money to go to a nightclub."

"Mel, sometimes you hold on to a nickel so tight you squeeze the shit right out of the buffalo," Andy said. "Come on, let's take the girls out and wine and dine them."

Mel hesitated for a second. "We'll go to lunch at Peters. That will only take half of my month's pay; that OK?"

Yoriko nudged her friend, and they talked back and forth so rapidly that neither Andy nor Mel had a clue as to what the two girls were saying.

"OK, lunch and then movie. You promise. Then I tell you. No can tell no one. OK?"

Mel grinned. "You sure you want to do this, Andy?"

"Goin' to be expensive. We'll blow everything on the date and have to ride out the rest of the month on base." But it would be worth it.

"We promise not to tell what you say about Mama-san," Andy said. "Cross my heart promise. Now you tell."

"First buy champagne. Then I tell little," she said.

Sumiko waved to the girl behind the bar and placed the drink order. She grabbed the guys by their hands and escorted them to a table in the far corner of the tavern, out of hearing distance of the bar. The waitress brought the drinks over, set them down, and held out her hand for the money. They paid champagne prices for the beverages, though the drinks might have been wine or plain soda, and then the waitress went back to the bar and left them alone at the table.

Sumiko began her story. "I know Mama-san long time, since war end, but she not talk much 'bout past till one winter night last year when we 'lone, after bar close. Very ... how you say, ridged outside."

Mel interrupted, saying, "No. Frigid, not ridged."

She ignored him and continued, "We stay overnight with Mama-san 'cause snow out, too cold walk all way home. Mama-san have much sake. She say wine keep her warm. She drink much, cry, an' say she miss family an' we like little sisters to her. Then Mama-san start tell us 'bout her life."

***

Mama-san began her story, saying, "My birth name is Shizuko, which means 'quiet child.' I was born in a small fishing village in southern Kyushu about 1915—I'm not sure of the year. I'm the youngest sibling of six girls and two brothers."

Tears began to form in her eyes, but she quickly wiped them away. "My father, an illiterate fisherman, was never successful in business. He struggled and labored, eking out an existence for us. His father and his father's father had all been fishermen before him and provided adequately for their families. My poor, proud father, his pride would not let him admit his failure at his occupation, and he always made excuses for his incompetence and dreamed of an easier and better life."

Mama-san stopped talking and reached over towards the sake tokkuri, but Sumiko's reflexes proved quicker, and she refilled Mama-san's cup. The older woman nodded politely, took a sip of the wine, and continued, "Perhaps I was six years old the year that had been especially difficult for father. With no money, he was heavily in debt for new fishing nets and boat repairs. At night after I went to bed I would lie awake, listening to my mother and father argue about the debt and lack of money.

"One evening, he came home from an unsuccessful day at sea and told my mother, 'Keiko, I've made an important decision today. I spoke with one of the town tradesmen, a man with many contacts among influential people in Kyoto. The person I talked with agreed to broker an arrangement where Shizuko will go to Kyoto and receive training as a geisha.'

"Tears began welling up in my mother's eyes, and he added, 'She will have excellent care and a prosperous life.'

"My mother wished to say something, but he held up his hand and said, 'Do not argue. The decision is final.' She clasped her hands over her face and bowed her head, both in submission and, I think, so that no one could see her weep.

"The tradesman was charismatic, and with elegance and charm he convinced my father that they would provide me with the best education possible. Later, I learned the man with whom my father dealt had lied about having real contacts in the geisha community; he only knew of a degenerate thief who trafficked in the human bondage trade.

"'We are going to send Shizuko away to be a maiko; she will be trained as a geisha!' Father proudly boasted to any who'd listen. 'We'll receive money now, and when she has become a renowned geisha, she will provide for us and help us in our old age.'

"He strutted like a peacock, for he thought he'd arranged for me, his youngest daughter, to thrive and become prosperous.

"The same servitude happened to hundreds of other Japanese girls, enslaved at a young age and cast into the shadowy realm of the geisha. Born female in that era of a male-dominated society, it was my fate that I be sold into bondage.

"The money they paid my father was far less than promised. The tradesman spun a web of deceit and lies about how the poor economy had driven more families than normal to sell their daughters. The surplus of young girls lowered the price he could pay. The man boasted that he'd bargained and argued until he'd sold my contract for an excellent price. My father had no choice but to accept the smaller sum of money, as he had already spent the expected funds on food and fishing gear. It was essential that my father repay the debt before the end of the year. It was a matter of honor, an obligation. He needed to settle his debts, and I think it was with a sense of remorse that he accepted the tradesman's offer.

"On the trip to Kyoto, the men talked of how easy it had been to cheat my father. Father didn't know his monetary commitment was to the same person to whom he was selling me. The tradesman had known exactly the amount of money my father had needed and had taken me as payment for my father's liabilities, giving him only a few extra yen to make the transaction appear proper. Because they'd paid my father less, they would receive a bonus when they sold me for a larger profit to a geisha house.

"I did not live up to the name of quiet child. Not wanting to leave home, I did so only kicking, screaming, and fighting to the point where they needed to bind me. On the trip to Kyoto, I tried to escape every time there was a chance. For a long time, they kept my hands bound and tied a rope around my waist. They dragged me behind them like an animal being led to slaughter.

"During the journey, only one of the original men who'd taken me from my home remained with me. Along the way various cohorts joined him, and they asked for money to pay for transport and lodging. The man I was with claimed he didn't have any funds to pay for such luxuries.

"Though but six years old, they made me walk long distances. I slept in the dirtiest of places. Many times I was forced to sleep on lice-infected straw mats and given the foulest of foods to eat that were inadequate to sustain even my meager needs. They forced me to endure ridicule, physical and sexual abuse, and beatings for misbehavior. They did not rape me, for they feared punishment, even death, at the hands of the tradesman if they were unable to sell me. After many days on the road, we stopped at a crossroads and waited there for two days until a group of travelers arrived who had an older woman and a number of young girls with them. The troupe of men dealt in the slave trade, but I was fortunate they sold me to a representative of a geisha house. Not all the girls went to geisha houses; most were sold as indentured slaves.

"The last man to buy me saw within me the promise to be a trainee, a maiko. The week before we arrived in Kyoto, he and the woman he traveled with let me bathe and gave me clean clothing. They fed me nourishing meals because I needed to be presentable when they delivered me to my final destination.

"The matron of the geisha house callously examined me upon my arrival to ensure I was still pure. All the girls endured the same shameful examination. They only allowed virgins to participate in maiko training. I was accepted and admitted.

"Like a bag of rice, once they determined I was free from vermin, the people of the geisha house purchased me.

"From my previous captors, the matron learned I was a difficult child to control. She put me to work doing hard menial chores to learn the value of discipline. For two years I scrubbed floors and did demanding tasks while striving to maintain control of my fighting spirit. They beat me for any slight mistake, and I learned to yield and concede to their wishes. Never did I lose my rebellious nature, and I pretended to be a docile girl. When they thought my resistance was broken, they began teaching me reading and writing, music, dance, and the tea ceremony. How I enjoyed learning to play an instrument, how to dance, and the subtleties of the tea ritual. As a handmaiden, a vassal to run errands for the older maikos and geishas, I learned about makeup and combs. I listened to stories about the world of the geisha, some of the tales were beautiful and romantic, others were of abuse and terror.

"By age thirteen, I excelled in music thanks to my superb singing voice. My agility and execution of the tea ceremony was flawless; I mastered the art to perfection. My intelligence, skills, and physical beauty assured them I would be a most-desired geisha. The one major problem was my nonconformist temperament, which I hid. Because of my talents, they traded me to an upscale geisha house. My training intensified, and I relished the attention I received for my performances. It was the first happy time in my life since my father had sold me. Everything was going well, and they treated me with care and respect, allowing me small amounts of freedom."

***

Sumiko hesitated as she recalled the rest of what Mama-san had told them. Mel and Andy did not need to know this dreadful part of Mama-san's life, so she decided she would not tell them, but sat in silence as she vividly remembered how Mama-san's voice began to tremble when she continued telling the story.

***

"Then came that terrible night, the night I bit off the patron's ear."

Yoriko gasped at the statement but did not question, to allow Mama-san to continue.

"As a teenager, my bodily features and womanly appearances were slow to develop. The matrons were disappointed I had not reached physical maturity by age fourteen, and that my deflowering ritual would be delayed. The postponement meant I would be unable to begin repaying the money invested in me. They put me to singing and serving tea and drinks. It wasn't until age sixteen that I matured enough to begin fulfilling my obligations to them. My deflowering ceremony was arranged, and a suitable price with a patron negotiated; I was not given a choice. They received a top price, and it provided more than a marginal return for the house.

"I was scared and unsure, but they schooled me on how to mentally remove myself from the act and become absent, a nonparticipant. They assured me this was what I needed to do and everything would be fine. Not believing them I refused to do their bidding, determined not to bed with a man against my will. My rebellious nature earned me a beating and a promise of worse, including physical harm against my family if I did not do as I was told.

"The man who they had contracted with for the deflowering was a prominent diplomat with immense wealth and power. As he was important, rich, and in a position to do many favors for the house, they bowed to his every wish. They commanded that I obey him and do as he asked. Again, they threatened me with painful punishment if I failed."

Both girls had fallen silent during Mama-san's homily, but Yoriko, no longer able to contain her silence, blurted out, "Why did you bite his ear off?"

"The night of the ritual was the first time I met him—a huge, fat, horrid man. He restrained me by squashing my arms hard against the futon. I struggled and fought, but he was much stronger than I. It hurt; the pain was excruciating. I asked him to stop and pleaded with him, but he only laughed. His bulk smothered me and, unable to breathe, I was suffocating. He yelled at me to quit fighting and cooperate. But I would not give in to his desires and continued to struggle. The man held my arms down to restrain me and, with the last of my strength, I bit his ear. I clamped down with all the strength and intensity I could and held on. He let go of my arms and started brutally hitting me on my face and head. The more he struck me, the harder I fastened on his ear with my teeth until I bit through the flesh.

"Unmerciful in his punishment, he continued beating me about the head and face until I was unconscious. There were many times after that when I wished he would have killed me. When I woke, the people from the geisha house were standing over me, screaming and calling me a wretched, worthless wench, exclaiming that my uncooperativeness and viciousness had cost them large amounts of money. The man had refused to pay, and he was going to seek damages from the house for the injury to his ear. My nose was broken, one of my cheekbones shattered, and two of my ribs cracked. I had shamed them and the honor of the house. No doctor was sent for; they merely let me lie, offering no assistance, intending that the broken nose serve as a reminder of my disobedience. One of my friends bandaged my ribs but could do nothing for my cheek and nose. She wanted to find a physician to help me, but they forbade her under threat of cruel reprimand. Later that day the matron marched into my room, trailed by all the young girls in training who lived in the house. She unmercifully whipped me with a bamboo switch until my body became nothing but raw flesh covered with welts and cuts, my sleeping kimono wet with blood. She made the girls and maikos watch as a lesson to them not to disobey and be rebellious.

"That night, when I slept, three men came into my room and tied my hands and gagged me. I fought and struggled. My injuries were painful, and the men, callous and cruel, raped and beat me repeatedly until dawn. The next night, other men came and bound and raped me again. It continued night after night until I had lost the will to resist. I was as a mindless person, not feeling or caring what happened. I was more dead than alive. I will never forget the viciousness of the painful attacks or the degrading humility and shame. In time, the ribs healed and my nose and cheekbone, never given any medical attention, mended, though not properly. Now I have a misshapen nose and cheek, which makes me look hideous."

"No, no, Mama-san, you don't look ... bad. No, not bad at all," stammered Yoriko. "You're very pretty."

Mama-san smiled at Yoriko and continued, "Once an attractive woman, now I use heavy makeup to hide my shameful appearance.

"After the incident, the owners of the geisha house, not wanting to invest any more money in my training, forced me to work as a courtesan. I was no longer a geisha but had been given the status of simple prostitute. My face was so disfigured so to drive up the fee for my services, they forced me to sing and play the *shamisen* behind a screen in order to intrigue and entice customers. When a patron agreed to the price, they'd sell him the use of my body.

"Sometimes they allowed me to serve tea. I enjoyed singing and playing the musical instruments and serving tea, though I never told them I did. But I hated the rest!

"One night in 1940, a group of high-ranking Japanese officers accompanied by their aides came to the house seeking an awe-inspiring time. Among this group was a particular colonel who wasn't a military man, but a political lackey who had received his rank through bribery and blackmail. Loathed by all the geishas for his fondness for abusing women, the colonel was a loud and obnoxious clod. The geishas plied him with an alcoholic drink until he passed out. The beverage was laced with a narcotic noted to provide realistic and pleasurable dreams. The other courtesans left with their male escorts, leaving me alone with the sleeping colonel and his aide, a young lieutenant. The aide asked me to help him move the colonel into a room where the drugged officer could sleep and recover.

"The lieutenant said he was smitten by the loveliness of my voice and musical abilities and wondered if I would honor him by singing and playing for him. We sat together all night. I sang and played the *shamisen*, and we talked. In the past, I had never met a man so kind and understanding. He spoke with me as a person, not a commodity, not as a piece of merchandise purchased for the evening and later summarily tossed aside, unwanted and unappreciated.

"In the morning, when the colonel woke, he did not remember anything that had happened past the time when he'd sat at the table drinking. The lieutenant wove a wonderful tale of mystery and romance for him about how the colonel had spent the night with the most beautiful and alluring of geishas, who'd told him how she'd fulfilled his every desire and that she wished him to return. As to why he did not recall all of the events, the wonderful elixir that he'd been served had made him irresistible to women but had also clouded his memory. A gullible man, the colonel returned the following evening to claim the woman he believed he'd captivated and to fortify himself with the delightful drink. Assured that when he was ready to retire the lady would again do his bidding, he enjoyed the evening. The officer was once again given food and drink laced with the narcotic, and his dreams became his reality. He awoke in the morning a happy man, remembering nothing but his dreams. The colonel became addicted to the drink, and his aide and I continued this ruse for six months. We fell in love. It was the first time I ever loved someone. Ashamed of my battered face, I tried to hide behind a fan or mask. Hitoshi—the lieutenant—told me, 'It isn't our outward appearance that matters. What we feel in our hearts is the path we must follow.'

"Hitoshi wanted us to be together. One day, he approached the owner of the geisha house to strike a bargain and purchase my freedom. He made a formal request, but the figure they gave him was quite absurd. They told him it was what I owed them for food, clothing, and lost income because of my rebellious nature. Hitoshi had a small inheritance left to him by his grandfather, it was not enough to pay for the transaction. Confident he could procure the necessary funds, he said he just needed a little additional time, so an agreement was made. The week before I was to be freed, Hitoshi was informed that he must accompany the colonel to Manchuria. The following morning, he arrived at the house. He did not yet have enough money to complete the agreement for my freedom and tried to strike a new bargain, but the geisha house owner would not settle for less. He pleaded with the owner, but to no avail. All was lost. Hitoshi left the house belittled and distraught.

"Hitoshi returned that evening. Having but a short time he could spend with me, we made arrangements for what to do if we were unable to locate each other when he returned. The first weekend in May of each year, if able, we were to travel to a small hotel he knew on the south shore of Lake Yoshi. We were to wait for two days for the other one to come, and if they did not, we would return the following year. We were to continue this routine until we were reunited or it was clearly hopeless to persist.

"As he departed, he handed me a small piece of delicate rice parchment on which he'd beautifully inscribed in kanji the characters 'love' and 'happiness.' 'These shall be ours when I return home,' he promised.

"I lovingly folded the paper and placed it inside my kimono, over my heart. I kept it safely there for many years in a small silk pouch I later made.

"With the prospect of ever being united with Hitoshi gone, even though he had offered them money, in retaliation for their callousness and for not releasing me from my bondage, I caused many problems. I became so difficult they decided to sell me to a brothel in a small suburb north of Nagasaki. The trip from Kyoto was worse than the one I'd made when I was a little girl. The men who escorted me to the new bordello looked upon me as a common prostitute and had their way with me. Beaten and tied up, I went without food and sometimes sleep. We finally arrived at the brothel, a run-down, poorly managed house, worse than anything in Kyoto. This poor brothel purchased me in the hope that my musical abilities would bring new trade.

"Hitoshi returned to Japan after a year in Manchuria. In Japan for but two weeks, he sought me out in Kyoto. They refused to tell him where they had sent me. My friend secretly told Hitoshi I'd gone somewhere near Nagasaki, but she did not know precisely where. He searched for me as long as he could. His limited time in Japan precluded an extensive search, and he returned to China with the colonel.

"On August 9, 1945, the Americans unleashed the bomb on Nagasaki; Hiroshima had been bombed three days earlier. The brothel was located north of the city but close enough that we heard the B-29's droning engines as it flew overhead. Hurrying outside, we could see the bomber drop its delivery of death. I felt the heat of the wind on my skin as the mushroom cloud rose and hovered in the sky. The fire's mesmerizing red glow held us spellbound for a moment. Then blazing tentacles of flame spread outward toward us, as if an evil demon were reaching and groping to engulf all. A little girl began to cry, and a young woman, overwrought with panic, screamed. Gripped with terror and not knowing or understanding the horror that had been unleashed on the city, the crowd of people ran hither and yon like a nest of alarmed field mice.

"Then a fire broke out in the bordello, and the matron demanded that we go secure all her possessions and bring them back to her. A few of the courtesans ran to do her bidding. I failed to react quickly enough, and she yelled that I was a worthless person, disobedient and lazy. Then, using the switch she always carried, she beat me about the head and shoulders. The matron shrieked at me, 'You miserable whore, I'll thrash you until you can't walk!'

"The rebellious spirit of childhood rose from within. Never again would anyone beat me; never again would I let myself be sexually abused; never again would anyone call me a whore. I tore the switch from her hand and flogged her with all my strength. Then I turned, still clutching the switch, and bolted from my captivity and the existence I had been trapped in for all but six years of my life. I ran and fled north, away from the flames, away from the bombing and the terror of the existence I had lived. The matron screamed for me to stop, but it was my chance to escape. I was no longer afraid of them; I no longer cared what happened. I wanted my freedom, to be independent. I knew they weren't going to chase me; they were too busy to be bothered with the likes of me.

"I sought an escape route away from my captors. I hid by day and moved by night. A family of women fleeing north who were traveling with a large group of refugees befriended me. Droves of people were fleeing from Nagasaki; some had been burned by the bomb's radiation, some by fire, and others were uninjured, all were frightened and scared. Many died, and all we could do was place their bodies beside the road and pray that someone would come and give their remains a proper burial.

"I won't talk anymore about that. I mingled with the refugees and sought safety in their midst until I arrived in Tokyo. There, I disappeared among the thousands of homeless people, found a new identity, and became a different person. Never again would I be a courtesan. It did not matter if there was no place to live or nothing to eat. I would never go back to that life.

"Like hundreds of other refugees, I ate whatever I could beg and rummaged through garbage and trash for scraps of food. I ate rats, mice, and bugs. I slept in alleys and doorways, doing whatever was necessary to stay alive as I wandered from place to place. Occasionally, I'd find a job and earn a few yen or some rice. The war ended, but there was still misery, illness, and death to be seen in the backstreets of Tokyo.

"I was one of the fortunate and found employment serving drinks and tea at a tea house owned by an unscrupulous man. He was not interested in the old ways of Japan; he wanted money and influence. He had come from a poor family and was now an entrepreneur, having made millions of yen on the black market. He wanted to be a legitimate businessman and a visionary. He didn't care who I was or what I'd once done. Lucrative in his enterprise, he expanded and strengthened his business and influence. He rewarded me for my work with money and placed me under his protection.

"Every year, I went to the hotel at Lake Yoshi and waited for Hitoshi. I always arrived a day early and stayed for two extra days afterward, allowing five days instead of two. In 1947, my wait ended.

He was there—war-wearied, haggard, beaten, a skeleton of the man I loved.

"When he saw me, he began to weep. I had never seen a Japanese man show his feelings so openly before. He repeated over and over, 'I was so afraid you were dead, that you had died in the bombing.' He took me in his arms and caressed and kissed me right there in public, which, as you know, Japanese men do not do.

"Hitoshi's physical appearance was different from when I'd last seen him, however inside he was the same person. He had only recently been released from a prisoner-of-war camp in Burma, having been incarcerated there the last four years. He'd been hospitalized for the six weeks since his return to Japan, but had slipped out and come to the hotel.

"He did not wish to return to the hospital, and since I already owned this business, which also included a comfortable house, I brought him here to recover."

"How did you get this bar, Mama-san?" asked Yoriko.

"Perhaps someday I will tell you, but not now.

"Japan began the war. I don't hate the Americans. I dislike the cruelty of the atomic bombs dropped on Hiroshima and Nagasaki, the bombing of Tokyo, the deaths of all the innocent Japanese people. Yet I owe them a debt of gratitude for giving me the means to be free from bondage. Although they may not realize it, they are shielding me now. When the war ended and after I finished my employment in Tokyo, I settled here because it was safer to surround myself with big-nosed foreigners than only Japanese. The house matron or her thugs will never find me or even look for me this close to an American base. If they did, they would be foolish to try to take me. I'm too well known in the military community, and there would be many questions."

"Did you ever see your mother or father again, or your brothers and sisters?" inquired Sumiko.

"No. After I ran away, I did not try to contact them. I was afraid that the people I'd run from would look for me there and that it would be dangerous for my family. I am not even sure where I would start looking for my parents or my siblings. I remember the name of the town where I lived and my family name, but that is all. I have no idea if they are even there or alive. I never heard from them after they took me to Kyoto. Perhaps someday…."

"Do you hate them for selling you?" asked Yoriko.

"I did for many years, but I'm over the anger now. My father did what he thought was right and best for me." She paused. "I often wonder what my life would have been if it had never happened. I am happy with Hitoshi, though. He is a wonderful man, though the war made him frail and withdrawn. The years he spent in prison and captivity in Burma were difficult. Before the war, his family was wealthy and owned a custom furniture company. Many of their beautiful pieces are in the most elaborate homes in Japan. Hitoshi spent more than a year constructing the bar counter that adorns this room. Working with his hands, building and creating beautiful furniture, has been therapeutic for him and has started to help heal the sickness of war.

"I'm tired now and am going to bed. Good night." Mama-san left the table and shuffled to her living quarters behind the bar.

***

"Sumiko, why did you stop talking?" Andy looked at her questioningly. "What happened after Mama-san said she was happy for the first time since her father sold her?"

Sumiko had not realized, being so absorbed in her own thoughts, she'd quit speaking. "That's 'bout all she tell us," she said. "She stay Tokyo after war for a while and then come here an' start bar. Now you buy 'nother champagne. I thirsty talking."

CHAPTER TEN
The Search Begins

Andy's attention abruptly returned to the present when he thought he heard the noise of a door opening. They stood for what felt like an eternity and became increasingly impatient as each minute passed. The urge to fling open the door and go inside kept nudging Andy, but he couldn't. This wasn't the bar; it was her home. So they waited. He thought of what Sumiko had told him of Mama-san's life. At no time had she mentioned that Mama-san had a husband. *Who was that man?* he wondered. *I think Sumiko held back on us and didn't tell us the complete story.*

Finally, the door slid partway open. *"Nan deska?"* (What do you want?) Mama-san stood squinting against the rays of the sun that shone into her eyes.

A soft expression adorned her features, one that depicted a gentler and more carefree person than when she was behind the bar. A sense of tranquility surrounded her as she stood there in a soft green cotton kimono, the intricate white flower pattern of her gown blending with the surrounding garden. The morning light silhouetted her beautiful, delicate features, while the direct sunlight accented her facial flaws, a raised area on her cheek and an imperfection of the nose bone. With the heavy makeup she used in the evening gone, she was naturally beautiful and not the artfully painted oriental doll he had come to know.

An expression of puzzlement crossed her face as she recognized them, and the expression changed to concern. She repeated, *"Nan deska?"*

Mama-san understood a little English, but to what extent they were unsure. In the evening there were always younger women, girls who assisted her with drink orders. Andy often noticed that if Mama-san didn't grasp a question, one of the girls who spoke English would explain the conversation to her.

"We're looking for Butler; is he here?" Mel blurted out.

Mama-san squinted at them. *"Nani?"* ("What?")

"Where's Butler? Butler, Oren Butler. Is he here? Do you know where he is?" The words spurted out in such rapid succession that no one with only a partial knowledge of English could have grasped his meaning. Mel was notably perturbed; he felt the pressure, and patience was not one of his virtues.

"Mama-san," Andy implored, "Butler-san, our *tomodachi,* our friend. Four stripes." He pointed to the chevron on his sleeve and indicated four instead of his two stripes. *"Wakaru?"* ("Understand?") Mama-san was perplexed. *I'm slaughtering the language, but I must keep trying.* He continued, "Butler-san, older. We here yesterday. He here. He...." *What's the word for "drunk"? Can't remember; I'll have to wing it.* "Stinko, pass out," he added, doing his best impression of Buster Keaton's silent film version of a drunken man about to topple over. "We need find him so he no be in trouble. *Wakaru?"* He struggled with the words and butchered what few words of Japanese he had in his limited vocabulary. He needed to try to make her understand, so he kept making facial expressions and waving his hands. *I need to learn some more words; I can't rely on this pantomime stuff.*

Finally, Mama-san broke into a smile and nodded. Perhaps he was funnier at impressions than he thought. *"Hai, hai,* stinko, GI. Butler-san." She waved her hand back and forth to signal no. She pointed to the interior of the building, saying, "Go," and placed her hands together, bringing them up to her cheeks and laying her head on them to mimic a person asleep. Then she pointed toward the air base.

"You." She pointed at Andy. "Tomodachi, no." Unsure of the English words she wanted to express, she gestured with her hands and rebuked him with a grim expression. Andy understood she felt they had purposely left Butler sitting there alone when they should have been helping him.

"Butler-san good," she criticized. "You no tomodachi." She pointed her finger at his chest, and the little lady stared up at him in total displeasure. She scolded him as a mother would when disciplining her offspring. The reprimand issued forth in Japanese and he understood not one single word, but the meaning came through loud and clear.

"Tomodachi help Butler-san!" Her tirade ended, and she stopped talking when she realized why they were there. A look of apprehension appeared in her eyes. "He no base?"

Andy shook his head no and, in pidgin English, said, "He no come base last night."

He was doubtful she even understood all the words, but she did fathom the meaning, and she forcefully executed her desires by pointing to the ground with her index finger. "*Koko ni, ite,*" she said and pushed her hand downward. Turning, she rushed back into the house, leaving Andy and Mel alone to stare at each other.

"Did you grasp all that?" inquired Mel.

"Enough. She wants us to wait," Andy advised.

Within minutes, Mama-san came rushing out. She had put a coat on over her kimono and she hurried down the path, her wooden *getas* grating against the gravel walkway. She motioned for Andy to follow her. Noticing they were carrying the little AWOL bags, she snatched them from their hands and hurriedly tossed the satchels inside the foyer before ushering the boys out of the garden gate and down the street. Mama-san moved with such speed that both Andy and Mel had to walk at a fast pace to keep up with her. She didn't speak, but every so often she would turn her head and peek at them to make sure they kept up with her. The shops were all open. People bowed and greeted her, and she courteously returned the gesture but never slowed her pace.

After following her for a number of blocks, Andy recognized the surrounding area. They were in the vicinity of where Sumiko and Yoriko lived. It all made sense; Mama-san understood Butler was missing, and she needed an interpreter to continue the conversation.

They arrived at an apartment building and ran up the stairs to the girls' rooms. Mama-san banged on the door and, after a short period, Yoriko greeted them. Although she was surprised to see Andy and Mel standing at her door with Mama-san, she didn't ask why they were there, only said good morning and flung the door open so they could enter. They slid out of their shoes, stepped up on the tatami mats, and observed Sumiko sitting at the western table in the kitchen area eating breakfast. Yoriko had left her place at the table to answer their knock.

The three Japanese women began talking so hurriedly that Andy had absolutely no inkling of what they said. However, he assumed it was about them and Butler.

The discussion paused, and Sumiko told them, "Mama-san think perhaps Butler left bar with girl named Peggy. Mama-san fired girl for stealing."

The name rang a bell with Andy, and he recalled he'd had a conversation with the barmaid the evening before.

"What was Butler doing with her?"

"Mama-san guessing Peggy hear her tell Butler she find someone help him back base. She guessing Peggy told Butler-san she was supposed to help him to base. Mama-san thinks Peggy up to no good."

Sumiko shrugged her shoulders. "Peggy not a very friendly person. We no associate with her."

"I no like her," Yoriko added spitefully. "She say bad thing about Mama-san. She not nice person. She streetwalker."

"If the gal is a hooker, she must have some friends. There must be girls on the street who know where she lives," insisted an anxious Mel. "Go ask them where she is."

"We no speak them type of girls," snapped Yoriko.

Mama-san voiced something to them in Japanese, and Sumiko translated. "We go now, make inquiries."

Mama-san shooed the boys out of the apartment while the girls got dressed, after which they all walked down to the section of town where the prostitutes hung out. This section of town was seedier than the area where the Brass Rail was located, and the shops were all a little dingier. The GIs had nicknamed the area Prostitute Row.

"You wait here, Mama-san says." Sumiko pointed to a sleazy teahouse, more of a coffee shop, that catered to GIs. "We go ask questions."

Andy protested and insisted that they should to go with the women; however, he later conceded it was best if they waited. The owner of the shop came and brought the coffee they ordered. "You on R and R from Korea?" he queried.

Mel gave him a negative shake of his head. "No, on pass for the weekend."

"You want something very tender and sweet for dessert?" the proprietor probed.

"No thanks," Andy replied politely. "I'm not hungry."

Mel promptly kicked him in the shins. "He's talking about women, you dope. He's wondering if we want to get laid. Andy, buddy, granted you're a hayseed, but how gullible can you get?"

"Guess I wasn't paying any attention to what he was saying," Andy murmured, trying to cover his blunder.

Mel leaned forward, put his elbows on the table, and scratched the back of his neck. "You think maybe Butler's just shacked up? That it's no big deal and he's fine?"

"Doubt it, especially if he was expecting a phone call from the States and he'd already alerted the CQ to the fact. He was planning on being back on the base," insisted Andy.

They roosted in the little café for forty-five minutes. After Andy had consumed three cups of appalling coffee, which necessitated a couple of trips to the *benjo*, the three women finally returned. The guys expected them to sit down and fill them in on what, if anything, they had discovered. Instead, they motioned for them to leave. The men paid their bill and walked briskly down the street, following the women. The warm rays of the sun had evaporated most of the water puddles that had lingered from the previous night's rain, leaving the street dry and even dusty in places.

Sumiko slowed her pace, allowing them to catch up with her. "We find out where Peggy live. She work for pimp name Koji." She quickened her steps and hurried after Mama-san and Yoriko. The men kept stride with her, and when she had caught her breath, she continued, "No one see him this morning, but not strange. Most time, he come around in late afternoon. We also hear him like sell stuff on black market."

"Where are we going now?" Andy asked.

"To where the girl live and see if she home."

Mama-san hadn't uttered a word since they had left the teahouse, but instead walked along in silence, absorbed in thought.

Yoriko noticed Andy had been watching Mama-san, and she interjected, "Mama-san very angry 'bout this Peggy and worry what she do with Butler-san."

"What can one girl do against Butler? The man's no slouch, drunk or sober," declared Mel. "Where does this Peggy live?"

Yoriko didn't answer; she pointed in the general direction of a cluster of houses and small apartments in the distance, down the road they were on.

When they arrived at the group of dwellings, Yoriko exclaimed, "She live here," and pointed to one of the buildings.

Mama-san barked orders at the girls, who both listened intently and politely bowed as the older woman turned and shuffled toward the steps leading to the building. Sumiko relayed, "Mama-san want you"—she gestured toward Andy and Mel—"stay where no see. Mama-san go talk girl."

When she came back shaking her head in disappointment, they learned Peggy was not at home. One of her roommates told them she had not come home yesterday, that she often stayed with customers all night. The other girls in the apartment wouldn't admit they worked for the pimp and refused to talk about him, although one girl admitted they were all afraid of him.

"Someone has to have some information," Mama-san told Sumiko in Japanese before she began canvasing the neighborhood food stalls, asking questions of anyone who would talk with her.

After numerous attempts at trying to get information, she told Yoriko to take Mel and Andy back to the teahouse and wait there for her. Mama-san was not getting the cooperation she needed with the GIs hanging around. Japanese were still reluctant to trust Americans.

They trudged back to the little teahouse, ordered more coffee, and waited while Yoriko attempted to keep them entertained by asking them about the States. She told stories of her home and about what her childhood was like growing up in Japan during the war. They dawdled around the teahouse, shifting restlessly back and forth in their chairs, anxious to discover what was happening and bored because they couldn't help. Not knowing what was going on made the time drag, and the bad coffee didn't improve the situation. "Why did Mama-san want us to wait here on Prostitute Row?" Andy asked Yoriko. "Butler was snatched over at the Brass Rail, not here."

"Mama-san not sure, maybe bring here," the girl replied as she waved her arm in a semicircle, indicating the general vicinity.

After an hour, Mama-san and Sumiko entered the teahouse. The older woman appeared exhausted and worried. She sat at the table and asked the shop attendant to bring her some tea, and she tasted the hot beverage while Sumiko imparted what information they had gathered. Someone had observed Peggy escorting a GI down the street, not that it was unusual for her to be on the streets so late. What struck the person as strange was why Peggy had taken him into that empty, dilapidated shack. The building was only a few blocks away.

"We go now and look." Sumiko waved them forward. Mama-san had finished her tea and had not waited for them. She had walked out of the building and continued moving hastily along the thoroughfare, kicking up little clumps of dirt as her wooden getas scuffed against the surface of the street.

"Well, at least Mama-san was able to get people to talk to her," Mel commented.

"She pay much yen for information and make many…," Sumiko groped for the words. "Threats. Mama-san many friends … *yakuza no* … from Tokyo days."

At the empty building, Andy vigilantly opened the shack. He found a stick and propped the lopsided door open. The sunlight flowed through the opening and glinted against a piece of glass on the floor. The reflective object proved to be nothing but a shard of glass, and Andy started probing about for some evidence to prove to him that Butler had been there.

Mama-san stooped, picked up the sliver of glass, and began sifting through the dirt and debris. From under a small scrap of newspaper, she retrieved a portion of the glass vial Butler had knocked out of Peggy's hand. Bringing the open end of the glass tube to her nose, she sniffed. "Butler-san drugged," she murmured aloud in Japanese, alarmed but not surprised by her discovery. She searched the dusty floor and found a cork stopper, which confirmed her suspicion. During her years of servitude in geisha houses, she had used similar ampoules of exotic narcotics to entice and control patrons.

Hearing what the woman had whispered, Sumiko raised her hand to cover her mouth and cried out in English, "They kill him!"

Andy, startled by her sudden outburst, spun around and stared inquisitively at her.

Mama-san was unsure what the emotional outpouring of words meant, and she looked up anxiously. *"Nani?"*

Sumiko, embarrassed by her lack of emotional control and composure, explained to Mama-san in Japanese what she feared. The older lady answered in the same language, "I don't think so, at least not yet."

Impatiently, Andy interrupted their conversation, asking, "What's going on? You find somethin'?"

"Oh, Andy-san, Mama-san think Butler drugged, but OK; still alive," cried Sumiko.

Mel had been listening to their conversation as he remained bent down, surveying the floor. He moved judiciously from spot to spot, examining and progressing on to assess different areas of the shed.

Andy grunted, "Mel, you're like a damn bloodhound the way you keep nosin' around."

"Kind of a habit. I've got a couple of uncles who are the crème de la crème of criminal lawyers in Philly, and they—"

Andy abruptly interrupted, saying, "They're not going to do us any good; they're in Philadelphia."

"Yeah, I know. What I was trying to tell you was since I was, I don't know, twelve or thirteen, every summer, when I wasn't in school, they let me tag along with them or sent me off with one of their investigators to different crime scenes so I could gain firsthand experience. They figured if I was going to follow in their footsteps and become a lawyer, I needed to learn the very basics, and the best way to do that was to crawl around on my hands and knees. They taught me some stuff."

"Stuff like what? I can track a rabbit after a snowstorm or follow one of our heifers if they wander off, but on dry ground it's damn near impossible. Just how the hell are we going to do it here?" exclaimed Andy.

"I don't know for sure, but I can guess. Look, I'll show you what I mean." Mel pointed out and explained his theory. "Looking at the shoe prints, there were three people in here recently, a woman and two men. The smaller man's print means he's probably Japanese. The other man was an American GI. Check the imprint of the shoe and compare it with ours—same sole type and heel. The American walked over here and sat down. Notice how the dirt's all messed up. They pulled him from here over to a wagon or cart, thus the lines made from his shoes as they pulled him. Why a cart? Because of the double wheel marks in and out of the shed. I think Butler walked in here, and then something happened: he passed out, was knocked out, got mugged, maybe they killed him, I don't know. And they loaded him in a cart and hauled him off. I know it sounds like a bunch of *Dick Tracy* comic strip bullshit, but that's what my uncles taught me to look for. Pure speculation, right or wrong it's a good guess unless you've something better."

"You're a regular gumshoe, Mel. You might be full of crap, but at least you have a theory. You might make a decent criminal lawyer after all," Andy replied. Then he crossed the area to where Mel thought Butler had sat. There, he noticed a dark splatter in the dirt and touched it. *Might be blood; might not. Something stained the dirt.* However, he didn't say anything because he didn't want to freak out the girls. "Can we follow the tracks of the cart outside?"

The shaded areas of the dirt street were still moist from the previous night's rain, but they revealed no immediate signs of the cart. *Either the rain washed away the tracks or someone covered them up.* In a solemn voice, Andy made an observation. "Well, all we can do is hunt around for tracks. I don't think they would have gone back toward the Brass Rail, so let's check up this direction," he said, pointing in the direction he wanted to go. They spread out and walked the alley, searching for any clues.

In the dirt sheltered by an overhanging eave, Sumiko remarked and pointed at a slight indentation. "Andy-san, maybe this them?"

After a look, Andy replied, "Possible, but let's keep lookin'."

They wandered down the alleys, catching a glimpse now and then of what might be tracks left by a cart, until their search led them to the nearby riverbank. Here, the busy street had been so crisscrossed with cart and foot traffic that it was impossible to tell which way they might have gone.

Mama-san stood stock still, staring up and down the street. Andy had stopped walking as a confused expression formed on his face. "Now what do?" questioned Yoriko.

Andy shook his head, unsure and trying to decide what their next move should be.

"I'm starving," exclaimed Mel. "Close to 1330; let's find some food and mull over what we want to do while we eat."

"Me hungry too," Yoriko and Sumiko both said, simultaneously indicating their need for nourishment.

Yoriko took Mama-san by the arm and spoke to her in Japanese. The woman nodded and signaled with her hand they were to follow Mama-san. A short distance from where they had stopped, she entered a noodle shop. The *noren* hanging in the entryway to the restaurant was clearly not built for Americans, and Andy and Mel both had to brush it aside as they ducked underneath. Mama-san and the girls were short enough it didn't interfere with their entry. With a sweeping motion of her hand, Mama-san informed them they were all to sit down at the table. She ordered a lunch of buckwheat soba noodles, rice, and tea, and the famished searchers ate in silence, each pondering their own worries and aspirations about the chase.

After they'd finished eating, Mama-san called the proprietor over to their table and relayed to him that they were seeking information about a cart that would have been in the vicinity last night and been pushed by a man and woman. She described the woman but, never having seen the man, could not give the café owner a description of him.

The proprietor was a talkative individual and eager to tell her about all the excitement in the area. "Last night, over at the bridge, they found the body of a man lying half in and half out of the water."

Alarmed by the news, Mama-san asked, "Was the man Japanese or American?"

The proprietor shrugged his shoulders, as there were rumors of both. He thought he remembered a cart, but wasn't sure; there'd been so much activity he couldn't be certain. However he said his next-door neighbor might have knowledge about any foot traffic that late, explaining the neighbor was an elderly man who had trouble sleeping and sat by his window, keeping watch over the street until the early hours of the morning. He was old but very observant. Leaving a young girl to tend to the customers, the proprietor went next door to speak with his neighbor.

Andy began speculating about the body they had found and if it might have been Butler. *"Doko denwa...."* He groped for the word he needed. *"Airi ... huh...."*

Yoriko slurred through a mouthful of noodles, *"Arimaska."*

"Doko denwa arimaska?" ("Where's a telephone?") he asked the girl who was minding the shop. She pointed outside and mumbled something in Japanese that he couldn't grasp.

Sumiko grabbed Andy's arm. "Outside, around the corner; I show you. Who you want to call?"

That was the quandary. At first, he'd intended to call Sergeant Bowman. However, Bowman would only end up calling Sergeant Jones. *We don't have that much time. I'll cut out the middleman and call Jones.* Something about those identical campaign ribbons the first sergeant and Butler both wore made him think they must have a history together. After finding the telephone, he gave Sumiko some money. She slid the coins in the slot and had the operator contact the base. When the chief clerk answered the phone, Andy said, "Hey, Borelli, it's me. I need to talk with the first sergeant right away."

"He's busy now."

"I can't wait. I need to talk to him."

"He's in his office chewing a guy's ass out."

"Well, interrupt him."

"If I do, he'll climb all over my back."

"Ya need to. It's really important. Come on."

"OK I'll try, but you owe me big time, Andy."

"Yeah, yeah, and tell the guy Jones is chompin' on that he owes me for ending his ass-chewing session early."

Borelli laid down the phone, and there was relative quiet for a while. Presently, Andy heard an undistinguishable conversation in the background and then the sound of a closing door.

"Anderson, this had better be important," stated Master Sergeant Jones briskly.

"It is. The American they fished out of the river last night, was it Butler?"

Silence.

Then: "You say they recovered a GI from the river?"

"That's what I'm hearing," Andy confirmed.

"Stay on the line; I'll check. Don't hang up, Anderson, you hear me? Don't hang up."

CHAPTER ELEVEN
Mama-san and Butler

Andy relaxed his grip. He had squeezed the telephone receiver with such intensity that his knuckles had grown white and numb. A thousand different scenarios played over in his mind. *Was it Butler in the river? Why did they snatch Butler in the first place? Was it retaliation against Mama-san? Why is this woman so intent on helping us track him down? Does this hijacked man mean more to Mama-san than a regular bar patron?* He was on the verge of asking Sumiko if she knew anything about the relationship between the bar owner and Butler when the first shirt came back on the line.

"Anderson, you there?"

"Yeah, Sarge, I'm still here."

"Where are you? Can I call you back?"

"I'm at a phone booth in town. Easier if I call you back."

"Give me about ten minutes. I need to do some checking on the identity of the person they found." The seriousness in his voice made Andy wonder again if the dead person was Butler.

"OK. I'll ring you again in ten minutes." He hung up the telephone and turned to Sumiko, who had been standing by him, listening to every word.

"Was Butler-san?"

"No information; I have to call back in a bit." Then he asked the question that had been haunting him. "Tell me, what's the relationship between Butler and Mama-san?"

"What mean relationship?"

"Why is Mama-san so intent on helping us?" quizzed Andy.

Mel and Yoriko had left the restaurant and huddled next to them by the phone booth to eavesdrop on the conversation. Before Sumiko could answer him, Mel interceded and said, "Yeah, and why doesn't Butler ever pay for food or drink at the bar? Does he run a tab?"

"Mel, what the hell does running a tab have to do with finding the guy?" countered Andy.

Sumiko, puzzled, asked "What mean tab?"

"It is the same as credit. You put down in a book what someone owes, and they pay for it later."

Yoriko hurriedly interrupted, replying, "Oh, no. Only money to buy! Must have yen, no credit."

"Only wondering," Mel continued. "One day, we drank a lot of hooch and ate food at the bar. We were pooling our money to make sure we had enough to pay for our extravagance. Butler was watching us and told us not to worry, he'd take care of it this time; his treat, as he had an arrangement with Mama-san. We all left the Brass Rail without paying. If Mama-san doesn't run a tab, how did he manage it?"

Sumiko didn't say anything for a few seconds; her beautiful bright eyes reflected the knowledge of a secret. She mulled something over in her mind. "I s'pose tell maybe OK. I there that day and translate for Butler-san. He give Mama-san money for future drink."

"You're telling me Butler paid for all his booze in advance?" Mel queried.

"Yes," acknowledged Sumiko. "But different."

"You need tell all story for them understand," Yoriko interjected. "Need to tell 'bout Mama-san when she go Tokyo from Nagasaki."

"OK, so tell us," urged Mel.

"I try tell. You no can tell no one," Sumiko insisted.

***

This was how Mama-san told her story as she, Sumiko, and Yoriko, shaded by the afternoon shadows, sat in the garden behind the bar, drinking tea.

"When I left Nagasaki, I met a group of refugees fleeing north. The people I traveled with were afraid of the big bombs; we walked day after day not knowing if more bombs would drop. There were rumors the Americans would destroy more cities. If peace did not come soon, we would either all die from the bomb blasts or the radiation. The war, however, ended while I trudged toward Tokyo.

"Times were hard when I arrived at the city. I think I mentioned to you before that I slept in doorways and alleys, anyplace I found dry and relatively safe. I begged for food and rummaged through garbage. We ate rodents if we could catch them, and I even munched on bugs.

"I kept seeking any type of work for money or for food. I did not care. One day, I heard on the streets about a man wanting to hire a woman who could perform the tea ceremony. It was also gossiped that he was a very corrupt and evil person, a man to fear. I went to him anyway and begged for the job. I pleaded with him but, after a short time, he dismissed me. I returned to the backstreets, where I lived in a bombed-out building that housed many other homeless people.

"Four days later, in the evening, I was holding a very sick young girl no one wanted. The poor little waif was so malnourished, needing aid but all alone in the world. I gave her what little food I'd hoarded and cradled her to keep her warm while singing her a lullaby, hoping she would sleep. As I sat huddled in a corner, the evening light became obscured by a shadow. I looked up; three men were staring down at me. One man, dressed in a business suit, was the one I had talked to earlier about the job. The other two were large, muscular men, very unpleasant and callous-looking. I was certain they were going to hurt me.

"The man—I will call him N-san—said to me, 'You can sing; I know because I just heard you. Can you play the *samisen*?'

"I was afraid, so I only nodded.

"'You are or were a geisha?'

"Again, I nodded yes.

"'Are you running away from someone?'

"Fear overcame me, and I had no voice.

"N-san again spoke in a very mellow tone, saying, 'I will not hurt you, but it is important you tell me. Are you running from them?'

"He had figured out I was in hiding and had already deduced from whom and why I was fleeing. He asked me these questions to find out if I would give him an honest reply.

"I was terrified to answer and scared about what would happen if I kept silent. I nodded again.

"'Is this your child?'

"I shook my head and found the courage to speak. 'I found her wandering on the street.'

"'Let me see her.' I moved the young girl where he could stare at her face. 'If you come to work for me, I will find a home for her, but it will be difficult.'

"That's how I found work at a teahouse. N-san wanted a person to serve his customers, a woman he could trust to not divulge what might be overheard. I was running and hiding and would not do anything to bring attention to myself.

"I'd associated with men like this before and their bodyguards; they were very dangerous men, and you did not want them angry with you.

"The teahouse, while not open to the public, was a meeting place frequented by men who were less than honest and honorable. The patrons were all deeply involved in the black market and many other illegal activities. These men were ruthless in their business dealings and conducted business in secret. Some did not want to drink alcohol, they preferred tea, and this was where they needed my skills with the tea ceremony. They may have been criminals, but they were civilized and appreciated the finer things in life.

"They were not a lot different from the men I'd met at the geisha houses. They were businessmen of wealth, and each commanded a large organization, modern shoguns with armies of cold-blooded thugs, and like samurai, they ruled their territories, their fiefdoms, with an iron fist. They were not patriots of Japan, and they did not care that Japan had lost the war; their interest was money and power. These groups controlled nearly all of the illegal activities in the Tokyo area after the war ended. The amounts of money they discussed and exchanged were staggering. What they spoke of doing was inconceivable for me to imagine. They talked freely when I was in the room, knowing I would not reveal any of their secrets. These were not men to cross; if I did, my life would be taken as quickly as a chicken's neck is broken. I did not betray any confidences and did my duty with skill and dignity.

"N-san wanted to build a Western-style nightclub in Tokyo. He wanted the biggest, most expensive and exclusive club in Japan. He told me, 'The war is over; the Americans will be here for a long time. The Western way of life will make vast inroads into the Japanese culture and our way of living. Our way of doing things will change forever. We either embrace these changes at the beginning and become wealthy, or resist and be trampled upon and become poor. The choice is ours, and we must take advantage of it while we can. I want legitimacy, power, and money. You have earned my favor by being trustworthy, and I would like you to stay and work with me while I build this dream. I want you to hire young, beautiful women to work at my club and teach them how to serve and cater to the guests and to me. However, no prostitutes. I will not tolerate prostitution. If one of the girls is found selling her body, she will be severely punished and dismissed as a lesson to the others. I am serious about this; it is a nightclub, not a geisha house, not a brothel.'

"I accepted his offer, worked for him, and learned many things. He promised me that as long as I worked for him, he would protect me. Well liked among the high-ranking American military and diplomatic circles, he prospered. As he became a powerful man, his partners in the crime syndicate market conveniently disappeared.

"My life became my own again, but I was still working for someone and being told what to do and when to do it. I'd experienced how precious independence was and needed to be my own master. I wished to be beholden to no one. My friends told me that the freedom I wanted was impossible for a Japanese woman to have, but I needed to try.

"I learned the nightclub business and wanted to open a little tavern near an American base. I felt safe around the Americans. However, money was a problem. I talked with N-san, and he offered to lend me the money I needed to start my business. I was leery of such transactions, so he suggested we go to a lawyer and have a legal document drawn up to protect me. But I still was concerned about the debt. I paid him as promised each month without fail. Because of the manner in which the loan was constructed, the last payment was larger than the rest, and I struggled to come up with all the money. N-san assured me that if I could not pay, other arrangements could be made. I knew the character of this man. He was a good man one minute, but he could be ruthless a moment later.

"I needed to be free of the debt. One evening, Hitoshi and I discussed the problem while standing behind the bar. Butler-san slouched at the far end of the bar on his usual stool; I thought he was engulfed in deep thought. Only two or three GIs were in the bar, and they were flirting with the bar girls. We talked openly about the money problem at great length, feeling safe from prying ears since we were speaking Japanese. Butler-san left a short time later.

"The next day, Butler-san came in and ordered his customary sake. When I went to collect the money for the drink, he discreetly slid an envelope to me that contained sixty-five thousand yen, the exact amount I needed to make up the deficit on my payment. In shock, I pushed the envelope back to him and said, 'No, too much money for the sake.' In his poor Japanese, he tried to explain to me that the money was for an investment in the future of the Brass Rail. I tried to decline his offer, as I did not want to be obligated. However, he insisted. The only agreement would be that the money would be paid back through drinks and food. He told me he would be in Japan for a long time and he'd probably consume more alcohol than the money would cover. 'Keep this,' he said, 'and when I have a zero balance, no money left, you tell me.' Butler now has a share in the Brass Rail until all the money is spent."

Mama-san ended her story and stared wistfully out at the green leaves and colorful hues of the garden.

***

Sumiko looked first at Andy before she started speaking again. "Butler-san understood Mama-san needed money and how much. He no understand exactly why she needed it right away. When I ask him why he do this, he smile and say, 'My lend-lease program, my way of saying, *domo arigatou gozaimasu* for taking care of me. A type of business arrangement for me.'" Sumiko hesitated. "I still not understand what lend-lease mean. Mama-san took money and told us Butler-san never again have pay for drink. Since, Mama-san look after him and take care him as member of her family. Butler-san, he understands more Japanese than we think." Sumiko sighed. "Maybe this explain relationship, Andy-san."

"Yes, that is the relationship," agreed Andy. *Mama-san paid her monetary debt to the man to whom she owed the money. Now there is a moral obligation, a kindness, that needs to be repaid. She will do anything in her power to fulfill her commitment of gratitude to Butler.*

"Well, how 'bout that!" exclaimed a surprised Mel. "That's why he didn't worry about paying for the sake. Both humanitarian and a philanthropist—boggles my mind."

Butler never worried about money, and the scuttlebutt was he was from old money and was a business bigwig in civilian life. Andy reminded himself that Butler was a reservist recalled to active duty and had a lucrative life outside the military. The man was not in the Air Force because he needed a job. Butler had never flaunted his wealth. Doing a fast calculation in his head, even with the exchange rate at 360 yen to the dollar, it was still a chunk of money to give to Mama-san. To put it in perspective, with that much money you could pay cash for a new Chevy back in the States.

"What happened to the little girl Mama-san was holding?" asked Andy.

"N-san found her home to live, but girl not happy there. Mama-san always kept close watch, make sure girl OK. When girl grow up, she go and work for Mama-san."

"The girl works at the Brass Rail?"

"That girl me." Sumiko lowered her eyes and stared at the floor. The words she spoke were so faintly uttered Andy barely understood them.

CHAPTER TWELVE
The Drunk and the Entrepreneur

More than ten minutes had passed when Andy made the second call. The first sergeant came immediately to the phone this time.

"Anderson, it was not Butler. The provost marshal is questioning how you found out it was an American, because that information hasn't been released. I covered for you for now, but you have some explaining to do when you get back. You have any luck with other leads in your search?"

"If it wasn't Butler in the water," Andy said, "I guess there's another possibility we can follow up on as to where he might be. I'll let you know how it pans out."

"Keep me updated, day or night, OK? Anderson, I don't want to call in the military police unless it is necessary. If you need anything call me, and I'll come to wherever you are PDQ. Anything else?"

Andy considered telling him about the drug vial and the blood spatters, but decided to keep the information to himself for now rather than stir up additional controversy.

"Not now, Sergeant Jones," Andy said. "I'll keep you informed. Thanks for the info."

By the time they went back into the café, the shopkeeper had returned. Mama-san had told the girls what the shop owner had been told by his neighbor. They, in turn, relayed to Andy and Mel that the neighbor had spotted a man and woman pushing a two-wheeled cart that appeared to be heavily loaded, and they'd continued down the road by the river that led out of town.

"That's not a lot of help; we can't keep running up and down roads banging on doors. We need specific information on where they might have gone," Mel growled.

"The pimp want sell stolen stuff on black market!" exclaimed Yoriko with a burst of excitement.

"So what?" Mel grunted, frustrated with the lack of information. "That doesn't help us."

"Yes, yes, it does. You need talk to Irish," Sumiko insisted.

"Irish, the guy that hangs around the Brass Rail? The character who was busted down to private for dealing on the black market? He's nothing but a washed-up drunk and braggart."

"You are wrong, Andy-san. Irish have many contacts in black market. He know much news. If there is any chatter, he hear."

"Where are we going to find him on a Saturday afternoon?"

"I think know where find out," Sumiko said as she rushed from the restaurant and hurried up the street. Yoriko and Mama-san pushed back their chairs and ran after her.

"Guess we wait again," Mel droned, and they tilted their chairs against the wall.

A short time later Yoriko ran back into the shop, out of breath, and blurted out, "Irish ha—have own rooms at a hotel; you go there and talk." She stopped stammering, caught her breath, and hurriedly uttered as she ran back outside, "Me show. Mama-san and Sumiko go check other place."

They followed the girl through the backstreets of the town until she stopped and pointed at a building.

"We here. You and Mel go now talk with Irish-san. I be at café when you finished." She turned and darted away.

The place sure didn't look like a hotel. It was a rambling, shabby one-story bungalow structure with a number of rooms. Andy thought it looked more like an old geisha house or a house of ill repute. The sign out front read, in English, Palace Hotel. The mistress, a woman in her fifties, answered their knock.

"We need to see Irish," Andy stipulated.

"He sleep; no want be wake."

"It is very important we see him now."

"Matter of life or death," said Mel.

"No, no can do. He come home late. He tell me no wake him. He not like if I wake."

Mel yanked out two thousand yen from his billfold and waved the money in the woman's face. "We pay."

She hesitated for a few seconds and then bowed. "Maybe Irish be mad," she said and snatched the money out of Mel's fingers. Then she motioned to them to enter the hotel.

"Thank you." Andy bowed. Mel followed suit with a sloppy, unsophisticated bow, and they followed her into the house.

"Off shoe," she demanded as they entered the foyer. Rules are rules, and customs are customs. "No shoe. Take off." She pointed out they could not step up onto the straw tatami mats covering the floors with their shoes on.

They pulled off their shoes. Andy mumbled, "Glad I don't have holes in my socks," as he put on the white cotton slippers she handed him. Mel followed suit.

Beckoning them to follow, she proceeded down the hallway. The *shoji* screen doors on both sides of the hallway stayed closed against the prying eyes of any intruders. Andy surveyed each door they passed, trying to detect any movement behind those thin paper enclosures, speculating there might be an unknown danger behind any one of the doors.

I'm jumpy, with the dead American in the river and all.

The woman continued along the hallway, stopped in front of one of the rooms, knocked quietly on the doorframe, and then slid the door open. Andy peeked around her and saw Irish lying sprawled on a futon, sleeping. Two very comely women were cuddled next to him.

The women woke up at the sound of the door sliding open, giggled, and pulled the blanket *moofu* up around their necks.

"Irish-san, *ohayo gozaimasu*. Sorry wake you. Two GI say they must talk with you, matter of great importance; live-die matter, must talk."

Impatience getting the best of Mel, he shoved his way into the room. "Come on, Irish, we need to talk with you," he said in a loud, demeaning voice.

"You're gonna piss the guy off. We need him to help us, not be mad at us," Andy chastised. Then, in what he hoped sounded like a pleading tone, he said, "Please get up, please, Irish. We need you to find out some information on a guy."

The man resting on the futon opened his eyes and stared at them with a cold look. "What da you want? Whatever it is will cost you." He shook his finger at them. "Gonna cost ya plenty for waking me up."

"We need—" Andy started to say.

Irish cut him off. "How about butting out for a minute so I can put some clothes on."

They backed out of the doorway, and the woman closed the door, saying, "Wait." She ambled down the hallway, and they stood there for five minutes until they heard, "OK, you two yahoos can come back in now." They reentered the room; the futon had been rolled up and put away. The women were gone; Andy supposed they had disappeared into an adjoining room. Irish sat on the floor, elbows leaning on a small table that had been placed beside him.

"Now, what the hell do you want?"

"We're trying to find a Japanese guy who deals in the black market with stolen stuff."

"Shit, that could be any of a thousand people. What are you two doing screwing around looking for someone in that crowd?"

"We need to locate him and find out if he has any information on a missing GI."

"Someone went AWOL, huh? Big friggin' deal; lots of guys cut out all the time."

There was a soft rap, and the door slid open. The woman who had admitted them to the hotel entered with a tray bearing a mug filled with coffee. She set the tray and its contents down on the table and exited the room.

Andy continued, "We think Koji is his first name; he's a pimp and buys and sells stolen stuff."

"Koji," Irish said, sipping his coffee. "Heard of him but never met him personally. He's a punk, a bad apple; thinks he's a big man, but most people don't want to deal with him. He is a street kid with a violent temper and loves to hurt people if he thinks they're weaker than he is, especially women. His weapon of choice is an eighteen-inch iron pipe with tape wrapped around one end for a handgrip. The nasty freak's trying to align himself with a group of Chinese smugglers. Stay away from him or you might end up hurt."

"Irish, we gotta find the guy."

"Well, it's your funeral. Like I said, the favor's gonna cost you."

Andy truthfully said, "We don't have much money, but—"

"I'm not after money; I can make dough. What I need is stuff, favors."

"I don't know what stuff you're talking about," Andy answered calmly. He had heard tales of how Irish would find a guy's weak spot and coerce or bribe him to pilfer military equipment for Irish. "You need to know I'm not going to steal property from the Air Force so you can sell it on the black market, Irish. If that is what you are suggesting, it is akin to extortion, and I won't do it." Forcefully, Andy blurted out, "We'll find Butler on our own." He turned around and started walking down the hallway toward the front door.

"Hold on there, troop, don't get your bowels in an uproar. Geez, kid, you got balls, I'll say that for you. But don't tick me off if you want help."

Andy turned back and glared at Irish, who said, "Butler, you say? What did he do, go off and shack up someplace for the night?"

"We're supposed to keep mum about the situation, but…," Mel mumbled.

Irish shrugged his shoulders and raised his hands, palms up. "I can't help you if you won't tell me. Butler's an OK guy, always treated me fair and square. Word is he was a good officer but got a bum deal at the end of the war."

"You were stationed with Butler during the war?" inquired Mel.

"No; he was in the European theater and I was always in the Pacific." He paused. "I'll see what I can do, first let me grab a quick bath and clear the cobwebs."

"We're in a hurry," insisted Mel.

"Well, if you want my assistance, you're damn well going to have to wait until I'm ready."

Irish yelled for the hotel matron and spoke softly to her while Andy and Mel listened, straining to hear the conversation.

He finished and turned back to Andy and Mel. "You only gave her two thousand yen to wake me up? You're a couple of cheapskates. I told her to ask you for at least five thousand the next time. Now, go with her. She'll make you comfortable until I'm finished." He walked off, signaling for them to leave.

The woman motioned for them to follow. She took them to a sitting room with a low table and pointed that they were to sit on the tatami-mat-covered floor. "You want drink? Food?"

They indicated no, and she disappeared down the hallway.

Twenty minutes or so ticked by before Irish wandered into the room, bathed, shaved, and wearing a freshly laundered kimono. He had the appearance of an entirely different person—confident, self-reliant, and in control of his surroundings. He sat down at the table. The sliding doors from an adjoining room opened, and the two young women who'd shared his bed brought in food and drink. "You guys want anything?"

Andy was impatient. "We gotta go if we're going to find Butler."

Irish held up his hand. "The inquiry has already begun, and I am waiting for an answer. While we wait, I'm going to eat." And he eagerly began consuming the tasty morsels of food which had been placed in front of him.

He pushed back from the table when he'd finished eating, grabbed a pack of cigarettes, and lit one. He sat back for a second, puffing on his nicotine stick. "While we have time, let's talk first payment."

Andy interrupted, saying, "I'm not stealing for—"

"No, let me finish," Irish broke in. "I've got less than eighteen months left in this man's military and then I'm out, free as a bird to do what I want, a civilian again."

"You're heading home and back to the States," asserted Mel.

"Shit, no," declared Irish. "I'm staying here in the land of cherry blossoms and geishas. Why in the hell would I want to go back to the crappy life I had in Trenton? In Jersey, I lived on the wrong side of the tracks in a run-down cold-water flat with one bedroom that was infested with cockroaches and rats."

Andy scrutinized him inquisitively. "No kidding—you're staying in Japan?"

"I own all this." He made a circular motion with his hand. "This hotel; it may not be the Ritz, but it's mine. I've got a thriving side business; granted it's a little shady, however it provides for me very well."

The two girls who had brought in his food still knelt beside him, and he put an arm around each of them and smiled. "I've been in Japan since 1946, and for me it's a great life."

"If you own all this, why do you hang around the Brass Rail?" Andy wondered.

"Business, my lad, pure business. The troops on R and R often need a place to disappear to when the curfew whistle blows. I steer them here, a safe location with booze, lots of food, women, and a place to bed down. Now, let's conclude our agreement. Before I get discharged, there is a big blast planned in honor of my becoming a civilian. I plan to be loaded for at least four or five days. I plan on taking leave, and the only remaining military commitment I'll have left is to report in on my final day, sign my release papers, and bid my adieus. The first of my requirements and your first obligation for payback for helping you will be … you will make sure I get to the base on that final day and get to Group Headquarters. You're going to make sure I am there presentable and sober enough to sign my name."

"Sounds easy enough," Mel proclaimed enthusiastically.

"It might not be as easy as you think; there are some logistical problems associated with the task, which we will discuss later."

A soft knock on the shoji screen door suspended the discussion, and the hotel mistress poked her head into the room. "He here now, Irish-san." She opened the door wide enough to admit a brawny Japanese man with closely cropped hair. A knife scar ran from his cheekbone down to his chin and presented him with a sinister mien. "*Konnichiwa,* Irish-san," he said as he bowed.

"Konnichiwa. What did you find out?"

"Koji seen on road one hour ago, going east to … think to *uchi* of Chinese scum. Informant think he come from village north and west; that where Koji born. He always go there when in trouble, but he no stay in village."

Mel, anticipating a negative outcome, blurted out, "Oh, shit."

Irish glared at Mel and motioned for the man to continue. "Koji's *ojiisan,* grandfather, before die, have a fishing *koya* close town by river. Informant think he go there, hide something."

"How good is the informant? How reliable is his information?" probed Irish.

"If informant no good, he suffer much pain." With a sadistic smile, the man smirked as he pulled out the lethal dagger he had concealed in his belt.

"You take these men and show them the place. Watch out for the police."

"*Hai!* Irish-san." The man bowed and left the room.

Irish's stern voice bespoke the seriousness of the situation as he looked at Andy. "All he's going to do is take you and show you where the fishing shack is, and then he will leave and come back. He won't stay with you. I don't want my man involved with any cops, understood?"

"Yeah, I understand," replied Andy.

"If you need the police involved, wait until my man's gone." He motioned with his hand for them to leave, summarily dismissing them before he returned to drinking his coffee.

CHAPTER THIRTEEN
The Chase
Saturday Afternoon

Andy located Mama-san and the girls at the grubby coffee place on Prostitute Row. Mel and Andy sat at the table and explained everything that had transpired at Irish's place. Now he needed to figure out how they were going to get to that small village eight kilometers away. Mama-san didn't wait for any further explanations and left the shop with a shuffling run. As she crossed the street, the clop-clop sound echoed each time her wooden getas encountered the compacted dirt surface. She yelled *"Busu, Busu!"* pointing at an archaic vehicle approaching them on the roadway.

Andy hollered, "The bus, she wants to ride the bus!" and they followed her to the spot where she stood flagging down their ride.

The transport was crowded, but they all managed to squeeze in. Black smoke billowed from the exhaust pipe of the bus as they began their journey. Andy grabbed one of the looped leather straps that hung from the roof of the conveyance to steady himself during the ride. Wedged in between other commuters, there was little worry he would lose his balance during the abrupt starts and stops. Yoriko was holding on tightly to his left arm, and Sumiko's arm was cozily draped around his right shoulder in the closely confined space. Their bodies pressed snugly against his, and if it weren't for the circumstances of their trip, he would have enjoyed the ride.

As the bus approached the town, Irish's man pointed to an old *koya,* a shanty. "That place; you walk back from where step off the busu in town, not more one kilometer."

They reached the outskirts of the small village and the bus jerked to a stop. Irish's man, not bothering to bid them good-bye, bounded off the vehicle and walked across the road to wait for transportation back to town.

Mel was on the verge of making a negative comment to the man as he walked away, but Andy put his hand on Mel's shoulder. "Let it alone; he did his job. It's best we're rid of him. He gave me the willies, anyway."

"Rude son of a bitch," Mel grumbled to Andy so quietly that no one else could hear what he was saying as he stood staring after the scar-faced man.

The afternoon sun grew warm as they made their way down the road. Mama-san removed her jacket and carried it loosely on her arm. When they reached the shed, it was obvious to Andy that someone had opened the door recently. He'd studied the wheel tracks leaving from the main road to the koya. Scrapes in the dirt in front of the door showed the entryway had been moved. The drag marks from the badly hung portal obliterated the cart tracks. Forcing the entryway open he glimpsed inside and, beside the cart, Peggy's body lay sprawled, the earthen floor stained with her blood. He yanked the weathered entryway open wider. Sumiko and Yoriko screamed in alarm as they saw the bloody and battered remains of the woman.

Yoriko moved out of the entryway and covered her mouth with her hand, trying to stem the nauseous response. Andy stepped over and gave her his handkerchief, and after she wiped her mouth, he put his arms around her.

Yoriko lifted her head, tears streaming down her checks. "Andy-san, maybe she no nice person"—she shook her head from side to side—"but no one deserve die like that. I so sorry I say bad thing 'bout her." Yoriko's slight frame trembled as she was racked with an uncontrollable sobbing. He gently drew her closer, wanting to shield the petite girl from the gruesome spectacle.

Mama-san stepped into the shack and stared down at the dead woman. She stood unmoving, without uttering a word. Andy looked closely for an emotional response and realized that the bar owner was saying a parting prayer for the deceased women.

"Butler!" Mel's yell terminated the moment of silence. He pointed to the rolled-up tarp, which lay off to one side of the room. The only thing they could see of Butler was the top of his head and the deathly pallor of his forehead and cheeks. The rest of his body was so tightly bound in the canvas roll that he, almost comically, resembled an unappetizing hot dog in a moldy bun.

Mel stumbled around the dead woman and rushed over, placing his fingers on Butler's neck as he tried to locate a pulse. It was only then that he saw the bloody mass of hair where the pipe had struck Butler. "Think he's still alive; can't tell for sure."

"Pull him out! Unroll him!" screamed Sumiko. "Pull him out!"

"Butler, can you hear me?" Mel shouted as he knelt down, trying to determine how to free the imprisoned man.

Andy dropped down on his knees next to Mel and said, "You hold the flap of the tarp down; we'll try to get him out." He motioned for Sumiko to come and help. With Sumiko at Butler's feet and Andy at his shoulders, they began unwinding the unconscious man as cautiously as possible. When Butler was free of his cocoon and lying on top of the coarse material, an overpowering stench filled the small shed. Before they'd unrolled Butler from the tarp, there had been the smell of blood and the stink of old fish and mildew, but now the odor increased to the point where the stench was almost unbearable. Butler had soiled himself repeatedly, and the noxious aroma filled the confined area. Andy stepped back as an unnerving shriek emanated from the unconscious figure.

**

Butler was drifting in a mental sea of distortions and illusions. He tried to open his eyes, but there was nothing except fog, and his movements were hampered. Striving to cling to reality, he failed and slipped back into the horror of the narcotic.

Like piranhas, a jumble of unrelated feelings fed upon each other, devouring all reason until no rational thought survived. Delusions invaded and plagued his subconscious; to submit to their power was simple, but to escape their ominous grasp—impossible.

The hallucinations carried Butler back to that endless January day in 1944. The weather was cold and damp, the sun masked by ominous clouds. Freezing sleet obscured the dreary Italian countryside ravaged by relentless shelling. Standing at the edge of a bomb crater, he stared, mesmerized, into the bleak depression filled with murky, putrid water. Knowing what would happen next, he strained to avert his eyes but could not. They were fixated on the reeking muck beginning to solidify in the crater.

A lifeless human body floated upward to the crusty surface. The thin layer of scum parted, revealing a cadaver shrouded in mud and decomposing matter that dripped from the torso and limbs as the figure levitated above the filth. The macabre form, stiff with rigor mortis, mutilated by bullets, and disfigured by the water, hung motionless in space. The lesions on the torso enlarged and burst open, oozing blood and gore, and the muddy brown water turned a dark crimson. The ghoulish facial features distorted, wavered, and altered to resemble men from his unit slaughtered in battle. The corpse's face then became recognizable as its vacant eyes stared directly at him. The grisly phantom's arm languidly rose. An emaciated accusing finger extended as a whispering voice pleaded, "Captain … help me, Captain."

The phantasmagoria dissipated, and he thrashed about in anguish and cried out in his drug-induced sleep. Suddenly he felt a hand wipe the perspiration from his brow and cover him tenderly with a blanket. Anna Mae, Anna Mae, the name rose in a crescendo and flooded his mind.

***

Mama-san, who had been standing behind Andy, now knelt down. "Butler-san, *gomennasai*. I'm so sorry." She took her handkerchief and sympathetically wiped the dirt from his face, trying to examine his wound. "He needs medical attention now," she exclaimed in Japanese. Stepping toward the door, she retrieved the coat she had laid down when they'd entered the building and protectively covered the injured man with it.

She tucked her coat tightly around Butler's shoulders. The garment still retained a slight scent of the perfume she was wearing. The bouquet of the cologne stimulated his senses and aroused a reminiscence from his subconscious.

In his junior year at the Citadel Military College, his aunt had arranged a blind date for him to accompany a young socialite to the annual Charleston Cotillion. On that occasion, he'd escorted the beautiful Anna Mae, debutante of the season. She was the sweetheart of Charleston and the darling of all South Carolina. How proud he had been walking through the ballroom with her on his arm. He recalled the young women had been lavishly dressed in exotic ballroom gowns of silk or satin as they'd danced with cadets attired smartly in uniform.

He still remembered the rustling sound of Anna Mae's gown as it swished and swirled in rhythmic motion to the music. The alluring lilac scent of her perfume and her lovely blonde hair, its golden radiance soft in the light of evening, pervaded his thoughts. At dawn the dance ended, but their romance flourished. The next year passed in a blur, their vows and adoration for each other enriched and deepened as they strolled beneath the clear, starlit southern sky. The passion they experienced grew into a pledge of marriage. The families, both of old aristocratic Southern lineages, approved of the match, and an elaborate wedding was to occur in the spring. Relatives and friends received invitations announcing the gala affair.

What they did not plan for was World War II. On graduating from the prestigious Citadel College in 1941, Oren accepted a commission in the Army as a second lieutenant, and his assignment came within weeks of completing his compulsory military training. Fluent in French and English, his assignment was to a US Army liaison office in England, working with the Free French.

Butler then wanted to delay the wedding, which led to their first argument. His fear was that if he suffered an injury during the war, Anna Mae would have the burden of caring for an invalid husband. She did not share his fear and wanted to continue with their plans. Oren prevailed, and the wedding was postponed until after the war.

How he loved her and wanted her; he yearned for her touch. An ephemeral image of Anna Mae surrounded him, and as he reached out to embrace her the vision faded, leaving him with a vast emptiness.

Butler tossed and turned, not wanting to let his mind drift as auras shifted to a summer's day in 1944. The ability of nature to regenerate vegetation and cover the scars left on the French countryside by the war was noticeable. A few green plants had begun to grow here where the soil had been torn and ripped apart by the shelling. Butler peered cautiously over the dirt embankment that separated him from the road.

He scanned the lush green foliage of the hedgerow. No movement. As he inched his way upward for a better view, a ray of sunlight momentarily penetrated the thick hedgerow and glinted for a split second off a rifle barrel. There was a muzzle flash and explosive bang. Then a hand grabbed his coat and jerked him down as the loud resounding ring of a bullet ricocheted across his helmet. The deafening, chattering report of the platoon sergeant's Thompson submachine gun rumbled in his ears as .45-caliber projectiles spat out of it, shredding the leaves of the hedgerow and stitching gaping holes across the torsos of the two German snipers hidden among the trees. "Lucky that time, Captain," the sergeant said. "Hard to replace a good officer.... Even harder to replace a friend."

The scene changed to a little bistro in a quaint village, where the wine flowed freely and the mademoiselles were friendly. He and the sergeant drank until they could drink no more. His facial muscles relaxed, and a slight smile formed on his lips as a curtain of darkness cloaked the memories. The nightmare drifted off into the void that captures all forgotten dreams.

***

Trying to determine what they should do, Mel said more to himself than anyone else, "How will we carry him? Make a stretcher?" He looked around the shed, and his gaze fell on the cart. "Nah, use this."

The soiled canvas was the only thing available for padding, so they reluctantly folded it and lined the bottom of the cart. Andy and Mel lifted Butler into the cart, trying to make him as comfortable as possible.

"Let's go; he needs medical attention. Should we try to get him back to the medics at the base?" Mel exclaimed with great anxiety.

"No, if there is a doctor in the little town, that's much closer. I'll call the base from the village and request an ambulance," Andy insisted.

They were ready to make their exodus from the building when they heard someone say, "It looks like you could use a little support here."

Andy, startled at hearing a strange man's voice, spun around and stared at the door. The light shining from behind made it impossible to distinguish the face of the intruder.

"You are Anderson, right?" The stranger pointed to Andy.

"That's right. Who are you?"

"I'm here to offer my assistance; I see you have your friend. What about her?"

"She was dead when we arrived."

The man stepped over and leaned down to inspect the body. "I'm not a coroner, but I'd say she's been dead for four to five hours." The man's face was still in the shadows; Andy thought the man was Japanese, but his speech patterns gave the impression that he was an American.

"Now, where you heading?" he asked.

"Do you have a car?" Andy urgently inquired. "We need to get him to the base and the hospital."

"No, I don't…. The only wheeled vehicle in the area right now is that." The man pointed to the wooden cart bearing Butler. "I suggest you disappear from the premises now. I'll clean up here and explain to the local constables when they arrive."

"Who the hell are you—" Andy started to ask.

But the man waved him off, saying, "Don't worry; hurry it up and take that injured man to a doctor. Go!"

They pushed the cart out of the shed and up onto the road. Mama-san was the last to leave the shack. She stopped and spoke in Japanese to the man. He replied, and she thanked him and hurried after Andy, Mel, and the girls.

Andy said to Yoriko, "What did Mama-san ask that guy?"

"She asked who he worked for. He tell her that he is a government policeman and not to worry, he make all OK. No one bother us on what happened."

Andy figured that if the Japanese government cop knew about the koya and knew his name, the local police and provost marshal knew about it also, and they would be around to question him about what had happened. Now, however, he needed to worry about getting Butler medical attention.

The road leading to the small town was pockmarked with ruts and holes, the cart was unavoidably jostled about by the rough road. Even with Mel pulling the cart and Andy pushing, the going was slow. One of the wooden cartwheels slammed down into a deep pothole, and the battered man whimpered in pain. Andy, hoping his talking would soothe some of Butler's anxiety and discomfort, said, "It's OK now. I've got you. You're going to be all right."

As Butler faded in and out of consciousness, the words slipped deep into the foggy recesses of his mind, where they triggered a recollection. Somewhere in the past, someone spoke the same words, but who it was eluded him, and his mind began to spin. The impression of being in a deep hole besieged him, and he attempted to pull himself out of the pit. Handholds on the circular walls were formed by words, and each time he grasped at a word to pull himself up, the word would collapse and disintegrate, and he'd fall farther down into the depths. It was critical that he maintain his hold on the words and their meanings. This was the key he needed if he were ever going to be able to climb out of the bottomless black well. He could see light at the surface, but he was powerless to reach the top.

The task was arduous, and he strained to recall. Billy had said those words *OK now*. That had been a long time ago in France. Now it was a different voice, but the words were the same. Alexander's voice, was that who'd spoken? No, not Alexander.... Butler lost his mental grip on the words and slipped back under the influence of the drug as the traumatic trek across the African desert during the war came rushing into his semiconsciousness.

The heat of the relentless sun was excruciating; his legs were heavy, and his back rebelled against the endless pain from the burdensome weight he carried. He needed to stop and rest, but he had to keep moving.

The clanking of iron treads in the distance filtered through the desert air. He feared the Germans had caught up with them. They were in an exposed position, with nowhere to hide and no energy left to fight. He still had the will to resist; surrender was not an option, but perhaps it was the only solution. He concentrated on the sound made by the vehicle. The noise was coming from the opposite direction of the German positions. A half-track crested a sand dune in front of him, creating a billowing cloud of dust that obscured its details. Veiled in dust and grime, the half-track rumbled sluggishly down the slope. It was American! The driver squinting through the grimy windshield was Alexander. He had carried out his task of getting the squad and the wounded to safety. Then, against the advice of the aid station commander, he had taken the half-track back to the barren wasteland alone to search for his comrades.

The desert sands quivered, wavered, and rippled as they transformed into a green lawn shaded by flowering magnolia trees, the Butler ancestral plantation. A young woman with fair hair, clothed in a flowing gossamer white dress and holding a wide-brimmed summer hat loosely in her hand, skittered across the grass. As she passed, he smelled the fragrance of fresh-cut lilacs, a scent that brought joy to his heart.

Then she was gone, the aroma of lilacs replaced by the rancid smell of rotten fish guts and human feces. Nausea overcame him as he began to sweat, and he fought the urge to expel the contents of his stomach. He could not breathe and strove for a lucid thought. He wanted to remember, and then he wanted to forget, for what he remembered was a hazy image of a pool of blood and the prostrate figure of a battered woman.

CHAPTER FOURTEEN
Stitched Up

Butler opened his eyes and found a filmy white veil blurred his vision. Hesitantly he blinked in an attempt to regain clarity, and the cloudy substance slowly cleared. He was staring up at a whitewashed ceiling. It was not any ceiling he recalled seeing before. *Sure the hell isn't the barracks.*

The feeling that someone was standing next to him instinctively compelled him to turn to observe the interloper. With that slightest of movements, he encountered a cold sensation, an icy numbness that impregnated his scalp. Alarmed by the feeling and that he could not remember where he was, the urgency of determining his surroundings grew stronger with each second of uncertainty. Hands, firm but gentle, held his head immobile.

"What's going on?" The raspy sound was unidentifiable as his voice. His throat was raw, constricted, making speech difficult.

"Nani?" A familiar voice, but his thoughts were muddled, and he was unable to recognize the speaker. A face moved into his field of vision as Mama-san, wearing a grim expression, attentively studied him.

"Butler-san wants to know what is happening," a voice from off in the distance said in Japanese.

Sumiko, at Mama-san's direction, stood in a corner away from the operating table. The young woman waited there until her English skills were required. She replied to Butler, "You're at the doctor's office. He put stitches in cut on head."

"Wha'... how was I injured?" Butler throatily whispered.

"You hit ... you go...." She hesitated. "Andy tell; he outside."

"Andy? What in the blue blazes is he doing here? Last thing I remember was following some girl that Mama-san had sent down a street."

His entire body ached. A whirlpool churned around in his gut, and a throbbing headache added to his confusion. His skin was damp and clammy, as if he had washed but not dried thoroughly. The coarse material that was draped over him clung to his naked body.

"Where's my clothes? I'm bare-assed naked" was all he could mumble.

His bewilderment was only amplified by Mama-san and the doctor's clamoring back and forth in Japanese.

Confused and frustrated, Butler appealed to the English-speaking person he knew was in the room. "Get Anderson in here, will you please, so I can find out what's happening." As he tried to sit up and see the person, Mama-san reprimanded him sharply, *"Ugoku na."* ("Don't move.")

"I go see," Sumiko answered, and he heard a door open and close.

Listening in an attempt to decipher what Mama-san and the doctor were discussing in Japanese, he caught the words "overdosed," "rest," and "twenty-four to forty-eight hours."

"Doko ni watashi no fuku wa?" ("Where are my clothes?") he clumsily said in Japanese.

"Your clothing was filthy and torn; we needed to remove all of your garments in order to bathe you," Mama-san replied tenderly in Japanese, trying to calm him. She had taken his putrid, ripped uniform and thrown it into the trash for burning. It would be easier to replace than to try laundering and mending his old clothing.

Sumiko opened the examination room door warily. Andy stood beside her. *"Haittemo yoroshii desuka?"* ("Is it all right if we enter?") she asked.

Without lifting his head to see who was speaking, the old doctor grunted, *"Un,"* and continued with the suturing.

"Hey, Butler, how you doing?" Andy inquired as he approached the examination table.

"You tell me, Anderson. I have no idea what's going on."

"Well...." Andy was unsure just where to begin. "You didn't show back up at the barracks last night, so they sent us out to look for you. It took some time, and when we found you ... you were kind of beat up and had a head wound that bled a lot and required stitches. Sumiko told me the doctor said it was only a superficial scalp trauma but you might have a slight concussion.

"However, the doctor is concerned about the overdose of narcotics. No one knows for sure how much or even what you had ingested." He paused and then continued, "The doctor can only assume it was a large quantity based on your reactions. You are going to have to lay low for a while, and your medical condition needs to be monitored for any adverse reactions. I've been talking with Sergeant Jones, and he seems really concerned. I'm going to call him back now and have him send a base ambulance to haul you to the base hospital."

"If I don't need to go to the hospital, I'd rather go back and recuperate at Mama-san's place, if she doesn't mind," Butler petitioned the young man. "Tell Billy … Sergeant Jones that I would like to take a couple of weeks' leave; I have the time coming. I would just as soon this incident doesn't become public knowledge if possible."

"Why do—" began Andy.

"Later, I'll explain it all to you later."

Andy slipped out and, with Yoriko's assistance, located a telephone. The operator connected him with the base, and he asked for the first sergeant.

"Hey, Sarge, we have Butler. He was drugged, robbed, and roughed up some."

"How bad of shape is he in?" asked the sergeant.

"Not the greatest. We took him to a Japanese doctor who patched him up and said he's OK to travel as long as he is lying down. I wanted him to go to the base hospital, but he doesn't want to. He said he can recover and mend at the Brass Rail."

"Is Butler anywhere close to a telephone?"

"No, and I don't think he could make it to one. The guy's requesting a couple of weeks' leave; says he has the time coming."

The silence on the line went on for so long that Andy began to think he'd lost the connection.

"I'll take care of it," answered the first sergeant, finally, and then he mumbled to himself, 'We've covered him this far…." Then, more distinctly he asked, "Can you move him to Mama-san's place?"

"Guess so. We'll give it a try."

"OK, bring him back to town. I'll be in to see him tomorrow."

"And by the way, Sergeant Jones, thanks for sending us the Japanese government cop; he helped."

"Cop? What cop? Never mind. Just call me when Butler's tucked in." The first sergeant hung up.

After the phone conversation ended, the question about the government police officer did not linger long in Andy's mind as he began formulating different scenarios on how he was going to move Butler to town. Using the old two-wheeled cart was not much of an option. He turned to Yoriko and started to explain what they needed to do when, across the street, he noticed a man parking his vehicle.

The merchant was about to enter a shop when Andy urgently said to Yoriko, "Ask that guy how much he would charge to haul us back to town on that." He pointed to a three-wheeled motorcycle. The auto bike consisted of a single front tire and the handlebars and engine of a motorcycle. The frame fanned out on either side of where the rear tire would have been and became, instead, a three-wheeled mini truck to haul produce.

Yoriko was at first surprised by the request, and she then smiled as she understood Andy's thought process. Hurrying across the street, she intercepted the man before he could enter the small store. A discussion between the two ensued, with a great shaking of heads and waving of arms, until Yoriko finally bowed, thanked the man, and returned to where Andy was standing.

"The man first want 2,500 yen, I tell him too much. And now he say take town for 1,800 yen." Yoriko looked at Andy for confirmation. "I sorry no could make him cheaper." Andy figured the price was steep, but they needed the wheels.

"He want money now. I say only half now and rest when back to Brass Rail. It OK?"

"OK, if he does one thing." Andy told the girl what he wanted and handed her nine hundred yen. Yoriko scampered back across the street, where more arm waving and pointing ensued, and finally an agreement was struck.

Returning to the house, they found Butler sitting in a chair dressed in a clean kimono, his head bandaged. He was holding a small bundle. Mama-san had removed the insignia and campaign ribbons from

Butler's uniform before tossing it and had tied the few possessions left in a silk handkerchief; his wallet had been taken in the robbery. Using a dusty stretcher they found in a closet in the doctor's office, they carried Butler out and loaded him onto the truck bed of the three-wheeled vehicle. Andy noticed the padding that covered the truck bed was a conglomerate of old tatami mats covered with a tattered blanket. The agreement was that the man needed to put some padding down. *Better than nothing*, thought Andy. Mama-san gathered some blankets from the building and wrapped them around Butler.

The little motorcycle truck was insufficient in size to haul all six of them back to town. Mama-san suggested that it would be less conspicuous if she accompanied the convalescing man and the younger people took the bus. They would meet at the bar.

"Hey, Butler, before you go, I've got a question that's been bothering me," Andy said. "Why did Sergeant Jones tell me to mention 'lay own' to you? What does it mean?"

"Lay own? Lay own? Doesn't mean.... Oh, it's Laon, Andy, not lay own. Laon is a small town in northern France; I was there during the war. Why did he—"

Their conversation was interrupted by Mama-san loudly urging, *"Hayaku isoide kudasai."* She prodded the merchant with her finger. *"Ikimashou."*

The storekeeper started the engine, slipped the motorized contraption into gear, and set off, leaving Andy standing on the road with the half-answered question. He listened to the putt, putt, putt and watched the puffs of smoke released from the motorcycle's exhaust as it disappeared down the road.

Butler dozed fitfully on the ride back to town. The effects of the narcotics had lessened, and the hallucinations had decreased. He thought about Andy's question. Jones had told the young man to ask him about Laon—why? The little motorcycle truck bounced about on the bumpy road, the jostling reminiscent of the uncomfortable ride along the shelled and bombed roads around Laon, France.

In 1944, he and four other soldiers had occupied the underground command bunker by the airstrip as intelligence reports of a pending air raid squawked over the field radio. The American forces had captured the airfield ten days ago from the Germans. In the weeks leading up to the seizure, American artillery had pounded the German garrison into submission and forced their withdrawal from this strategic position. In retaliation for the loss of the airfield, the Germans were intent on completing the destruction that the Americans had started, and they renewed their blitzkrieg.

The Luftwaffe launched a squadron of Dornier medium bombers in a predawn air raid against the US forces. The Dornier's bomb bays were loaded with sinister cluster and incendiary bombs. Others carried the SC500 and SC250 ordnance. Intent on completing the destruction that the Americans had started, the German mission was to obliterate the airstrip.

The eerie wail of the air raid siren awakened the sleeping soldiers, warning them of the imminent attack. They ran from the building and tents and sought safety as they huddled in crowded bomb shelters and foxholes. Antiaircraft battery crews ran to their assigned stations and prepared for action.

Butler and his group were already in the underground command post when the alarm sounded. With him were Second Lieutenant Ryan, fresh out of Officer's Candidate School, with the unit for six short days; Sergeant Munson, a linguistic expert who had transferred in last year; and Private Felix, the runner and courier, five months out of basic training.

The radio operator was Sergeant Alexander, who had been Butler's radioman since North Africa. He sat hunched over the battery-operated field radio on the opposite side of the bunker. Of the small contingent of brave men Butler had led into North Africa, some had died in battle. Others had been evacuated because of wounds. Only two remained in his command—Sergeant Alexander and the platoon sergeant. These two men were the last of the companions with whom he had shared both dusty and muddy foxholes. They'd eaten gritty, sand-laced C rations together and read each other's letters from home. As comrades they had tramped through the hot, dry desert, sloshed across rainy, muddy fields of the frigid Italian countryside, and now were in France. Alexander was the only one of the two from the African campaign on duty with him that night. Ack-ack fire burst and blossomed, the molten shrapnel fragments of the exploding shells seeking out the marauding aircraft. Brilliant lights from the bursting shells added an unnatural sheen to the red and yellow rays of the dawning sun.

The Luftwaffe planes swept overhead, the sound of their droning engines filling the sky. Incendiary and explosive devices released from the bomb bay cradles emitted a high-pitched scream as they plummeted to earth. The rain of metal canisters struck in indiscriminate patterns, delivering their messages of death and destruction. Butler's group in the command post listened with apprehension as the detonations grew closer and louder.

Minutes after the attack began, an explosion shook the command bunker. The ordnance detonated on the already weakened structure, raining dirt and debris down upon those hunched in the enclosure. Light from a sputtering lantern revealed a growing irregular fissure in the cracked center of the concrete ceiling. The bunker, in immediate danger of collapse, creaked and groaned, sections of concrete scraping and shifting as they rubbed together.

"Out of the middle; seek cover!" Butler yelled as they all dove to the floor and scrambled for protection near the exterior walls.

A thunderous explosion sounded as a second projectile struck, and the ceiling began to separate. Minute fractures and cracks in the concrete widened, and the reinforced roof crumbled and began to collapse. Sharp shafts of steel reinforcement rods and rubble tumbled into the room, burying the defenseless men.

Butler regained consciousness to find himself engulfed in darkness, a tumultuous ringing in his ears. With no knowledge of his immediate surroundings and uncertain of his fate, he lay listening. He could hear no sound other than the humming in his ears.

He called out, "Hello, anybody? Can anyone hear me? Lieutenant, Sergeant Alexander, Sergeant Munson, Private Felix, sound off!" His voice sounded muted by the chaotic buzzing in his head.

A heavy weight pushed down on his thighs, pinning him to the floor. He twisted his body and struggled against the weight to release his legs. Groping with his hands, he touched the obstruction. The total darkness felt like a heavy cloak, suffocating him, and a relentless terror surged, his pulse beating rapidly and his judgment unclear.

Realizing he was trapped, panic reared its insidious head as anxiety tried to conquer reason. But the fear at last subsided, and logic prevailed.

Light. He needed to see, needed to find out why he was immobile. He was able to sit up, and his hands were free. Rummaging through his pants pockets, he found his Zippo cigarette lighter. Pulling the lighter from his pocket, he flipped the top and turned the wheel. Sparks shot forth from the flint and glared brightly as a searchlight in the dark but failed to ignite the wick. Again, he spun the wheel. The flint sparked and offered its reward, a glaring glow of flame. His eyes adjusted, and the immediate surroundings of the chamber became visible. His thighs were trapped under a collapsed metal table overlaid with heavy concrete rubble. The legs at one end of the table, though bent, were ridged enough to support the weight of the wreckage and had kept the tabletop from crushing his limbs.

He'd need help to extricate himself from the obstruction. "Hello, anyone there?" he called out. "Sergeant Alexander, can you hear me? Alexander!" No answer.

"Lieutenant Ryan? Anyone?" Silence, deathly stillness, permeated the demolished bunker.

In the dim glow of the lighter, he surveyed the obstacle imprisoning his legs. The top of the table slanted, angling down to the center of the bunker where the ceiling had caved in. That portion of the table had collapsed to the floor under the weight of the rubble. The table legs at the end where he was still provided support, and perhaps there was eight inches of clearance between the tabletop and the floor. The metal top lay across his thighs; his right leg was relatively loose and moved slightly, but his left leg was solidly trapped. With his hands and the muscles of his left leg, he moved the limb a little to the right and stopped. He took a deep breath and lifted, straining, and with a gut-wrenching push, his right leg came free, but with a price: a perceptible increase of weight from the table on his left leg.

The yellow flame flickered. There wasn't much lighter fluid left. He shut the lighter, extinguishing the flame. Wisely, he put the lighter in his shirt pocket and buttoned the flap. It was imperative that the Zippo not be misplaced or lost. The oppressive mantle, the fear of blindness, again enveloped him. Fear flared for an instant then ebbed away as he evaluated his situation.

The mental picture flashed in his mind of how the table pinned his leg. His left thigh served as a partial support in holding up the tabletop and rubble. If removed, more of the ceiling might collapse.

Concentration on the problem became difficult. The forbidding environment stifled his thoughts and sought to suck out his strength and eradicate his ability to reason. He shook off the bizarre imaginings and delved into the problem. With the use of his hands, he sought pieces of concrete the size he thought he needed. Fumbling around in the darkness he searched, pulling and dragging the jagged pieces with his fingers close to where he thought he should place them. He considered various scenarios countless times on how to free his leg and escape from his entrapment.

Waiting until he felt he had gathered enough rubble, he lit the Zippo. The pile of concrete fragments and rubble seemed larger in the dark; not nearly enough to fill the void under the table between his left leg and the floor. Glancing around, he sought larger chunks that he might manage to move. With arms stretched back over his head, he searched for additional concrete fragments. He bent and twisted his upper body so that he could view the part of room that lay behind him. Spotting a few blocks that would work, he reached back and shifted the first one and dragged it toward himself. Grappling, he seized the second piece with his fingertips and pulled; it moved for a few inches and stopped. In moving the fragments, he exposed a trouser-covered leg and boot sticking out from under a massive concrete slab.

Not lingering on the sight, he went back to his task of searching for useable rubble. Finished with his survey, he closed the lighter and securely tucked it in his shirt pocket, forcing himself to focus on what he needed to do. The vision of the human limb and boot protruding from under the concrete flooded into his mind, and a mental struggle ensued to block that image. He said to the darkness, "Whoever you are, or were, I'm sorry. May you rest in peace with God. Forgive me; I failed to keep you safe…. Now I must focus on how I'm going to survive."

***

The three-wheeled conveyance recoiled roughly against the uneven dirt road, and the jarring pain brought him out of his reminiscence. He looked at Mama-san, whose attentiveness seemed unending. *"Neru, Butler-san. Neru* (sleep)," she said.

He closed his eyes, and his weary mind and battered body succumbed to her counsel.

CHAPTER FIFTEEN
Back to the Brass Rail

Andy waited until Mel and the two girls scrambled aboard the crowded bus. Then he bounded up the steps and squeezed in between the other commuters. Jockeying for position, he twisted around until he could watch out a window as they neared the old fishing koya. He couldn't tell if the person who'd said he was a government cop was still around or not. The shack looked deserted. Just then, the front tire of the old bus dropped down into a pothole, jostling the passengers, and Andy's view of the shed became obscured as they pushed and shoved to regain their balance. Not more than ten minutes later, he thought he heard the clanging of a fire bell. He bent down and peered out the rear window of the bus, catching a glimpse of what might have been smoke coming from the spot where the koya was located. It was difficult to tell in the fading light of the evening.

It was 2200 hours when they arrived back at the Brass Rail. Mama-san had gotten Butler tucked into bed, and he was asleep. Sumiko and Yoriko said good night and went back to their apartment.

Tired and hungry, Andy and Mel wandered over to a hamburger joint on the other side of the tracks; it was named Wimpy's after a comic book character. The American décor of the Japanese restaurant provided a touch of home, plus they cooked a tasty hamburger. Andy wondered at times where they got their beef, or if it even *was* beef, but the burgers were tasty, so he didn't linger on where they purchased their meat.

He was munching away on a burger when he heard a sarcastic, "Hi there, Andy."

He stopped chewing and glanced up to see Irish standing next to the table, looking down at them.

"Interesting day, huh? Found Butler and took him back to the Brass Rail, right?"

Andy nodded and went back to eating, keeping an eye on Irish and wondering if the guy were fishing for some specific information.

"The way you handled stuff today makes a guy curious why you didn't take him to the base hospital … makes a guy wonder."

Andy purposely took a huge bite and then mumbled a few words incoherently while chewing and shrugging his shoulders.

"Who was the Japanese guy who cleaned up the mess? You gave me the impression when we talked earlier that you didn't have any contacts. That guy knew his stuff. Really makes me skeptical that you're telling me everything. Do you have some pull someplace, kid, and held out on me?"

Andy stared at Irish in puzzlement. *How did he find out all this? I never spotted anyone tailing us.* Andy maintained a straitlaced expression and shrugged his shoulders; he wasn't going to let on that he was as buffaloed about the events as Irish.

"You're going to clam up on me now and keep mum? OK, but you two better eat up and clear off the streets. It's near curfew. Head over to my place and bed down for the night. You can't afford to be picked up by the military police; they might ask you some questions you don't want to answer."

Irish walked out of the little food place, and as soon as he stepped out the door, two of his henchmen joined him. One was the guy with the scarred face and wicked-looking knife who had escorted them on the bus trip.

Chewing the last bite of his sandwich, Andy said to Mel, "Let's go," as he slid his chair back and stood up. Until then, he hadn't he realized how tired he was.

***

A soft rapping on his hotel room door woke him, and before he even said "Come in," the door slid open, and one of the young women who had served Irish's food the previous day slipped into the room. With a polite bow, she approached the futon where Andy lay and knelt down, placing a tray of food on the floor beside him.

"Irish-san say give you. He tells me you hungry from all your travel yesterday. He say to tell you 'member deal; you no forget."

"I no forget." He sat up on the futon as she arranged the tray to enable him to select the food he desired.

"You want bath after eat? Your uniform all washed and iron, an' have clean skivvy for you wear. Want maybe massage?"

Two hours later, Andy strode along the street bathed, clean, and refreshed.

Mel sauntered along beside him. "I wish we'd discovered Irish's place earlier. I, for one, plan on making a return visit."

It was Sunday afternoon when they returned to the Brass Rail. The front door was open, so they wandered in and looked around. A couple of guys perched at the bar nodded to them as they entered but did not speak. There was only one barmaid working they could see. Pulling out a couple of barstools, they sat down and motioned for her. The girl seductively sashayed over to them, smiled enticingly at Mel, and said, "Mama-san instruct me tell her if you come in. You want something drink?"

"Just coffee for me. You want some?" Mel asked Andy, who nodded yes, and Mel said, "Two coffees."

She returned with two cups of the hot brew, placed them on the bar, and said, "I go tell her you here." She swooped her skirt up to expose her shapely thighs as she turned and left the bar area.

"I think the little woman has thoughts about your prowess with the ladies. Better be careful, or she's going to have you in the sack," joshed Andy.

A couple of minutes later, Mama-san opened the door between the bar and the kitchen and motioned for them to join her in the rear rooms. As they got up from their stools, she pointed to their still-full coffee cups and said, "Bring, *daijobu.*"

They grabbed their coffee mugs and traipsed along behind the older woman as she led them through the kitchen. Before they entered the hallway, they removed their shoes and proceeded to the room where Butler lay convalescing.

"Hey, Butler, how are you doin'? You look like hell," Mel taunted as he entered the room.

"Hello, guys." Butler managed a slight smile and wave of his hand. "You two look like you found someplace comfy and cozy to spend the evening."

"Did we ever," said Mel, and he began to deliver an account of last night's lodging and the morning visit with the masseuse. After a half-hour of chitchat, they exhausted their banter for the day.

They were startled by a voice behind them. "Good afternoon, gentlemen."

They turned and saw that it was Sergeant Jones.

"Afternoon," greeted Andy.

"I'm very appreciative of the work you did yesterday in getting Sergeant Butler back safely. Excellent job. If you don't mind, I have a few things I need to go over with him in private. Then we need to all discuss a couple of things. Give me a few minutes."

"Sure thing," Andy said as he stood up and waved for Mel to follow him. He started out to the bar when Mama-san motioned him to follow her out to the garden area. "*Dozo*," she said as she pointed to a place on the porch prepared with sitting pillows and a small table. There, all set out for them, was a tray with green tea and rice crackers.

Sitting cross-legged on the small porch, Andy took a sip of tea while Mel continued to describe his morning massage. He could just hear the first sergeant through the open porch door saying to Butler, "You're lucky you didn't get yourself killed. What in the hell were you thinking?"

Mel put his finger up to his lips. "Shush," he said as he scooted closer to the partially open sliding paper and wood door to Butler's room.

"That was the problem, Billy, I wasn't thinking, or I would have never drunk that Mickey and gotten suckered into that position."

The first sergeant said something that was undistinguishable, and Butler continued: "You bailed my ass out again. Smart having those two come looking for me. Andy's reliable, intelligent, and will go far given the right opportunities. Mel's a good egg. They both can keep a secret, and I want this little escapade to be kept quiet if possible."

"Why did you want to come here of all places instead of going to the base hospital?"

"I don't need the publicity and notoriety and don't need this type of a screwup on my military record. I want to keep a low profile until I find out—"

"You have something in the works? Something I'm not aware of? Is that why Anna Mae is calling?" The first sergeant was in a bit of a snit and continued ranting. "Why the hell did you come back on active duty, anyway? You had everything you wanted in Charleston—a home, a business, a great woman. You don't need a job, and for damn sure you don't need money."

"Why, Billy, my pride, my damnable pride. They took away what was mine. You know the kind of physical shape I was in after the war. Cashiered out of the Army and stripped of my rank because I was a little torn up. Damn right I'm pissed. I am going to use anybody and anything to get back what they took away from me, and I'm not going home until I do."

"Butler, I'm not going to argue with you today. You're in no physical condition to become upset and infuriated. Just sign this leave request so I can cover your ass, all right?"

"Billy, I'm sorry," Butler murmured as he scribbled his signature on the paper. "You've been taking care of me since '41. You have to be getting tired of it by now."

"Well, it hasn't been all one-sided. You hauled me across the desert; I owe you my life. Guess it's a kind of mutual admiration society."

"Have you heard anything from home?"

"Anna Mae called twice, once on Friday night and again early yesterday morning. She's suspicious that something's wrong. That gal has a sixth sense when it comes to you. I don't feel my answers are fooling her any. When are you going to marry that woman? You should."

"Yeah, I will, and I am. She said she would call. I'll need to have access to a telephone and give her a ring back."

"What's going on? Why is the State Department calling you?"

"I imagine that Perrier is trying to reach me."

"Perrier.... Oh, yeah. Wasn't he one of the Free French you worked with in the underground that time you parachuted into France? The time I was laid up in the hospital in England?"

"That's him."

"What's it all about?"

"Don't know for sure, since the end of the war we've kept in touch. He has some friends in the State Department, and that's been the easiest way to keep track of each other. I imagine he's just touching base, that's all. The reason I want to recoup here is that, as you know, I am still pushing to have my commission reinstated. I don't think it would be of benefit if the word got out that I was involved in a stupid drunken escapade."

"OK. I don't agree with you, but I follow your line of thinking. Now, I'll let you rest. I need to talk to Anderson and Schultz. I'll be back tomorrow to see how you're getting along. I brought clean clothing and shaving gear. Give me a holler if you need anything else."

Jones left the room and pushed the outside door of Butler's room open wider so he could walk out onto the garden porch.

When he realized that the sergeant was going to exit through that door, Mel—who had scooted closer to the open door—scurried backward in a crab walk to his seat. Grabbing a rice cracker and his teacup, he acted as if he'd never left the table.

Jones spotted where the two younger men were sitting and walked over to the table. "What I wanted to ask you is to not say anything to anyone about what happened yesterday. Some of the events are bound to leak out, however I want you to keep it as quiet as possible. You two did an excellent job. Now I have to return to the squadron area."

Do I need to tell the sarge about Irish's involvement? Andy was still deliberating this when he felt Sergeant Jones's hand on his shoulder.

"This whole incident was caused by a series of freak circumstances, but by a streak of good fortune and your tenacity, Butler managed to survive. I'll see you two tomorrow. Thanks for a job well done." Turning, he went down the back steps, where he retrieved his shoes and walked down the path and out the garden gate.

Overhearing the conversation, Butler thought, *"Managed to survive." I said those words once in an improvised prayer. I'd almost given up hope, and I prayed for those lost souls to forgive me and rest in peace because I needed to figure out if or how I was going to survive.*

***

He recalled the darkened man-made tomb in Laon and how he'd stretched his arm out behind his head as far as he could reach. He had given a massive sweep of his arm, only to plunge the palm of his hand down on a protruding shard of steel. The metal ripped into the palm of his hand, and the sudden pain from the injury stirred him from his despondency. He stopped and then continued, his penance paid. He resumed the sweeping motion, being careful each time he contacted a piece of rubble so as not to inflict further damage. As he found other pieces of debris, he shifted them to where he could push the rubble under the tabletop. He rested and then returned his arm behind him and searched again, first with his right and then with his left, until he found no additional fragments.

When he had finished gathering everything within his reach, his fingers were stiff and sore from the cuts inflicted by the jagged concrete. In the cursed blackness, he tried to assess the collected amount of rubble. It wasn't as much as he had hoped for, but it would have to suffice. The job of pushing the debris and cramming the rubble between the floor and the underside of the tabletop began. He wedged the rubble from the point the table touched the floor over and up to his left leg. He could only reach part of the way under the tabletop from his position, it was going to have to do. His sore fingers pushed and shoved the concrete bits and pieces, not seeing, only feeling, until he'd used everything moveable within his reach. He felt the mound he'd built under the tabletop. The rubble felt solid and substantial, but would it work? He wanted to see what he had accomplished, but knew he shouldn't waste the precious fluid in his lighter.

He bent his freed right leg until his knee touched the underside of the table. As he sat up, he placed the palms of his hands flat on the floor. Pushing down on his hands and with an upward push of his knees, he exerted all the pressure on his knee that he could rally. There was a slight movement, or was it his imagination? His leg did not respond when he tried to move it.

I need to use my hands to move the leg, he thought. Once more using his hands to gain purchase against the floor, his right knee pushed upward until his strength waned and the pain became excruciating. Dust and gravel from the ceiling sifted down on his head. The loosened gravel proved that something had moved. He lifted his left hand from the floor and pushed it against the imprisoned leg. His strength ebbed away, and he released the pressure on his knee. He lay exhausted, out of breath. Finally he sat up, moved his hand to investigate, and felt a discernible difference in the location of his leg. He felt to examine the wedge built under the table and repacked the rubble with his hands. Lying back down, he reviewed the problem in his mind and rested. He sat up, placed his palms on the floor, and with bended knee, he again pushed, exerting all the pressure he was humanly capable of to the underside of the metal top. More dust and gravel sifted from the ceiling; he strained to maintain pressure on his right knee as he grabbed his left leg and tried to slide it over. The leg moved, but he only felt the movement of flesh as his hand pushed. Again he tried, the pain in his knee excruciating as he let out a yell of despair. Spent, Butler lay back down, breathing heavily, his heart pounding from exertion.

"Captain, Captain, help me," a muted voice called out, or was it just his imagination?

His senses now more alert, he listened. Everything was quiet except for a few particles of falling gravel that tumbled down onto the floor.

"Alexander—Sergeant Alexander, is that you?" No reply. "Whoever, answer me!"

Stillness, absolute quiet. Was someone out there alive and needing help?

Adrenaline surged through this body. He positioned himself again and, with a herculean effort, pushed. The tabletop hesitantly moved upward. With his left hand, he slid his leg over until it was free. With both palms down against the floor, he pushed himself backward with all the force he could rally until his movement stopped as he reached an obstruction. Reaching out with his arm, he felt the tips of his boots but not the table. He was clear. The movement of the table had dislodged fragments of concrete, and as dust began to clog the air, he started coughing and fought to breathe. Lying still waiting for the particles to clear, he perceived a slight movement of air and felt the circulation of fresh air and life-sustaining oxygen.

With his strength regained, he needed to get a visual of his surroundings. Taking the lighter from his pocket, with painful aching fingers, he struggled to move the small flint wheel. He held the lighter up over his head, and it cast enough light to allow him to survey his entombment. In front of him was the table, still supported by the rubble he had jammed underneath it. On the opposite side of the table was a small area clear of debris. A jumbled pile of fallen concrete blocks lay beyond that point. His tomb extended to his right, just beyond his reach, to one of the exterior walls. The total space was around ten feet in length and eight feet in width. Reluctantly, he looked behind at the barrier that had impeded his backward shuffle when he'd pulled free from under the table. From his new position, he saw Lieutenant Ryan's grim, gray face, blank eyes staring unseeing at the ceiling, the upper portion of his torso exposed. Another dead man lay behind Ryan, though Butler was not sure who he was. He averted his gaze swiftly, but the image was burned forever into his memory. He spoke the short prayer again, "May you rest in peace with God." *So many men under my command have died.*

He swung his gaze to the exterior wall. Partly covered by concrete dust was a torn map. Unable to use his left leg, he placed his palms flat on the floor, raised his buttocks up, and pushed his body sideways. Then he propelled himself forward with his hands, making a wide berth of the protruding leg and boot.

He scooted to the paper map and picked it up out of the gritty dust. Sensibly, he tore the map in half and formed a cylinder with the paper, touched the paper to the flame of the lighter, and made a small torch. With a quick snap, he closed the lighter and slid it back into his pocket. With the aid of the burning map, he looked for anything else that might burn but saw nothing. The map burned gradually, flakes of charred paper floating in the air, until the final glowing charred remains burned to ashes. The air was heavy with the scent of smoke, and the aroma floated away gradually on the current of air. He moved so he could lean his back against the outside wall. Exhausted, he tried to remain awake and listen in case someone called out, but he slipped into a troubled slumber.

When he awoke his leg was stiff, and the chill of the concrete floor penetrated his body. The soreness of his fingers and the throbbing of his leg allowed for little comfort. His left thigh caused him notable discomfort when he moved, but the pain reassured him that he still had sensation in that portion of his leg.

"Captain?" It was an extremely faint cry.

"Sergeant Alexander, is that you?"

"Help!" The voice was muffled.

Where had the appeal for help come from? He listened, hoping to focus on the cry.

"Captain!"

He pictured the interior of the collapsed bunker. The sound had come from the corner on the far side of the table. Using his hands to grope his way in the blackness of the bunker, he scooted around the jutting piece of furniture. Not sure where he was, he again used the lighter. The flame was growing tinier and weaker with each use. Believing he was at the right spot, he snuffed out the flame.

"Alexander, is that you? Alexander, can you hear me?" In silence, he waited.

An exhausted whisper: "Captain!"

He began furiously attacking the concrete blocks, digging, pushing, and shoving the rubble out of the way. "No more of my men are going to die!" he screamed an oath, and the resolve pierced and seared in his mind. "Alexander, hold on, I'm trying to…."

No reply.

Fragment after fragment, chunk after chunk his fingers shredded, fingernails torn past the cuticle, hands bruised and cut, he relentlessly dug and scraped out fragments of concrete. Hour after hour he toiled, until he collapsed.

"Got to take a break, Alexander. Need to rest. I'll keep digging later, I promise." No answer. "Alexander, I promise I'll find you."

Feebly he scooted back against the wall, exhausted. He slept fitfully. Visions of Anna Mae floated through his subconscious. Her image was fleeting, replaced with the grim, dead face of Lieutenant Ryan. His face became commingled with that of Sergeant Alexander, trapped and pleading for help. This image faded into the gruesome depiction of a dead, mutilated corpse in a muddy foxhole. The images continued, fast and fleeting, in a never-ending horror show. Butler woke screaming and sweating, clawing for breath. He opened his eyes and stared into the nothingness; somehow, the darkness soothed his terror.

How long he'd slept he couldn't tell; it was cold, and he put his hand down on the floor to shift his position. The floor was damp. In the stillness of his confinement he could hear a drip, drip, slow and steady. It must have rained, and water was dripping into the bunker. He touched and felt along the floor and wall, seeking the source, but couldn't locate it. Thirsty, parched, he wondered how long it had been since his last drink—hours, a day? In desperation, he took out the lighter. It was impossible for him to turn the wheel with his maimed fingers, so he resorted to using the backside of his thumb. He made a few tries before a flame appeared, the fluid all but gone. The wick smoldered. With the lighter placed next to the floor he searched, and in a small depression a foot or two away, he found a small puddle of water. Lying on his stomach he inched the distance, and with his lips pursed over the hollow he sucked grimy, filthy liquid into his mouth, allowing the cold water to soothe his raw, sore throat. The water was alkaline and full of chemicals leached from the concrete, polluted and foul, but it was water. The flame burned dim and went out. The wick glowed red for a second and then extinguished itself. He placed the Zippo back in his shirt pocket and buttoned the flap.

Refreshed by the water, he worked his way back over to the wall of rubble and recommenced digging. The pieces he could handle now with his torn hands seemed insignificant. The work was tedious and slow, and each handful of rubble extracted increased the pain, but he kept digging. He called repeatedly for Alexander, with no answer. Time passed. He dug, slept, dug again.

Propped against the exterior wall, he was jolted awake by a cracking, grinding noise. Crouching down, he huddled to make himself as small as possible and sought protection next to the wall. His immobile left leg stuck straight out, as he was unable to bring it back to his body. The concrete slab began to slip. As the rebar separated from the cement, sharp shards of rubble propelled across the enclosure and pelted him as if shot by a cannon. Fragments of concrete and rubble plummeted and filled the small hole he had so determinedly dug, obliterating all his work. The tomb became smaller. After the rumbling ceased, he reached up and touched the ceiling from his sitting position. He stretched his arm forward and encountered a slab of concrete. Hours elapsed and then days. He became delusional, and the nightmares—always the terrible nightmares.

A blinding light penetrated his eyelids. He wanted it turned off, and he wished for darkness and the apathy of not being able to see. Slowly he opened his eyes and stared at a concrete slab over his head, visible by the beam of a flashlight shining through an opening between blocks of debris. An arm pushed its way through the fragments and into his crypt, and a hand—a rough and callused but gentle hand—touched his forehead.

"Captain, it's OK now. I've got you, and you're going to be all right. We'll get you out. You're safe." Butler recognized the familiar voice, and it calmed and reassured him. "Don't give up! I'm here. Remember our deal; we take care of each other—you take care of me and I'll take care of you."

The next hours were a blur of different hands, fresh water, food, calming medication, people talking, and sleep.

The well-known voice, Billy's voice, said, "Hang in there, Captain Butler! Oren, listen to me: the medics are here, and they're going to take you to a hospital."

Then came the sensation of him being lifted and the words: "You owe me a bottle of bourbon, and I intend to collect. Meet you in Charleston after the war."

The scene shifted to a field hospital outside Paris with everything blurred, elusive images, and the unbearable pain. A comforting female voice assured him, "Here, Captain, the morphine will help." A shadow covered his memory, and the pain subsided.

The hospital ship; he was going home, his hands wrapped in bandages and his left leg splinted. The pain in his fingers was horrendous to the point of being unbearable. He asked for relief, and they gave him more and more morphine to soothe the discomfort and block the memories.

He had survived the bombing after being trapped in that burial chamber for six days.

The rescue efforts had officially ended after they'd spent three days and nights sifting through what remained of the bunker. Everyone had stopped looking, everyone except for that stubborn platoon sergeant, who'd relentlessly continued with the search when others had given up hope. Billy would not take no for an answer and had located him in that small enclosed space on the fifth day. It had taken another twenty-four hours for them to extract him from the confines of the bunker.

He remembered how useless his hands were then, the flesh shredded from tearing at the concrete shards in his attempt to rescue himself and from his failed effort to extricate Alexander. The infection was so bad the Army doctors even considered amputating his mangled hands.

***

CHAPTER SIXTEEN
Visitor

Andy was resting his tired backside on a barstool at the Brass Rail that night. Butler had been recuperating in the rooms in the back of the bar for about a week. He grinned to himself, admitting that Butler was receiving a lot more attention from the girls in the Brass Rail than he would ever have received from the nurses in the base hospital. The sponge baths he received were definitely far superior to those he would have gotten in the hospital. The bar was humming with the normal noise of the night when there was an increasing amount of commotion, feet shuffling around, and chairs being roughly pushed and scooted along the floor. His first thought was *A fight's brewing*, and he intended to ignore the hubbub. A chorus of whistles and catcalls sounded. *A woman must have walked into the bar to have caused such an uproar. These guys are all so horny if someone's grandmother walked in, she would be greeted with a series of hoots and hollers.*

He looked up at the reflection in the mirror panel at the back of the bar but could only see the reflection of a couple of Army grunts with their mouths agape, staring toward the front door. He caught a fleeting glimpse of Yoriko, her lips slightly parted, staring openly in the same direction. Andy swiveled around on his stool to see what attracted their attention. A woman, an American judging from her clothing, in a fashionable light gray traveling ensemble, stood in the entry way with two pieces of stylish Samsonite luggage by her side. As she glanced despairingly around the bar, a perplexed, questioning expression traversed her face.

He concentrated on Yoriko, whose expression had turned from surprise to hostility. The sweet, gentle Yoriko's reaction to the American woman reminded Andy of a feline in a defensive posture. She was the epitome of a wildcat ready to protect her litter and territory from an invader as she approached the stranger and, with a haughty snarl, said, "What you want here?"

"I'm looking for a Sergeant Butler; I understand he frequents this bar." No one immediately answered, so she continued, "If he isn't here, perhaps a person by the name of Andy … an Andy Anderson or ah … a Mel Schultz might be here, and I could speak to them."

A stool toppled over and crashed against the floor. "I'm Mel Schultz, and it would be my pleasure to provide you with any assistance I can," the awe-stricken man said with all the schmaltz he could muster as he hurried over to where the woman stood.

"I'm looking for Oren. My name is Anna Mae, Anna Mae Du Frère. I came here from South Carolina to see him. Is he here?" Her voice was as delicate as a flower petal as she asked for help.

Anna Mae Du Frère was possibly the most gorgeous woman Andy had ever set his eyes on. She was in her thirties, with blonde hair and blue eyes, dressed exquisitely and impeccably groomed, as if she'd stepped from the cover of a fashion magazine. The awareness of who she was rolled over him like a Sherman tank. *Anna Mae from South Carolina, the woman in the stories about Butler, the man's fiancée.*

Andy slid off his stool, walked over, stuck out his hand, and said, "Hey, I'm Andy." *I'm acting like I'm some schmuck at a barn dance with a piece of straw sticking out of my mouth. I can't believe I just stuck out my grubby hand and said, "Hey."*

She held out her hand and said with a smile that warmed him clear down to his toes, "I feel already acquainted with you and Mel…. Please, call me Anna Mae."

In the few minutes they had been talking with Anna Mae, Yoriko burst from the bar and ran into the back rooms, yelling, "Mama-san, American woman here in bar. Want see Butler-san."

Mama-san, gathering her kimono about her, rushed out to the tavern, motioning for Yoriko to follow her, and hurried to where Andy and Mel stood.

She bowed politely. "*Konnichiwa, Irrashaimase.*"

Anna Mae looked at Yoriko, hoping for a translation.

"She say good day and welcome."

The injured man's stay in a back room was not a closely guarded secret. But it wasn't exactly common knowledge, either, and they tried to keep it that way so as not to invite unnecessary inquiries.

The patrons in the bar were straining to listen in on the conversation, and Mama-san, aware of the inquisitive listeners, motioned to the group standing by the door to go outside. The older Japanese woman whispered something in Yoriko's ear. The younger woman motioned for Andy to bring Anna Mae and follow her. Shocked and confused, Anna Mae frowned and began to protest when she understood she was going to be escorted from the tavern. "I need to see Oren. Please, Andy, you need to help me. I won't leave until I find him."

"I understand," Andy said in a comforting tone. "You'll see Butler, don't worry. Please, just follow me."

Mama-san disappeared back into the rooms behind the bar as they followed Yoriko out of the bar and around the building to the fenced area. There, they found Mama-san standing by the open gate, ready to admit them in through the garden area.

As they reached the back entrance to the living quarters, Yoriko commented, "Mama-san go now and tell Butler-san you here."

"Please, I wish to surprise him; would you take me to him?" Anna Mae pleaded elegantly.

"Don't think good idea; maybe he no like surprise." Yoriko was still in a defensive mode.

Andy interceded. "Yoriko, I think it will be OK." *What's gotten into her? She has never acted snippy before.*

Yoriko reluctantly relayed Anna Mae's request, and Mama-san took the American woman in tow as they walked to the rear door of the structure. As they began to step up from the foyer into the hallway, the command "Off shoes" came, giving Anna Mae her first lesson in Japanese customs.

As Mama-san shuffled down the hallway, Anna Mae stuck to her like a shadow until the older woman stopped at the entranceway to a room. Gesturing to the American woman to be silent, Mama-san then slid the door partly open, bowed, and motioned for Anna Mae to enter the room.

The two guys were told to stay on the narrow wooden porch which ran the length of the building.

Andy and Mel removed their shoes, put on slippers, and stretched out on the porch floor by a low table. Andy was speculating on how the impromptu meeting would go between Butler and Anna Mae when he felt a tug on his sleeve. He looked up to see that Yoriko had slipped up to him and jerked on his arm to get his attention. She whispered incredulously, "That woman Butler-san's *okusan* (wife)?"

"No, his fiancée. She is the woman who is going to be his wife," Andy replied.

"So, she no wife, what she do here? Why she come Japan?" she asked in a pretentious and testy manner. "Why she think she can come here? This bar not for her. It only for Japanese girls and American boys. No American *onna* belong."

"Hard to explain," he said, and then he maneuvered the conversation to other topics.

Sumiko unexpectedly appeared, giving the impression that she'd just happened to wander by. "Who's the woman that came in here?" She nodded toward the living area where Anna Mae and Butler were.

"Butler's fiancée," mumbled Mel.

Sumiko, very casually and with total indifference to the situation, shrugged her shoulders. "Oh! She very pretty," she said and then left as if it were a common, everyday occurrence.

Mama-san stepped out on the porch and scowled when she saw that Yoriko still stood there. The younger woman jumped up and hurriedly rushed to the tavern area, fearing a violent tongue lashing from the proprietor. Andy started to stand up, but she motioned for both him and Mel to stay seated. She had retrieved the unfinished drinks left in the bar, and she set the beer bottles down in front of them and departed without saying a word.

"Look, this is great," said Mel quietly, pointing to the still partially open door leading from Butler's room to the porch. "Maybe we can overhear what they're talking about."

"Come on, listening in on what Butler and the first sergeant were talking about is one thing, but eavesdropping on a guy and his girl is something else."

Mel pretended to sulk at Andy's rebuke. The polite pretense of minding one's own business only lasted a few minutes as both of them strained to listen to the muffled conversation drifting out through the open door.

***

Butler had been lying with his face toward the inside door with his eyes closed when Mama-san slid the door open. Anna Mae entered the room, crept forward on her tiptoes, knelt down, and kissed him tenderly on his forehead.

Without opening his eyes, he said, "It is you. I smelled the scent of fresh lilacs. I thought it was all a dream." His eyes opened, and he looked at her with disbelief.

Watching him through misty eyes, she said, "Yes, I'm here. I needed to see you, and I wanted to be with you. I've missed you so much."

He took her in his arms, holding her tight while he caressed and kissed her. Her presence poured new life into his body. He uttered, "I'm happy you're here, so delighted to see you."

The reality and realization that she was there in Japan hit him. In an inquisitive tone, the questions came. "But why—why did you come all this way?" He paused. "How did you find me here at this bar? How did you get here? You were supposed to call last Friday night."

"Slow down, Sherlock. You sound like a detective questioning a suspect. I did call, and you weren't around. Finally I contacted Billy, and his explanations were not enough to convince me everything was all right. I know I'm impulsive; I was worried, and so I called the airlines and booked a reservation on the first flight out. I already had my visa; I planned on coming next month anyway, after Carol Sue settled in."

Butler kept staring at her as she continued.

"When I arrived and called the base from the airport, they said you weren't there. I was unsure what to do. I remembered you wrote me the name of this place, so I had the taxi bring me here to this, ah ... little tavern. I asked for you, and when I received no response, I asked for Andy or Mel—and bingo, they were right there. Both were such gallant young gentlemen, and along with a Japanese girl and

Mama-san—I think that is what you call her—they brought me back here to you."

"You didn't travel from South Carolina to Japan by yourself, did you?"

"I'm a big girl now, Oren, and I can take care of myself." She fidgeted, trying to find a comfortable position, the cut of her dress not allowing her to sit easily on the floor.

"Don't take it wrong. I'm happy to see you and glad you're here, but why did you decide to come all the way over here?"

"What did you expect me to do? I couldn't get you on the phone; you didn't call me back. What did you presume I would do, sit at home and not worry? It's not like during the war, when we couldn't travel overseas. This time I could do something, so here I am. I felt something bad had happened to you. I was uneasy that perhaps you'd become depressed or troubled, perhaps you were attempting to find solace in a bottle. Even you had written me you were drinking more than you should, and I was concerned that alcohol could become a problem. Do you remember my Uncle Jack and his difficulty with Jim Barleycorn? My Aunt Laura should have intervened long before she did; maybe he would still be alive."

"Not a problem for me, I assure you," Butler countered. "Perhaps a setback."

"If that were the truth, how did you become all beaten and bruised? Why are you here, hiding out in the back of a bar, for heaven's sake, instead of receiving care in a hospital? It doesn't make any sense to me."

Andy, overhearing her words, thought, *Funny, her attitude toward drink reminds me of Aunt Bessie. She always used the term Jim Barleycorn when referring to alcohol.* That was OK; Aunt Bessie was one of his favorite people, and as a teetotaler from the Bible belt, she was appalled by the idea of someone drinking spirits. *Anna Mae's right to be worried. True, Butler drinks a lot, but so do a whole bunch of other guys here.*

There was the GI gin guzzler in the hangar office. He would go on sick call, fake a cough, and the medics would give him cough syrup. The syrup was a clear liquid with a low alcohol content and clear color, hence the nickname, GI gin. The guy would empty out the cough syrup, fill the bottle with vodka, and stick the modified prescription in his desk drawer. Every hour or two during the day he would start coughing, almost to the point of suffocation. The guy was such a great actor he could have won an Academy Award for his portrayal of a man on the verge of death from choking. Then he would pull out his prescription bottle full of vodka, take a healthy pull, cough, and go back to work. Everyone knew what he was doing, but he never became inebriated and it didn't interfere with his job. Andy didn't think Butler's drinking was such a big deal. Guess you could call it a problem if you wanted to. Then he started thinking about the town drunk they had back home, wondering if the guy was still hanging around the saloon. The joker was a transient, somewhere between thirty and fifty years old; hard to guess his age with his face so weather-beaten, wrinkled, aged because of all the booze and his way of living. He was a railroad bum who'd literally fallen off the train when it had come through town. No one cared what happened to him except for the ladies from the church's temperance society; his Aunt Bessie was one of them. These compassionate women tried to help the bum, but he didn't want any help. The guy drank anything he could beg or steal and loafed around all day. He'd become a curiosity to the kids, almost a celebrity in the small town. Now, *there* was a drunk with a problem. The railroad station was a short three blocks from the saloon, yet the drunk never sobered up enough to find his way back to the train tracks.

"How long are you going to be able to stay in Japan?" Butler asked Anna Mae.

"Depends on what you want—a week, two weeks, or more. If you can get leave, perhaps we can go somewhere, a secluded place, one that is quiet and romantic. I would like that," she whispered seductively.

"Me too," whispered Oren. "I'm already on leave and still have a week left. Plus, a week's extension of the leave is a possibility."

"Well," she said and then hesitated. "Are you well enough to travel someplace?"

"With you by my side, I would venture to the ends of the earth—or to the limitations placed on me by the military within the confines of the island of Honshu."

"Mount Fuji or Nikko will do fine, Romeo."

"I'm a real mess right now. And you're right—I'm drinking more than I should, and I'm not taking care of myself physically or mentally. I'm better than a few months ago but still having a relapse now and then." He took her hand and caressed it tenderly. "You're taking a chance with your reputation just to be seen talking with such a messed-up specimen of a man like me."

"My reputation is already in question with my coming to Japan alone. Only you can make an honorable woman of me. Oh, Oren, I want to be able to help you, but you have to let me in. I can't help you if you keep shutting me out and won't tell me what's bothering you. I love you, and I want you to come home. I realize the killing and death you saw in the war was terrible and the memories are horrible. Please, why won't you confide in me? Please talk to me about what the problem is."

Butler smiled at her. He knew she was right and needed to understand what bothered him, instead he pushed his explanations aside for another day and said, "We will leave in the morning. Your suggestion of Nikko is perfect. The temples are mystifying and inspiring. The landscape is beautiful, the exact place to go."

Anna Mae wasn't going to let him off so easily. "Tell me what happened and why you're hiding out in this room."

He skimmed over of the details of his mugging and divulged little of what had actually happened. Then, as if to justify his actions, he said, "Guess I let my guard down and was snookered, as they say."

Her blue eyes probed and questioned with a stare that penetrated his defenses and pried open the barriers that had held in his trepidations for all these years. His reluctance to divulge his feelings burst, and all that was tormenting him poured out like water pumped from a well.

"The fighting didn't bother me…. After the war was over, they stripped me of my pride, my self-worth. They took away everything I had worked for." He stopped. Now that the confession had been voiced out loud, the reason sounded rather pathetic. However, it was how he felt, robbed of what his future might have been. He tried to explain it to her as he rambled on.

During this interlude of conversation, Mel poked Andy with his elbow and mouthed, "Listen up, this should be good." Then he bent forward, trying to lean a couple of inches closer to the open door to improve the audibility of the tête-à-tête.

"The Army told me they were giving me a medical discharge because of the condition of my hands. They felt I was no longer medically fit to hold a command position. Granted, my hands were such that I couldn't handle a gun. I was barely able to use a pencil when they released me from the hospital … kicked me out of the Army, and told me to go home."

He paused and took a deep breath. "While I was a patient in the hospital, they pumped me so full of morphine to quell the pain that I depended upon the medication to see me through the day."

Anna Mae remained quiet while he talked. She shifted her sitting position so her body pressed tightly against him, and she firmly held onto his hands, not wanting to release him.

"The Army told me to go home; the report said that I was no longer a viable Army officer. They discarded me like an old broken cup, threw me out, and I was left alone to pick up the pieces."

He looked away from her. "I'm almost ashamed to admit it, but they destroyed my pride, my dignity. Despite all I had gone through during the war, all I'd done, I was summarily dismissed. It sounds like sour grapes I know, but it is how I felt."

Anna May squeezed his hand, and he continued, "Billy, as you remember, came to Charleston on a thirty-day leave to help me. I could not remember everything that happened in Laon during the bombing, and he worked me through the blank spots. He supported me through the hard times as I weaned myself off the medication. The Butler family has a proud history of military service in the Americas going back even before the Revolutionary War, all serving with dignity and honor. And then they threw me out like yesterday's garbage."

His voice grew a little angry. "The concept that someone who'd never met me could destroy my life with the stroke of a pen gnawed at the very essence of my being. I needed to prove to the Army and to myself I was a valuable, worthwhile individual and not an empty shell. This need became a compulsion, and I shut you and everyone else out while I pursued my quest. It was something I thought I needed to do alone. I overcame the handicap and, other than the scars, I have complete use of my hands. They hurt sometimes, but I don't let on."

"Excuse me," a soft voice from the doorway in the hall said. "Mama-san told me bring you tea." Sumiko entered the room and placed a tray down on a low table. "Mama-san also want tell dinner be ready in short time. I come for you then."

Sumiko bowed and left the room, closing the door behind her.

"Who's that girl?" asked Anna Mae. "She doesn't look ... Japanese, at least not...."

"She is Eurasian; one of her parents was Caucasian. That's all I know about her lineage, and ... ah ... she's kind of a ward of Mama-san," Butler answered.

Mel and Andy were still listening in on the conversation as Mel pointed to their empty glasses and mouthed to Andy, "I'm going to try to find us something to eat and get a refill on the drinks."

Andy nodded and stayed seated, wanting to hear the rest of what Butler might divulge about his past.

Anna Mae and Butler moved over to the small table in the room, and she poured them tea as she said, "Please continue telling me...."

Butler stared down at his cup, wisps of vapor rising from the hot liquid. "What bothers me the most was someone made an arbitrary decision that I was no longer physically fit for duty. I spent months trying to track down the official reason, but all the government red tape kept stopping me. I corresponded with congressional representatives and military officials, pleading my case. The people who'd decided my future were out of the military. Their written justifications and reasons for my dismissal were all poorly and scantly documented. My perseverance partially paid off, and my commission was reinstated in the inactive reserves. It wasn't what I wanted, but it was better than nothing."

He stopped, lifted his cup, and took a sip of tea. "I admit I can be stubborn sometimes, and I was not giving up this pursuit. I joined the active reserves as an enlisted man as a way to regain my commission on active duty, only it hasn't quite worked out the way I had anticipated."

"Why don't you just come home, quit the military, and stop chasing this ... dream or quest or whatever you want to call it," Anna Mae pleaded. "We want you back in South Carolina; you have a family business to run. Heaven forbid, you're not in the military for the money; you don't need money, and if you did, I would give it to you," she cried.

"I needed to find myself, to be back in touch with my wants and needs. I want to feel whole again; I need to regain my self-esteem. People don't seem to understand that even if you have money, you still need to have your pride and your honor to feel that you're of value to yourself, your family, and your community."

He paused. "Money can't buy that, at least not for me." He changed the conversation by saying, "If we are going to have dinner, I'd better freshen up at least a bit. Remember, I was napping when you arrived." He went to a closet and took out some clothing, and as he left the room, he called out, "I'll be back in a minute."

Butler had hardly departed when Sumiko reentered. "You wish to wash up before dinner?"

***

Out on the porch, Mel slipped up to Andy and faintly said, "Hey, Mama-san wants us to clear out of here and go back to the bar. I got us a table and food's coming, so let's move it."

"Why do we have to leave? The conversation is starting to get interesting."

"Sumiko said the old lady wants to use the space and for us to vamoose, to clear out of the garden."

***

Anna Mae followed Sumiko down the hallway to a room where there was a washbasin and a smaller adjoining room with a deep tub and a separate toilet area. The fixtures were all recognizable yet different from the American version, and it took a few minutes for her to work out how they functioned.

As Anna Mae left the bathroom, Sumiko reappeared along with Mama-san, who smiled, bowed, and waved for her to follow, also signaling Sumiko to accompany them.

The older woman led them to the rear of the house, where the sliding doors were open to the outside. The twilight had deepened, and various-sized candles placed in strategic locations illuminated the pristine garden. The flickering flames of the tapers cast a wavering light, creating mystic shadows that ebbed and flowed, heightening the captivating atmosphere of the delicate garden.

Mama-san invited Anna Mae to sit on one of the pillows placed by a low table. The American woman glanced around in uncertainty, and Sumiko reassured her, "Butler-san be here in minute."

The dinner was elegant and decadent; the foods were strange and exotic to Anna Mae. The kimono-clad young women who attended them served the food with poise and efficiency while never uttering a word. In the background someone played a koto, and melodic songs were sung in Japanese. The garden setting captured the American woman's imagination, and she was enchanted by her surroundings. She exclaimed, "Oh, Oren, I'm beginning to understand how you can be fascinated by the beauty and charm of Japan and its people."

At 2300 hours, Sumiko interrupted them. "Curfew in one hour," she reminded Butler. He hadn't realized it was so late, and he said to Anna Mae, "I would like for you to stay at a Western-style hotel tonight, one that caters to military wives and dependents. You'll be comfortable there. In the morning, we will leave to go to Nikko. I'll be there at 0900 to pick you up."

"Would you please call me a taxi," Butler asked Sumiko, who still stood next to them. "And also ask Andy and Mel if they would escort Anna Mae to the hotel for me."

"Why do I need to go someplace else? I'll just stay here with you. I didn't travel all the way to Japan to be shuttled off," replied Anna Mae with a formidable tone and determined expression.

"But—" he said, attempting to protest.

She placed her finger on his lips. "No argument. I'm sleeping right here."

***

CHAPTER SEVENTEEN
A Lesson Learned

The following morning, Sergeant Jones drove to the Brass Rail to pick up Anna Mae and Butler. The two discreetly left the Brass Rail by the secluded garden gate, and the first sergeant took them to Tokyo. Perhaps it was at the insistence of Anna Mae or, more likely, Butler finally realized he needed the woman and she was the most important thing in his life, they made a stop at the American consulate. At the consulate, a civil ceremony joined them together in marriage. The newlyweds departed Tokyo and traveled by train to honeymoon at a resort in the vicinity of Nikko.

Three weeks later Anna Mae left Japan, returned to Charleston, and began making plans for the day Butler would be returning home.

Butler, with only a few months remaining on his active duty commitment, resigned himself to counting the days he had left in the service. The whirlwind visit of Anna Mae and their marriage had triggered a realization that his elusive quest for reattainment of his captain's rank was becoming an impossible task. With the acceptance of this insight, his attitude became more relaxed.

Butler kept himself scarce; Andy would see him at work, chow, and in the barracks, and occasionally at the Brass Rail. The first sergeant's family had arrived from the States, and Sergeant Jones had moved from the barracks to family housing. Andy surmised that Butler hung out with the Joneses in the evening more often than not, although there were still times at Mama-san's when he drank heavily, as old habits are not changed quickly. Before he left the bar, Andy would check on the man's condition; however, Butler never asked for assistance.

As the months elapsed, on the evenings when Butler did stop by the Brass Rail, he made a concentrated effort to curb his drinking. One evening instead of heading directly to the bar and his customary stool he stopped by the table where Andy and Mel sat, pulled out a chair, and wedged in between the two younger men, saying, "Evening, gentlemen, and how are you all doing tonight?

The sudden intrusion by Butler caught Andy by surprise, and as he began to stammer out an answer, Butler continued, "I thought it was about time that I joined you and bought us all a round of drinks."

From then on, when Butler entered the bar and it appeared that the ex-captain was heading towards his favorite stool, Andy would jump up from his chair, intercept Butler, and steer him towards the table. Once while doing this, Andy thought, *Geeze, I'm turning into my aunt Bessie, shepherding the man away from his daily ration of booze.*

Butler kept their interest by telling them stories not of combat and war, but of the people he had met and his experiences with them. His tales captivated and interested the younger military men as he related the stories of human nature, including mischief, and some were extremely humorous.

When they first started their round-table conversations, there were just the three of them. Then slowly the number of interested participants in their group increased, along with the laughter and amusement at the tales and anecdotes being swapped between the participants. It was no secret that Butler had once been a captain. In the eyes of the troops, that elevated him to the counselor category, and guys began to seek him out for guidance. Most of these guys had either seen or heard about Anna Mae coming to the bar looking for Butler. They figured that he must know all about women to have a looker like Anna Mae for a wife; thus, Butler became the soothsayer of the lovelorn. Anytime someone received a Dear John letter from home or had women trouble, they ran to Butler for advice. He told them he didn't understand women any better than they did, but that didn't stop them from seeking his counsel. Butler appeared to relish the attention.

The longer he conversed with the troops, the more his advice was sought, and the less time he had to drink. He'd order his customary sake, but seldom had the chance to consume the entire contents of the small tokkuri.

Several weeks later, one evening when twilight had given way to darkness, Andy and Mel poked about town, trying to find something interesting to do. The number of coins in their pockets had diminished to only a few as the end of the month had grown nearer, but payday was still a week away. Any entertainment that interested them needed to be inexpensive, so they were thinking about going to a movie or a *pachinko* parlor. If worse came to worst, they'd go back to the Brass Rail and have one drink before they headed back to the barracks.

They walked by an alleyway and, from the recesses of the darkened passageway, Andy heard a groan of some sort. He spotted a brief movement in the shadows fifty or so feet from the entrance.

"Mel, something's going on in there," he said.

"Probably some guy getting a quickie and didn't have enough cash to pay for a room, so he's ripping off a little in the alley."

"Nah, don't think so," Andy replied hesitantly.

The obscure image strained to push itself up off the dirt surface. *The guy's hurt.* The unknown person struggled to stand and awkwardly stumbled toward Andy. A man, for sure, but Andy wasn't able to distinguish the individual's features, as the person was bent forward, clutching his stomach. As he neared, Andy could make out that it was a GI, his face battered and clothes torn and dirty. Whoever had gotten to him had worked him over good. As the man approached, Andy saw his face and realized he had seen him before but couldn't place exactly where.

"You OK, fella? Need some help?"

The battered man glared at him and snarled, "What's it to you?"

The guy's eyes were almost swollen shut. His lip was cut, and blood was crusting around his mouth and chin. He peered at Andy through bloodshot and puffed-up eyelids.

Then Andy recognized him. *He's the big guy who was in the truck with Skeeter.* "I know you. I saw you with Skeeter one day. You work with him, don't you, at base supply?"

The battered man struggled to remember the man who stood in front of him and mumbled, "You're ... you're his friend, ain't ya?"

"What happened? Someone rob you or something?"

"Yeah, well…. Yeah…. Yeah … that's what happened. Three Japanese guys jumped me and beat me up. Took my money."

Mel interjected, "Better report it. The Japanese cops will find them; they're good at doing their job."

The man didn't say anything for a few seconds and then declared, "I should, but maybe the whole thing is best forgotten."

Mel spat out, "Forgotten? What do you mean? If you don't report those creeps, they'll keep on robbing Americans. You got to make a report; if you don't want to, I'll do it for you."

The man explored the looks on Andy's and Mel's faces for a second and said nothing.

Andy saw the fear in the young man's eyes and the apprehensiveness in his countenance. "What is your name?"

"Phil," he said as he squinted through his one good eye. With a great deal of hesitation, he said, "Skeeter told me you was a decent guy and trustworthy, an' he could always depend upon you when he got in a pinch. Told me you helped him out a bunch. He told me ... told me that if I ever got in trouble and you was around, I should get you to help me."

Andy didn't reply; he just nodded.

"I didn't get robbed. I'll tell you what happened if you promise not to tell anyone," Phil confessed.

Andy and Mel both indicated they understood and for Phil to continue.

Phil began, "Didn't have any money, and I wanted to be with this girl. She's ... ah, a streetwalker. I like her a lot; she's a nice girl, just having a rough time making a go of it. She is only working on the streets to get some money saved up, and then she is goin' to quit. I wanted to spend the night with her, but no money no girl. I had an unopened carton of cigarettes I could sell on the black market that would get me some money, but the girl cost more than I could make from selling one carton. A guy at the motor pool told me how to fix an empty carton so it looked full. He swore to me he fixed the cartons the very same way all the time and never had any trouble selling them, always worked. I didn't think it was right to cheat, but he said the black-market guys are criminals and it wasn't unethical to cheat criminals."

He wiped some of the blood and drool off one corner of his mouth and spat some bloody saliva onto the dirt roadway. Then he swallowed and continued, "I needed the money and decided to try it. I took five packs of smokes out of one carton and filled the bottom of both cartons with folded cardboard so it would look full. Then I put in the top row with packs of cigarettes an' sealed them up good; you couldn't tell I'd monkeyed with the cartons."

Phil went tight-lipped for a second as a trio of GIs wandered up the street and passed by them. When the group was out of hearing range, he continued his account.

"The black-market guy," Phil continued. "I'd been to him before to sell smokes. He hefted the weight of the box and peeked inside at the top layer. I figured there was plenty of time to make the transaction, take the cash, and clear out of there before they realized I'd pulled a fast one on them. Everything went smooth; I exchanged the cigarettes for money and took off down the street to the girl. With the money in my pocket, I ... planned to stay the whole night." Here he hesitated, possibly not wanting to tell the rest of the story but knowing he must. "Only, it went wrong. They caught me when I reached the alley; that was about 1900. Three of them jumped me. I'm a big guy an' figured I could take care of any trouble they could dish out. These Japanese men are little and I can handle one or two, no problem," he bragged. "But all three of them jumped me at once, and they were a hell of a lot faster and stronger than I thought they'd be."

Phil paused and moistened his lips with his tongue. The kid needed a drink of water, but they didn't have any.

Then he continued, with a bit of humility, "I was OK as long as I was standing up. I'm holding my own. Then they hit me with sticks of some sort, knocked my feet out from under me, and pinned me to the ground. After that, I didn't stand a chance. I got beat up good; they took back the money, kept the cigarettes, and warned me not to tell the cops. One of them must of hit me with a sap 'cause I've been out for a while an' I got this big lump on my head."

Mel mumbled, "Probably beat you with short pieces of bamboo. You're lucky they didn't kill you. You should know better than to screw with the black market."

"You guys gotta understand," Phil pleaded. "If I report what happened, the Air Force can bust me and put me in the stockade for dealing in illegal activities."

He wanted Andy and Mel to say something, but when they didn't, he gave them a hound-dog look. "I ain't gonna do it no more, I can tell you for sure."

Dumbfounded that the kid was so gullible, Mel shook his head in disbelief. "Don't believe all the advice you hear floating around. Much of the crap they feed you is to find out how naïve you are. Don't take what they're telling you seriously; they're yanking you by the short hairs."

"You need to head back to the base," Andy said. "Your face looks like, ah … I've seen roadkill that looks better than you do. Better clean you up a little."

"Bet we can find some water and a washcloth at the Brass Rail," Mel said.

With Phil in tow they trudged off toward the bar, hoping they didn't run into someone they knew. The kid, shaky and sore, kept grabbing at his side and stomach as if he conceivably had bruised or cracked ribs.

They managed to reach the side of the tavern unobserved, or at least without attracting a lot of attention. Andy said harshly, "Phil, you wait outside by the fence over there while I go in and secure what we need. Stay by the fence and don't go wandering off. Mel is going to stay here with you, OK?"

Inside, Yoriko was serving some Army types, and he waved her over to where he stood. It took her a couple of minutes to extract herself from the group, she rushed over and threw her arms around him with a passionate hug. She seemed so happy to see him, and he felt so guilty afterward he had not taken more time with his greeting. Instead, he burst out with "We need a pan of hot water and a washcloth. Our friend outside was in a big fight, and we need to clean up his face. Don't tell anyone. *Wakaru*?"

"Big problem, maybe. Mama-san no like. I got to work, maybe not OK." She hesitated. "Me try."

"Yoriko, bring small sake, *dozo*."

She peered at him, and an unpromising expression manifested on her face.

Andy said, "Mama-san understand," and he gave her a quick peck on the cheek, hoping it would make up for his being inconsiderate.

She favored Andy with a quick hug and scurried off to the kitchen.

Outside, Mel stood looking down at Phil, who slumped piteously against the fence. The guy was in bad shape and in need of a doctor.

Yoriko came sneaking out the bar's back door a short time later with a pan of warm water and a cloth as well as the sake.

"Here, drink this. It'll help," Andy told Phil as Yoriko handed him the sake. The poor guy's mouth was so sore he could hardly press the cup to his lips.

Yoriko touched Andy's arm and revealed in a whisper, "Sorry, I have tell Mama-san. She say OK but you to pay for sake. An' Irish-san, he kept tell me if I see you to tell that he want talk with you."

He smiled understandingly at her. "It's all right. Don't worry about it."

Yoriko lingered and cleaned the blood off Phil's face and hands. She was far gentler than either of the guys would have been. Phil relaxed and seemed to relish the attention of the beautiful girl cleaning up his cuts and bruises. Andy was sure that Yoriko's presence and tender touch boosted the injured kid's deflated morale.

"OK," Andy concluded. "I think it's as good as we're going to get. Time for you to head back to your barracks."

They hoisted Phil up; Mel held onto him while Andy gave Yoriko what yen he had left for the sake. As an extra measure, he planted another quick kiss on her scrumptious lips. "Thanks for your help," Andy said, and they began their trek up the street to the gate.

The progress was slow; the kid was hurting more than he would admit. Andy could tell Phil was in pain by the way the kid walked and breathed, but the beaten man neither complained nor whimpered.

When they arrived at the base, one of the guards was the same sergeant who had been on duty one night when they'd brought an inebriated Butler through the gate. They handed him their passes, and the guard eyeballed first them and then Phil. The cop, with a half-grin on his face, said, "You two again. You part of a church mission rescue group? Every time I see you, you're dragging in some derelict. Last time, it was a boozer. Now this guy."

Andy smiled back. "No, they attach themselves to us like puppies, and we bring them home like stray dogs."

"Might be best if you take him back to the barracks or the hospital; he don't look any too good," the guard said as he handed back their passes.

They caught the bus and rode in silence, Andy sitting next to Phil and Mel in the seat in front of them. They were within a block of the hospital when Mel turned around and faced Andy. "You think we ought to get off at the next stop? I'm worried about Phil's condition!"

Andy agreed. "I think so. It won't hurt for him to see a medic."

They piled off the bus at the hospital stop, escorted Phil inside, and then left him alone to make his way over to the admitting desk. They departed, not needing or wanting any further involvement in the incident, their good deed for the day accomplished.

Standing at the bus stop for ten minutes, before the next one came along, Phil's quandary reminded them of a little risqué jingle that was going around. The ditty, sung to the tune of "My Darling Clementine," summed up Phil's dilemma:

Chocolato, cigaretteto, chewing gum a ten a yen.
Short time o no presento, sayonara, come again.

Only, Phil had not even managed that. The only thing he'd been the recipient of was a shellacking for his efforts.

***

CHAPTER EIGHTEEN
Rendezvous at the Laundry

Andy strolled along the dimly lit street, his mind preoccupied by events of the past. A three-wheeled motorcycle truck loaded with produce rattled and bounced across the deserted intersection, reminding him that only five months ago, they had loaded an injured Butler on a similar contraption and then had snugly tucked the weakened man away in a back room of the Brass Rail.

There was still ample time to beat curfew and be on base before midnight, but the hour was growing late and he couldn't dawdle. *Sure not much going on at the bar tonight,* he thought. *Mel's off chasing that cute little skirt he's become infatuated with over at Chibi's joint, and Yoriko had to work.* He hadn't wanted to go to Chibi's, and in spite of all Mel's pestering, he'd decided he might as well head back to the barracks and hit the sack. The sound of his leather soles grating against the loose gravel jarred him from his woolgathering as he walked across the darkened dirt street.

Andy was focused more on his destination than on his present surroundings. Ahead of him, the entryway of the small street was bathed in eerie shadows. A quarter moon, periodically obscured by clouds, momentarily left the backstreet mantled in a cloak of black. As he passed the center of the intersection and entered a darkened area, a hand shot out of the shadows and clamped over his mouth, preventing him from yelling. A muscular arm encircled his shoulders and roughly yanked him back into the gloomy passage. Andy's immediate gut reaction was to twist out of the hold and kick the son of a bitch in the balls.

A hushed voice whispered, "It's me, Remmey. Be quiet."

Andy stopped struggling, and the hands released him. He turned and faced his accoster, "What the f—" he uttered.

Remmey put a finger to his lips, indicating silence, and motioned for Andy to follow him. They slipped farther back into the darkened alley and halted in an isolated space between two buildings.

Remmey put one of his big meat hook hands on Andy's shoulder. "I need your help, kid."

"Bullshit! No 'Hello, how the frigging hell are you?' No 'What you been doing?' Just, 'I need your help!'" Incensed, Andy blurted out exactly what was on his mind. "What kind of a greeting is that, and what the hell do you mean you need my help? Is that all you got to say? The last time I saw you in Yokohama, you'd stripped off your Air Force stripes and sat looking like a peacock all prim and proper in an Army Jeep as a second lieutenant. Where the hell you been? What the hell is going on?"

"I'll answer all your questions; keep your voice down. I'll tell you everything, but right now I require assistance. I need your help, kid; everything else can wait. Calm down and listen to me, OK?"

Andy squinted at the darkened silhouette of the man standing before him and nodded his assent.

"In a shop down the street, four Chinese espionage agents are having a meeting. They've stolen sensitive military information and are passing it to the Chinese government. We also suspect they killed that Air Force OSI guy and dumped his body in the canal. Crucial we nab these people, and it has to be tonight. You're going to be my partner and help me; I've got no one else to turn to right now!"

"Come on, Remmey, cut the crap. Horsing around on the boat was one thing, but what's with all this cloak-and-dagger baloney? Quit screwin' around; it ain't that funny anymore."

"I'm not messing with you, Andy. I'm dead serious."

"Well then, if you're not jerking me around, then what are you up to, and who the hell are you—Army CID, Air Force OSI, or some damn fed, a G-man?"

"Something like that. What I'm not is Jack Armstrong, the all-American boy, and I can't do this alone. You trust me?"

Andy's temper had cooled slightly, and he was listening. "Yeah, I trust you, but I'm pissed too. Why'd you have to rough me up?"

"Look—I'm sorry, and I'll explain everything to you later. I promise. Right now I've got a job to finish, and I don't have the time to go into a long explanation. The people that were supposed to be here to provide backup support haven't shown up. Look, Andy, I can't go into this alone. If I tried, I'd be killed. If I don't do the job right now, within the next five minutes, it will be too late. I must stop these people now or thousands of American troops in Korea could die as a direct result of allowing these men to escape. I'm up a creek; I know I'm asking a lot, but the only one I could think of that I trusted was you."

"How did you know where I would be?"

"You are the epitome of consistent behavior. Ninety percent of the time, you take the same route to the base when you've been at the bar."

"You've been here watching me?" Andy's exasperated mood quadrupled as he spat out, "All this time, you've been keeping tabs on me? Why didn't you say some damn thing? Why didn't you let me know you were here? I thought we were supposed to be friends!"

"I've been under orders to keep out of sight and … never mind. Now, I must stop these four guys tonight or eight months of surveillance goes into the *benjo*. I don't have time to find someone else; you're all I have. I'm asking a lot of you, and it could put you in a perilous situation. Are you game or not?"

"Sure I'm game, and you knew that without asking. What do you need?"

"On the ship coming over, you told me you could shoot the eye out of a running jackrabbit with a .22. Now is the time for you to show me and not just tell me."

"Well, maybe I exaggerated a little. I'm a good shot, and most of the time I can pop them in the head or close, but hitting 'em in the eye, that only happened a couple of times. I might have been lucky."

"Well, it's a little too late to go to confession now, buddy, and there are no priests around for you to tell your sob story to. I can't do this job without help, and you're elected." Remmey pulled a small penlight from his pocket and clicked it on. "Here." He slapped a pistol he had just removed from his coat pocket into Andy's palm. "Your weapon."

Andy stared down at the gun. "I knew you were feeding me a line of crap! This isn't even a real pistol, it's a—"

"Yeah, a dart gun, a tranquilizer pistol. We need these guys alive; they're no good to us dead. It's imperative we know their source and where they're delivering the information."

Remmey dug down in his pocket and pulled out four deadly looking darts, handing Andy two of them. Then he brought forth two small CO_2 cylinders.

Sticking the little flashlight in his mouth to free his hands, he aligned the tiny beam of light on the pistol. Mumbling, slurping, and slurring as he spoke around the cylindrical tube stuck between his lips, he said, "This is how you insert the CO_2." He took the pistol and demonstrated the procedure. "Understand?"

"Yeah," acknowledged Andy.

"Watch now." Remmey took one of the darts, removed the protective cap from the needle, inserted it in the chamber, cocked the pistol, slipped on the safety, and handed the gun back. Removing the penlight from his mouth, he continued, "Simple; the CO_2 charge is good for four shots, or so they tell me. Don't bank your life on that info. If you can switch out the cartridge after two shots, do so. Don't depend on having enough compressed air to push out a third dart after you've used it two times. Got it?"

Andy nodded.

"OK, stick the extra darts and CO_2 in your pocket."

"What are you going to use?"

"I still have one dart I can use as an injection needle."

"That's all you have?"

Remmey smirked. Andy knew the guy could handle himself in a tight situation: he had the physique of a wrestler. Remmey flipped open his jacket, and in a shoulder holster hung a service-issue M1911, a .45-caliber semiautomatic pistol.

"I don't want you to kill anyone," he said. "Shoot them in the ass or thigh and let the sedative in the dart do the job. Butt or leg, a fleshy part of the body. The stuff is potent, and if you hit a vital organ, it might be deadly, lethal."

"Yeah, how fast does it work?"

"Not sure; it's a new formula, a vecuronium base, with some other ingredients like curare to speed up paralysis. Might even contain rat poison for all I know. Lab people say it should only take a few seconds. They've tested it on animals but never on a human. How long it really takes—that, my fine young friend, is for you to figure out. You sure you're up for this, Andy?"

"Think so."

"These guys are also looking for an American airman who was standing on the bridge talking to a woman the night they killed the lieutenant, because they think he might have seen them. The guy is as good as dead if they find him."

"Oh, crap, I bet that was me. I didn't see anything, but I was on the bridge that night!" Andy exclaimed.

"Yeah, I figured it might have been you by the description. Now this little mission's become personal; there is more than one reason to eliminate these SOBs."

Andy didn't have an answer; he swallowed and became acutely aware of everything Remmey was telling him.

"Never mind the reasons; here's the facts. The espionage agents are meeting in the back room of a laundry. When you get inside, there's a service counter that runs along the front of the building." Remmey knelt down and, with the help of the penlight, found a small twig and began sketching the floor plan of the laundry building in the dirt.

"It will be dark in there, so feel your way along the counter to your right."

"Here"—he pointed to the diagram with the stick—"is an opening between the counter and the side wall. Behind the counter, eight rows of laundered clothes hang on racks parallel to that wall. The people we want are in the room behind the clothes." He continued his drawing. "In the back wall there's a doorway, which will be to your far left, with a half-door. It may be open or closed, there should be enough light from the back room for you to be able to see it once you're near the door. When you are at the door, sneak a look and determine your targets."

For reassurance, Andy gripped the butt of the dart pistol. It didn't ease his concerns, although it was some comfort.

"You take the two guys closest to you. Andy, be careful. I'm not certain your training adequately covered this kind of work, but you know how to hunt. You're not out trying to creep up on a deer. You're stalking prey as deadly and unpredictable as a rabid coyote or wolf. These men have little regard for human life. They're as mean and vicious as any rattlesnake you might have encountered out on the prairie, and they can strike just as fast."

"Where are you going to be?"

"I'll be coming in the rear door. Wait until I take out the first guy. Then you start to work with the dart gun. You OK?"

Andy didn't say anything; he just nodded his head.

"Give me at least three minutes to get around to the rear door and be in position."

Rubbing out the sketch marks in the dirt, Remmey turned the penlight and shoved it back into his pocket. He stood up and moved down the small street to the laundry's front entrance while Andy followed. There, he motioned for the younger man to stand fast as he took a lock pick out of his pocket, swiftly undid the simple door lock, and then soundlessly pushed the door partially open. "Any questions?" he whispered.

"Nope."

Remmey slipped into the shadows and disappeared around the corner of the building.

Andy edged in through the door, his heart pounding to the point where he was certain the men in the back room could hear it thumping. The room was shrouded in darkness, and he groped his way forward little by little until he touched the counter. Warily, he moved to his right and slid around the end of the counter. Reaching out he searched, feeling around in the dark, and after a few tries he touched the wall. As noiselessly as possible he moved forward, inching along at what felt like a snail's pace. The smell of the freshly laundered clothes was pleasant and fresh, and he felt calmer and more self-assured now that he was on the move.

Abruptly, he smacked into the wall. The room was smaller than he had imagined. To his far left, a sliver of light from the half-open doorway pierced the room's murky interior. Hugging the wall he ventured forward, stopped, and wormed closer, the closed half-door providing a screen. The sound of voices drifted from the adjoining room in the melodious singsong of the Chinese language.

Dropping down, he crawled along the floor until he could peer through a crack between the half-door and the doorframe. Four men stood around a table, examining a document. One was a large guy, much bigger than anyone he had expected to see. *Won't be any trouble shooting him in the ass.* The second man, thinner but muscular, and a third skinny Chinese man of medium height stood with his back toward him. The fourth man stood on the far side of the table; it was hard to get a good look at him in the dim light. This man was younger and perhaps Japanese; Andy couldn't tell.

Over the table hung a single shaded lightbulb providing a dim circle of illumination. The rest of the room was masked in shadows. *Which one first,* Andy thought, slipping off the gun's safety. *The more body mass, the longer the tranquilizer is going to take. The easiest shot is the skinny guy.*

When Andy had first entered the laundry he'd started his count, *one one thousand, two one thousand.* The three minutes were over, and he waited for an indication that Remmey was ready. As the seconds ticked by, he strained for a better view through the small crack. The three men still gathered at the table, concentrating on the document that lay in front of them. The fourth agent had moved away, out of the dim sphere of light. Andy glimpsed a shadowy arm grab the man and a hand jab the dart into the agent's thigh. *How long will it take? I should have counted the seconds.*

He raised his head above the half-door as he brought up the pistol, picked his target, and squeezed the trigger. *Phutt.* The dart short forth and penetrated deep into the left buttock of the smaller man. Andy ducked behind the doorframe to reload and cock the tranquilizer gun. *Now count the seconds, one one thousand, two one thousand, three one thousand.* Andy looked though the open gap. The heavyset man had realized something was wrong and was looking around. *Four one thousand, five one thousand,* the skinny man staggered and then collapsed.

Time for the next shot: he stood and peeked around the doorframe at the same moment the hefty guy stared at the door. Spotting Andy, he came charging toward the door with the force of a raging wild bull. Andy swung the pistol and fired. The dart hit the man in the upper thigh, but it didn't faze him or slow his onward rush. Andy retreated behind the wall and dove into the mass of hanging clothing. The goliath thundered through the half-door, splintering and crushing the wood. The brute stood wheezing in the demolished doorway, furiously trying to determine where Andy had fled.

Concealed between the narrow rows of clean uniforms, Andy clumsily fumbled to change the CO_2 cylinder by feel in the dark. *I should have taken the pen light.* Finally, the cartridge clicked in place. More than ten seconds had passed, and the man still stood upright, snorting like a winded horse. With a grunt, the big guy started to rip though the dangling clothes, hunting for his quarry. Andy's adversary's methodical search kept bringing him closer. *I must have missed; no, I hit him. I saw the dart stick. He's a big guy, but its taking way too long for the tranquilizer to metabolize into his system.*

Andy lobbed the depleted CO_2 canister over the top of the clothes racks. The cylinder smashed against the opposite wall and tumbled, clattering to the floor. The portly agent, alerted by sound, stormed toward the source of the noise. While his foe ransacked and searched, Andy pulled the last dart from his pocket, loaded the gun, and slapped the chamber shut. Keeping perfectly still, he tried to control his breathing while he listened. He heard the sound of clothes being pulled from the racks and a muffled thud. Andy held his breath. There was a slight rustling of sound and then quiet. *Has the tranquilizer finally worked? The noise might have been the man falling.* He breathed again. *How much time has elapsed?* He'd lost count from the firing of the dart. *At least a minute and a half to two minutes.* Slipping from his hiding place, he crept toward the spot where the CO_2 canister had landed. The big man lay motionless, slumped on the floor.

Moving to the destroyed entryway, Andy cocked the gun as he advanced. Framed by the wrecked doorway, he observed Remmey and the remaining Chinese agent engaged in deadly struggle, both battered and bloody. Remmey had the upper hand when, suddenly, his opponent grabbed and flipped him with such force that when he slammed onto the floor, the whole building shook. The espionage agent pounced on the prone man as swiftly as a panther and, using his knees, pinned Remmey's arms against the floor. A double-edged dagger of lethal proportions appeared in the muscular Chinese man's hand, and he raised the knife in preparation for a downward strike to Remmey's chest.

Four seconds, minimum, for the serum to take effect. That's sufficient time for the guy to plunge the knife into Remmey more than once. I've only got a profile view of the bastard, an ass or thigh shot, too slow, won't work. Kill shot, must be a kill shot, only where? I can't see his chest. The man drew his head back to gain momentum for the downward thrust and exposed his neck.

The carotid artery is a pathway to the brain. At this distance and under these conditions with a dart gun, damn near an impossible shot. Put the dart in as close as possible. One chance in a hundred that I can even hit the neck, let alone place it one or two inches under the ear. If it works, a kill shot. Relax, breathe, let it out, hold, confirm aim, squeeze.

Phutt. The air rushed from the barrel as the dart sped forward. The knife hung motionless, Remmey's antagonist still keeping him pinned to the floor.

The empty gun slid from Andy's grip as he sprinted into the room. *One one thousand,* the knife wavered, *two one thousand,* his shoulder slammed the man and knocked him off to the side, and the dagger clattered to the floor, *three one thousand.* The momentum of his rush rolled Andy over the agent and onto the floorboards. He clambered up to regain his feet, not knowing what to expect. The Chinese man lay silent, staring out of unseeing eyes.

As Andy scampered over on his hands and knees to check on Remmey, the rear door banged open. There was the ominous click of a gun hammer drawn back, and he cringed in trepidation and fear as he felt a cold steel muzzle pressed to the back of his head.

It felt like an eternity before he heard, "Put the gun away, Pete! Put the damn thing away!" A gruff command rasped from an exhausted

Remmey. "Andy's a friend. About time you two showed up. Where the hell you been?"

As the iciness against Andy's neck fell away, the chilling terror dissipated from his spine. He let out a sigh of relief as he heard the lowering of the hammer into its cradle.

"The new honcho pulled us off and put us on another job. We told him you were waiting for us," Pete explained. "We got here as fast as we could."

"What do you mean he pulled you? You report to me, not him," growled Remmey. "I could have gotten creamed in here if I hadn't commandeered Andy."

"I'm afraid you're going to have to discuss that with that new honcho; we're just the worker bees."

"OK, Pete, not your fault. There's another one of these guys down in the laundry room," Remmey informed him. "And one schmuck over in the corner and another at the table. Check on them."

"This character's got a broken vertebra!" Pete exclaimed, checking the man in the corner.

"Yeah, had to snap his neck; the serum was taking too long. And Mister Atlas here," he said, pointing to the man lying beside him on the floor, "was ready to jump me."

Andy looked over at the dead man with the broken neck and, for the first time, noticed the length of lead pipe lying on the floor with tape wrapped around one end for a handgrip. Although he had never seen the man before, he knew the corpse was Koji. If, as they suspected, Koji had killed Peggy, the punishment meted out did not seem sufficient to atone for her brutal murder. Koji would never again bludgeon another woman.

"The one by you has a dart stuck in his neck. Our instructions were to only shoot them in the ass," Pete commented in a critical tone.

"Tough!" snapped Remmey. "He got exactly what he deserved."

"The skinny fellow by the table is breathing but needs medical treatment, pronto."

A different voice from the adjoining room called, "The big slob in here is still out. I've cuffed him. He'll be coming around soon. Need to give him a hypodermic before he wakes up."

Andy had listened to the northeastern accent before, and he turned to see the same Japanese man who had appeared at the fishing shack. "You work with Remmey.... He sent you to the koya...."

"Good to see you too, Anderson. You seem to be mixed up in all sorts of crap, don't you? You must be bored." He stooped down, pulled the dart from the dead man's neck, and moved over to the outside doorway.

The solemn expression on Andy's face communicated his emotion as he stared at the man he had just killed.

"You did what was necessary. Without your help, I'd have blown this operation." Remmey paused. "The lab boys sure fed us incomplete information on the use of those tranquilizers; they took way too long to work." He reached out his hand. "Here, give me a hand up." Staggering to his feet, he said to his cohorts, "OK, clean up these vermin. Load the ones who are breathing into the truck and I'll take them in. Call in a crew to clean up the place, and leave no evidence the Chinese or we were here. If you have to, burn the place down. Move Andy to a hotel for tonight and provide transport for him to his squadron early tomorrow morning.

"Andy, you can never tell anyone about this operation, understand?"

Andy nodded.

"Right now, it's imperative I take the two live ones in for interrogation. I'll catch up with you as soon as I can and go over everything." Remmey placed his hand on Andy's shoulder. "You're a great pal, Andy; thanks for saving my skin." Then he walked out the door, leaving Andy with a thousand new questions, all unanswered.

***

CHAPTER NINETEEN
Tranquility and Surprise

The war in Korea languished on, men fought and died, and the peace talks stalled. The constant need of replacement and maintenance of aircraft continued. As boring as Andy felt his job was, it was a never-ending task. The routine continued: work six days, a day off; work six days, a day off. One of the non-duty days found Butler, Mel, and Andy all free at the same time. They had gotten together and gone to the chow hall and the Post Exchange.

Walking back from the PX to the barracks, Andy spotted Sergeant Jones's car. An attractive lady waited in the front passenger seat of the Ford. A little girl, about five, fidgeted and jumped around on the backseat. The little child spied them and screamed at the top of her lungs, "Uncle Oren! Hello, Uncle Oren! Over here, over here!"

She waved frantically to ensure he'd see her. Oren strolled over to the car, leaned his head in the front passenger's side window, and gave the woman a kiss on the cheek. The little girl jumped up and down on the seat. "What 'bout me?" She leaned out the window and threw her arms around his neck, giving him a big hug and a wet, sloppy smooch. Mel and Andy stood and stared stupefied at the scene.

Butler smiled at their look of amazement. "Guys, this is Carol Sue, Billy's—rather, Sergeant Jones's—wife, and this cute little lady is their daughter, Betsy." He reached through the open rear car window and gave her a big squeeze.

They had never met Sergeant Jones's wife, which was not strange. There are distinct worlds on a military installation, and among them are family housing residence and those of the barracks compound. The communities are adjoining, yet the populations seldom meet.

Then little Betsy exclaimed, "Oh, Uncle Oren, you funny."

"In case you're wondering about the familiarity, Carol Sue is my cousin."

She responded to this with a sweet smile and said to Butler, "You're coming to dinner on Sunday. We won't take no for an answer. Sunday, church, mass, and dinner, don't y'all forget."

"I'll remember, and I'll be there, promise. By the way, Carol Sue, this is Andy and Mel, friends of mine."

She smiled at them. "Pleased to make y'all's acquaintance, gentlemen."

As they continued their slow, meandering walk back to the barracks, Oren explained that after the war, Sergeant Jones had come to South Carolina. At a Butler family gathering, he'd introduced Billy to Carol Sue. The two of them had connected and begun dating. Six months after they'd met, they married.

Andy thought, *That explains a great deal. So, Butler and the first sergeant aren't just friends ... they're family.*

***

The days of midwinter were brisk and cool, and the nights cold and chilly. Andy looked forward in anticipation to spending the weekends with Yoriko. The last time he had spent any time with her had been the trip to Tokyo. He and Mel had gotten weekend passes and proposed the idea of the girls meeting them in Tokyo. After all, they had promised the girls a weekend out. Since both Sumiko and Yoriko were scheduled to work on Friday night, he arranged to meet them at the train station close to the Ginza at 0900 on Saturday morning.

They went to lunch at Peter's Restaurant, as promised, and then saw a movie at the Ernie Pyle Theater. The girls wanted to go to the American military movie theater, and which was fine with Andy, it was cheaper and the movies were in English. The movie shown that day was *The African Queen* with Bogart and Hepburn. Yoriko and Sumiko sat in awe and watched the film intently. Even after a big lunch, they ate popcorn until Andy thought they would surely burst. After the movie, the four of them strolled along the Ginza, and the girls gazed longingly into shop windows at dresses, gowns, and kimonos.

Late in the afternoon, they walked along the boulevard surrounding the Imperial Palace. Then they were off to Shinjuku for the evening, where, at a small Japanese restaurant, they dined on sashimi and sushi. Sumiko had not wanted to spend the night in Tokyo. She became adamant Mel take her home right after the evening meal.

That night, Andy took Yoriko to a small, inexpensive nightclub. They danced and partied until the midnight curfew. Arm in arm, the affectionate Yoriko cuddled against Andy as they strolled back to Shinjuku. They spent an amorous night at a quaint, comfortable Japanese hotel, enamored with each other.

Sunday afternoon, riding the train back to the base, they were mostly silent, each absorbed in their own thoughts. Andy sat holding Yoriko's hand. She had burrowed close to him and lay her head on his shoulder, her eyes closed. He gazed out the window, deep in thought, as the countryside slid by in a series of blurs. The little escapade to Tokyo had taken most of Andy's measly monthly pay, but the weekend jaunt away from the base and with Yoriko had been worth every yen he spent.

Monday morning, Andy caught up with Mel at the chow hall for breakfast. Speaking between mouthfuls of scrambled eggs and toast, he asked, "What was the deal? Why did Sumiko want to go home Saturday night?"

Mel, gulping his coffee, replied, "We had a difference of opinion, a falling out. You know I'm always out looking for a good time. She's not into doing that, so we parted company; still friends, just not going to go out together."

Andy's eyebrows rose. "Is that all that happened?"

"Nah," said Mel. "After I left Sumiko, I hooked up for the night with that cute babe from Chibi's."

***

Andy had been working double shifts with no days off for the last month, plus the lack of funds had effectively restricted him to the base and limited his going to town. Three weeks had passed since he had last set foot on the scrubbed floorboards of the Brass Rail. His luck had turned this weekend, and he had Friday night and all day Saturday off. Boarding the bus, he hustled to town after chow on Friday evening and slipped into the Brass Rail. As he ordered a beer, he looked around for Yoriko, wanting to surprise her. After three minutes, he gave up his search for the petite object of his hunt, and as one of the bar maids walk by, he stopped her. "Where's Yoriko?"

The waitress gave him a strangely terse reply. "She no working. Must go now. Have drinks to serve."

Andy scowled at her. "Will she be here tomorrow evening?"

"No" was the quick retort.

The following week he was off duty at 1700 hours on Sunday, but he had to be back on duty by 1600 on Monday. Using these free hours, he went back to the bar in search of either of the two girls. He spotted Sumiko when he walked in; she was running the till. In reality, it wasn't a cash register but a cash box where she made change and collected money from the barmaids. "Yoriko went to her parents' house. I don't know when she will be back" was the answer she gave Andy. Then she excused herself, saying it was a busy evening and she had to get back to work.

A month had passed since that conversation, and every time he had spoken to Sumiko about Yoriko, the answer was always "I don't know; too busy to talk now" or some other excuse.

Determined to find out what was going on, one evening, Andy went to the bar and firmly but gently grasped Sumiko by the arm. "Even if I have to revert back to the old 'I'll buy a bottle of champagne' guise, we are going to sit down, and this time you are going to answer my questions. Where is Yoriko?"

Sumiko sighed, waved her hand for Andy to follow her, and led him over to a secluded table in the far corner of the room. "Sit." She pointed to the chairs at the table. Andy pulled out a chair and dejectedly plopped down; he vigilantly studied Sumiko's face as she sat in the chair beside him.

She took Andy's hands in hers and squeezed them. "Yoriko must go home. Her father sent her brothers to get her, take her home."

"Is something wrong … someone sick…? Is she sick…? When is she coming back?"

"She isn't...." There was a long pause. "She now married ... three weeks ago. Her father make a marriage for her. It is done; she is married, and she will never be back."

Andy was flabbergasted at the news. He stuttered, "Ma-ma-make a marriage? You mean an arranged marriage? I thought that only happened in stories ... archaic! Couldn't she have refused?"

"Remember, Andy, Japan is an ancient civilization. Our customs go back many centuries. It is difficult for a Westerner to understand our customs, just as it is difficult for us to understand Western customs. Her father arranged the marriage, and she had no choice. She had to obey." She hesitated. "Yoriko get married to an older man, a wealthy landowner. He will take care of her."

Andy lowered his eyes, staring at the floor, and said nothing as he shook his head in disbelief. "Why didn't you tell me this before, when I first asked you where she was?"

Sumiko said in a sympathetic voice, "I thought you might do something stupid, go to her father's home and try stop marriage. If you had done this, you would have brought unbearable shame upon Yoriko and her family. I could not ... could not chance that happening, and I could not tell you."

Andy looked so dejected that she wanted to comfort him, but all she could do was whisper, "You don't have to understand our customs, only accept them."

"Did Yoriko have an idea that this might happen? That her father was going to arrange this type of marriage?"

"Perhaps she did; not sure," answered Sumiko.

"Did she know about this marriage when we went to Tokyo for the weekend?"

Sumiko only shrugged her shoulders and looked away.

Andy sat mutely in the chair, exasperated, struggling to fathom what she had just told him. As incomprehensible as it was to him, he knew he had to accept the facts.

Over the following weeks the days were filled with work, and the evenings were empty. Then Mel suggested that Andy needed to do something to get his mind off Yoriko. Andy agreed it was time to focus on the future and get his mind off past events. When he happened to get a day off, Andy tried to soak up some of the local culture by going on trips to parks, shrines, and temples. He found sightseeing trips were more enjoyable when he had a companion, so he cajoled Sumiko into joining him on the excursions, on a purely platonic basis. He had the experience of going to his first sumo wrestling match. Then he turned the tables 180 degrees and attended a kabuki theater presentation, which he found interesting and even enjoyed. However, there was an emptiness that lingered with him, and he wondered if the feeling would ever dissipate.

***

CHAPTER TWENTY
Return

The news came that the North Koreans might release some of the Allied prisoners of war. In April 1953, Operation Little Switch, the return of sick and critically ill American POWs from North Korea, swung into high gear. The medical air evacuation planes began arriving at the base, transporting sick and injured American prisoners of war to the base's medical facilities for treatment.

The hospital had asked for volunteers to help and to serve as general grunt labor in providing support for the operation. A gnawing feeling in Andy's gut told him that he needed to participate. What difference did it make if he emptied bedpans or cleaned up crap? He needed to contribute. Volunteering was something he wanted to do; he needed to be part of the group of men on the flight line when the POWs arrived. He asked Sergeant Bowman for permission to go, and after receiving the sarge's OK, he found someone else to take over his normal duties for the day.

He was assigned to the job of backup litter bearer, which, in essence, meant he would do anything they needed. He was filling in for some medics while they were taking a break, carrying the released POWs on stretchers between the hospital plane and the ambulances. The task was humbling; these injured men had given so much. He felt that helping was a gratifying experience, even if it was physical labor. For the first time since Andy had enlisted in the military, he finally felt he had contributed something. At last he was helping, doing his part for the Korean War effort.

After assisting in placing a young soldier into an ambulance, Andy walked back toward the medevac plane. The kid looked extremely young and had probably lied about his age to enlist in the Army. Andy thought he wasn't more than seventeen, and now he was an amputee: the kid had had his leg amputated while he'd been interned in a POW camp. Besides having lost a limb, the young man suffered from acute malnutrition.

The ambulance sirens blared as it sped off, rushing the unfortunate soldier to the hospital. Andy was deep in thought about how unlucky these men were to have been sent to Korea and how fortunate he had been to have been in Japan all the time. Staring straight ahead, his concentration was fixed on the medevac plane as he avoided looking at the frail bodies that lay so helpless on the stretchers.

As he passed alongside one of the litters, a frail arm reached out. A thin, gnarly hand scrabbled toward him and snatched at his sleeve. "Andy."

It was so soft that at first he thought he had imagined his name being spoken, and he literally froze in his tracks.

The strained voice forced out, "Andy," a second time.

Overcoming the initial shock, Andy started backpedaling. Shuffling backward to stay even with the stretcher, he peered down to find out who had spoken to him.

Intently he searched a pallid, emaciated face for a clue to the man's identity. Hollow, deep-set eyes looked up at him, and within their depths he found his answer. He stared down at the stretcher in disbelief, not wanting to accept whom he saw.

"Remmey? Remmey! You, you're.... What happened? How?"

Remmey mouthed, "Wrong place, wrong time."

Andy's mouth gaped open in shock, and he mumbled, "What...?"

The two GIs carrying the litter stopped walking to give Andy an opportunity to speak with the shattered returnee. But when they came to a standstill, the gruff-looking master sergeant in charge came over. "Keep the line moving. We need to get everyone off the plane as fast as possible." The old sergeant regarded Andy and said in an understanding voice, "You can visit your buddy at the hospital later, son."

Andy nodded his acknowledgment.

As he turned and started to move away, he said, "Remmey, I'll be over to see you tonight as early as I can, I promise."

Having only enough strength left for a slight movement of his hand, Remmey raised his fingers an inch or two, and his arm fell clumsily down on the stretcher. They carried him toward the medical conveyance, and Andy hustled back to the plane and his task, his thoughts a blur, wondering what torment his comrade had suffered in North Korea.

When he was released from duty that evening, Andy rushed to the barracks, showered, and went right to the hospital, forgoing the evening meal at the chow hall. Remmey was the priority; his stomach could wait. He would grab something to eat at the snack bar later.

As he hurried into the hospital that evening, questions flooded his mind along with concern for his friend's well-being. "Sorry," said the medic at the front desk. "They're not allowing the POWs to have visitors tonight. Why don't you come back tomorrow?"

Disappointed, and knowing that arguing or pleading was futile, Andy headed for the barracks. The questions he had so prudently formulated to ask his friend remained unasked and unanswered.

Mel, who'd hung around in the barracks by his cubicle, asked Andy as he walked in, "Where you been? I've been waiting for you to find out how the day went helping out with the medical detail."

"Been over to the hospital; went to visit a guy, a released POW I know. He came in on the plane. I had no idea the guy was even in Korea, let alone had been captured. He looked like hell; they must have done terrible stuff ... torture. He used to be muscular and robust, and now he looks.... But I couldn't get in. They wouldn't let me see him tonight."

A couple of airmen who were playing craps by one of the bunks had stopped to eavesdrop on the conversation. Andy didn't want them to hear what he had to say, so he poked Mel. "Let's get out of here. I need to get something to eat, and I'll tell you what happened."

It was too late to go into town, so instead they hiked down to the enlisted men's club. Andy needed to relax, unburden, and vocalize to someone about what had transpired during the day. Mel, by virtue of just being there, was elected as the sounding board. As they walked toward the club, Andy began relating the physical condition of his friend. The club wasn't very busy, fifteen or so guys lounging around. After ordering a sandwich and a couple of brews, they found an acceptable table and sat down.

Andy took a couple of quick swallows of the cool liquid and then began filling Mel in on the rest of the details. He recounted how he had met Remmey on the boat and why they had paired up. He ended the story by saying he hadn't seen Remmey after leaving the boat. He omitted the parts about seeing Remmey in the Army Jeep as a second lieutenant and their having reconnected in Japan during the encounter with the Chinese agents.

Listening to Andy, Mel had leaned forward and placed both of his elbows on the table, and he now asked, "What happened after you docked in Yokohama?"

"Nothing," Andy said. "Until I saw him today." *Little white lies don't hurt anyone, I hope.*

He took a swallow of the American beer he had gotten, noting that the brew didn't have quite the same zing and taste the Japanese beer did. *Wonder if I'm going native? Oh, what the hell difference does it make?*

They stayed at the club until it closed at 2300 hours and then strolled back to the barracks. The clear night air refreshed Andy, and getting all the pent-up emotions off his chest had helped. It had been a tiring day, and he had needed to unwind. The physical condition of the POWs had impacted him more than he wanted to admit. When at last he climbed in the sack, he had trouble dropping off to sleep.

He rose early, and instantaneously the unanswered questions from the night before began whirling around in his mind. What treatment had his friend been subjected to during his confinement in the North Korean prisoner-of-war camp? Haunting images of what the man might have endured flashed in Andy's brain all day. After work, he went to chow and then to the barracks, took a shower, and headed out to the hospital.

As he approached the front desk, he noticed the corpsman on duty was a different medic than the night before. "How you doing?" Andy asked. "I'd like to visit one of the POWs. A friend of mine, a guy named Remmey."

The medic didn't say anything as he began thumbing through the patient locator files. "How do you spell the name again?" he asked without glancing up.

"R-e-m-m-e-y," Andy told him.

The corpsman pored through the files once more. The old master sergeant who had been in charge of the detail yesterday came out of his office and walked over toward the admissions desk. As he approached, he recognized Andy. "Thanks for the help yesterday; you're...?"

"Anderson," Andy replied.

"Anderson, we appreciated you volunteering to give us a hand. By the way, did you get to see your friend?"

"No, not yet, Sarge. I'm trying to it do now."

The sergeant leaned over the shoulder of the corpsman and checked the patient list. "What's his name?"

"Remmey."

The corpsman glanced at the sergeant. "I don't find anyone by that name. Sure the spelling's right?"

Andy spelled the name for him again, knowing it was right. *I stared at the nametag sewn on Remmey's fatigues for fourteen days onboard the troopship; I ought to know how it's spelled.*

The master sergeant picked up a clipboard and read a message fastened at the top. He lifted his eyes off the board and glanced at Andy, pulled the note off the board, stared at it again. "Go over and take a seat for a minute. I'll be right back." He disappeared for five minutes or so, returned, and motioned to Andy to remain seated. "Lieutenant Smith will be out here to talk with you in a couple of minutes."

All types of scenarios pounded around in his head—*Remmey is in a coma, he's unable to speak, or he's in the operating room, or he died during the night.* Gloomy thoughts rushed around and threatened to overwhelm him as he waited.

The door of one of the wards opened, and a nurse, a stunningly beautiful angel of mercy with luminous red hair, walked out. Her fresh, dazzlingly white starched uniform completed the heavenly aura. *If I were sick, she would be the Florence Nightingale I'd long for to nurse me back to health.*

"Anderson?" Her voice floated over him like a summer's mist blanketing a lush, green meadow. He almost forgot why he was there.

Smitten, he wanted to ask her out on a date. *Alas, she's an officer, and I'm only an enlisted man, and ne'er shall the twain meet.* He stood. "Yes, ma'am."

"Your friend—they transferred him to another hospital. Before he left, he dictated this note to me. In his present physical condition, he could not hold a pencil and write it himself. He said you would be asking for him as Remmey; that's a different name than we had him listed. He was insistent you receive his message. I made him a promise that I would deliver it to you in person."

She handed him the note. He took the folded sheet of paper from the unsealed envelope and read.

Andy,

I wanted to talk with you and I was looking forward to having a long conversation with you. Sorry we didn't have the opportunity to catch up on all that has transpired in our lives these past months. After my ordeal in the POW camp, my spirits lifted when I saw your homey country-boy face. I needed to see the face of a friend. I hope not all the cow manure has scraped off your boots. I need to think some of that country sociability remains, because that's what I admire about you.

All the stories and yarns you told me about growing up on the farm in eastern Colorado helped me keep my sanity during my internment in North Korea. In my thoughts I retreated in time and space, reliving some of the zany stunts we pulled onboard the ship and recalling your childhood. I lived with you through the story you told me about when you were twelve or thirteen. You and a friend sat under a tree by a creek and smoked handmade cigarettes with dried corn silk substituted for the tobacco.

If life became rough and the pain of physical suffering became unbearable, I learned to transport myself mentally to a better place. The places and events of your childhood fascinated my imagination and drew me in. I sat on that creek bank and listened to the rippling of the water. I fished and smoked, and sometimes you were there, and we talked. The shade of the big old cottonwood cooled me, and I slept. When I was cold, I visualized a golden sun as it filtered through the green leaves and imagined the heat of the sun's rays as it warmed my chilled bones.

They never broke me, Andy, and that was because of you and your farm boy stories. One day, you and I will sit on that creek bank under the tree and smoke a cigarette. I don't know if I can handle corn silk, but I can do a Lucky or a Camel. The happy times are what you remember and from which you gather strength when everything is bleak and dark.

I'm sorry I could not be completely honest with you about my past and apologize for the deception. When the time is right and I'm able, I promise I'll contact you. You're a great friend. Take care of yourself.

Remmey

Andy read the note twice, and the number of questions he had increased. "Lieutenant, where did they send him, what hospital?"

"I don't know. All I can tell you is an ambulance with a security escort came for him and another POW returnee early this morning. They transported them to Haneda Air Base in Tokyo for medical air evacuation to the States. I don't have any other information. Sorry."

She turned and started to leave. Then she swung around and stood facing him. "Andy—I hope you don't mind me calling you Andy. I realize it's not proper military procedure, but that's how he referred to you and how I think of you. I wouldn't worry too much about your friend's health. I'm sure in time he's going to get better and be all right." With a smile so bright and warm it could melt the snow of a Colorado blizzard, she turned around and left him standing there.

He stood silent and still for a few seconds. The questioning look he shot at the corpsman seated behind the desk must have shown how perturbed he felt.

The young corpsman quietly complained, "That's usually the way it is with the OSS or CIA spooks, whatever you want to call them.

Those counterintelligence guys breeze in here, and the doctors patch them up and stabilize their condition. Next thing you know, they're whisked out of here all hush-hush and secret-like. Their paperwork goes with them. Their identification is always false, as though they'd never existed, never been here."

Andy said nothing in reply to the medic, only shrugged his shoulders.

"Tough luck that you didn't get a chance to see your buddy." The corpsman hesitated. Then he asked, "How come you know a CIA guy, anyhow?"

Andy resisted the urge to blurt out, *None of your damn business. Maybe he's CIA, maybe not. All I know is he is simply Remmey to me, a plain, ordinary guy from Chicago. A person I met coming over on the ship, a good friend who has returned from an incarceration in Hell.*

Andy fought to control his annoyance at the questions asked by the guy at the desk. *I'm concerned about his physical condition; his vocation has nothing to do with my frustration about his well-being.* Andy had to take several deep breaths and count to ten a couple of times before he regained his composure. The corpsman, by telling him there were CIA personnel in the hospital, had already told Andy more than he should have revealed.

"Thanks for the help," Andy said. Then he jammed the note into his pocket, shoved open the door, and walked out into the emptiness of night.

CHAPTER TWENTY-ONE
Skepticism and Reward

Toward midmorning, Butler was in the process of wrapping up the daily aircraft maintenance report. In an adjoining room, the recently arrived assistant production control officer, Second Lieutenant Creigmeyer, arose from his desk chair and went to the open door. The doorway opened into the office where the bulk of the enlisted men had their desks and workstations.

He stood there a few seconds, looking out upon those he felt were his minions. "Have you finally compiled the figures yet, Butler?" he said loud enough for everyone to hear him question Butler's competency.

"They'll be ready for the lieutenant's review before noon," Butler answered. Then, in a caustic tone, he added, "Sir."

"They'd better be, Butler, and they'd best be correct and not sloppy." Creigmeyer turned around, and as he went into his office, he spat out in a demeaning tone, "I'm never certain what to expect from a deadbeat like you. How the hell you were ever an officer is beyond my understanding." He gloated inwardly; he had made his point and accomplished his intention of embarrassing and discrediting Butler in front of the enlisted men. He slammed the door closed behind him to emphasize his disfavor.

The lieutenant, a ninety-day wonder fresh from college and OCS, hadn't a clue how to conduct himself as an officer, gentleman, or even decent human being.

With the heat of bitterness burning deep in his gut, Butler fumed, *You've no right to insult me, you snot-nosed SOB. I've never given you incorrect or shoddy information. You don't need the statistics until 1500, and that should give even you more than enough time to look at them before they're due.* He shrugged off the cloak of resentment toward the young second lieutenant and concentrated on the paper. He had already completed the analysis and just needed to check the figures again for any possible errors.

Engrossed in finishing the work, a few moments passed before he sensed a presence standing by his desk, staring at him; he glanced up and saw Sergeant Bowman.

"You got time for a quick cup of Joe?" asked the sarge.

"Sure, I could use some right now, or maybe even something stronger." He glared at the lieutenant's closed door.

As they walked across the hangar and entered the break room, neither spoke. Each drew a cup of coffee from the battered, stained aluminum urn. The coffee was dark and bitter. Sergeant Bowman laced his with cream and sugar and stood stirring the unsavory beverage with a wooden swizzle stick. Butler, who drank his black, finished topping off his chipped, discolored mug with the dark sludge. The small break room was crowded, and when they finally spotted an empty table, they went over and sat down.

"Been having any problems lately? I mean, with your, ah, bad memories?" Sergeant Bowman asked hesitantly. "I hope you don't mind me asking. Just curious how you're holding up."

"No," replied Butler. "I don't mind at all. The flashbacks are not a concern; once in a while the nightmares still bother me, but they're getting less frequent." He sensed the sarge had something else on his mind. "You ever have any difficulty, any problems with bad memories, Bowman?"

"Not really. In the past it wasn't a problem. But when I start to get stressed now ... I'm starting to. Once in a while, I relive some incidents from Saipan—rough there, lost good friends." The sarge hesitated. "For the most part, I'm OK. When I do, what I recall materializes quickly, painfully. Not physical pain; we were raised to control our emotions, to suck it up, be men. We don't talk about what's ... kind of needed once in a while ... best I can describe it as mental…. Hard to describe the emotions and put them into words. Is it like that for you? The memory pops out of nowhere and confronts you?"

Knowing the unpleasant sensations and how reluctant one was to admit the problem, Butler said, "Sometimes it helps if you have someone you're comfortable talking to; a person you can trust will keep your confidences. Having Billy—Sergeant Jones—around helped me a lot. He lived through most of the experiences with me and can understand."

The sarge nodded.

Butler then added, "You ever talk to anyone?"

Sergeant Bowman stared at his coffee, stirred the wooden swizzle around, and answered, "A couple of guys at HQ were on Guadalcanal and the Marshalls. I met them after I arrived in Japan. We gather for a beer once in a while and talk. For the most part, our discussions are about broads and booze and such, not so much on what happened or how we feel."

"If you need, I'm around," said Butler. "And I'm sure Billy will sit down and have a beer with you. He's a good listener; give him a try, why don't you? No one will give a second thought about you talking to our first sergeant, and nothing would be more natural."

The sarge nodded in agreement.

Butler continued, "Difficult to admit you need to confide in another person, and to find someone you trust is essential. Billy saw a lot of action, more than you can imagine. After the fighting was over in Europe, they transferred him to Okinawa. I believe he was there the same time you were."

"I didn't realize Jones had been on Okinawa. Been meaning to talk to … to ask you, Butler, did you do something to tick off the new lieutenant, the assistant maintenance officer? He's sure on your case a lot. He seems to enjoy badgering you."

"Nah, he found out I was once a captain, and I think he gets his cookies off by giving me a hard time because I'm now an enlisted man. He's young, feeling his oats; it's a kick being able to give people orders. Perhaps the thrill is in bossing me around. Hopefully, he'll learn someday it takes more than shiny gold bars on his shoulder to lead men. Better he rides my back than jump on the young guys like Andy and Mel."

"I've mentioned … discreetly … I've tried to talk to him about the need to develop leadership skills once. Got me nowhere except for an ass chewing. Tell me if it gets too bad and I'll try talking to him again. But I can't guarantee you any positive results."

"That's OK, Sarge. I can handle the problem. Appreciate you trying to help," said Butler.

They finished their coffee, rinsed out their cups, and walked back over to the production control office. Butler rechecked his calculations one last time, found no errors, and took the document to Lieutenant Creigmeyer.

"Here is the completed tally of the figures, Lieutenant," he said.

"About time, Butler; you took long enough," snarled Creigmeyer.

"Yes, sir," Butler mumbled as he spun on his heels and exited. He glimpsed the clock on the opposite wall—1115 hours. He shook his head and wondered what Creigmeyer expected from him.

***

The Call

A few weeks later, at 0830, they were settling down to their duties when Sergeant Bowman walked over to where Butler sat and tapped him on the shoulder. "I received a call from the orderly room, and you're wanted by the wing commander. Now!"

A bewildered Butler looked at the sarge. "Wing commander? Why?"

"They didn't give me an explanation and I didn't ask. They just said go. So move it."

"OK!" answered a confused Butler. "I'm on my way. Can't think of any reason they'd call me upstairs. I guess I'll find out when I report to the colonel."

"Butler, wait!" The sarge pointed to Andy, who had been standing a few feet away from them. "Anderson, commandeer a vehicle and give Butler a ride up to headquarters. Don't wait for him; I want your butt back here pronto."

During the ride to headquarters, Butler spoke little as he sat deep in thought, wondering what the wing commander wanted.

When the weapons carrier screeched to a stop outside the HQ front door, Butler jumped out. "Thanks for the lift, Andy; if I need a ride back, I'll give you a call."

"OK." Andy stepped on the gas pedal and swung the small truck out onto the street.

Butler entered the wing commander's office; an American civilian female secretary glanced up at him. "What can I do for you, Sergeant?"

"I'm Sergeant Butler; the wing commander wanted to see me."

"Oh, yes. Take a seat and I'll inform him you're here." She nodded to the vacant chairs on the far side of the room.

Butler strode over and sat down. He'd seen the captain in an adjacent office watching him. Must be the colonel's aide. *Wonder what the deal is and why I'm here,* thought Butler.

He sat on the gray metal chair for fifteen minutes before the secretary said, "Sergeant Butler, the colonel will see you now." She nodded toward the commander's door and resumed her typing without saying another word.

When Butler knocked, a gruff, unpleasant voice from the other side of the richly paneled door rumbled, "Enter."

Butler opened the door, approached the colonel's desk, snapped to attention, and gave a smart salute. "Staff Sergeant Butler reporting as ordered, sir."

The colonel returned his salute and grumbled, "At ease." He returned his attention to the file in front of him. "You're wondering why I've called you to my office." He tapped his finger on the folder atop the desk. "A communiqué from the State Department, via the Pentagon." The colonel stopped talking and studied Butler. "It seems the French government is going to be honoring you. They are giving you the French Legion of Merit for services with the French Resistance during World War II." He read, "Your presence is requested at the French Embassy in Tokyo two weeks from today, when you will be presented with the award."

The air went out of Butler's lungs. *French Legion of Merit?* He took a deep breath in.

The wing CO kept staring at the documents in from of him, continuing, "All this says is the commendation is for outstanding services while attached to the French Military Delegation in London. What did you do during the war, some plush job in England with the

French? Dining out, eating escargot, drinking fine wine, hobnobbing with the brass? You must be friends with a high official in the French government; they sure pulled some strings."

Why the negative crap, Colonel? What's in the folder you're reading? I recognized you when I first walked in. Older, hair is gray, you were a major then. I did not intend to mention that I remembered you, but you're starting to piss me off, and I'll be damned if I'm going to let you impugn my character. "Wasn't a plush job the night outside of Marseilles when we plucked you out of that barnyard." Then he added with emphasis, "The German patrol had found your downed P-38 fighter and were breathing down your neck just as we reached you ... sir." The word came forth with razor sharpness.

The colonel's expression froze; he squinted, unblinking as he scrutinized Butler's face. "Who the hell are you? How do you know about that?" He abruptly stood up and peered at Butler across the desk for more than a few seconds. In disbelief, he whispered, "I'll be damned. I'll be damned. How could I have failed to recognize you? I thought I would always remember your face, bearded or not. 'Le Rebelle.' I always believed you were a French patriot. I didn't realize you were an American. The word was you'd been captured and executed by the Germans! You are The Rebel, are you not?"

Butler had not heard that name in years. Only those inside the French Resistance or those helped by the resistance called him by the code name Le Rebelle. Butler did not verbally respond to the colonel, only nodded his affirmative.

The wing CO sat down hard in his chair, fixed his eyes on Butler, and didn't say anything. He just kept staring. Then he leaned forward on his elbows, looked Butler in the eyes, and spoke with the utmost sincerity. "Your real identity was never revealed to us, none of us; those you rescued never figured out who you were. The military shrouded you in secrecy.... Le Rebelle's exploits with the French Resistance are legendary." The colonel took a deep breath, paused, and continued recalling the incident that happened years in the past. "I crawled into the sloppy muck of a pigsty and covered myself with mud and animal feces to conceal my location. My leg bone had been shattered in the crash. I couldn't walk and wasn't even able to stand. I lay there waiting, expecting death or capture. The German patrol was already searching the barnyard, probing all possible hiding places with their bayonets. They kept moving closer to me; I thought I was doomed. Like shadowy ghosts, you and your men appeared out of the darkness. You dragged me out from under all the pig shit, picked me up and carried me into the obscurity of the night, right under the eyes of the Germans." He paused, as if to recall the events. "You took me to the camp, bathed me, patched up my wounds, fed me, and nursed me back to health. When I had strength enough to travel, you smuggled me to England via your underground railroad. If it weren't for you and your band of men, I'd be dead."

He stood up. "I apologize for those remarks. Please forgive me. I glanced at the file and saw the letter from the State Department informing the DOD the French were giving you the French Legion of Merit, and the DOD-ordered reinstatement of rank. I only assumed political influence. I had no right to judge before I reviewed the facts. I'm sorry."

There was a moment of silence, and then the colonel spoke again. "I'd consider it a privilege to shake the hand of Le Rebelle."

Butler held out his hand, but instead of reaching across the desk, the colonel walked around and grabbed Butler's hand with both of his. He grasped it firmly and, in a nonmilitary moment, put his arms around Butler in a manly hug. "Indeed, a pleasure to meet you again, Le Rebelle—Major Butler."

At first, Butler couldn't comprehend what he had heard—*What did he just say? Something—he said something earlier about reinstatement of rank.* Thoughts about the French Legion of Merit and memories of the French Resistance had been racing through his mind vanished like a puff of dust. He tried to focus on what had been said, but the colonel returned to his desk and continued reading from the file. "Your inactive reserve status as captain is hereby changed to active reserves, promoted to the rank of major, and recalled to active duty on ... let's see...." He looked at the document. "The effective date was three days ago. So much for government efficiency. Welcome aboard, Major Butler."

Butler, in desperate need of clarification, tried to speak, but the colonel kept on talking. "The French also asked for you to serve as a US liaison officer with their military delegation in French Indochina. In addition, the Pentagon's requested we send a small contingent of men to French Indochina, or, as some call the country, Vietnam. The French have a few C-119s, and they've asked for our support in maintaining the aircraft. You'll go as a liaison and as the commander of the detachment. We've asked enlisted men to be volunteers for this mission. Under your command will be an adjutant, a lieutenant, twenty aircraft maintenance men, two administrative personnel, and a team of five security men."

The colonel finally took a breath, but he didn't give Butler a chance to ask questions as he continued, "A Lieutenant Creigmeyer—I believe he is in the same squadron you're currently assigned to—was suggested as the adjutant." The colonel looked at Butler. "Will he do? Or is he a problem?"

Without hesitation, Butler replied, "There could be a certain level of difficulty."

"The final OK on who you wish to take belongs to you. You're to be in Saigon in six weeks. Not a lot of time to mold a group together and get ready for embarkation. Your French counterpart—a Colonel Perrier Lafount—will meet you in Saigon."

"A good man," observed Butler.

"I assume, then, you've met him."

"He's one of the Free French patriots who helped carry you from the farm that night."

The colonel's eyes glazed, the hazy stare of a man remembering the past. "Major Butler, I'd like to get together with you at the Officer's Club for a drink and perhaps to discuss … what happened. I don't remember much. I was in and out of consciousness the first few days after my plane was shot down. I'd like to talk, if you don't mind. I've several questions I need answered…. I've only glanced at what little service information they sent on you. The document states you were medically forced out of the service after the war. Why…? Never mind, my questions can wait.

"Right now, I want you to get settled into the BOQ. We need to locate a proper uniform and insignia for you to wear. I … we'll talk later. Please speak with Sergeant McConnell; he'll assign someone to give you a hand in getting everything set up. We'll work out the other details tomorrow. If you require anything, call me."

All Butler could think to say was, "Yes, sir." He left the office full of pride, delight, and unanswered questions. He knew the French were having problems in Indochina and that the Vietnamese communist government wanted to overthrow the French colonization. *What did Perrier need him for? Why had the French requested him?*

Making the Adjustment

Sergeant McConnell arranged Butler's assignment to billets in the BOQ. A Jeep with a Japanese civilian driver was delegated to take him to pick up his clothing and personal belongings from the barracks. Everything was moving quickly; he needed to slow down and take stock of what had happened.

"May I use the telephone for a moment, Sergeant McConnell?" Butler asked. "I need to make a couple of calls."

"Please do so, Major," acknowledged the sergeant. "And I'm having a fatigue shirt with major insignia brought in for you."

Butler dialed a number. "Production Control Sergeant Bowman, sir," said a voice on the other end of the line.

"Sarge, this is Butler. Unexpected developments; not sure when I'm going to be down to the shop. You'll need to put someone else working on the reports."

"I've already taken care of those, Major. Congratulations."

"You know already? The speed of the grapevine never ceases to amaze me. Who else knows?"

"To my knowledge, no one except Sergeant Jones and me, the squadron CO, and, of course, those at Wing HQ. The word can get around fast if scuttlebutt is interesting. If you want me to try to keep the news quiet a while, I'll do the best I can."

"Yes, try to slow it down. I need to mull over some things. Give you a call in a couple of hours."

Butler dialed another number. He hesitated for a second and then said, "This is Sergeant Butler; may I speak with Sergeant Jones, please?"

"Just a moment," murmured an uninterested person.

"Billy, it's Oren. You heard?"

"Yes, congratulations on both the promotion and French Legion of Merit—long time in coming, and you deserve them, old friend. I'm not sure about the French Indochina bit. Nor do I think Anna Mae is going to be too happy about you not coming home next month, but things have a way of working out. Anything I can help you with right now? Anything you need?"

"No, I'll give you a call at your quarters tonight."

As Butler hung up, Sergeant McConnell came in with a shirt bearing major leaves on the collar.

Butler slipped out of the one with staff sergeant stripes and put on the one handed to him. That surge of pride and sense of rebirth flashed through him again.

The sergeant reached for the discarded garment, saying, "I'll take care of this for you."

"No, but thank you anyway," Butler insisted. "Those chevrons have a special meaning, and I'm going to keep them."

The rest of the afternoon was a whirlwind of paperwork, moving into new billets, and becoming used to the fact that he was an officer again. Butler was shown to his new temporary office and introduced to the administrative assistant who would be aiding him during the transition.

Lieutenant Creigmeyer's application was a concern. The chief maintenance officer had suggested Creigmeyer for the mission not because Creigmeyer was an astute, capable officer, but because he felt the assignment would be a learning experience for the lieutenant. Butler deduced that the maintenance officer just wanted the lieutenant out of his hair, and for good cause.

During the afternoon, Butler phoned the sarge and told him he'd be down at the hangar in the morning.

He lay in his BOQ room that night and remarked to himself how quiet the building seemed. There wasn't the endless hubbub, noise, and laughter of the barracks. The stillness and solitude was welcoming, but he felt alone. It was going to take getting used to.

At 0500 the next morning, Butler rolled out of the sack. After checking the time difference, he phoned Anna Mae.

When she answered the phone, she was bubbly and full of enthusiasm. "We have the house all ready for your return next month. We have parties planned and a big family reunion scheduled. Everyone's excited to have you here again."

Uh-oh! This news is going to burst her bubble. "Well, honey, I have some news. Yesterday, I met with the wing commander and...." He proudly explained the events that had occurred.

"This means you won't be coming home next month" was the first thing she said when he finished talking.

"I'm going to French Indochina, so I'm not going to be able to."

"Why—why can't you? I don't like the idea of you traipsing around in some jungle carrying a gun!" was her immediate, imploring plea.

He started to explain, but Anna Mae interrupted him, asking, "Did you ever think of saying no?"

He hesitated. *I hadn't even considered saying no; how could I? This is something I wanted and something I have to do.*

"They need me there," Butler replied.

"I need you here, at home."

"I have to—"

"You have to what?" she asked in a hurt tone.

"I have to prove to myself that the medics who cashiered me from the Army after the war were wrong. I am still medically and physically capable of holding down a command."

"This is just some male ego thing," she murmured, almost in tears. "The house is ready; we're just waiting for you to come home."

Her disappointment tore at his soul, and he tried to reassure her that they could still be together. "There are French dependents in Saigon. We could rent a villa and set up housekeeping, and I could be with you on the weekends."

"I've no desire to go to Indochina; I don't think I'd like it there. I'd be miserable worrying about you all the time. If I have to fret, I'd rather do it from here." Anna Mae sniffled. "Well, if the French are going to give you a medal, I'm going to be at the Embassy in Tokyo for the presentation."

"I don't know. I'm only going to be in Japan for a short time. You'll have made a long tr—"

"I don't care," she said. "I'll catch the first plane I can tomorrow, and my visitor's visa is still valid. See you in a few days. Tell Carol Sue I'm coming. Love you." She hung up before he could think of a rebuttal.

That's my wife, he thought, *an intelligent, gorgeous, and determined woman. I love her. She's a strong-willed individual and will not take no for an answer.*

At 0900, Butler walked into the hangar office. As he opened the door, those working inside looked up; when he closed the door behind him, most returned to their duties.

He walked into Sergeant Bowman's office, and the sarge began to stand as he entered.

"Sit down, Sarge—no formality between friends." He smiled. "Not in private, anyway. Is Creigmeyer in? Excuse me, I should have said Lieutenant Creigmeyer."

The sarge grinned at him, aware of the significance of the slip up. "Yes, sir, and once again congratulations on the promotion, Major."

"Thanks, Sarge. Coming from you, that means a great deal to me. You're a true friend. You've helped me over some rough spots and I won't forget it. Thanks."

"You're welcome. Lieutenant Creigmeyer yelled for you yesterday afternoon and this morning. He didn't like the way Airman Wright did the analysis report. He even telephoned HQ and asked why they wanted you up there. They refused to give him any information—made him even angrier. The man's in a nasty mood."

"I'll take care of it. He doesn't know, then?"

"Nope, not a clue." The sarge added, "Everybody else does, but not him."

"No sweat, Sarge." Butler grinned as he turned around and headed to Creigmeyer's office door. He knocked, and an arrogant voice answered, "Come in."

Creigmeyer was ogling the pictures in a dog-eared men's magazine. "What do you want?"

Butler, in a soft, low tone, responded, "I understand you've been asking for me. *Lieutenant.*"

Recognizing the voice and not looking up, Creigmeyer spit out, "Butler, where the hell have you been? The information I received yesterday was terrible. I should bring you and that Wright up on charges for being inefficient. What did the wing commander want you for anyway? Why didn't you ask my permission before you left?"

Then he finally glanced up. An outraged amazement distorted his facial features as he became aware of the oak leaves on Butler's collar.

"What the wing commander wanted me for is obvious. Do you think you should be reading a girlie magazine during duty hours? I don't believe it sets the right example for the young men. Put the magazine away." *He didn't realize how good the feeling would be to reprimand Creigmeyer; he really wanted to ream the SOB out.*

Creigmeyer's face flamed with anger and resentment as he sarcastically answered, "I don't think you set a stellar example either, being the barracks drunk!" As he spit out the words, the gold oak leaf clusters on Butler's collar caught the light and gleamed like a pair of bright headlights. Creigmeyer realized there might be consequences for his outburst and added, "Sir."

"Point taken, Lieutenant, but we are talking about you, not me. I understand you're considering going to French Indochina?"

"How do you know about that?" snapped Creigmeyer, his anger heightening the redness in his face.

"Because, Lieutenant, I'm assigned as the detachment commander, and if I select you as my adjutant, you'll be answering to me. How do you suspect you'd find such an arrangement? Weigh your options, Lieutenant. I need an answer within the next three days. You can reach me through the wing commander's office."

Butler started to leave, but then turned back. "A word of advice: I'd let Airman Wright become familiar with the reporting system. He is an intelligent, meticulous young man. Give him an opportunity to display his talents."

As the newly appointed major left the lieutenant's office, Andy stood blocking his way. *Strange,* Andy thought, *to see the officer's insignia pinned on Butler's collar, yet they look right; they fit him. Butler seems more natural sporting the major leaves than wearing stripes.* Andy stuck out his hand and said, "Congratulations."

Butler grasped the extended hand and whispered back, "You deserve credit for keeping me out of trouble," and he walked out the door.

***

CHAPTER TWENTY-TWO
June 18, 1953
1630 – Thursday

Andy was grateful he had only one more day of work and then two days off. The tempo at the hangar had been hectic, almost chaotic, the last few weeks. Getting off the base for the weekend, away from the rigors of military discipline and protocol, would be good. He needed a break. While driving the tug back to the shop pulling a load of aircraft supplies, he cruised down the flight line at a modest five miles per hour. At that leisurely pace, there was plenty of time to fantasize.

Memories of how he once had snuggled with Yoriko on Friday and Saturday nights penetrated his awareness. He felt a pang of a forbidden lover's pain as he envisioned the two of them sprawled contentedly on a futon in a secluded mountain inn. In his contrived illusion, he could smell the clean fragrant scent of her raven hair as it fanned across his torso. She would nestle next to him, her head resting on his chest. The softness of her body and the tenderness of her caresses were warm and affectionate, and they burrowed together under the warm blankets, uncaring about their surroundings, conscious only of each other.

The romanticized mental picture shattered, and the shards of the scene were replaced by an image of an old Japanese farmer roughly disrobing the small, delicate Yoriko, the woman he had grown so fond of. There was nothing he could do; she was married to another, and all he had now were the treasured memories of their times together. He missed her and only now was beginning to realize how much she had meant to him.

His attention was diverted back to reality by the rumble of engines as the noise penetrated his daydream. He stopped and watched as a C-124 Globemaster II lifted off from the ground and took flight into the afternoon sky.

Veering the tug off the tarmac, he swung over to the paint shop down a narrow paved access road between two hangars. He dropped off some lacquer, thinner, and aircraft fabric, turned around, and headed back to the hangar. It was his last run of the day, no need to hurry, so he let the little tractor idle along.

He at last pulled into the usual parking spot and shut off the motor. Then he noticed Mel frantically waving at him as he ran in Andy's direction. "The sarge wants everyone now," Mel puffed breathlessly.

"Why?"

"A 124 went down in a rice paddy just off the base; they need recovery and rescue people now! Let's go!"

"How bad?"

"Really bad; plane's buried in the mud they say!"

"One took off a few minutes ago. Wonder if it's that one."

"Don't know; Bowman said there is a six-by waitin' for us at the east door, and to get a move on."

Men were darting back and forth running around like scattered sheep, figuring out where they were supposed to be going. He tried to listen in on as many conversations as possible to pick up a little information about the crash here and there.

"All the troops on board are dead; everyone killed in the crash," one person said.

"Wasn't in a rice paddy but a melon field."

"The plane plowed in and was covered with dirt and mud."

"The C-124 was loaded with guys heading back to Korea from R and R."

They all piled into the truck, and when they arrived at the crash site, organized confusion reigned. Fire trucks, ambulances, doctors and medics, firefighters, and crash crews all performed their assigned tasks. The crash crews were moving in enormous amounts of heavy equipment. Other men milled around while those in charge shouted orders.

Many of the medics were the same ones Andy had worked with on the POW release. One of them grabbed Andy and told him to help. He did, completing each task given him as instructed without belaboring or thinking of the tragic aftermath he was dealing with. He didn't want to think; he just helped carry out the dead. Then he went back and helped pick up personal belongings. The scene was neither a sight nor an experience he wanted to remember. The total number of fatalities was 129 souls; all those aboard had perished in the accident, the largest loss of life in a single crash in military aviation history to date.

The next day, everyone was still talking about the terrible incident. Andy was deep in a discussion with a couple of mechanics about possible engine failure being the cause of the crash when Sergeant Bowman called him over. "Anderson, take the tug and trailers up to the end of the flight line where they're stacking items from the C-124 and help them haul the stuff to the containment hangar."

As he drove, he couldn't help but think of the carnage of the plane wreck and the haunting scene he had witnessed. He thought of the GIs who would never see home again. The sons who'd perished and would never again greet their parents. Husbands who'd never hold their wives or be around as their children grew to adulthood. All those young lives cut short by the horrific accident.

When he pulled in to the designated area, there were several trucks and trailers already in line. He asked the sergeant in charge what he wanted him to do. The sergeant gestured. "Pull in over there by the six-by and wait; I'll have a load for you in a minute."

Andy fixed his eyes forward along the hood line of the tug. They were all there to do a specific and solemn task; no need for conversation. He focused on the air cop handling traffic control, who motioned for him to pull up in line in front of the truck. Andy swung the tug and pulled in tight along the right-hand side of the deuce and a half. A big burly guy was slouched in the passenger's seat of the truck, looking in the opposite direction. Andy didn't give him a second glance as he maneuvered the tug and trailers, parked, and cut the engine. He sat alone, wrapped up in his thoughts for a few minutes, thinking of the people who had perished.

A sudden movement to his right startled him, and he caught a glimpse of a figure. Next to the rear of the tug stood the big kid from the six-by; it was Phil, with a paper coffee cup in one hand and a Thermos bottle in the other. At the same time Andy become aware of Phil, someone tapped him on his left shoulder, causing him to swivel around and stare into the familiar face of Skeeter.

"Hey, Andy, I didn't notice you until you moved in front of my truck." With his thumb, Skeeter motioned behind them.

"How you doing?" Andy said as he glad-handed Skeeter.

"Phil"—Skeeter pointed to the big man—"said since you were a friend and we had extra, we wondered if you'd like to have a cup of coffee while we're waiting."

Andy remarked, "I could use a cup." He turned to the big guy. "Thanks for thinking of me."

Phil handed Andy the paper cup and then unscrewed the Thermos and filled the cardboard receptacle with hot coffee.

"Thanks again, Phil."

Then Phil, with a slight whisper that only Andy could hear, said, "Welcome. You helped me out; least I could do," and walked back to the truck.

"Takes him a while to get to know people, be comfortable around them," Skeeter said. "He's a real thoughtful kid, and once you get to know him, he grows on you."

Andy didn't say anything about Phil's little problem in town. The guy must not have told Skeeter about the shellacking he had taken and that Andy had taken him to the hospital.

Skeeter sat down on the fender of the tractor, and they chewed the rag until Andy was called to proceed.

"They're telling me to move up now. Later, Skeeter." He turned far enough around so Phil was visible through the windshield of the truck and held up his hand. "Good coffee; I owe you one."

Phil waved back but didn't say anything.

Moving forward, Andy was directed toward a stack of pallets laden with equipment and some boxes filled with personal items, duffel bags, and suitcases. The sergeant in charge of the loading signaled for him to stop and motioned to the GI running the forklift, indicating which pallets he was to load. Andy glimpsed up at the lift jockey; his face was somber and grim. Andy nodded to him, and the guy lifted the boxes of personal belongings and stacked them on the trailers. With a responding nod, the forklift driver backed the lift away, giving Andy more than enough room to maneuver around him. Andy then recognized him. He was the same Neanderthal who'd tried to run him down in the hangar more than a year ago, only this time they were not rivals but had a common somber task to fulfill.

***

CHAPTER TWENTY-THREE
The French Embassy

Butler invited Mel and Andy to attend the awards ceremony at the French Embassy in Tokyo. Of course, they accepted; having never been in an embassy before, let alone a French one, Andy wasn't going to miss the opportunity.

Anna Mae had caught the first flight she could over to Japan. She was with her husband every minute possible, determined to spend as much time with him as she could until he left for French Indochina. The wing commander, with other top-ranking US officers, stood among the French and American diplomats. Anna Mae, Sergeant Jones, and his wife, Carol Sue, were there with Sergeant and Mrs. Bowman.

The pomp and circumstance that went with the awarding of the medal and the grandeur of the ceremony made an indelible impression on Andy. The memory of the day was one that would linger with him for the rest of his life. As he viewed the proceedings, he thought, *The French sure know how to put on a show.*

Afterward, at a private lunch in an upscale Tokyo restaurant, he mingled with the crowd of brass, embassy officials, and foreign dignitaries. He was a little uncomfortable at first, but the uneasy sensation disappeared and he had an astonishingly good time and met some nice people. The guest of honor might have been Butler, but Anna Mae and Carol Sue were the belles of the ball. Their sparkling personalities mesmerized the luncheon group. After the meal concluded, everyone went their separate ways, to the base or in whichever direction they needed to go.

He kept thinking of the events at the French Embassy, of the lavishness of the ceremony and the extravagance of the luncheon. The manner in which the participants and guests had dressed and conversed kept running through Andy's mind. *I enjoyed myself and could get accustomed to living in that style; a lot different than life on a farm. If I want this type of life, then I need to concentrate on my future. It's not going to be handed to me on a silver platter; I'll have to work and earn it.*

Andy did not have a great deal of contact with Butler over the next few weeks. The recently appointed major had the task of getting the group ready to leave for Indochina. Andy's routine duties kept him busy buzzing around on the tug, driving between the hangar and supply, picking up aircraft parts. Whether or not the episode at the French Embassy triggered it, he decided to enroll in the after-duty college education program.

Late one afternoon, there was a phone message from Anna Mae. She invited Andy and Mel to a small bon voyage dinner with Butler, Anna Mae, Sergeant Bowman and his wife, and Sergeant Jones and Carol Sue.

Two days later, they stood on the tarmac in front of base operations, watching the contingent of men finish loading their gear aboard an air transport C-54. One person was noticeably absent. Creigmeyer had wisely rescinded his request for consideration for the assignment in French Indochina.

During the hour they had been there, the wing commander had arrived and given his farewells and good wishes to Butler and his men. Other well-wishers had come and departed. On the ramp were only those who had personal reasons to wait until all the men had boarded the plane, except for Butler.

Anna Mae and Carol Sue stood apart from the men. Butler walked over to the two women and gave his cousin a hug. Then he turned and embraced his wife. They stood clinging to each other and then he kissed her, and they reluctantly released their hold. He turned and walked over toward the men.

The revving engines of the C-54 made it difficult for Andy to hear the conversations going on around him. Butler first stepped over to Mel, shook his hand, patted him on the back, and quietly said some departing message. Next, he grasped Sergeant Bowman's hand; they talked for a couple of minutes and then shook hands. Butler looked at Andy and smiled, walked over, and grabbed his hand. Andy detected the roughness of the scars left from his World War II injuries, but the man's grip felt like an iron vise. He didn't let go of the handshake as he put his left hand up on Andy's shoulder. With the noise of the engines roaring in the background, he leaned forward and spoke into the young man's ear. Andy strained to listen as Butler said, "You're a great kid; you've a bright future ahead if you take the right paths life will offer you. Just a suggestion, I think you would make a great officer. You might want to consider applying for OCS or an ROTC program."

Andy moved his head so he could look at Butler's expression as the man continued, "I've on occasion taken the wrong path, but as if by a guiding hand, I've found the correct way. If not for you ... I might not be standing here. For that, you have my undying gratitude. If you need help or if I can ever be of assistance, contact me. Keep in touch."

He let go of Andy's hand and moved over to Sergeant Jones, who was standing next to him. The two friends embraced each other. The pilot cut the C-54 engines to idling speed, and Andy overheard Jones say, "Good-bye, old friend.... Be careful ... you're on your own this time. I won't be around to cover your back. As soon as my tour of duty is over, I'm going to retire and go back to South Carolina with my family. I'll be there waiting for you when you're finished in Vietnam."

Sergeant Jones stepped back, stood at attention, and laid the sharpest salute Andy had ever seen on Major Butler, and they all instantly followed suit. The major snapped to and returned their salute, executed an about-face, and walked to the waiting plane. As he boarded he turned, waved a final good-bye, ducked his head, and entered the plane. They closed the hatch, and the C-54 taxied out to the runway. No one spoke as the plane sped down the runway, lifted off the ground, and took flight. The new major and the small contingent of men headed south to Southeast Asia and Saigon.

The group stood gazing at the sky until the C-54 vanished from view. Then they went back to the hangar, with little conversation passing between them.

After that day, Andy started following the news of the war in French Indochina, which he had previously ignored.

***

The rough, boisterous voice of Sergeant Bowman yelled from across the hangar, "Anderson!" The sarge was motioning Andy over to the office.

Oh crap, déjà vu. Now what?

Andy put down the rag he was cleaning the tug with and hustled on over to find out what was on the sarge's mind. "The first sergeant wants to see you when you have time. It's 1100 hours right now, so why don't you go to chow and stop by the orderly room on your way back?"

When Andy arrived at the orderly room it was noon, and the first sergeant was in his office. Anna Mae was with him. He signaled Andy to join them.

"I received word," Sergeant Jones said, "that Mama-san would like to see Anna Mae this afternoon. I can't go with her, as I have another obligation, and we were hoping that you would accompany her. I'm going to entrust you with my car to drive her down there. I'll square everything for you at the shop, so go change out of your fatigues and come right back."

Andy hustled off to the barracks at a gallop, went to his bunk, and changed into civvies. It was good to be able to wear civilian clothes off base now. He hurried back over to the orderly room; everyone had gone to lunch except for the CQ. Andy nodded to the guy who was watching the office during the lunch hour and went into the first sergeant's office.

Anna Mae was sitting there alone.

Seeing Andy's expression as he sought the whereabouts of the first sergeant, she said, "He had to leave. He was concerned there might not be enough gasoline in the car and went to the gas station. Sergeant Jones should be back in a minute."

Neither said anything for a few seconds. Then Anna Mae spoke up. "I greatly appreciate your escorting me down to Mama-san's. I'm not quite sure what she wants. I know Oren had some business dealings with her, but I'm not sure of the details. She was quite adamant that I come and see her before I return home tomorrow."

The woman's voice quavered as she spoke, and Andy fretted that she was going to tear up as her eyes were misty. He was about to offer her his handkerchief but stopped. He couldn't remember if he had stuck a clean one in his pocket or not, and he was imagining his embarrassment if he pulled out a dirty old snot rag.

She stopped talking, cleared her throat, and took a very delicate hanky from her purse and dabbed the tears that were forming in her eyes.

Is she going to cry? What do I do now? Come on, I need some help here. Andy asked her, "Would you like ... something to drink?"

"A glass of water would be perfect, thank you."

Andy popped up from his chair and walked out of the office, closing the door behind him, uttering a sigh of relief. The CQ thought he was expressing a different sentiment and said, "Good lookin' chick, ain't she?"

The comment took Andy by surprise, and he nodded. "You have any clean cups around here so I can get her a glass of water?"

"Yeah, water's in that tin pitcher over there." The CQ pointed. "And cups are by the coffee pot. What you see is all there is, Mac. You're gonna have to make do."

Selecting the cleanest of the chipped and stained coffee mugs, Andy filled the mug with water and went back into the office.

Fortunately, Anna Mae had regained her composure. "Thank you, Andy." She smiled as she took the cup from his hand and sipped the water. "I'm so sorry,..." She took a couple more sips. "That's enough," she said and put the cup down on the desk. She rewarded Andy with an enchanting smile. "Now, tell me a little more about yourself. I believe Oren told me that you're from a small town in Colorado."

"Yes, my folks have a farm outside a ... guess you could call it a town or village, more like a wide spot in the road."

"What made you join the Air Force, and what's in your future plans?"

At first, he hesitated. He didn't think his problems or what he wanted to do were of any interest to her, so he gave her the standard pitch. "Like thousands of other guys, I joined up because I was about to be drafted into the Army. I'm not sure what I'm going to do after my hitch is up." He stopped talking, but she looked at him in such a way that he couldn't help but trust her; perhaps she was interested in his future. "I'd like to go on to college, although I need to figure out the finances. If I can't work it out, then I'll go back to the farm." *Go back and toil on the land as did my father, grandfather, great-grandfather, and his father before that. My dad was the first of my family to ever graduate high school, and that might be as far as I'm going to go.*

For a few seconds, Andy waited for her to ask another question. *This might be an opportunity to have some of my questions answered.* "Perhaps it's none of my business, but how did Butler and Sergeant Jones meet?"

Hesitating briefly, Anna Mae smiled. "I don't think it is a secret, and I'm sure they won't mind if I told you. Oren was just out of college, which was in the spring of 1941, and as a newly commissioned second lieutenant, he was sent on assignment to England. He was assigned to an American-French liaison office because he is fluent in French, as you know. After the US declared war with Germany, Oren's next position was to command a platoon of men going to North Africa. This was when he met Billy, who was the platoon sergeant. Billy had been in the Army for a few years, and he'd been in Panama at the end of the Banana Wars and already had some combat experience. He and Oren became friends and developed a bond, a special kinship which grows stronger even today."

Andy interrupted, saying, "I understand they were together in North Africa." He hoped that by stating he had prior knowledge of the fact, it would elicit a detailed response. He then could fill in some of the blanks from his eavesdropping about Butler hauling Sergeant Jones across the desert.

"They don't talk much about the war except to each other," Anna Mae continued. "What I know is that from England, they went to Africa, where they both were wounded, Billy rather severely. Then they were sent back to England to a hospital to recuperate from their injuries. Billy was hospitalized for quite a time. Oren was reassigned to the French liaison office where he had worked before and then later sent to work with the French underground. I don't know exactly what happened in France, but the Germans somehow learned his name and had a picture of him. They placed a bounty on his head, but he managed to make his way safely back to England.

"Oren and Billy, they never tell us—Carol Sue or me—many of the details about what—" Just then, Sergeant Jones opened the office door.

"OK," Jones said. "It's time to go; my car's parked outside."

They cruised down the street and past the runway out to the front gate, where the guard on duty waved them through. *Sure is a lot easier driving through the base entrance in a car than taking the bus.* Andy pulled the Ford in along the street by the bar and parked by the fence. He walked around and opened the door for Anna Mae.

The gate was unlocked, and they walked up the groomed path and stopped at the back entrance. Mama-san, always vigilant, must have had someone on watch, and before Andy could knock, Sumiko opened the door. "Konnichiwa."

Andy bowed and replied, "Konnichiwa."

"Please follow me," Sumiko said. "Mama-san is waiting for you." Slipping off their shoes, they stepped up into the hallway and tagged along behind the young woman to a room where a table had been set up with refreshments. Sumiko motioned for them to enter the room and sit down at the table. Once Anna Mae was comfortable, Mama-san entered and knelt, and Sumiko followed suit. Mama-san began speaking in Japanese.

"Mama-san English not so good, so I translate for her," Sumiko said.

Mama-san cradled a small tissue-wrapped packet in her hand and kept glancing at the package.

"Mama-san says this given her long time ago by her … friend." Sumiko stopped. "No, not right word … her love, her sweetheart. He told her the words he inscribed on parchment are our future when he returned home to Japan from war. The words he wrote are love and happiness. Mama-san says that she kept the words next her heart all time he was gone. He came home, words came true. She found happiness.

"Now it's time for you to find happiness. You keep parchment, good karma. When Butler-san comes home to States, you will see.

Words will come true if keep talisman next heart. Keep safe, believe; all the time, believe. Butler-san is good man, care about others. He drinks much because he fights war demons deep in his soul. My Hitoshi the same; he fight war devils deep inside him all the time. Someday he'll win. Someday Butler-san will conquer but not with drink. Alcohol is no help. Butler-san will find his strength and return to you."

The older woman hesitated for a few seconds and took a sip of tea. Then she spoke again as Sumiko translated the words into English. "Butler-san is part of my family; he helped me when I was in need. I have no family to help, but Butler-san asked nothing and assisted me from the generosity of his heart. Butler-san needs now is a good woman to love and be loved. You take care him."

A tear rolled down Mama-san's cheek as she finished talking, and with a slight bow, she extended both hands clasping the packet and offered the present to Anna Mae. Anna Mae graciously accepted the parcel and unwrapped the soft paper covering the silk pouch. Opening the tiny satchel, she removed the rice paper parchment and studied the intricate writing. "Beautiful," she declared, closely examining the present. Carefully refolding the parchment, she placed it in the pouch and slid the small silk pouch into her bra, next to her heart.

Anna Mae bowed delicately. "I shall keep it here next to my heart...." She touched her left breast. "Until it comes true. Thank you."

Mama-san bowed in return. Very softly, almost to herself, she said in Japanese as she left the room, "As with all the others who have befriended me over the years, I may never see him or you again in my lifetime. You will become as wisps of mist floating in and out of my memory. Sayonara."

Sumiko hesitated for a second and wisely only said, "Mama-san says she wish you health and happiness. May the future bring you peace and joy. Farewell. She wishes you a safe journey home."

**

CHAPTER TWENTY-FOUR
Irish to the Base

Eighteen months had passed since Butler had been tucked away at the Brass Rail. Andy and Mel had advanced in rank to E-4, and Andy thought the three chevrons on his sleeve made him look impressive—a little bit, anyway.

The day arrived when Andy needed to drag Irish, the soon-to-be civilian, back to the base. Why Irish needed anyone to escort him back to the base was a question for which Andy could find no answer. The man was physically and mentally capable of taking care of himself, so why did he need a chaperone? The only thing Andy could surmise was the guy wanted to show he could throw his weight around and coerce people into doing his bidding. However Andy had made Irish a promise: in payment for Irish's help in locating Butler, Andy would escort Irish to the base. Andy anticipated accomplishing this chore would be an easy matter. If he and Mel left the base early on Monday morning, they had ample time to arrive in town, round up Irish, and be back to Group Headquarters by 1300.

Andy's name popped up on the duty roster for Monday, and it proved to be more difficult to swap for the day off than he anticipated. He managed to swap around the duty schedule, but the price was high: he had to pull the midnight shift on Saturday and the mid-shift on Sunday. Too many aircraft were sitting in the hangar needing repairs, and he was on the run picking up parts from base supply every moment of his shift. Mel, on the other hand, whom Andy commandeered to assist him, was able to weasel the day off. Such were the differences in duty assignments.

Early Monday, Andy rousted Mel out of the sack, and they managed to hop on the first bus to town. Figuring they would have a leisurely breakfast and coffee when they reached Irish's little hotel, they felt there was no need to rush.

As they ambled along the path to the hotel, all appeared tranquil. However, as they approached the front door, before they set foot on the front step of the flophouse, the door slid open, and the hotel matron summoned them to hurry. Her bow was quirky and solemn. "Ohayo (morning)," she said. "I worry you no come. Irish no good; he drunk all week. Come back hotel maybe one hour ago, no want take bath or wash clothes, now no want get up." She pleaded, "He upset all time when I go room. He be big trouble no get base on time. He my *hogosha,* protector. He get in trouble, I no place go, no place sleep. You help."

They hurried after her. She abruptly stopped, turned, and double-checked to ensure they had removed their shoes. Then she continued along the hallway, stopped in front of the familiar door, and knocked quietly on the doorframe. Gently, she slid the paper-covered door partially open. Andy craned his neck to gawk through the crack and spotted Irish sprawled on a futon. He resembled the remnants of an abandoned scarecrow in a harvested field. The reek of alcohol, stale tobacco, and body odor that permeated the room slowly wafted out into the hallway.

"Ohayou gozaimasu, ohayou gozaimasu, ohayou gozaimasu (Good morning)," she said loudly yet very respectfully to Irish.

Andy assessed the bedraggled form. *The guy was in the sack the last time we were here. Only this time, there's no women in the bed with him.* He wondered how they were going to provoke that sodden lump of human flesh awake enough to even talk to them.

The only reaction from Irish was to curl up into a fetal position.

"Out of the sack, Irish!" Mel shouted. "Get the hell up! Haul your ass out of here."

Nada, nothing. Mel went into the room and nudged the sleeping glob's shoulder with his foot. "Rise and shine." His efforts were rewarded by the continued slow, rhythmic breathing and non-melodious snoring from the inebriated man.

Mel had curbed his irritation up to this point, but his veiled ire was on the verge of eruption.

Deciding he'd better step in, Andy moved in closer and said to Mel, "You're gonna piss the guy off. We need him to cooperate, not be mad at us." He reached down, grabbed Irish by the shoulder, and none too gently shook him. "Roll your butt out of bed; we need you to wake up. You're going to be a civilian today, you need to stand up and walk."

The answer, an eye-watering flatulence, was expelled from Irish's gastrointestinal tract. The odor slipped out silently, but the reek would have done a polecat proud.

Involuntarily scrunching up their faces, they attempted to block out the noxious fumes swirling in the air as the hotel mistress bolted from the room. She reemerged, her nose wrinkled up as she scrutinized the messy bedding, unkempt room, and the lingering, unwholesome stench. By her disgusted expression, Andy knew she would be happy to be rid of the drunk for at least a while.

Irish's eyelids fluttered for a second, and he turned back on his side, facing away from them.

Mel's voice rose in frustration. "Come on, Irish, up and at 'em."

The soon-to-be civilian remained motionless for a couple of minutes, the sodden effects of the alcohol he had consumed affecting his physical movements. He shifted his body, reached out his hand, and threw off the blankets. Rolling over, he managed to struggle to his knees. Holding himself in that position for a few moments with his head hung toward the floor, he uttered, "If you're not going to leave me alone, then give me a hand up."

Straightening up on his haunches, he leaned his head back and took a deep breath. Mel reached down, grabbed Irish under the armpits, and yanked him upright.

Precariously the guy got up, wobbling and staggering. The sensation of the room revolving made him nauseous. As his throat clogged with ascending vomit, Irish piteously mumbled, "I'm going to be sick." Clutching his stomach with one hand and clasping his other hand to his mouth, he doubled up. His legs gave way, he opened his mouth, and just before his knees hit the floor, the mistress shoved a bucket under his chin. From the gaping hole in his face hurled forth the vile smelling and disgusting remnants of last night's binge.

Andy stepped backward, wanting to be out of range and avoid the regurgitated mess.

From the stream of bile spewed out, miraculously not a splash of the vomit landed anywhere but in the bucket. When Irish finished his bout of puking and the dry heaves had subsided, he started to wipe off his mouth with the back of his hand.

The mistress, who still knelt beside him, had removed the bucket, and she held in her hand a moist, warm washcloth. With a gentle touch, she moved Irish's grungy fingers away from his mouth and, with care, wiped away the lingering bits of vomit that clung to his lips and chin. Finished with the chore, she placed the soiled cloth in a pan beside her, produced a second damp cloth, and handed it to Irish so he could finish cleaning his face.

At what point she had brought the bucket and washcloths into the room Andy wasn't sure, yet they were there when she needed them.

Irish started to lie down. Andy grabbed one of his arms and forced him to stand. Mel rushed over and grabbed the other arm. Together they held the limp mass upright.

Flexible as a rag doll, Irish did a one-man balancing act until his equilibrium stabilized and he managed to stand alone. With a strained plea, he pronounced, "I believe I must make a sojourn to the lavatory."

They gingerly walked him out to the hall. Irish nodded with his head. "This way." He knew where he was going. Following his lead, they held onto him until he reached the toilet door.

Peering through gaunt, inflamed eyes, which gave him the appearance of a weary basset hound, he forced a small grin. "I can take it from here, gentlemen. Thank you." He staggered into the toilet and slid the door closed behind him.

The mistress set about fumigating the room. She opened the screen-covered windows, picked up the futon mat and blankets, and hung them on the porch rail outside the window, where they would air out. Then she disappeared down the hallway, the puke bucket in one hand and the washbasin clutched in the opposite one.

Irish stumbled out of the toilet fastening his trousers, his uniform disheveled and wrinkled from having been slept in. The growth of stubble accentuated his haggard appearance as he nonchalantly leaned against the wall, yawned, and scratched his crotch.

0830 hours

"Irish, we must leave. We can't fiddle around all day," Andy said. "We need to get you back to the base or you're going to be AWOL. You have to sign your discharge papers at 1300 hours. We need to go now!"

"Presently, presently" was Irish's sardonic reply, and with great flair, he continued, "We shall be on our way. But before I depart, it would be prudent for me to appear somewhat in the realm of normalcy. Would you not agree, gentlemen? The only manner in which I can assure you it will happen is with a wee bit of the essence of the grape, a sip of the nectar from the fruit of the vine."

Irish's attempt at sophistication was hilarious, and Andy smirked to keep from laughing out loud.

"But alas," Irish continued, "in this fair land so far removed from the great vineyards of Europe, I must concede I will but partake of the liquid of the rice. The bitter sweetness from the grain yields forth, through fermentation, a consumable elegant liquid as no other. A tiny bit of the clear, palatable drink created from the grain of the plant so meticulously cared for, nurtured, grown, and harvested in the rice paddies."

He took a deep breath. "I need to be rid of the fuzz implanted on my tongue and the cotton that seems to have sprouted in my mouth, to clear the cloudiness that has permeated my vision and the veil of haze that has encompassed my cerebellum. Once I've accomplished the task, we shall be on our way with great haste and no further ado."

"Irish, you're blowing smoke out of your butthole; not funny," complained Mel.

"That was my Cary Grant impression. I take it ya don't like it." Irish gave a deep sigh. "In other words, guys, I need some of the hair of the dog that bit me. My head is ready to explode. Give me a hand here, will ya?"

"What's next?" groaned Mel. "How the hell can you want a drink? You had enough last week to fill a bathtub, and you act as if you're still wasted. You need to snap out of it!"

Irish slipped back into his terrible impersonation of the Hollywood movie star. "What you say is true. I am sorry for my soliloquy, but it does me good to spout off once in a while; it makes me feel a little civilized, more alive, more in tune with my surroundings."

He looked at Andy and pleaded, "I am not leaving until I have a shot of sake, and I need it now…. Please?"

The matron returned and stood patiently beside Andy as she listened to the dissension between Mel and Irish.

Andy said, "Mel, let's let him have his drink; we'll never get out of here if we don't." He motioned to the woman, saying, "Irish-san needs sake," and then, remembering his manners, he added, "Dozo."

She nodded and seemed not at all bewildered by the request, probably having dealt with a multitude of drunks in her day. She signaled for Andy and Mel to follow her, and they grabbed Irish by the arms, dragging and pulling him as they trailed the mistress through the hall to the opposite end of the hotel. There, they entered a room that housed a small pub room and an exit to the street. Once they were in the little bar, they let go of his arms and let him lean on the counter for support.

Unhurriedly, Irish made his way around the bar, putting each foot down gingerly and grimacing each time his foot made contact with the floor. Although there were only four stools at the bar, it took him forever to find his place. Finally reaching his destination, he stopped and climbed up on the stool with the effort a person takes to climb Mount Everest. Neither Mel nor Andy moved a muscle to aid him. It was his hangover; let him suffer.

Situating himself, he propped his right elbow up on the bar and rested his head in his upturned palms. "Sorry I snapped at you guys. My head's pounding like there are fifty *taiko* drums beating away inside my skull. I realize you're trying to help me." Irish's soft, slurred voice was almost inaudible.

Anticipating Irish's needs, the woman had everything prepared, and she noiselessly placed a sake cup in front of him on the bar's highly polished wood surface. Judiciously, she began to pour the sake from a newly unsealed bottle into the empty cup.

"Iie," Irish pleaded, *"Atatakai sake kudasai."* ("I would like warm sake.")

She nodded and, with graceful, diminutive movements, disappeared through a door into what Andy believed was a kitchen to warm the sake. While he'd been engrossed with Irish's actions, Mel sat down on a chair at the only table in the room and motioned for Andy to join him.

Andy plopped down in a chair as Mel moaned, "Now what the hell's goin' on?"

After a couple of minutes, the woman reentered the room holding a decanter filled to the brim with the warm rice liquid. Irish's eyes took on a slight glow; he was already anticipating the effects of the drink. Deftly, she filled his small cup with the warm, golden rice wine.

Even in his post-drunken state, Irish's manners did not elude him. He acknowledged her exquisite service with a slight bow of his head. *"Domo arigato gozaimasu."* ("Thank you.")

With great respect, she bowed back. *"Do itashi mashite."* ("You're welcome.")

A sake cup is slightly smaller than a shot glass, and when filled, it requires some dexterity to maneuver the cup to your mouth without spilling the contents. Irish reached out and attempted to take hold of the small cup, but in his avidity he snatched at the cup rather than taking a firm hold. The sake sloshed, and in futile desperation he shifted his fingers, lost control, and knocked the cup over. The wine poured out onto the bar top. The expression crossing his face was that of a pitiful and forlorn man. Irish studied the small pool of spilled rice wine despondently. For a second, they thought he would bend his head down, stick out his tongue, and lap up the sake the way a thirsty canine laps up water.

The woman produced a clean cloth from under the tiny bar and wiped up the liquid. Satisfied that the spill was taken care of, she disposed of the dirty cloth and then turned her attention back to Irish. With the tolerance of a sympathetic and caring friend, she refilled his cup. After she finished pouring, his hand trembled as he lifted the cup from the bar and moved it warily toward his lips. Mindful to keep his movements slow, he maintained his composure and managed to lift the cup halfway to his mouth before impatience got the best of him and he lost control. His hands began to quiver, first trembling slightly and then more intensely. The cup tilted in his hand. Sake cascaded down onto his crotch and left a stain on his trousers as if he had urinated in his pants. The cup clattered to the floor. Irish folded his hands on the bar, and his pleading eyes focused on her.

Taking a clean cup from the shelf she poured the sake, however she filled the cup three-fourths full this time. Not a man to give up, Irish clasped the small ceramic cup firmly with fingers from both hands, and with a steady motion, he began to raise the warm, soothing liquid toward his lips. Eagerness again derailed his efforts; as the cup touched his mouth, his hands started, and sake plummeted down onto his shirt.

He set the cup back down on the bar and began brushing some of the spilled sake from his shirt and tie.

The hotel mistress pondered Irish's actions not with amazement, but with compassion and pity. Abruptly, she turned and padded back into the kitchen, returning with a small miso soup bowl. The bowls are fashioned in a manner that enables one to grasp it with two hands. The accepted way to partake of miso soup is by sipping straight from the bowl. She exchanged the sake cup with the miso bowl. Irish smiled at her as he comprehended the meaning of her actions. She poured in a small amount of sake and slid the bowl over to him. His hands shaking, quivering, and desperate, he grabbed the bowl with both hands and struggled to establish a firm hold. His fervent lurch for the bowl caused it to wobble, and the beverage sloshed around, but it stayed contained within the vessel. He knew this time, his endeavor would be a success. Ever so slowly he negotiated the bowl the short distance from bar top to his mouth and never spilled a drop of that precious alcoholic beverage.

Through the lips and over the gums, look out stomach, here it comes. The old saying popped into Andy's mind as he observed the way Irish savored the drink. He was amazed at how the man's appearance changed as the warm liquid ran down his throat.

Irish uttered a sigh of relief and satisfaction as the alcohol entered his system. His eyes started to clear, the misty gaze of melancholy disappeared, the trembling hands steadied, and his face started to relax.

The alcohol-craving man petitioned the woman, summoning the saddest and most pitiful look he could muster. *"Sake mou sukoshi onegai shimasu."* ("Sake, little more please.")

She poured him half a bowl of sake. With a slight tremble in his hands, he took the refreshing drink to his lips and let it caress his throat.

Irish was on the way to recovery after downing his third round of booze. The mistress poured him a fourth of a bowl of sake. He lifted the bowl, and the sake disappeared faster than a drop of water on a hot griddle. They both regarded Irish with inquisitive frowns, he shrugged off their questioning stares and announced, "I'm ready to go now."

Boom—just like that, he was ready to go.

Andy eyeballed him critically and thought, *We can't even go out on the street with him looking that raunchy.* "Irish, you gotta shave and clean up. You resemble a piece of crap, somethin' that slopped off the honey bucket cart."

Rubbing his hand over his chin, Irish nodded. *"Kamisori kudasai."* ("Razor, please.")

The mistress bowed, said "Hai," and motioned for Irish to follow her.

They were back in less than five minutes, and he looked more presentable in the dim light of the bar.

Relieved the wait was over, Mel slid back his chair and jumped to his feet. "Well, la de da. 'Bout time. Let's move."

Irish sat back down at the bar and said to the mistress, *"Sukoshi* (Little amount) sake, dozo."

The mistress complied with his request and poured him another drink in the soup bowl.

"Irish!" Andy harshly ordered. "Speed it up. Shift your butt into gear; we gotta go, now."

"Yeah." He swallowed the sake in one gulp, stood up, and proceeded toward the door leading outside.

The woman grabbed Irish's hat from the bar, where she had placed it earlier. *"Anata no boshi."* ("Your hat.")

He took his hat from her and bowed slightly. "Domo." Then he placed the hat on his head and adjusted it in a rakish manner.

Mel and Andy had been wearing their hats all this time, but they didn't have their shoes. Andy turned to Mel. "We can't go barefooted; we left our shoes at the other entrance!"

Irish was halfway to the front door before it dawned on him that he didn't have any footwear either. They were all still wearing slippers. Irish turned to the woman and asked, *"Watashi no kutzu wa doko deska?"* ("My shoes, where are they?")

"Ah, so deshita," she muttered, giving that quick little bow of hers as she shuffled out toward the living quarters. Mel started to follow her, but she pointed for them to remain in the bar. In a minute, she was back with three pairs of shoes. Graciously, she handed each of them their own shoes with a little bow and saying, "Dozo." How she knew whose shoes belonged to whom Andy couldn't guess. They all were the same, just different sizes. In the short minutes she'd been absent, she had found the time to wipe away the mud spots, and one pair was shined better than the other two.

There was an area just inside the exit door with a lowered stone floor. It was one place you could wear street shoes. Andy slipped on his shoes while keeping a close eye on Irish, who leaned against the wall by the front window. Sunlight filtered in through curtainless window and shone on the spot where Irish stood, affording Andy a good look at Irish's uniform. It was filthy and really in bad shape. The front of his shirt and crotch of his pants were wet from the spilled sake, and what Andy assumed were crusty bits of food or puke were splattered on Irish's tie. He might have shaved, but there were splotches of stubble on his face; he hadn't stood very close to the razor. Andy knew they weren't going to be able to slip Irish past the front gate of the base looking as rough he did without receiving some sort of admonishment from the gate guard.

"Irish, don't you have a clean uniform?" Andy asked.

"This is the last one I have. I got rid of all the rest of them; don't need them after today."

"I so sorry ... I so sorry. He no let take clothes off last night. He drunk and fight like crazy man, no let us touch, angry. No could wash clothes," the matron sobbed. "So sorry."

"I have a tendency to be that way sometimes when I've had too much to drink; I can be a mean drunk," admitted Irish. "I do have clean kimonos."

"You can't just go waltzing up to the gate in a kimono, you dumb...," grumbled Mel.

Hanging on the coat rack by the front door was a military raincoat that someone had forgotten. Mel rushed to grab the coat, and he flung it at Irish. "Put the raincoat on."

Grudgingly Irish caught the coat and, with a caustic voice, asked, "Raining outside?"

"Geez, Irish, we gotta cover you up some way. You look like...." Mel was so disgusted he didn't even finish the sentence as he turned around.

Irish mumbled some words under his breath, but Andy ignored what he had said as the man reluctantly threw on the coat. Irish buttoned up the rain gear and stood slouched over, his hands stuffed deeply inside the coat's pockets. The garment was a couple of sizes too small for him and made him look hilarious. However, at least some of the filth on his uniform was covered up.

Andy was out the tavern door in a flash, followed by Irish, whom Mel had forcefully shoved out the door after Andy. Mel seemed to be unaware of the incensed glare in Irish's eyes from his resentment of the rough treatment. They took off up the street in the direction of the base and the gate. If they could make it back to the hangar in an hour, they would have time to spare. Andy had an idea how to clean Irish up a bit and still have him to Group Headquarters on time. He picked up the pace and realized Irish was not keeping up with them. Turning around, he saw Irish lagging a quarter of a block behind them, strolling along at a leisurely pace. It was then that he spotted two of Irish's henchmen behind them, lurking in the shadows

"Come on," Andy yelled. "We need to make up some time!"

"Go screw yourself, Anderson," Irish replied evenly. He then added, "I am not as young as you two; don't rush me."

Andy hollered at him, "You've gotten a lot of breaks today, you old fart. You and your goons could rough me up anytime you want but we have a deal, and I'll live up to my part of the agreement to get you to Group HQ. Makes no difference to me if you're pissed off or not; we need to keep moving."

Irish caught up with Andy and poked him on the arm. "Andy," he said with a sense of urgency. "Stop; stop here. Duck into this store; I have to level with you." As he spoke, he kept looking up and down the street.

"We can't screw around. We need to make it to the gate and to a bus if we're going to get you back on time."

Irish grabbed Andy and pulled him off the street and into a little alcove. Mel grudgingly followed them. "That's what I need to talk to you about. The reason I wanted you to come and escort me back to the base is because there are people who want to see me … well, out of the picture."

"What the hell do you mean?"

"My competitors in the … let's call it the resale market, want me out. They assumed I was heading back to the States when I received my discharge, and they are ready to move in on my little enterprise. I'm already on shaky ground with the military; one wrong step and I'm thrown out with a less-than-honorable discharge. If my foes can discredit me and the provost marshal tosses me into the stockade, I'll end up getting a bad conduct discharge. Then the Japanese government can revoke my visa, my request to remain in Japan. They can declare me an undesirable and deport me back to the States. My resale business, hotel, even my stash of yen will be up for grabs."

Andy hung his head in disbelief at what he was hearing. "You have your own gang of goons to protect you; what are you worried about?"

"The men I hire to protect me are just that, hired hands. They watch out for me as long as I'm the top bidder. I doubt that any one of them is loyal enough they wouldn't sell me out to someone else with a bigger purse. Something is going to happen to me very soon—a fight, an accident, something. Too much talk going on. Might even be the cops are on my tail. I have information my competitors have paid money to a few American guys as well as Japanese to see to my demise as a player in the black market. Everything has to be handled very discreetly. One fight or brawl, or if they can stop me from getting to Group Headquarters by 1300, that will be enough to put the screws to me. They paid off people on the base to intercept me and cause trouble. They are onto my habits, like what gate I enter, and they are there watching."

"Why didn't you tell me this sooner?"

"I wanted you to escort me for a couple of reasons. They won't be so flagrant in their attempts to try to stop me if I have witnesses with me. You are unknown to them, an enigma; they have no idea what you'll do. I'm in the dark on what you might do. That's the beauty of the plan. The ones on base will now have to rethink their strategy if you're tagging along. The word is they could try anything short of killing me."

"Irish, I think you're blowing smoke," Mel blurted out. "None of this is true, and you're making a melodrama of this whole damn thing."

"What do you want me to do, Schultz, go up to the main gate and cry to the military cops like a little baby, 'I need help; someone is trying to hurt me'? Yeah, then they would check me out, investigate, and my ass would be in a sling and on its way to Leavenworth for dealing in stolen government property. If you ever rat me out, I'll guarantee there will be an inquiry into what happened in that little koya, and you two yahoos will be my cellmates."

"Hey, guys, knock it off. You can take potshots at each other later," demanded Andy.

"I still say he's full of crap," complained Mel.

"Think what you wish, Schultz. I have two of my men tailing us. There are two adversaries waiting on the next corner, two more on the street by the gate, and perhaps others."

He turned back to Andy. "Your actions have to be spontaneous, unexpected, and unpredictable if this is going to work."

"You really stacked the odds against me for getting you to the base. Look at you; you're in no shape to fend off or even run from an attack. You're hungover, weak, sick, and you can't even think straight."

"When I get to drinkin', I just keep puttin' them down one after the other. Yeah, I didn't plan it this way, but if I am going to go, I might as well go drunk and happy."

"We can't go in the front gate, for sure, not if they are waiting for us. What about the guys following us, are they at all trustworthy?"

"As far as I can guess they are, or at least they were last night."

"OK, let's see." Andy began thinking of ideas and speaking out loud as he thought about them. "Today is Monday. Monday ... what goes on Mondays? Maybe it will work. We're going in the back gate, where the logistics warehouses are located."

"Whale of a long ways. How are we going to—" Irish started to question, when Mel butted in.

"No buses run back there, no transportation. If you go in that gate, you either have to bike, walk, or have a car. It's the better part of ten miles to where we need to be; I think we ought to chance the main gate."

"Let's start and get the lay of the land and make our decisions as we go." Andy stepped back out on the street with Irish and Mel following him. As they approached the corner, he spotted two Japanese men and wondered if these were the two he had been warned about. One way to find out. He glanced at Irish and slightly moved his head back toward where Irish's two men were and nodded.

Irish picked up on the idea, and with his hand behind his back, he motioned to his thugs following them. The hired men moved swiftly and covertly between the shops and merchandise on the street, reappearing behind the Japanese ambushers. There was a tussle, and the commotion caused pedestrians to stop and stare as all four disappeared into a building.

They needed to shag on out of there. Andy guessed it was at least five miles to the back gate and then another ten miles to Group HQ. *Why should I care about helping this guy; except, I have an obligation to fulfill. We need some type of transportation,* he thought as he took another careful scan of Irish's appearance. The guy looked exactly like what he was, a slob coming back to the base after a week's bender. The raincoat covered some of his soiled uniform and helped his appearance, but very little. Irish still resembled the south end of a northbound horse.

"Did they say for you to be in Class A's when you report to Group Headquarters?" Andy asked.

"No, not that I can remember."

"Mel, we need to mix this up a little bit. I'm going to take Irish and swing back to his place. You head to the front gate and grab one of those taxis that hang around there. Go to Mama-san's and see if Butler left any clothing at the Brass Rail. We need some clean clothes for Irish. Afterward, have the cab take you to Chibi's. Irish and I will circle around a few blocks, make sure we're not followed, and meet you there."

"Sounds like a plan to me," Mel said and started to hurry off.

"When you're by the gate, snoop around and see if it looks like there's anyone lingering outside it who might be out to intercept us. Don't raise any suspicions. These people aren't informed of who is with Irish, and I think we can further confuse them if we split up."

"Roger that," Mel said, and he continued up the street. Andy turned and yelled at Irish, "Let's go! You created this mess; now you're going to have to keep up with me. Sick and hungover or not, damned if I care. Just stay with me."

CHAPTER TWENTY-FIVE
Run for the Gate

He shoved Irish into the breezeway between the two buildings and squeezed in after him, effectively blocking anyone from seeing the sought-after GI now dressed in traditional Japanese garb. After they left Mel, Andy doubted the wisdom of returning to Irish's hotel. Instead, they doubled back, went into a small store, and convinced the owner to sell them a nondescript used man's kimono and headgear along with a pair of gaiters. They dumped the blue raincoat which was easy to spot since it wasn't raining, and used the worn Japanese clothing to cover Irish's rumpled uniform. He rolled up his trouser legs and carried his shoes in a cloth bundle. If anyone was looking for all the men to be in uniform, perhaps Irish's change of attire would give them an advantage. Anyone looking closely could tell the guy wasn't Japanese, but it seemed their best option.

Irish's two henchmen had returned from their encounter with the advisories by the main entrance to the base, and Andy and Irish sent the men to check out any possible problems at the back gate. Across the street, the area around Chibi's joint appeared absent of any challengers. Now all they needed to do was wait for the cab Mcl was sending to pick them up.

Where the devil is the cabbie? Did he just pocket our money and take off? It wouldn't be the first time that's happened. Then, hearing the sound of an approaching car, Andy poked his head out of the narrow access way to obtain a better look, hoping the vehicle was the hack he expected. A blue Plymouth buzzed across the intersection. A brief glimpse of its occupants, two Japanese men, was all he caught of the automobile as it sped by.

He quickly forgot about the car as a shadow fleetingly crossed in front of the narrow opening, snapping him out of his trance and forcing him to concentrate on the present. The figure passed by and then returned and stood in the opening, obscuring the small amount of light that penetrated between the two buildings.

"Irish-san, you come out now and we no hurt," growled an unpleasant-looking man who stood straddle-legged, slapping a nunchaku against the palm of his hand. "You come out now."

"The back way!" Irish yelled as he tried to turn in the cramped space and retreat. He never took a step, for blocking the other end of the breezeway, another nunchaku-swinging ruffian stood waiting. Andy shifted his position slightly to see why Irish was still rooted in the same spot. Then he swung back to face the first adversary. Irish said, "OK, farm boy, let me see what tricks you have up your sleeve now. You've gotten us trapped by hiding in here with no place to run."

Irish was right. There was no place to go except straight forward. Andy's adrenaline started pumping as he contemplated how to overpower his challenger. Suddenly Mel appeared around the corner with a baseball bat held high over his head. He delivered a blow to the man's head that caused the assailant to crumple to the ground.

Andy charged into the empty space vacated by the fallen man. Irish, in his anxiety to escape from the small confines, rammed against him, and he tripped as his feet became entangled in his kimono when he endeavored to leap over the unconscious attacker.

Standing motionless, Mel stared down at the guy he had just coldcocked with the bat, mumbling over and over, "Did I kill him? I hope I didn't kill him."

"No, too damn bad, sport, you didn't," Irish said. "You only brained the bastard, he'll have a helluva headache when he wakes up."

Andy abruptly swung around and looked to the rear of the enclosure; the second man was hightailing it out of the alley. "Way to go, Mel. I guess three-to-one odds didn't look very profitable to him, so he took off. Where did you pick up the Louisville Slugger?"

"While I was searching for clothing at Mama-san's, I found it along with other gear stuffed in the closet used at the bar for lost and found. Somebody must have been playing ball with the local kids and then decided to have a drink and forgot and left it there. Figured I'd bring it along with me in case it might be useful."

"Hey, I thought you were going to send a cab for us. We've been waiting a long time," Andy impatiently bitched.

"I couldn't locate a second one. The only reason this cabbie stuck around was because I promised him a five-hundred-yen tip," explained Mel. "We're wasting time with all this jabbering. Can we start moving now?"

The three of them piled into the back seat of the small cab that Mel had left waiting for them in front of Chibi's, sandwiching Irish in the center between them.

"What about clean clothes?"

"Wasn't anything there. Butler cleared out all of his stuff."

"We'll just have to make do," mumbled Andy, unsure how.

No sooner had Mel told the cabbie where they wanted to go than Irish began complaining. "Give me some room. I gotta breathe." He fumed and griped as the cab sped down the street, the driver making a valiant attempt to avoid potholes while dodging the pedestrians trying to step around the obstructions.

"Irish, can't you shut up and quit complaining for a second? We need to figure out what we're going to do. You keep feeding us half-truths and only part of what is going on, and you expect us to keep you comfy and cozy like a little baby," seethed Andy. "It would be nice to have an idea of how many people are after you and why. For once, tell us the damn truth; no more horseshit, OK?"

"Not going to add much," Irish slurred. "You don't need to be privy to everything. Let's say some items, priceless heirlooms, have come into my possession over the past few years. The fortunes of war, shall we say. There are some influential Japanese families who don't want to see me ship the antiquities and their valuables out of the country, and their price…. The stuff is worth … well, maybe killing for."

"Fortunes of war, my Aunt Milly's bloomers. What a bunch of crap. You're nothing but a thief and a con artist. You're just a damn lowlife."

"Geez, Anderson, you don't have to get nasty. Hell, I don't want to guess how many are after me; just get me to the base like you promised," hissed Irish. "Quit bugging me…. Stop the damn cab; I'm going to be sick."

The car careened around a corner, flinging them about on the rear seat. The abrupt change in direction bounced Mel up off the seat, and he cracked his head against the top of the doorframe, triggering an eruption of profanity. The cabbie abruptly stopped, and Irish shoved Mel out of the door and followed. Most of the puke went outside, but some ended up on the kimono and the inside door jamb.

Irish slid back in, wiping his mouth with the kimono sleeve as he said, "You guys just don't understand, do you? This black market isn't going to last. After the occupation is over for a couple of years and the Japanese get their manufacturing going again, the market for stolen property is going to disappear. Right now I'm riding high, and if I don't maintain my status within the circle of marketers, I'll be nobody. Now I'm a big enough threat they're worried and are throwing a lot of muscle to chuck me out and take over my operation."

Hesitantly Mel reentered the cab, saying, "Why don't you go home like everyone else, go back to the States and get a job?"

Irish spat back, "What kind of job—dishwasher, swinging a mop swabbing out some dive? Why should I when everything I have is here?"

"You could find a job selling stuff; you're not stupid," growled Mel.

"How am I going to do that? I've got no background, no formal training. Running a black-market operation in Japan isn't a recommendation for a job on Wall Street."

"You have the GI bill; go to college."

"You're a damn dreamer." Irish laughed. "I never finished high school; how do you expect me to go to college? Hell, I never even made it out of the eighth grade. The only thing I might graduate from would be from smoking Mary Jane to poking needles in my arm with the hard stuff. I told you I came from the slums of Jersey. My old man slapped me around most of my life, until I was old enough and big enough to pound on him. And when that happened, I was out on the streets. If the war hadn't come along, I would be in the big house, staring out at the world from between iron bars. That was where my life was going. I can't go home a stupid nobody. What doll would look at me? I would be just another loser. Here I have my choice of beautiful women and a cozy lifestyle. I'll stay till they toss me out. Why should I go home and become a saloon bum and roam the streets?"

He paused. "The way you two been hanging out with the locals, I thought you understood the kind of life a guy can have in Japan right now ... if you have cash."

The cab roared around a couple of blocks, up and down unpaved streets, and then skidded to a stop in front of a small public bathhouse. The car doors swung open, and they piled out.

"Money!" yelled the cabbie, "give money." Mel handed over the yen, and the cab's rear tires spewed gravel as the cabbie stomped on the gas pedal. The car sped down the street with the open back door swinging back and forth.

Andy surveyed the man in his safekeeping. *The thing now is to get Irish out of the kimono. He's still wearing his raunchy clothes underneath with the trouser legs rolled up. Doubtful the slob will be even remotely presentable; all we can do is take a chance and hustle him onto the base.*

Irish looked at him and then turned his head and puked in the street. "Something's not settin' too good in my gut; give me a second."

"Could be the oranges you stole from the shopkeeper when we picked up the kimono."

"I was hungry."

"You could have paid the man. You didn't have to swipe them."

"Up yours, Anderson."

The old bathhouse, which had seen better days and a better clientele, was now primarily used by GIs and the girls they picked up as a place for copulation and companionship. Inside, Andy bodily shoved Irish into the dressing area.

"Take off those gaiters, put your shoes back on, and try to at least straighten your tie. Come on; move your butt, Irish, or I'm going to leave you here at the mercy of those you say are chasing you."

"You wouldn't do that; I'll squeal on your boy Butler."

"Don't threaten me, you hungover SOB. One more word out of you that sounds like a threat and I'll call the provost marshal. If I repeat even half of what you've told me, you'll be in the stockade a hell of a lot longer than I will be for helping Butler. The only thing that interests me now is getting your sorry ass to HQ and then forgetting that I ever met you.... I'll wait for you outside." With that statement, Andy stomped out the door.

Mel, who had remained silent for a while, now joined in the verbal fracas and hollered as he followed Andy outside, "Irish, quit screwing around and rid yourself of that damn kimono!"

He turned toward Andy and said, "You must have a scheme for getting transportation or we wouldn't have come in this way. What is it?"

"I do; I'm sure we can flag down a ride. We'll have to wait a few minutes, but he will be here."

"How the hell do you figure that? You already talk to the guy?"

"Nope, but he's a creature of habit, always leaves the same time, always takes the same route, and never misses getting to the chow hall for lunch by 1230. You can set your watch by his eating habits."

"I don't understand a thing you're talking about," uttered Mel, doubting every word he had heard so far.

"Have a little faith; it will work out, and we'll secure a ride and dump Irish."

Peering back at the bathhouse entrance, Mel yelled, "Irish, come on! We don't have all day to fart around waiting for you."

Irish mumbled a vulgarity as he staggered out the door, his uniform somehow looking worse now than it had earlier. Andy caught a glimpse of two Japanese police officers slowly pedaling their bicycles toward where he stood. The junsa or keikan were looking into every doorway and nook they passed so that it was obvious they were searching for someone or something. The police officer in the lead spotted Irish and yelled something to his partner behind him. Irish did an abrupt about-face and hightailed it back into the bathhouse, yelling, "These guys ain't cops, they ain't cops! Help me here, Andy! Give me some friggin' help!"

The two bodyguards Irish had sent ahead, along with a beefy third man, emerged from a nearby building and ran to the *ofuroya*, bathhouse, in Irish's defense. Andy was on the verge of starting to dash forward when Mel grabbed him by the arm and pulled him back.

"Damn it, Mel, let go. I've gotta see if I can give that stupid Irish a hand."

"Let it go, Andy. Stay out of it. The odds are in Irish's favor four to two, Irish and three hired hands against the two cops, if they are cops. You don't need to get involved; let it play out."

Reluctantly Andy conceded and stood with his eyes fixed on the bathhouse door. The sounds of a struggle were heard from inside the building. Loud voices mingled with Japanese expletives were shouted between the foes as they tussled. A hush fell upon the scene, and Irish strolled out of the ofuroya looking no worse for the episode, his appearance unkempt, raunchy, and filthy, but he didn't seem to mind.

He walked up to Mel and Andy as he said, "Good damn thing I had my crew standing by, and they took care of the creeps for us. Didn't see you two wimps pitchin' in to help. Boy, I could use a drink. I'm dying right now; need some hooch."

"What did they want?" Mel asked. "Were they real cops?"

"Nah, they weren't for real, just dressed up like cops so they could roust me. They didn't find what they were looking for," Irish sarcastically boasted. Then he said, "Get me on the base."

As they walked down the street, Andy shook his head in disgust at the man's filthy apparel and rundown physical condition. *We just have to chance it. Hope for the best and trust we don't get a ration of crap from the guard as we go through the gate.*

The closer they got to the gate, the more Andy became concerned about the air cop who would be on duty. Some guards could be real nitpickers about appearances and passes. However, many of the APs considered duty on the isolated back gate to be punishment. It was a crappy assignment, and they didn't really pay much attention to you.

Usually, the guard on duty at this gate was one who had screwed up or been busted down in rank, but this one was a three-striper. Andy handed him his pass, and the cop gave him the once-over and handed the pass back. In the same basic motion, the guard reached over and took the pass out of Mel's hand, glanced at Mel, and handed it back.

The expression on the air policeman's face became sterner as he reached out his hand to Irish. "Pass." Andy started worrying.

Irish pulled crumpled leave papers out of his pocket and handed them to the cop. The AP checked the document and surveyed Irish up and down. "Tough leave, huh, pal? You look pretty rough. Better crawl back to your unit and clean up before anyone else sees you. Wow, you stink like a brewery and look like leftover garbage scraped out of the gutter."

"Shouldn't I remember you from someplace?" The guard glanced down at the pass again. "Your name's Flanagan, huh? Don't you go by some sort of a nickname?"

Irish just stood there and didn't say a word.

"Hold it a minute," the AP said. He went into the gate shack and rifled through a sheaf of papers attached to a clipboard. Then he came back out and handed the leave papers back to Irish, mumbling, "Guess I'm mistaken. Couldn't find any flier on you. Do me a favor—don't come through this gate when I am on duty looking like you do now; I hate writing people up, but you're a disgrace to the uniform. Now, move the hell out of here."

They walked through the gate, Irish fuming under his breath, "Next time I have to go through a gate I'll be a civilian, and I won't have to put up with all the military garbage; I'll be a free man."

Andy spotted a truck just as the vehicle was pulling out from the street corner a half-block away. He yelled and waved as he frantically tried to flag down the driver of the olive drab tarp-covered truck, but he was too far away and the driver didn't hear or see them. *I hope like hell that wasn't him; still too early. He has recited his routine and schedule to me a bunch of times. It's at least a half-hour before he normally would head back.* A couple of seconds ago, he'd been so positive everything was going to work out OK. *That little hiccup with the cop at the gate shows how everything could go south in a flash. Maybe I should have come in the other gate. My dad once told me shouldas, couldas, and wouldas don't count in real life. He was right, because what I could have done is past and doesn't matter in this situation. It's what I'm going to do that counts.*

With no need to hurry now, they took their time to walk over to the intersection. Even at that leisurely pace, Andy needed to continually badger Irish about keeping up with them. When they arrived at the corner, Irish plopped down and sat on the curb. As he made himself comfortable, he stretched out his legs, his feet sticking in the street, and then closed his eyes in anticipation of a nap. Mel leaned against the street signpost while Andy began pacing back and forth, looking up and down the street for a hint of the truck he was searching for.

Waiting—how Andy hated waiting. The unofficial slogan of the military is "Hurry up and wait," but thirty minutes is an incredibly long time when you're in a hurry. There was no one to blame but himself for the predicament he was now in. He'd made the agreement with Irish. If he didn't get the guy there on time, what were the consequences? Guess Irish could rat out Butler. Perhaps one of Irish's goons could break his kneecaps. He had read someplace that was what mobsters in the East did for nonpayment of a debt, be it verbal or monetary. On the bright side, at least they'd made it through the gate and it wasn't raining.

The base had two different operations, so in a matter of speaking it was two different bases. The corner they were at was on the logistical side, and the maintenance hangars and their barracks were on the operational side. They were stranded at an intersection of a road which ran from the warehouses and connected the road going south from the logistical side of the base. It then intersected a road going west, past the runway. Simply, the main roads made a large rectangle surrounding the flight line and runways. They were still a long, long way from where they needed to be, and the clock kept ticking.

Irish was asleep, or pretending to be, his head hung loosely against his chest. Mel fidgeted about and constantly kept checking his watch to the point where it was irritating. Andy poked him with his elbow. "Looking at the time every two seconds isn't going to make our ride arrive here any sooner."

"I … I need to do something. This waiting is driving me nuts," Mel said. "I'm going to be a nervous wreck before whoever you are waiting for shows up. I'm not even going to ask you who it is. I don't need any long drawn-out explanation, because I don't think we have a chance in hell of getting Irish there in time."

"Nothing we can do now…. Why don't you make a wish or say a prayer. Time seems to go faster when you do something positive."

Andy stopped pacing at the stop sign and, clasping the edge of the metal hexagon, he stared down at the sidewalk, hoping a bug would stroll by to keep him amused. He nervously started drumming his fingers against the sign until Mel glared at him to quit the repetitious tapping.

I have to admit, Andy thought, *maybe I blew it. I should have pushed Irish to move faster and not lag behind instead of giving in to him. If that was the truck, we needed to be five minutes earlier, and now, poof, like a magician waving his wand, the time's run out. No, quit doubting yourself; your strategy is sound. Don't let Mel's discouraged state get you down.*

Irish managed to move and shift around until his back was propped up against the signpost and he slumped, sprawled like a wet gunnysack, napping with his head resting against the pole.

The mood of doubt and failure tugged at Andy. He was at the mercy of someone else. He could do no more except to stand there and wait. Patience is a virtue, he remembered his Aunt Bessie telling him. It seemed so long ago now that he'd sat on the porch of the farmhouse and listened to her expound on the lessons of life. When a small flock of birds flew overhead, memories of Kamakura materialized. He recalled the words of the old peddler … divine intervention from God or Buddha…. Things would work out; he just needed to be patient.

CHAPTER TWENTY-SIX
The Ride

A high-pitched, deafening screech of truck brakes jarred him from his melancholy trance, and he squinted in the direction of the noise. No other vehicle in the world has brakes that sound like a six-by-six, a distinctive, classic, two-and-a-half-ton military truck. He thought if he heard that singular sound with his eyes closed, he still could have identified the noise as a deuce and a half. He found himself peering at the canvas-covered truck which was shuddering to a stop at the intersection.

With both hands glued to the steering wheel in a death grip was the person he was waiting for, Skeeter. Andy had met this likable character back in supply school in the States; he'd been in the same class as Andy and had shipped out to Japan a couple of weeks earlier.

Andy gave Skeeter a high sign. "Hey, ole Buddy," Andy said, "what are you doin' way over here on this side of the base?" *Yeah, Skeeter, I know what you're doing, and I've been waiting for you. Today is Monday, and you always make a truck run over here to the logistics side for supplies on Monday morning. However, I want it to look like our meeting is accidental.*

"Working!" shouted Skeeter. "Had to come over to the logistics depot to pick up a load of supplies, and I'm headin' back now."

"Hey, how about a ride? We could sure use a lift."

"Can't do that. If I got caught giving you guys a ride, my ass would be in a sling."

"Come on, Skeeter; no one's going to find out."

"Can't. Be in trouble for sure."

You're leaving me no choice; I don't have the time to be diplomatic. I hate to do this, Andy thought, *but he's not going to voluntarily consent.* "Damn it, Skeeter, don't give me a bunch of bullshit. Come on, guy, you know you owe me. I bailed your ass out in tech school. I said it was OK and we were square, but I need help."

With a hangdog expression, Skeeter began to protest, "Andy, but if—"

"Don't but if me…. If I hadn't passed you the answers on the final test, you would have washed out. It was your third and last try to pass the exam; they'd have tossed your butt out of the Air Force. If I had gotten caught helping you, what do you think they would have done to me?" There was a pause. "We need a lift. You're not going to get caught. Now, quit trying to weasel out."

Andy watched Skeeter's facial expression and thought how Skeeter was a decent person, a hard worker, just not much for academia. If it wasn't something the guy could touch with his hands or pick up in his arms, the concept eluded him. Andy had wondered how the kid from the Ozarks had even passed the entrance test for the Air Force. Skeeter had confided in Andy that he had not even finished the third grade and had lied on his enlistment papers about getting through high school. He supposed either the recruiter hadn't met his quota of enlistees for the month or he'd felt sorry for the kid. "Come on, buddy; I need a favor. No one is going to find out."

As quickly as a cow can flick its tail and knock a fly from its back, the disagreement was over, and Skeeter simply said, "OK. Hop on, then. Time's a-wastin'. I got to get this load back to supply. I ain't had lunch yet, an' I'm hungry. By the way, this here…." He pointed to the guy sitting in the passenger's seat. "Ah … is Joe. He volunteered to come along to help me load the truck." Skeeter punched his companion on the arm to get his attention.

Joe looked up from the comic book he was reading and gestured with a slight motion of his hand, saying, "Hey."

"How're things, Joe?" Andy said. Then he pointed to the two with him. "That there is Mel, and the guy sleeping is Irish."

Joe acknowledged the introductions with a nod. He and Skeeter eyeballed Irish's unkempt appearance, but they didn't make any comment.

"What happened to Phil?"

"They shipped him out to another base; got tangled up with some girl or something in town and asked to be transferred. He never said much about it," Skeeter replied. "Now I don't have help unless someone just wants to go along for the ride, like Joe. My question for you, Andy, is why are you over here in Class A's in the mornin'?" he carped. "I'm workin', and you look like you're goofin' off, ya lucky son of a bitch. You just gettin' back from an all-nighter in town, sneaking in the back gate?"

Joe interrupted and said, "While you guys are chewing the fat, I gotta take a piss. Be right back." He motioned to a building that bore a small sign that read: "Squadron Day Room." "They gotta have a can in there."

Andy turned his attention back to Skeeter and said, "No, no overnighter. We had to...." He faltered. "We had the morning off and went to town to pick up some stuff, but we're running late and need to get back. I'm on duty this afternoon."

Listening to the conversation, Mel was aware they were getting a ride and had started moving toward the truck. Irish remained motionless, sitting on the curb. Whether the guy was asleep or awake, Mel didn't care as he snatched him under one arm, and Andy moved over to help him, seizing Irish's other shoulder. They lifted their charge off the curb and dragged him out to the street, ushering him over to the back of the truck. They unlatched the tailgate, and it dropped down with a resounding clang as it slammed against the steel bumpers. Irish clenched his eyes closed, the expression on his face evincing the pain in his head. The noise touched every one of his tender, alcohol-impaired nerves. They boosted him up to the bed of the truck as if they were loading a sack of potatoes. Now was not the time to be compassionate.

Packed with various boxes of parts and equipment, the back of the truck was crammed. They managed to squeeze in and found places to sit on the ends of the wooden benches mounted along the inside of the truck bed. Irish sat down and placed his hands over his ears as if trying to hold his head steady on his shoulders. Oh, the joyous aftermath of a weeklong binge.

"OK, Skeeter, let's go. Drop us off at the maintenance hangar, will you?" Andy called out.

"OK. Here's Joe's coming back now. Let me know exactly where ya wanta pile off when we're there," Skeeter responded. Then, as he double clutched and wedged the gearshift into first gear, grinding off a pound of metal in the transmission case, he said, "Ya feel better now, Joe?" He let out on the clutch, and the truck jerked, jumped, and started to roll forward.

"What're you looking so worried about, Andy? We're moving; we're on the go!" Mel yelled over the noise made by the gears being slammed into second. The six-by gathered momentum, and Skeeter jammed in the clutch again, popped the truck into third, and off they went.

Andy stared at Mel and replied, "I don't know; probably worried about nothing, but that guy Joe up front; I can't figure him being here." He reached up and pulled the back flap down. The heavy canvas tarp darkened the interior of the truck, with the only light creeping in between the slits opened by the wind when it flapped the tarp as the truck sped forward. "Skeeter generally makes these supply runs without a helper. He has told me a number of times there are people at the supply depot who do the loading and unloading, so he doesn't need a helper on this run. Yet this guy Joe volunteered to come along."

The truck sped along without any incidents down the road. Then Andy felt the motion of the truck slowing, and the brakes screeched as Skeeter slowly brought the truck to a stop. He heard the gears shift, and as the man let out the clutch and turned the deuce and a half onto the perimeter road that ran past the flight line, something slapped against the tailgate. Andy's first thought was it was the tarp beating against the metal. Then he noticed fingers working to wrap around and get a grip on the rim of the tailgate. A second set of fingers appeared as another pair of grubby hands grabbed onto the metal rim. Andy heard grunting and groaning as the intruders tried to pull their wearying bodies into the back of the truck. The back road they traveled was empty of traffic and spectators this hour of the day, and the assailants' struggle to breach the tailgate was unobserved by others.

Mel jumped up off the bench and lifted the edge of the tarp, exposing two GIs who were grappling to maintain a grip on the tailgate. One had managed to get a foot up on the extended bumper of the frame, and the other guy was running like a fatigued antelope, seeking an opportunity to make his leap.

A quick glance at the two showed neither wore stripes on their sleeves. They looked like a couple of tough characters right out of the stockade. Andy didn't hesitate; he popped up, and while Mel held up the canvas flap, he stomped on the fingers of one of the men with his boot. The guy let out a yell but held on. Andy stomped on the man's opposite hand, and there was another screech as Andy's boot heel smashed at the fingers. Four or five hard stomps were needed before the guy hollered and let loose. Precariously, the interloper balanced one foot on the truck frame for a fraction of a second before falling back onto the roadway. The second man maintained his grip on the truck, running as hard as he could to keep up with the vehicle as the truck slowly gained speed. Irish ineffectively hammered on the second man's fingers with his fist. The guy finally let loose of the tailgate not due to pain in his hand, but because Skeeter had the truck going fast enough now that he could no longer hold on. As they sped away, "You F***** bas****, Irish; we'll get you yet!" was heard in the fading background. The two accosters stood in the road, shaking their fists at the escaping six-by.

"How did they figure out we were in the truck?" Mel asked, puzzled.

"Same way they figured out we went in the back gate ... money, bribery, and a network of spies. These guys are smart and have connections," jeered Irish.

They plopped back down on the benches, seeking a few minutes of relaxation. The wood benches were hard, like sitting on concrete blocks. Every time the truck tires hit a hole or a bump, the impact pounded their bodies like a sledgehammer. They were jostled up and down, sideways, crossways, and every other way while the deuce and a half roared down the road. The heavy-duty treads of the tires sang a sorrowful wailing song against the pavement.

Irish's face had turned a light shade of green, and he looked like he was going to vomit at any minute. Andy hoped he could hold it back, but any sympathy for the GI-turned-black-marketer had long since faded. *Let him be sick, as long as he doesn't upchuck on me.*

After twenty-five long minutes of bone-jarring and teeth-rattling bouncing, the truck swung around a corner and headed north. Only a few more minutes and they would be at the maintenance shop.

"Hey, Skeeter, let us off at the next hangar!" Andy yelled. The truck didn't slow but kept moving at the same speed. The noise of the exhaust and the wind whipping the tarpaulin had muffled his voice, so he bellowed, "Let us off here!" They were racing down the road like the truck was running the Indianapolis 500. Andy stood and leaned as far forward toward the truck cab as he could and yelled louder, "Skeeter, stop the damn truck! Now!"

This time, Skeeter understood the message and slammed on the brakes; the tires shrieked and skidded on the asphalt pavement. The brake lining met the steel wheel drums and produced a high-pitched squeal that sounded like a pig with its tail caught in a gate. The truck lurched to a stop, and Andy catapulted forward, resembling a rock shot out of a slingshot. His shoulder collided with a huge wooden crate. He careened off boxes like a beach ball and found himself face down, eating dirt off the floor. Mel had slid off the seat and ended up spread-eagled on top of boxes, his hand tangled in the loose paraphernalia that had been neatly stacked beside the crates. Andy started to sit up and spotted Irish, still on the bench, staring at him with a half-ass smirk.

With a disdainful look, Irish chuckled, "You guys comfy?" The abrupt stop had propelled him forward a few inches, but he'd stuck to the bench like a rodeo bronco rider sticks in the saddle.

Andy's uniform was suddenly as grungy as Irish's, having absorbed all the muck and grime from the truck bed like a damp sponge. Gingerly he got up from the floor and attempted to brush off the worst of the dirt as he recovered his hat.

The truck had careened to a stop a block past where he'd wanted to get off. Skeeter hollered back, "Sorry about that; the friggin' brakes stick. You guys all right?"

Sarcastically Andy answered, "We're fine ... a little bloody, bruised, and beaten up, but nothin' you need to worry about." Then he added, in all earnestness, "Skeeter, you'd better write those bad brakes up on your trip ticket so the motor pool mechanics look at them before you kill somebody."

"Great idea, Andy. I'll do that for sure."

Mel untangled himself from all the jumble of odds and ends, muttering streams of profanity under his breath, and brushed off his clothes. For Andy, it was another case of I'm-glad-I-couldn't-understand-what-he-said.

They unlatched the tailgate and let it swing down with an explosive crash, increasing the intensity of Irish's headache. Hurriedly they jumped down, pulled their hungover protégé off the truck, and made their exit.

Looking over his shoulder, Andy spotted Skeeter's reflection in the outside rearview mirror. He signaled that they were clear of the vehicle and said loudly, "Owe you big time. You saved our butts!"

Skeeter waved back. "You can buy me a beer the next time ya see me in town."

The kid's already forgotten I shamed him into giving us a ride. "You bet, buddy, catch you later." As Andy turned, there came the sound of grinding gears as Skeeter tried to find first. *By the time he makes it back to base supply, there isn't going to be any transmission left.*

Mel, irked by their slow progress, had placed an iron grip on Irish's arm and was hustling him down the street. Running to catch up, Andy reached out and latched onto Irish's free arm, and they picked up the pace.

Irish was like an anchor, dragging his feet against the ground. The faster they went, the heavier his feet become. He started objecting. "Slow down, fellows; we're here. You got me back. Now, give me a breather."

They paid no attention to him.

"Come on, men, you can slow down, can't you?"

"Why did we get off here?" Mel asked between gasps for breath. "We still have some ways to go to haul this sack of crap to HQ."

"Who you calling a sack of crap?" Irish spat. "You damn snobby, prissy-assed mama's boy."

Irritated with the incessant arguing between the two, Andy shouted, "Both of you knock it off! We're here to grab a change of clothes for Irish."

It was lunchtime, so except for a skeleton crew, everyone had gone to chow. It was an opportune time to sneak Irish into the hangar. They whisked him in through a side door and ducked into the latrine-shower room combination.

Andy went to the row of lockers at the far end of the room. "I always keep an extra pair of one-piece fatigue coveralls in here." He opened the locker and handed the fatigues to Mel. "Pull off the stripes for me and then give the coveralls to Irish, would you? Remember, the guy's been busted all the way down."

Mel was still wound up tighter than an alarm clock, and he took a small pocketknife out of his pocket and savagely ripped off the stripes. He tossed the coveralls at Irish at the same moment Andy pitched him the fatigue hat. Not expecting the fatigues to fly through the air across the latrine, Irish made a snatch grab. He juggled the incoming clothes and managed to hold onto the hat, but the coveralls landed on the floor. He bent down to retrieve the fatigues, and as he started to straighten up, he rocked back and forth, trying to keep his balance. Andy started to go over and grab him, but stopped. He didn't care if the guy fell on the floor or not.

"Get changed," Andy grunted.

Irish stood, clothes clutched in his fist like a beggar on a street corner awaiting a passing philanthropist to bestow some gift upon him. "I will," he said, disgusted, "but it would have been nice if you two could have considered giving me some clean underwear and socks." He gave them a cheesy grin and entered one of the toilet stalls, closing the door behind him.

"Can you believe that?" Mel spat between clenched teeth.

Andy thought the comment was funny, but didn't say anything because he didn't want to rile Mel or encourage Irish. He caught a glimpse of himself in a mirror. His clothes weren't as filthy as Irish's, but they were dirty after the incident in the truck, and he hoped the laundry would clean them.

Andy left the john and was over at the water fountain, getting a drink, when Mel came out. Straightening up, he wiped the water drops off his chin with the back of his hand. "How's Irish doing?" Andy asked in a low voice.

"Don't know," Mel voiced back. "He's in the can with the door closed."

"You think we need to go and roust him out?" Andy murmured.

"I think he's about done." Then, in a hushed tone, Mel added, "While Irish was changing clothes, he threw his grubby trousers over the stall door, and a small cloth bag fell out of one of the pockets. When I reached down to pick it up, Irish opened the stall door and snatched it out of my hand."

"What was in it?"

"Strange, it felt like, uh … a couple of marbles. The bag was velvet material or something, with drawstrings like a Bull Durham sack."

"Marbles? What the heck would he be doing with marbles?"

"Perhaps not marbles; maybe small rocks. He was in a big hurry to snatch it away from me; must be something important in there."

"Interesting, but we've no time to be concerned about that now."

"How are we going to get him up to Group HQ?" Mel inquired.

"We are going to borrow that weapons carrier over there," said Andy, pointing to a three-quarter-ton truck.

"You can't just take the truck; you're not on duty today."

"My name's on the trip ticket, and we'll have it back here before they need it. No one's going to be the wiser. I'll sign it out nice and legal like…."

"Where the hell is Irish?" asked Mel. "I'm going to go roust him out, and I don't give a tinker's damn what he's doing. I'll have him out here dressed or butt-ass naked while you bring around the truck."

As Mel began to make a fast pivot on his heels to hightail it back to the latrine, a shallow, pathetic clearing of the throat came from behind them. They did a quick about-face, and there stood Irish; he'd snuck in without Andy or Mel seeing him.

"Just listening to see if you were going to say anything nice about me," he said sarcastically.

Mel and Irish climbed in as Andy pulled the weapons carrier out toward the hangar door. Three figures stepped into the opening to block the truck's passage onto the flight line—the two guys who had been chasing the truck and Joe, who evidently had bailed from the six-by as Skeeter had driven back to his work area. Andy stomped on the accelerator, and the weapons carrier lurched toward the three men. It was a game of chicken, who would flinch first. The assailants jumped aside at the last second as the truck bore down on them. Andy swung the steering wheel, and the vehicle careened around the hangars over to the street and kept moving. Not looking back, the three rode in silence, and it wasn't until Andy pulled the vehicle in front of Group Headquarters that he finally spoke. He turned to Irish and said, "You're here on time and presentable, although, theoretically, you're not supposed to wear low quarter shoes with fatigues. I figure you'll manage. Now, get out."

"Whoa! Wait a minute; not so damn fast," protested Irish as he jumped out and held onto the side of the truck. "It should only take forty-five minutes or so for the paperwork to be finished. You'll be here when I come back, right?"

"The deal was to bring you here, not wait and take you back. We've lived up to our part of the bargain," exclaimed Andy.

"Yeah, guys, I need you to do me one more favor and mail a package home for me."

"No dice," countered Mel.

"What about your clothes, Anderson? You need these back." Irish grabbed onto the sleeve of the coveralls.

"Keep them. I don't need them, and I don't want them!" Andy shouted as he pushed on the gas pedal and left Irish standing alone in the street in front of the building.

"It just dawned on me why the goons were chasing Irish today," said Mel. "Irish even told us why, and we were too stupid to figure it out—stolen jewels. The bag he dropped in the can sure reminded me of a gem bag. Bet you he had loot in there, stolen precious stones or something of value he planned on smuggling out of the country today. By having us mail a package for him, it would have been our asses, not his, if customs discovered what was in the package."

"Sensible theory," Andy replied. "That might be why he wanted us to escort him to the base. We can't prove it, but your idea makes good sense. Let's hope we're rid of the son of a bitch for good." Andy smiled as he slapped Mel on the shoulder.

CHAPTER TWENTY-SEVEN
The War Is Over
July 1953

Even before Andy arrived at the open front door of the Brass Rail, the noise of the enthusiastic chatter streamed out onto the street, indicating the mood of the patrons. The war in Korea was over; they had signed the peace accords. The speculation had begun, and the GIs were sure their tours of duty would be shortened and they could go home. Troops in the bar on R and R from Korea were all wondering if they should cut their time in Japan short and get back to their units, because they might miss the opportunity for an early return to the states. Rumors were flying, spirits were high, and everyone was happy.

The armistice ended the fighting in Korea. It was not a peace treaty, just an end to the open conflict. As anticipated, the downsizing of the number of troops in Korea began; men packed their bags and headed home to the States. For Andy, the routine continued. War or no war, his job remained constant, and the end of the hostilities had little impact on his daily routine.

A month passed with nothing extraordinarily exciting happening, and Andy began settling into a groove. One day, as usual after work, he'd checked his mail before going to chow. In his mailbox, he was happy to find a letter from his sister as well as an outdated brochure from his local 4-H club on the year's livestock awards.

As he removed the pamphlet, a second letter caught in the folds of the pamphlet toppled out and fell to the floor. He reached down to grab the envelope and, as he did, the slight scent of freshly picked lilacs wafted up faintly. No question, he knew the letter was from South Carolina, but he had no idea why Anna Mae would be writing him. Typically, if there were any messages from the Butlers, he would find out secondhand from Sergeant Jones.

He tore open the envelope, unfolded the delicate stationery, and read the short but life-changing message:

Dear Andy:

You mentioned to me once how you would like to go to college after your enlistment is over. You had, however, some concerns. I think that perhaps we have found an answer to some of your problems. My father is on the Board of Trustees for Citadel Military College. He has arranged for you to receive a full scholarship. There are conditions, of course, the main one being that you must meet the school's entrance criteria. You'll receive a packet of information from the college outlining all the details within the next month.

I do hope this pleases you. You were such a huge help and such a good friend when I visited in Japan. Perhaps this will in some small way help repay some of your kindness. Oren sends his regards.

Best Wishes, Anna Mae Du Frère Butler

He gulped as he reread the letter. The excitement in him swelled, and he burst out, "Mel! Read this!" as he shoved the perfumed paper under his friend's nose.

"Give me a second while I finish what I'm reading…. Oh, from Anna Mae, fantastic-smelling perfume," he said, catching a whiff of the lilac scent as he grabbed the letter.

After he finished reading, he exultantly said, "A great deal; what's terrific is we will both be going to school on the East Coast, not far away from each other. It couldn't have worked out better unless you were going to Harvard with me." To others, perhaps news such as this was not life-changing, but to Andy, it meant a different future. The prospect of knowing he was going to go on to college put a different twist on his life.

***

The fighting in French Indochina made newspaper headlines. In May 1954, the battle of Dien Bien Phu brought about the defeat of the French troops.

Major Oren Butler returned home to South Carolina and to his wife with a few cuts and bruises as souvenirs of his time in Vietnam. The scars went unnoticed by most who attended the hero's welcome home celebration hosted by Anna Mae. The French government and the State Department lavished him with accolades for his service. The Air Force promoted him, and Lieutenant Colonel Butler's plans for a military career were back on track.

Farewells

On December 3, a chill was in the night air as Andy pulled open the door of the Brass Rail. Mel barged in before him to get out of the blustery wind. Pausing for a second, Andy's thoughts drifted back, and he allowed the door to close behind him, eliciting some crude remarks about being born in a barn. Mel would be shipping out to go home in two days, Butler had left last year, and Andy had no idea where Remmey was. The closest friends he had in Japan would soon be gone. He looked around at the bar and reminisced about the hours he had spent in the building over the past years.

The Brass Rail: a Japanese version of an American western saloon with a footrail that ran along the base of the elaborate handcrafted bar, and fake spittoons that adorned the ends of the footrail.

"*Konbanwa,* Mama-san," Andy greeted with a bow and a smile.

"Konbanwa. Good evening, Andy-san. Konbanwa, Mel-san." Mama-san bowed with elegance.

Mel bowed in return. "Konbanwa."

Payday had been only a few days ago, and the bar was full of people. They found a couple of empty barstools, and by chance, the one Andy grabbed happened to be in Butler's old favorite spot at the bar. They plopped down on the shabby and cracked blue padded seats and put their tired feet up on the brass rail. Two cute young barmaids hustled over to take their drink orders, and they were eager to engage the two young ladies in conversation. However, Mama-san shuffled over to where they sat and shooed the girls away. Ever since the episode with Butler, Mama-san insisted that only she, Sumiko, and of course, Yoriko, before her departure, tended to their needs at the bar.

Having Mama-san's exclusive attention was great, but in many respects it was like having your mother breathing over your shoulder all the time. Andy revered the strong-willed woman who treated him as if he were family.

"Beer, sake?" Mama-san asked.

"Tonight, sake," Andy replied.

Mel said, "Me too, dozo." He looked wistfully at the two girls who had now captured the attention of two other guys.

Mama-san padded away with that delicate shuffle of hers. She returned and placed two decanters of the warm wine on the bar in front of them. She was the epitome of charm, poise, and refinement as she served them, moving with a simple elegance and sophistication. She might have been serving tea to the Emperor of Japan, so delicately smooth and graceful were the quality of her movements. He wondered what her features had been like when she was younger, before her facial injury. *She must have been a knockout when she was one of the lovely elite geishas of Japan.*

Turning to look at Mel, Andy raised his cup. "As I'm perched on Butler's old stool, I think a toast to Oren Butler is in order. Good luck to him. *Kanpai!*"

In response to the toast, Mel raised his cup of sake, and the two cups touched. Awaiting a soft chiming sound to resonate through the room, Andy was disappointed. *In the movies, when two wine goblets touch, you always hear a pleasing musical note.* Instead, his reward was a dismal clunk. Ceramic cups just don't have the same qualities as fine crystal glasses. He wanted music, a crescendo. Butler, despite all his problems and faults, deserved a musical tribute or at least a drum roll. *With all he's been through—the war and his struggles to forget the horrors of battle—at least we should have the ringing bells of Notre Dame Cathedral on his behalf.* Andy had to admit he admired the guy more than a little. When Butler drank, he was one hell of a drinker. When Andy had gotten to know the major, he'd found the man to be a classy, elegant person. He had learned from Butler what loyalty to your friends meant.

Mel reiterated Andy's salute. "To Butler; good luck. Kanpai."

"You know, Mel," Andy despondently voiced. "The next three months are going to be a little empty without your ugly puss around here. You realize we've been coming here to this bar together for damn near three years? Since we were nineteen."

"Yeah." Mel smirked. "Now we're old men, twenty-one, and can legally drink when we get home."

"Two days and a wake-up and you'll be stateside, in Philly for Christmas."

"I'll make you a promise, Andy. When my family gathers around the tree for our annual Christmas Eve toast and my turn to give the toast comes around, I'll include you. Hell, it's not like we're not going to see each other; you'll be down at the Citadel, and I'll be at Harvard. We'll have spring breaks and summers."

"You're right. But time for another toast now." Andy refilled the sake cups. "To you. Kanpai."

Mel interrupted, saying, "My turn. Who would ever think I would get mixed up with some hick kid from a farm in Colorado and discover the best person I've ever known? Kanpai."

They tossed down the sake; the river of rice liquid warmed their throats.

"Sayonara, ole buddy; Godspeed," Andy uttered under his breath.

The following months, he tried to amass as many transferable credits as he could so he would not have to begin his studies at the Citadel as a freshman. Having been granted an early release from active duty, and with the approval of the college, he attended a college summer session in June.

The last time he had been promoted, they had changed his duties. With the stripe came extra responsibility. They took away his tug and gave him a Jeep and the services of a Japanese interpreter. He'd been given an additional job in procurement that included traveling back and forth to Tokyo to have equipment repaired by local firms. He spent time at different companies and had to wait when items were not ready for pickup. Inevitably, they would serve green tea and rice crackers while he waited. Often, a young executive would join him for tea and engage him in conversation. Andy imagined they took the opportunity of his being there to practice their English language skills, and it gave him the chance to work on his Japanese, which was going nowhere fast.

One day, Andy came out of a contractor's office in Ueno and noticed a man loitering alongside the Jeep. It was not a common occurrence to see someone doing this, but it happened regularly enough he was not wary of someone trying to steal something. Generally, it was just a curious person looking at the vehicle. He walked around to the passenger's side, where the man stood.

"Hello there, Anderson. Long time no see."

Andy was stunned to see the same man who had posed as a Japanese government agent at the koya and had been part of Remmey's late-arriving backup group at the laundry.

"What are you doing here?" Andy continued without pausing. "Where's Remmey? Is he in the States or here in Japan?"

"Don't know; couldn't tell you if I did...." After a pause, the man continued, "What I need is some information. Do you know an ex-GI who goes by the nickname Irish?"

"Yeah, I know him."

"Your buddy Remmey, as you call him, told me that if I needed your help, all I had to do was ask. I need your assistance. Are you game?"

"Doing what, and why me? You have other resources; what do you need me for?"

"Can't go into details unless I know you're in, and if it matters, it's because Remmey asked me to contact you. I realize that it's like jumping into a dark pit without knowing how deep the hole is. I can't divulge any details; it won't be as dangerous as the scrape at the laundry."

"So, you talked with him when?" asked Andy.

"No, I didn't speak with him, but I have had communications with him through a ... uh, a source, a third party, and Remmey wanted you to be part of this. Can't tell you why. He seems to be doing OK healthwise," answered the man.

"Good to know he's getting better. If you can't tell me why you need me for this job…it puts me in a blind spot not knowing. But sure I trust Remmey; he must have a reason, though I don't know why. I'll do it. Sounds more interesting than hanging around the hangar. Why not? You helped me out of a jam once. I don't even know your name."

"You can call me Boston ... and you're sure you want in? There is no backing out once you have agreed."

Andy hesitated for a second and then nodded his assent to the arrangement.

"The Japanese government has an interest in recovering missing treasures stolen after the war. We have information that this man called Irish may have knowledge of the location of some of these items." Boston waited for a reaction from Andy, and then continued, "They know Irish did not steal the items originally, they came into his possession through trade and barter."

"From what I know, that is a very reasonable assumption," Andy remarked.

"We've established a buy with a group of black marketers for next Thursday night, and we want you there."

"What happens if I'm scheduled for duty that night?"

"Don't worry; tomorrow you will be on assignment with the provost marshal. The pretense will be an assignment to an auxiliary base security force which will mean you'll be going through training the rest of the week. In reality you will spend those days with me and the crew, getting ready for the proposed buy. I want you to bring civilian clothing when you come. I assume you have some civvies."

"A couple of pairs of pants and shirts."

"What you don't have we'll pick up for you. I don't have to remind you that this is classified and must be kept secret."

"I understand," Andy assured him.

"There will be a security forces truck to pick you up at the barracks at 1300 hours tomorrow. Have your gear ready." With that statement, Boston turned and walked away.

The following week went by like a whirlwind for Andy. They moved him to a hotel and allowed him to only wear civilian attire. In an indistinct car, they shuttled him in and out of an Army post to an isolated firing range. Under the scrutiny of an instructor, they evaluated and commended his competency with .45 and .38-caliber pistols. *Like popping tin cans at home.* They took him to a training facility in a warehouse, where they had constructed mock rooms of the location the buy was to take place. He was instructed on when and where to enter and where to stand as well as which door other people would be entering through. He studied and rehearsed basic search, interrogation, and negotiation procedures. The day before the event, he still was not sure of his role in the operation, or even if he had a role to play. Boston had told him that he would not be carrying a weapon, he would only be an observer. This information made Andy wonder why they had given him all the training. The answer they gave him was: "We want you prepared, and we need to know your skill level, just in case."

Late in the afternoon, four Japanese government agents arrived. They were greeted by Boston, who spoke to them in Japanese. The men kept looking at Andy. First, they would nod their heads yes, and then they would shake their heads no. Left out of the conversation, Andy took a seat in a chair by a table on the far side of the training room and waited there until the men left.

When they were alone, Boston walked over to where Andy was and sat on the edge of the table. He peered at Andy and said, "Here is what they want. Very simply, they want the stolen heirlooms. They want to know who Irish's contact was then and is now for this type of stolen merchandise."

Andy began to ask, "What am—"

"Hold on, don't get so anxious," Boston said. "Let me finish.... They are going to shut down Irish's illegal business and confiscate that hovel he calls a hotel. They want to deport him from the country without a big fuss. If they can't do this and if Irish refuses to divulge his sources, they have enough evidence to arrest him and throw him in jail along with the rest of the crowd."

"What am I supposed to do?" asked Andy.

"Get Irish to comply. The fine details of how you are going to do it are up to you. I'll be here to give you a hand with the language and suggestions, but you call the shots," Boston said.

"You're asking me do a lot. I'll give it a try, but I can't guarantee the results. I know Irish, however I'm not his friend, and I have no leverage over him," griped Andy.

"Figure it out, Anderson. I don't give a rat's ass what happens to the guy. I'm only here out of courtesy to the Japanese government. You'll have the night to mull it over." Boston gave Andy a friendly pat on the shoulder. "Let's call it a day and go get something to eat. And having a drink sounds good."

The following evening, Japanese police surrounded a small building on the outskirts of Tokyo. Seven Japanese government agents and Boston, with Andy in tow, entered the building. Irish and three other black marketers sat in a room exactly like the mock training room.

A scuffle ensued as the Japanese agents entered the room and the vendors in the illegal goods trade tried to flee. The culprits were subdued, arrested, and moved to a different part of the building, leaving Irish in handcuffs, standing with two Japanese agents, Andy, and Boston.

"OK, Andy, the stage is all yours. You know what they want."

Up to this point, Irish had maintained his silence; he had noticed Andy and raised a questioning eyebrow, making inquisitive facial expressions but had not said a word. Andy motioned for Irish to follow him over to the corner of the room, where they might have a bit of privacy.

"What the hell's going on?" snarled Irish. "I knew you must have some friends the way the koya mess with Butler was covered up. You a cop or some sort of a damn snitch?"

Andy ignored the remark and said, "This isn't about me, Irish. Your ass is in a sling, not mine. You've been busted by the police for trading in the black market and dealing in stolen antiques. They're going to slap your butt in prison for a lot of years unless you cooperate with them."

"Bullshit; what do they want?" protested Irish.

"They want to know where you bought the heirlooms and who your contact was. They want all the antiques you have or know about returned. Your black market days are over; you're shut down, and you're out of business."

"What if I don't give them what they want?" Irish countered.

"You get to go to prison. They're willing to make a deal with you if you give them the stuff and the info they want."

"What kind of deal?"

"You can go home. Leave Japan and go back to the States, but you can never come back. No jail time."

Irish's face took on an expression of disbelief and total dismay. "What the hell?! Might as well go to jail. Can't go home with my pockets empty; gotta have some cash. I'd just be a bum again." A flicker of hope was evidenced in his expression. "Maybe if I do my time, I can sneak my money out then."

"Won't work," said Andy. "You go to jail, they will take possession of your money. You'll never get it out of the country."

Irish began pleading, "Anderson, I want to stay here in Japan; I don't want to go back to Jersey. I still have my hotel."

"No, you don't. They've taken that too. You've got nothing. I have an idea, though. Let me go talk with them," suggested Andy.

Irish's shoulders slumped. Beaten and forlorn, he leaned against the wall for support after hearing they had taken his hotel.

Andy went over to where the group of men was standing and talked with Boston, who, in turn, spoke with the Japanese officials. He then relayed the information to Andy, and Andy walked back to Irish.

"Here's the deal they are willing to make: you give them everything they want, and you leave Japan."

"I can't leave without money. Without cash, I'm a nobody," whined Irish.

"Shut up for a second. They don't care about your money. They want to get rid of you without a big political hullabaloo about jailing an American. The only restriction on the money is that it be lawfully transferred from Japan to the United States via legal international banking channels. The Japanese and American governments will extract the necessary taxes and fees."

"Screw you, Anderson. I want all my money. If they start taking taxes, it'll be all gone," Irish objected.

"What they told me to tell you is the feds are going to extract their due from your stash regardless. That's the deal. Take it or go to jail. You're not going to beat the rap; they have a pot full of evidence against you." He paused before finishing with "Irish, I don't care what happens. Do what you want. You can go to jail or you can go home. They hauled me into this mess because we know each other and you told me about the stolen property."

Irish hung his head and groaned. "They sure got me by the short hairs. I either become a stoolie and a fink or else."

Andy watched Irish's posture and put his hand on the man's shoulder. "You know, if you give them everything they want, perhaps they will let you stay and keep the hotel and some of the money. You know, Irish, this is more than just about you. Those women at your hotel, they depend upon you to keep them safe. Think about them for a change."

Andy paused before continuing. "No more dealing on the black market, no more of your shady deals, everything on the up and up. You'll be an innkeeper and that is it, and if the Japanese government needs additional information, you will give it up freely, or all bets are off."

Andy turned and began walking away. Then he looked back at Irish and, in a hushed tone, added, "I know they will deal. I overheard Boston talking with them about it. You created this pile of crap you're buried in and you have to dig your way out of it. They just gave you a shovel."

CHAPTER TWENTY-EIGHT
Gaijin

Andy mulled over what he needed to do that day as he finished breakfast. He looked over and scrutinized the men advancing through the chowline with their metal food trays held in front of them. They filled their trays, found a table, and gobbled down their morning meal. Then they rushed off to their various duty stations. Some were people he had known or seen for a few years; others were obviously just off the boat from the States. He wondered if he had been so easy to identify as a greenhorn when he'd first arrived.

After three years and ten days in Japan the time had come, and he would be heading stateside the following morning. The bus left the base for Tokyo at 0700 hours in the morning, and he would catch a plane to Travis AFB in California. A couple of more months on active duty and then he was off to a summer prep school session and on to the Citadel, the war college of the South, and the ROTC program.

"Mind if we sit here, Sarge?" asked a younger airman, gesturing to the vacant seats next to Andy.

Sarge, Andy thought, *sounds good.* He still hadn't gotten used to the title, having been advanced to the rank of staff sergeant on the last promotion cycle.

"No, go ahead; no one is sitting there," he said, immersing himself in resurrecting past memories of the friends, girls, loves, and all that had occurred during his tour in Japan. *I need to go find Sumiko; that's a priority. She wasn't at the Brass Rail when I stopped in last night to say farewell to Mama-san.* He decided that he would make a quick trip into town and see her. After all he needed to say good-bye, they had been friends for close to three years. *Then get back to the base to finish my base clearance.* The day was his to wrap up any unfinished business and clean up last-minute details.

Andy had not planned to go into town that night; instead, he intended on sticking tight in the barracks. He'd known of a couple of guys who had gone on a bender the night before they were to leave and missed boarding the airplane the next day. He had taken every precaution so nothing would screw up his going home. *Tonight I'll have time to cram clothes and junk in my duffel bag before I hit the sack. Then, in the morning, voila, I'll be ready to roll.*

Finishing the last of his coffee, he went back to the barracks, threw on some civvies, and caught the 0730 bus to town. He ambled through the maze of streets to the residential area where Sumiko still lived in the tiny apartment she had once shared with Yoriko. The streets were virtually empty. Those residing within the buildings had withdrawn back into their respective homes and businesses after completing the customary task of cleaning the vicinity in front of the house. It fascinated him how the people would go out every morning to complete this ritual. A few latecomers were tidying up, sweeping staunchly away with worn brooms made of straw. With weathered wooden buckets, they would douse water on the street and sidewalk to settle the dust. They nodded or bowed to Andy as he stepped around the corridor of their toil.

Arriving at his destination, he climbed the steps to the second floor of the small apartment building and rapped on the door. He anticipated a speedy good-bye, perhaps a little emotional, with a quick hug, maybe a kiss, and then he would be on his way. He and Sumiko had grown supportive and, in a sense, devoted to each other, though they were never romantically involved. He stood waiting in front of a Western-style door with hinges rather than the traditional sliding Japanese-style *amado*. There was no immediate answer, so he knocked again. A muffled voice said in Japanese, "Who is it?"

"Andy."

The door opened a crack, and Sumiko peered around the opening between the door and its frame. Her hair was disheveled, and her eyes red; it appeared she had been crying. "Andy-san, I just get up," she choked.

"Sorry, Sumiko; didn't mean to wake you up. I came by to say good-bye. I'm shipping out tomorrow in the morning."

As soon as he mentioned leaving, she burst into tears. Sensing the worst, he asked, "What's wrong? Did something happen?"

She didn't answer, just stared regretfully at him.

"You want to talk, tell me about it?"

First, she shook her head no. Then she bobbed her head yes and held the door open wide enough for him to enter. She whimpered, "I know you go States. Air Force say must go…. I wish you stay forever, but know you no can do." She began crying pitifully.

Sumiko hesitated for a second and stepped out of the entrance foyer and back up on the tatami mats, giving Andy space to enter the foyer. He stepped inside, and as he closed the door behind him, the room darkened since shades still covered the windows. The morning light sought to find entry into the simple one-room flat, stray beams of light creeping through gaps in the shades. In the tiny kitchen nook, a ray of sunshine peeked under the window shade, and specks of dust danced in the sunlight. The faint illumination left the main room, which functioned also as a bedroom, bathed in a soft, dim light.

Andy slipped off his shoes and followed her into the room where she stood looking at him, tears running down her flushed cheeks in little rivulets. Her chest heaved with enormous sobs. He closed his arms about her and drew her in tight, endeavoring to comfort her. She readily accepted his embrace and desperately clung to him in her anguish.

Holding the young woman, he suddenly was aware of the heat of her body and the realization that Sumiko was wearing only a thin silk sleeping kimono and nothing underneath. Even though she was fully clothed, he could feel the firmness of her breasts, the suppleness of her limbs, and the softness of her body as she clung against him. They spoke no words as they clutched each other. He was ready to ask her again what was wrong when she raised her head, studied his face for a second, and kissed him with intense longing and fervor. Andy returned her embrace with an explosive surge of passion and desire, yet he worried that her affection toward him was wrought out of her despair and despondency.

As they clung to each other, her sleeping kimono became untied. The sheer garment slid from her body. She stepped back in an attempt to retrieve the robe that lay in a rumpled heap by her small feet and stood before him, unhindered by clothing. Then Sumiko pressed her naked body against his chest, and he felt the fullness of her bosom as they kissed. The image of her unclothed silhouette was that of an impeccable sculpture: the well-shaped legs, firm buttocks and hips, her slim, tight stomach, beautifully rounded breasts, and slim neck so inviting to be nestled and kissed. Sumiko's extraordinarily exquisite face and tousled flowing hair were a beautiful vision to behold.

In his mind, he romanticized one of her arms sliding from around his neck and her fingers unbuttoning his shirt. He didn't resist and slipped his arms out of the shirt sleeves; the T-shirt followed. Somehow, while unbuttoning his shirt, she unbuckled his belt and undid his trousers. She placed her hands in his and guided him to the still warm futon, which she had left moments earlier to answer his knock. They clung to each other and, as in a single motion, they dropped down onto the mat, their naked bodies feverish with anticipation. He dreamed of holding her as he lay exhausted, not wanting the moment to end. Content and relaxed, he wanted to remain there with her in his arms.

The trance was broken as he sensed uneasiness in her, yet she did not let him go but clung tightly to him, unwilling to let him withdraw. Not saying a word and with great sensitivity, he carefully broke from their embrace. Reaching down, he picked up her kimono and gently placed it around her soft ivory shoulders. In an unconscious movement, she pulled the kimono around her body and knotted the belt about her waist as she wistfully gazed at him. For the first time, he admitted to himself their relationship was more than friendship. *It would be so easy*, he thought, *so easy*. He was infatuated with this beautiful caring woman, this lovely person whom he cherished so profoundly.

The burning desire that needed to be quenched with the physical joining of a man and woman flared inside him. However, this was quite unlike any he had experienced before; arguably, it become more emotional than physical. He cast the thoughts aside; it was wrong, he was leaving, and he would only be taking advantage of her emotional distress.

Sumiko lowered her gaze and said, "You stay, Andy. I make you some coffee, some *ocha*." She walked to the small kitchen area and busied herself with the task.

"I can only stay for a few minutes," he replied as he followed her to a small table and sat in one of the chairs.

The girl brought over the beverage and placed it before him. She took a seat in the opposite chair so they were sitting close enough for their knees to be touching.

She reached over, clasped his free hand, and quietly said, "I will miss you, Andy-san, I will miss you not here with me."

They spoke very little and then only of the memories that they shared. The mood was subdued and solemn, and they held hands in this moment of parting.

It was late and imperative Andy leave and return to the base. The time had slipped away, and he had stayed much longer than he had intended. He felt Sumiko had relaxed a bit, and with a wary and measured movement, he stood up from the chair.

She lifted her head, propped her chin on her elbows, and disappointedly asked him, "You go now?"

"Must ... must go, Sumiko. I need get back to the base. I don't have much time; sorry, but I must go. I have no choice."

Sumiko rose from the chair as impetuously as a tornado and pulled her kimono tighter around her as if she could squeeze out the anguish. "You go home, Andy," she said bitterly. "You go home, all go home! Mel go home, Butler-san go, even Yoriko go. You like butterfly: drink the sweetness of the flower and fly away, leave flower to shed tears in loneliness. You fly away. You fly to America; you have home. I no have home, no country." She seethed with sharp resentment.

He didn't understand what she was trying to say. "You are home. Japan is your home."

"No, it not. I born Manchuria, not Japan." Then her story came in a rapid wave. "They say my mother conscripted to work in Japanese soldiers' pleasure house. She comfort woman, an *ianfu* in Manchuria, where I born. Not all who use comfort stations Japanese; others use too. My father maybe no Japanese, might be Russian. Or my mother maybe white, a prisoner who forced to work as ianfu, and my father Japanese. I no know. I never see; no one knows.

"I born one year when some girl children born in comfort houses in Manchuria were sent back to orphanage in Japan. They want see if raise and train girls to become ianfu when older. They no check babies close, so they not know me not all Japanese. When get older, the girls at orphanage spit at me and hit me, call me *inu,* dog. They scream at me, 'ced *Gaijin inu,* foreigner dog, you no belong, leave.' I no Japanese. I no Chinese. I no Russian. I *gaijin.* I outsider, like you, foreigner. I Eurasian. I no white. I no Asian. You have home; I not have." Tears flowed down her flushed cheeks, and her chest heaved heavily as she wept.

Sumiko wiped her eyes with the sleeve of her kimono as she regained her composure and continued, "I run away from orphanage when maybe six, seven years old. Christian British missionary family take me in and care for me, start teach me English. The Japanese soldiers come arrest them, say they spies, put in prison camp for gaijin. I no more see after. Christian Japanese families hide me but move me much round. Place to place, always go new house. They 'fraid to hide gaijin, an inu like me. They in big trouble if get caught."

Tears welled up in her eyes, and she fought valiantly to stem the emotions. "After war over, I still little girl, but hear about job at American bar for scrub girl. I ten years old, go try to find work where there are gaijins, but I sick, very sick. Mama-san finds me. She understands, take care me, make me well, and find me new home. When I grow up, Mama-san gives me job. I have no home. I gaijin but have no country." She sobbed uncontrollably. "I have no family." Catching her breath, she continued, "Yoriko have home. She have mother and father live Honshu; now she have husband. She no worry 'bout you go home."

Andy was at a loss for what to say or do. *I think she wants me to stay, but I can't. I have to get back. I have PCS orders.*

He reached out to hug her, but she roughly pushed him away. "Go now, gaijin; you outsider, no belong. Go now. Go home to mother, father, brother, and sisters. No think me no more. I survive…. Go, gaijin, 'fore I get angry." Sumiko swung the door open wide and held it open. "Go!"

Hastily he slipped on his shoes, not even bothering to tie them as he grabbed his coat and stepped out of the entranceway.

The door slammed forcefully behind him. Her sobbing voice, choked with tears, cried out to him, the muffled voice tormented with loneliness, "Go home, gaijin. Go home, Andy. I always think you. You no know but I love you. I love you, and I no forget." The words she moaned were barbed arrows piercing his heart, where they embedded deeply; the pain would someday subside, but the words would forever remain.

Had he been blind all this time and unable to see how she felt about him? The sweet, lovely Sumiko; they expected her to be there for them, and she was. She was there when they needed her, and now there was no one here for her. Unhurriedly and with great chagrin, he walked down the steps and out onto the street, fighting the urge to go back, knowing he couldn't. He kept walking as her memory and the words burned deeper and deeper into the recesses of his mind.

No think of me no more. I survive. I love you. I love you, and I no forget. Go home, gaijin. Go home. Think of me no more.

EPILOGUE
Citadel

Three years had gone by since Andy had left Japan, and the time at the Citadel had passed swiftly. Adhering to the military discipline enforced at the college was not difficult after four years in the Air Force. Credits from night school and summer sessions allowed him to enter the Citadel as a sophomore. Andy adjusted to the academics, settling into the groove of studying full time again. Although older than most cadets, he did find other veterans attending the school, and having a common background, they established a bonding friendship and camaraderie.

Butler—now Colonel Butler—was on assignment with the American embassy in Paris. Taking full advantage of his military and State Department connections as air attaché, Butler was living in the best of both worlds. He'd chosen his path wisely. Andy had spoken with Butler and Anna Mae a few times after he'd become a student at the Citadel. Whenever the Butlers were in Charleston, they invited Andy out to dinner. In the autumn, they had held a large Butler and Du Frère reunion and invited him to the family home for the festivities.

The spring of his junior year, Andy received a beautifully embossed letter with no return address. Inside the envelope was an engraved invitation to attend the Charleston Cotillion. Pulling out the announcement, a slip of paper caught his attention.

Andy:

I am delighted that you are on the guest list to this year's Cotillion. You are to escort Marline Jane Magee, who is my niece. You met her at the family reunion last year. She is the same age you are. Marline Jane's debutant ball was a few years ago; this year, you two will be attending as honoree chaperones. A limousine will pick you up on the night of the ball at 8:00 p.m. Have a wonderful time.

Best wishes, Anna Mae

He pondered the message and debated if he really wanted to attend such an affair. He wrote Mel to tell him of his good fortune. They'd kept in contact since Japan, and had even gotten together a few times. Mel had integrated back into his Philadelphia and Harvard lifestyle; his speech and mannerisms were different, as were his dress and appearance. Andy noticed the subtle change in him each time they got together, but underneath he was the same old Mel. After an hour or so, he'd act the same as he always had when they'd been in Japan.

Andy had met Mel's family and spent an enjoyable Christmas week with them in Philadelphia. Mel's grandfather's stories had kept him intrigued and thoroughly entertained throughout his stay. Mel had made a journey to the farm in Colorado during the summer and spent a carefree vacation with Andy, roaming around on the prairie.

Invariably, when they got together, the conversation would slip back to Japan. They would reminisce about Yoriko, Sumiko, and of course, Mama-san and the Brass Rail.

About a week before the ball, a package arrived. The parcel contained a wrapped packet and a message. The note, written in Anna Mae's beautiful script, said:

Dear Andy:

I am passing this precious and lovely gift on to you. You were with me when Mama-san gave it to me.

I have found my life's partner. The sentiment expressed on the parchment is for those who are still searching for the fulfillment of love and life.

Do with the packet as you wish.

May the future bring you only happiness and joy.

All my best,
Anna Mae

He undid the wrapping, held the silk pouch in his hands, and speculated about Anna Mae's motive in giving him the parchment now. *Is she trying to play matchmaker?* He tucked the pouch in a small cardboard box in one of his dresser drawers. The box once had held a pound of chocolates; now it contained memorabilia he considered important—memories of Japan.

The day of the Cotillion, a telegram arrived.

> Mind your manners this evening. You're stepping out into high society. Behave yourself. You'll do excellently. Remember, don't pick your nose in public. I am proud and envious of you. Wish I was there. Let me know what happens. Mel

The evening of the ball, Andy stood by the dorm entrance dressed in his finest uniform, waiting for the car. His nerves were on the verge of besting him as he worried about what his venture into this different world would be like. He observed other cadets standing around waiting for their rides, and they all appeared as nervous as he. A long black Lincoln pulled up in front of the dorm. The chauffeur exited the vehicle and politely said, "Cadet Anderson?"

He gulped and replied, "Yes," and he stepped down off the stoop.

He was still unable to recall anyone he had met at the Butler get-together named Marline. There had been so many people and several attractive young women came to mind, but he couldn't match the name Marline with a face.

The chauffeur opened the back door. The loveliest of creatures greeted him as he stooped to enter the car. A Southern beauty with auburn hair and light gray eyes that sparkled like the stars sat gracefully in the backseat. Clothed with exquisite taste and appeal she wore a tantalizing smile, and he noticed she had some of the same facial features as her aunt Anna Mae.

He remembered meeting her but not the name; she had been polite, pleasant, and was with a male escort. Andy hadn't spoken with her for any length of time.

"Hi, Andy; I'm Marline Jane McGee. Remember me?"

He hesitated for a brief second, so bewitched he'd forgotten his own name. "Hello. It is my extreme pleasure to make your acquaintance again, Miss McGee." He had been practicing the introduction sentence repeatedly; now it sounded stiff and stupid.

"Please, don't be so formal. Call me Jane. All my family does."

The introduction at the Butlers' was Jane, not Marline.

He entered the car and sat down, oblivious of everything but her. The motion of the Lincoln told Andy the journey had begun.

"I feel I've known you for years," she said. "My Auntie and Uncle Oren have told me a lot about you."

"You have a distinct advantage; I know practically nothing about you." He speculated about what they had told her.

"By the end of the evening, we shall know significantly more about each other" was her soft, sweet reply.

"Just curious," Andy asked. "Who escorted you to the reunion?"

"Just a friend, not a beau or anything such as that, a boy I've known for years," she answered. "Do you have a girlfriend?"

"No, not currently. I'm afraid studying takes up most of my time and leaves very little opportunity for a social life."

The conversation went back and forth, mostly chitchat.

Jane smiled. "I must admit I asked my Auntie and Uncle Oren a lot about you and about what you did in Japan, about the girls there."

I wonder if the cat is out of the bag and they told her about the Brass Rail.

"He told me you and your ... buddy—is that the right term? I forgot his name—were both gentlemen and behaved well."

Andy went out on a limb. "Perhaps on our next date, I'll have an opportunity to tell you about Japan." Then he waited for her answer.

"I think that would be wonderful; I am anxious to learn of your experiences there."

Wasn't too hard; got another date.

The conversation continued, and the more she talked the more enamored with her he became—and the more he found out what Butler and Anna Mae had told her about him, which was a lot.

Perhaps it was the music on the radio. On the other hand, the soft moonlight peeping through the car's windows created a romantic setting. Japan seemed far away, an elusive memory that could fade as quickly as a cloud drifting on the night's breeze if he were to allow it to escape.

THE CONCLUSION

It took a lot of persuading to get Andy's dad to leave the farm and travel to South Carolina for Andy's graduation. Being the first of his family to finish college made the ceremony a special occasion, and his mother insisted that they attend. The family stayed in Charleston for three days before going back to Colorado. Even with their neighbor looking after the farm while they were away, his dad stressed about the crops and livestock and rushed right back home.

Andy, soon a newly commissioned second lieutenant in the Air Force, was to report to an air base in Texas for training in August.

As he had some free time before law school was to begin, Mel worked on luring Andy to Philly. Mel wanted him to bring Jane and come to Philly and then go on a trip with him and his fiancée, Bernice. They had planned an ocean voyage on the Schultz family yacht, and Mel was pressuring them to go along. The other guests were friends of Mel and Bernice's from Harvard and Radcliffe. It sounded more like a frat party than a cruise to Andy, and if he was going to go, he needed the proper clothing and gear for the trip. That meant he would have to be in Philly a few days earlier than the sail date so he could be outfitted. He was uncertain whether he even wanted to go on the ocean trip.

His attachment with Jane was laced with tenderness and affection, but it had not become a serious romantic relationship yet. Although he admired her tremendously, his future was uncertain. He needed to complete his military training before making any plans. Her family had invited him to their home for the weekend or longer if he wished to stay. However, Andy decided that during his break between school and reporting to the base in Texas, he wanted to go back to the farm for at least a few weeks.

Most all the other students had left the dorms. Only forty-eight hours before he had stood on a stage, and they had presented him with a diploma for his achievements. Now he was packing his suitcases. He pulled the cardboard candy box from his dresser drawer that held the memorabilia from Japan and placed it in his suitcase. Then, on second thought, he picked up the box, took out the silk pouch, and removed the parchment. He remembered the sentiment Mama-san had expressed and her belief in the power of the words and the irrefutable positive karma given to the person who possessed the parchment. He knew what he had to do; there was no question in his mind the talisman he held in his hand belonged to only one person. If anyone deserved the quality of life described on the message, it was Sumiko, the gentle soul who'd bestowed her friendship and love on others but, in the end, received so little in return.

Andy never mentioned the last time he'd seen Sumiko; it was a memory he wanted to keep to himself. That last day, both bitter and sweet, and those heart-searing words as he'd left were still fresh in his mind. He thought of Sumiko often and wondered what her life was like. He never wrote her, although he actually started letters to her more than once. Andy always found reasons to procrastinate, using such excuses as he didn't know if she lived in the same apartment or even whether she wanted to hear from him. He made up a thousand lame pretexts not to write, but always knew he should. He knew regardless of how old he was or where he lived, part of him would forever remain with those in Japan. He could only hope they were all right, but he was afraid he would never know.

He wondered if his feelings were because of guilt for walking out on her that last day in Japan. He knew it wasn't that; it was something deeper, and one day he vowed it would get to her. He wasn't sure how, but he felt it was imperative he hand it to her in person. When and where the exchange would transpire only time would tell. He made certain the small silk pouch containing the thin rice paper on which Hitoshi had inscribed love and happiness was tucked securely and safely away in the chocolate box and placed it back in his suitcase.

Someone knocked at his door and expecting another cadet, he called out, "Come on in; door's open." Andy turned to see who his visitor was, and there, dressed in a dark three-piece suit looking like a Washington lawyer, stood a healthy and vigorous man. Alongside him stood another person dressed in similar garb.

"Remmey!" Andy yelled. "What the hell are you doing here? Good to see you. Where the heck have you been? Why didn't you write me?

Sorry, I'm getting ahead of myself. You're looking a lot better than the last time I saw you."

"Andy boy, you're a sight for these old eyes. You looked sharp at graduation, all decked out in your uniform. A lot classier than those rumpled old fatigues you wore on the troopship."

"You were there, at the ceremony?"

"Yeah, you think I would miss your graduation? Stood in the back. I wanted to be here when they awarded you your diploma." He turned and motioned to the man standing behind him. "Andy, this is Don Miles. I wanted him to meet you."

Don Miles stepped into the room and extended his hand. Andy took the offered hand and they exchanged a friendly handshake. "Glad to meet you, Andy. I've heard a great deal about you and hope to get to know you better."

Don Miles had a mysterious, elusive, even a little sinister air about him. The man reminded him of a spy. Miles turned to Remmey. "I'm going to leave you two alone to reminisce while I grab a cup of coffee; might even have a Danish or two. Pick me up at the coffee shop when you're finished," he said to Remmey as he left the room.

"I forgive you for a hell of a lot, but why didn't you tell me you were in the CIA instead of stringing me along? Handing me that line of crap about being from Chicago."

"It was not all made up, Andy. I am from Chicago, and I like history. Actually, history was my major in college."

Remmey didn't want to talk about Korea and would not volunteer any details, but he did answer Andy's questions and told him a little of his experiences as a POW. Mainly, they talked about their time on the troopship and in Japan.

"Sorry you made the trip to the hospital for nothing. The CIA moved me out of Japan as soon as my condition stabilized."

"When I went to the hospital to look for you, they told me there was no patient named Remmey," Andy said. "So, what is your name if that's not it?"

"Perhaps someday I'll be able to tell you, but for now Remmey is as good as any. I like the handle."

An hour later, Remmey glanced at his watch and announced, "Must go, Andy. Perhaps, next summer, we can go sit under that tree of yours in Colorado. I would really like that."

They stood up and said good-bye, and as Remmey reached for the doorknob, he said, "Andy, we've been keeping up to date on your activities. You proved yourself while you were in Japan. There's a job for you with the Company if you would like it." He handed Andy a business card.

Andy was floored and exhilarated by this proposal to work for the CIA, and he didn't utter a word. The idea had caught him by surprise.

Remmey grinned, turned, and held out a second card. "Think it over, and if you want to talk about it further, here is Don's phone number; give him a call and he'll set up a meeting."

Andy took the card that read: "Donald Miles, Recruitment and Personnel," with two phone numbers.

"What about you? Will I catch up with you again?" Andy inquired.

"Yes. When, where, and how soon depends on if you make the phone call or not." Remmey smiled and turned the door handle. "Either way we'll cross paths with each other. See you around, Anderson." He walked out of the room and closed the door behind him.

The End

Printed by Libri Plureos GmbH in Hamburg, Germany